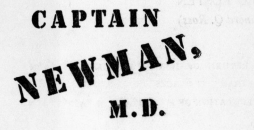

CAPTAIN NEWMAN, M.D.

BY LEO ROSTEN
(*Leonard Q. Ross*)

Humor

THE RETURN OF H*Y*M*A*N   K*A*P*L*A*N
THE STRANGEST PLACES
THE EDUCATION OF H*Y*M*A*N   K*A*P*L*A*N

Fiction

CAPTAIN NEWMAN, M.D.

Social Science

HOLLYWOOD: THE MOVIE COLONY, THE MOVIE MAKERS
THE WASHINGTON CORRESPONDENTS
A GUIDE TO THE RELIGIONS OF AMERICA (EDITOR)
112 GRIPES ABOUT THE FRENCH (WAR DEPT.)

Novels of Suspense

SLEEP, MY LOVE
THE DARK CORNER
ADVENTURE IN WASHINGTON
DATELINE: EUROPE

Screenplays

WALK EAST ON BEACON
THE VELVET TOUCH
LURED
SLEEP, MY LOVE
THE CONSPIRATORS

CAPTAIN NEWMAN, M.D.

by

LEO ROSTEN

HARPER & ROW, PUBLISHERS
New York and Evanston

CAPTAIN NEWMAN, M.D.

TO ZIMI

ACKNOWLEDGMENT

To Romi and Hildy: In whose house this book began, with many thanks for "kindness and salami."

CONTENTS

CONTENTS

Canst thou not minister to a mind diseas'd,
Pluck from the memory a rooted sorrow,
Raze out the written troubles of the brain,
And with some sweet oblivious antidote
Cleanse the stuff'd bosom of that perilous stuff
Which weighs upon the heart?

—MACBETH

CAPTAIN
NEWMAN,
M.D.

I

THE

FURNACE

We left Kelly Field in a bucket-seat C-47, nineteen officers in all, I alone headed for Colfax. I was outranked by all the others, who were going on—to Yuma A.A.F. base, March Field, and the vast installation at Santa Ana.

The officer next to me was a roly-poly Major who described himself as "a retread from the old Rainbow Division." He was wearing a Special Services shoulder patch and kept craning his neck to drink in every speck of scenery. "If that port engine doesn't catch on fire," he said cheerfully, "we ought to see plenty of mesa and desert. Know the Southwest, son?"

"No, sir. Until this morning, I was never west of Maxwell Field."

"Maxwell? Where's that?"

"Alabama, sir."

"Oh. Well, wonderful country we're heading into. Fantastic. Beautiful. Terrible, too. No place in the world like it—not even the Sahara. You never get to know the desert, really; that's why it never ceases to be fascinating. Where you headed?"

"Camp Colfax."

"The Furnace?" He made peculiar noises in his throat. "They fry by day and freeze at night. How long you visiting?"

"I'm not visiting, sir. I've just been assigned there."

"Oh, God. Sorry." He gave me a pitying sigh and rummaged in his brief case, in which I caught a glimpse of many Hershey bars and a .45. "Well, I suppose it could be worse. An overnight pass can take you to San Diego—pretty, but all Navy and intolerable; a three-day ought to mean Los Angeles. Silly town, but it will look like heaven after Colfax."

I was twenty-four, a second lieutenant in the Air Corps—and it was the Air Corps, not the Air Force, in those days, as the original words in the song about "the wild blue yonder" drummed into us. We wore our caps in that dashing pancake style, with the grommet removed, which distinguished us from the plebeian Army of which we were a rebellious and clearly superior province. I had been in Officers' Candidate School when the Japanese sent their planes and midget submarines to massacre our fleet at Oahu that terrible Sunday morning in December. A week later, I was flown down to the first P. R. and T. unit, at Maxwell Field. P. R. and T. means Psychological Research and Testing—and my head soon swam from both.

I was initiated into the mysteries of more aptitude tests, personality diagnoses and psychological "inventories" than I ever dreamed existed. I learned how to work up AGCTs (Army General Classification), how to score performance on the Porteus Maze, how to code CIs (Classification: Intelligence). I mastered instruments which measure everything from visual perception to psychomotor co-ordination. Now, over a year later, I was reporting to Lieutenant Colonel Michael Larrabee, C.O. of the hospital at—I call it Camp Colfax to spare the sensibilities of men who might recognize one or another of the wacky, tragic, weird, foolhardy episodes which, so many years later, I am setting down here. Colfax was a training base for fighter pilots and gunners on a godforsaken stretch of desert, some forty miles north of the

Mexican border, in the southwestern part of the United States. It was an operational training base, where the fledgling graduates of other flight and gunnery schools learned how to use aircraft as combat weapons. Their instructors, for the most part, were men returned from the war zones. . . .

Beside me, the Major pulled some Esso maps out of his brief case and spread them across both our laps. "Just look at these names!" His finger traced a path across Texas and Arizona. "Right out of a storybook."

And they were: Sombrero, Christmas, Quijotoa, Organ Pipe, Sunglow.

Soon we flew over desolate mountain ranges, high over the 7,680-foot Apache Peak, skirted the lesser Baboquivaris. Then endless miles of barren, rippled ground unrolled beneath us. For an hour I could not see the slightest sign of life: not a tree, not a shrub, not a stream, not a trickle, and surely not a living creature. Then the earth became a geologic graveyard, a fastness transplanted from the face of the moon: tremendous boulders, massive juts of rock and shale, accrusted peaks and battlements and colors such as I had never seen—burned russets, smoky blues —colors accented, in sudden and unexpected places, by stabs of white: chalk? limestone? bleached brontosaurus bones?

We crossed this ossified world and began to lose altitude, dropping toward a glare of yellowing plain. Soon I saw a car crawling across the earth, a beetle, puffing dust behind. As our ship banked and came lower, I saw a donkey plodding along an *arroyo*, all caked and cracked with alkali, as a man in a wide-brimmed hat flicked his hind with a branch.

The plane began to bounce around. The cocky little sergeant in the flight crew asked us to strap ourselves in. The chatter in the plane died away. A flash of tin roofs in the distance stabbed my eyes.

"There," the Major chuckled evilly, "is the Gehenna of your dreams, the gay metropolis of Colfax."

I studied my destination with that heightened awareness and,

I suppose, uneasiness that possesses any of us when we approach an alien place in which we know there is not one friend or voice to greet us. What I saw was not designed to nourish the soul: water towers and adobe walls, a cluster of shacks patched with Nehi signs, some glossy palms and gaunt saguaros, a Spanish mission from which a gilt cross rose out of the cracked, brown tiles, faded rodeo posters on a scabrous garage wall. My heart sank.

High up, in that crystal, cloudless, powder-blue sky, a squadron of fighters came rocketing out of space, and then another, maneuvering in the dazzling acrobatics of engagement and evasion. On an opposite arc of the horizon, a B-24 towed a drone target; two-engined craft were layered up in formation behind the flying coffin, peeling off, one by one. I could not hear the guns, but their tracer bullets stitched the sky.

Our buggy bumped the field so hard that a captain from G-4 grunted, "That son-of-a-bitch must own stock in a tire company."

We taxied down the runway. I saw the wooden struts of the control tower and rows of hangars and maintenance sheds. You could see the heat shimmering off every roof and runway.

"Don't forget to keep your head covered when you're out in that sun," said the Major.

"Thank you, sir."

"It hits your eyeballs first!"

"Yes, sir."

"Good luck, I hope."

The sergeant slammed the door back, tossed my B-4 bag to the ground, and extended his hand in an Indian grip, to help me down the no-ramp route. I stepped to the open door. I gasped as the heat hit me: a fist in a pillow.

"Lucky you got here during a cold spell, Lieutenant," the sergeant snickered.

"You are a born comedian," I said, and took the Indian grip and let myself down.

The sergeant grinned, "Geronimo!" slamming the door shut before I had staggered ten feet.

A corporal drifted toward me from the shade of a hangar.

The heat was ghastly, merciless, but the air was incredibly dry and light. Everything stood etched, razor-sharp, all the outlines astonishingly crisp. Far off, beyond a wire fence, feathery cottonwoods relieved that sun-drenched landscape.

The corporal led me off the baking field, out of the deafening clatter of propellers and riveting guns. I saw some advanced trainers and B-17s moving into formation on a far edge of the field. Beyond one of the runways a burned-out wreck of a plane, its bent propellers still clawing the sand, reminded me that death was not reserved for the men overseas.

The corporal heaved my bag into a jeep. "Take it away, Bronco." The driver, a charter member of that sullen breed from which jeep jockeys are recruited, got me to headquarters a good deal faster than I like to get anywhere. I signed in, then drove over to the hospital.

In Lieutenant Colonel Larrabee's office, a dimply WAC picked up the phone: "Sir, Lieutenant Alderson is—" She never finished. "Ouch." She wrinkled her shiny nose and put the phone back in its cradle. "You'll have to wait. Do you want to see the local paper? It stinks."

"Thank you."

She gave me a startled look and began to bang away on the typewriter.

A big electric fan on the wall was droning in a 180° arc. I leaned forward to let the wind cross the shirt that was sticking to my back, and browsed through the Colfax *Courier*. There was one movie house in town, a grain-and-feed store, a volunteer fire company, and a night-spot called The Blue Cave: "No Cover or Minimum Charge at any time. All Men in Uniform WELCOME!"

The news columns did not brighten my mood. Two Mexicans and a Negro had been arrested in a brawl in *El Cortez* Saloon.

Four new addresses on Sam Houston Street were declared off-limits to military personnel. A widow had broken her leg chasing a goat off the roof of her outhouse. A box on page 1, bordered by fluttering American flags, touted a forthcoming "gala" benefit dance for the U.S.O. at which Brigadier General Armstrong, our Commanding Officer, would join Mayor Garcia O'Leary as co-sponsor.

A double buzz suddenly signaled the WAC, who straightened her khaki tie and darted into Lieutenant Colonel Larrabee's office. She left the door slightly open and I heard a hard-bitten voice bark, "It's one hell of a way to run a hospital is all I can say, Larrabee!"

Through the opening I could see Lieutenant Colonel Larrabee, standing behind his desk, while a full colonel with steel-gray hair, a trim mustache, the bearing of a drillmaster and a chest-load of decorations paced back and forth before him, and in and out of my path of vision. "Who the hell's in charge, anyway—you or Captain Newman?"

I pricked up my ears. At Maxwell, my chief, Major Sibley, a clinical psychologist who despised "head shrinkers," had warned me: "You're going to an installation where there's a psycho-analyst in charge of the N.P. ward. His name is Newman and he acts as if it were Newton. He doesn't know the difference between characteristics and causes. He confuses his intuitions with facts."

"Does he cure his patients?" I asked naïvely.

"Cure or 'change'?" Major Sibley had snorted. "Oh, he's got lots of razzle-dazzle, and can charm the socks off a psychopath. I hear he gets transferences the way a movie star attracts school-girls. But he thinks he's got a cure when he only rearranges the symptoms. Hell, I've seen men 'cured' by prayer, frogs, friends, the passage of time or the application of the rarest wizardry of all: common sense. . . . Keep your wits about you with Captain Newman. He's a character. My guess is you won't like him."

My recollections were obliterated by the brassy thunder of the Colonel: "Goddamit, Larrabee, we're in a *war!* You've got the slowest return-to-duty rate in Ward Seven in the whole damn area command. Washington keeps putting the heat on me to step up training, grind out fighting men. Every C.O. on every base in every goddam theater of action around the *world* is practically on his knees, begging for pilots, gunners, navigators—and your man Newman keeps holding the hand of every little squirt who wets his pants on an instruction flight! He won't certify them for combat, won't let us send them overseas, until he's given every Nervous Nellie on the post a year's 'ther-a-py'! Ther-a-py, for Christ's sake! It's not ther-a-py, it's a goddam rest cure, is what it is. It's getting so that every time a GI hits sick call with a belly-ache or a runny nose, that joker finds some goddam 'psy-cho-gen-ic *syn*-drome' and pulls the guy out of training and takes him into Sunnybrook Farm. Every odd-ball, every gold-brick, every feather-merchant and malingerer and yellow-belly on this post thinks that all he has to do to get grounded is run to New-man with some cock-and-bull story about having the sweats every time He Thinks of Mother!"

At this point, the WAC backed out with a telegram, shutting the door, but not so carefully as to blot out that metallic voice. She jabbed her thumb downward. "Corsets is on the warpath."

"Who?"

"Colonel Pyser. Exec to the C.O. and a prize s.o.b. You're not supposed to eavesdrop." She went to her desk but did not resume her typing. Smiling dreamily, she listened with no pretense of disinterest.

We heard Lieutenant Colonel Larrabee's voice, so quiet as to be indistinguishable, then Colonel Pyser's vocal bugle: "He worries about their goddam 'neu-ro-ses' while the Japs are knocking our goddam ears off and the Germans are pounding hell out of England. Just *look* at his ward! Newman has them all weaving baskets and playing ping-pong and getting their goddam breakfast in bed while the men they started out with, right here at Colfax, are getting their brains blown out!"

Again Lieutenant Colonel Larrabee's voice made obscure explanations.

Again Colonel Pyser's trumpet took command. "Then send him overseas, for the love of God, and get a psychiatrist on this post who will!"

The door opened. I got to my feet fast and went into a brace. Colonel Pyser swept by me like a blast of wind. His face was dark; he was biting his mustache. His spine might have been cast in cement.

The WAC fanned herself.

In a moment, Lieutenant Colonel Larrabee came out. He looked like a pleasant man, ruddy, avuncular, considerably overweight. He handed some papers to the WAC, saying, "Six copies. Air Surgeon's Office." He saw me and smiled. "Come in, Lieutenant."

I gave him my transfer orders.

He scanned them carelessly. "I'm glad you got here. We need help all over the hospital. Your office will be on the ground floor, 109. I want every new patient to get a careful once-over. It ought to be routine. We're getting too many wash-outs around here because we just haven't enough personnel to button up every angle. Your predecessor, by the way, went off his rocker. His name was Drubeck. Did you happen to know him?"

"No, sir."

"You didn't miss anything. Bright fellow, but hard-drinking and a bit of a fool." He sighed. "I just don't understand some people. My exec will brief you on the S.O.P around here. I guess that's about all." He poured himself a Coke.

I rose and saluted. I was at the door when he called, "Lieutenant." He came over and put his hand on my shoulder. "Don't get things fouled up around here."

I did not know what that meant, but I said, "I'll try not to, sir."

I went down to Room 109.

My name was already on the door. It was the first time I had ever seen my name on a door, or had an office entirely to myself, and I won't deny feeling pleased. The office opened into the "Psychological Laboratory" which contained the CM701D chair, stick and foot pedals, a two-hand Graphic Recorder, a Single-Dimension Pursuit Meter. Everything was stencilled "M.C."— for "Medical Corps."

I explored the desk. The top drawer had a mound of sand in one corner and a snapshot of a Cape Cod house with snow on the roof and snow all over the ground. I felt sorry for Drubeck. The other drawers housed chits from the Officers' Club, some lottery tickets, elaborately lettered in Spanish, and some questionnaires.

In the bookcase I saw the *Interviewer's Handbook* (Adjutant General's Office, Supplement to AR 615-25). I thumbed through it. My eye fell on this passage:

> It is well to remember that the man you are interviewing is probably sizing you up, too. . . . He may appear surly, when in reality he is shy; he may chatter to cover up embarrassment; he may be silent because he resents anyone in authority. . . .
>
> After the new soldier has seated himself, preferably at the *end* of your desk rather than the desk-width away from you. . . .

I could not help smiling. I remembered the first GI I ever interviewed: a strapping Oregonian who blushed furiously when I asked him to take the chair at the end of my desk and politely declined. He declined to sit in the chair across from me, too. He just did not want to sit down anywhere. Convinced I had encountered an interesting case of Hostility to Authority on my very first foray into the field, I began to ask him questions. I thought I was being quite subtle about it, even getting some revealing responses which I could report to Major Sibley, when the red-faced son of the Northwest blurted: "Sir, I got a boil on my ass is driving me crazy."

My reverie was broken by the harsh *"Hut,* two, three, four;

hut, two, *hut,* two!" that punctuates the air of every army post in the world. I turned to the window. A platoon in olive-green fatigues, shovels on their shoulders, marched toward the barracks beyond the parade ground. From the distance, I heard the Comanche yell of men ending their calisthenics. I was turning away from the window when I saw something, no more than a shadow, scuttle under a prickly barrel cactus. I watched and waited, and at last it emerged—a hideous, purplish, scaly creature (reptile? lizard?) with vile pinkish blotches. I did not know then that some of the children on the post kept the Gila monster, that desert atavar, in cages, along with tarantulas and chuckwallas and the hideous, but harmless, horned toad. I felt queasy.

And suddenly, a wave of unbearable loneliness welled up in me. I was further from my past, my family, my friends, than I had ever been before, an exile in the desiccated sands ten thousand miles from an elm or a meadow or a fishing stream.

I wanted desperately to talk to someone.

I stepped into the corridor, almost colliding with an orderly who was pushing an operating table down the hall; a white-faced boy was strapped to the table, silent, crying, and a second orderly was walking alongside, holding a bottle of blood plasma in mid-air. He gave me a queer look as I blurted: "Where's Ward Seven?"

II

CAPTAIN
NEWMAN

I went down a corridor that bisected the main wing of the hospital, past Emergency, past Laboratories, past an arrow that read "Ward 7," through some swinging doors and down the incline of a long, open, screened-in ramp. At the end of the ramp was a set of double doors. I pushed one open—and stopped short.

Looming ahead, just beyond a reception area, some offices, and half a dozen rooms for patients, was a great iron door. It had heavy bars and a big, square prison lock. To the right was this sign:

WARD 7

—

NO VISITORS

—

RING BELL

Is it the uncaught criminal in each of us that stirs and sounds uneasy warning when we see a barred window, a Black Maria, a prison gate? Is it guilt that triggers apprehension, or are even the innocent made grateful, as I was then, to be free?

There were four offices in the reception area, two on each side, and a long waiting-room bench against the wall between each pair. Name plates stuck out at right angles above the doors: "Lt. Grace Blodgett, Chief Nurse," "Captain S. O. Mathieson," "Captain Josiah J. Newman, Chief, N.P. Section."

His door was open.

He was hunched over the desk, his head propped between his hands, reading. His khaki blouse was open at the throat; a khaki tie hung across the back of the chair. A cigarette drooped from one corner of his mouth, the smoke curling up into his eyes. He was so lost in concentration that he was completely unaware of my presence.

There are some men about whom you seem to know a great deal after a few moments' observation. Captain Newman, to me at least, was such a man. Even in repose, his features suggested a commitment to the sardonic. He looked distinctly unmilitary: his hair was thick and longish (most officers affected crew cuts, in an effort to look young or accent their virility); his sleeves were not creased in the knife edge that is the martinet's pride; his gestures, as he read, were singularly expressive: he rubbed his chin, frowned, scratched his cheek, scowled, ran a hand through his hair. At one point he grunted in disgust and crossed a savage "X" down half a page with a red grease pencil.

I cleared my throat, but he did not seem to hear it. I knocked on the open door.

Captain Newman looked up. He stared at me absently, silently, for an uncomfortably long moment, then nodded. "Hi."

I wasn't prepared for that casual "Hi," nor for the fact that, having said it, Captain Newman said no more, but proceeded to gaze at me in penetrating and most disconcerting appraisal.

"I'm—Lieutenant Alderson, sir."

"Well, come in. Admission is free." He waved me to a chair, leaned back, and—never before nor since, I think, have I been scrutinized with such unnerving *directness*. That is the only way I can describe it. His eyes probed mine as if I were the most interesting and important human being he had ever laid eyes on. "What's on your mind, Lieutenant?"

"Nothing, sir."

"That's dandy," he said dryly, "but hardly plausible. Tell me more."

"I—just thought I would come by—introduce myself," I stammered.

"How do you do?" he nodded, ironically polite. "I'm Captain Newman. How do you feel?"

"I? Quite well, sir."

He groaned. "Okay, okay. Let's play games."

It suddenly dawned on me that he thought I was a prospective patient, waiting to be interviewed, so I said hastily, "I just arrived, sir, from Maxwell. I'm the psychologist Colonel Larrabee requested—"

Delight lighted up his eyes and he flung his head back with a burst of laughter. "I'll be damned. I was just finishing a brilliant spot-diagnosis, and thinking you were possible material for Ward Seven. Too polite, guarded, a little tense; too well-bred to have a healthily tough, resilient ego; real party manners, but not as secure as you'd like me to think you are." He crossed his legs on top of the desk. "I was wondering where you stored your anxiety, and from which direction your ambivalence would pop out. And all those 'Sir's!'" A crook of displeasure moved across his lips. "'Sir!' You're one of the few guys who says it as if he means it. You're not from West Point, are you?"

"No, sir."

"Thank God. I guess you just love the Army." He extended a hand without changing his position. I had to rise from my chair to reach across his shoes to shake hands with him. "Welcome. You look pretty young to be the man we put in for. Maybe you're a genius. What are you, about twenty-one?"

"I'm twenty-four, s—" I caught myself in time.

"Attaboy. Where did you go to school?"

"Harvard."

"That figures. I suppose you majored in psychology?"

"No, sir."

He sighed. "What did those hot-shots at Maxwell teach you?"

"Tests, mostly."

"What kind of mostly?"

"I beg your pardon?"

"Skip it. What kind of tests?"

I rattled off the list, trying to sound impressive and professional, but I felt annoyed and extremely foolish.

He let me go on and on, nodding, alternately solemn and quizzical, and when I finished, he said, "You won't need half of that stuff around here. Would you like some coffee? My boys make the best on the post."

"I'd like that very much."

"Cream? Sugar?"

"Black, please. One lump."

"Lump?" he echoed. "Why, Lieutenant, where have you been? Don't you know there's a national *crisis* in lumps? The War Production Board is saving all those little pieces of paper they wrap lumps in, so they can make one roll five thousand miles long and then we can all make nine copies of everything instead of only eight. That's how we'll win the war. Carbon copies. Our secret weapon." He picked up the phone. "Do you spell your name with two 'ls' or one?" Into the mouthpiece, he said, "Sergeant Kopp, please."

"One, sir."

"Did you hear about the sign they've got in the Pentagon cafeteria? Six feet high and thirty feet long and it says 'FOOD WILL WIN THE WAR!' To which some bright boy cracked, 'Sure, but how can we get the Japs over here to eat it?' " He laughed. "I'd give that guy a medal. . . . Hello, Arkie? Forgive me for disturbing your beauty nap. This is your lovable and hungry superior officer. . . . No, of course, I didn't recognize your voice. You sound as though you're eating taffy apples—under water.

How about some Java on the double? Make it two this morning. One black, with sugar . . . Roger." He hung up and glanced at me sheepishly. "Sergeant Kopp loves to have you say 'Roger.' It makes him feel like a hero. He's scared to death of flying, which is fine with me because he's a hell of a wardmaster . . . Would you excuse me for a minute? I've got to finish reading this."

I took the opportunity to take a longer look at him. He was tall, very brown from the sun, slightly round-shouldered. He looked around thirty-five. He had heavy-lidded, hazel eyes with deep rings under them. The mannerisms he had already displayed, that unpredictable interplay between the wry, the weary, the impatient, the disenchanted, made me think of Major Sibley's phrase: "razzle-dazzle." He was certainly quick, intelligent, spilling over with responsiveness. He also struck me as vain. I wondered whether, like many gifted men who relish their intuitiveness, he was not insensitive to the vulnerabilities of those with whom he could not identify. I was in no mood to be charitable.

He looked up suddenly, catching me by surprise, and grinned. "If you don't see what you want, ask for it."

I could feel myself flush. He was exasperating.

"What's your first name?" he asked.

"Belden."

"Belden? Where did you ever get a name like that?"

"I was named after an uncle."

"Okay, where did he ever get a name like that?"

"It's been in our family for several generations, sir."

" 'Sir,' " he growled. "Is that what people actually *call* you—'Belden'?"

"My friends call me Barney."

"Congratulations. You've got fine friends. . . . I suppose you're a protégé of John Sibley's?"

"He—trained me," I said cautiously.

"He's smart as a whip—too rigid, for my taste, but a whiz with charts, extrapolations and all the hocus-pocus of statistics.

They reassure him. Like most systematic anal types he has a need to prove that numbers are superior to insight. Did he, by any chance, let you monkey around with the projective tests?"

"N-no, sir."

"No TATs?"

"No."

"Any sentence-completions?"

"A few."

"But no Rorschachs?"

"I'm afraid not."

"Don't be afraid," he said dryly. "And I think you ought to cut down on clichés like that around here. My patients latch on to the damnedest little revelations of the unconscious. 'I'm afraid' means just that to the anxiety cases. They hear the word, not the platitude. Even 'I think' can get you into a hassle with the compulsive neurotics. I recommend 'I feel.' A small point, but useful. No one can quarrel with how you *feel*. Even the doctors over in Main are wising up to the advantages of that bromide."

At this point a nurse came in, carrying a tray. There were lieutenant's bars on her uniform. I rose; Captain Newman didn't. I could not help wondering how much ribbing he took at the Officers' Club with a nurse as pretty as that around. Her eyes were china-blue; her mouth was wide, lazy; her hair was the color of wheat; her skin was fair and quite marvelous. "Good morning," she smiled. "Don't blow your top, Joe."

I started to help her with the tray.

"You *are* new around here," she said.

"Very funny," said Captain Newman. "Since when are officers on K.P. around here, Francie? Has someone shot all my orderlies?"

"Arkie was bringing the tray in, but I wanted an excuse to barge in on you and ask about that gunner who was referred from Interceptor Command."

"This is Lieutenant Alderson. Lieutenant Corum. She outranks you, Belden; she was commissioned before the war." He took a coffee mug off the tray and put it down before me. "What's worrying you, Francie?"

"He's hallucinating again. He dived under the bed before breakfast, yelling the Japs were here, and he won't come out. He keeps screaming and shivering and begging to go home."

"Did he get his medication last night?"

"Yes, but it's worn off."

"Have you tried to coax him out?"

"Blodgett spent half the morning on the floor, Joe."

"Blodgett isn't you. A man would be a fool to come out for Frozen-Puss. Has he eaten anything?"

"No."

"Does he have any special favorites in food?"

"Chocolate malts."

Captain Newman sipped some coffee moodily. After a moment he said, "Yeah," to himself, and turned to Lieutenant Corum. "You put a nice big chocolate malt and some cookies on the floor, right near the bed. Let him see you. Tell him he'll hurt my feelings if he isn't back in his bed when I start morning rounds."

"That's in twelve minutes."

"I know, I know. Don't nag me."

"And you've got a conference in Ward Two—"

"I can hardly wait. What rabbit am I supposed to pull out of what hat?"

"They want you to orient Major Eberly's staff on Pentothal."

"That will gratify my exhibitionistic quota for the day."

She laughed. "So long, Lieutenant. Don't let Joe forget all about time." She left. She had long legs and lovely ankles.

Captain Newman noticed me looking after her. "You're not married?"

"No, sir."

"I'd better introduce you to Captain Jarvis. He never got over reading a book on Don Juan. But don't waste your time looking in town, no matter what Bill tells you; the local women are female impersonators. . . . What weird tales have you heard about me and Ward Seven?"

"None, really."

"No?" He sounded amused. "Then I'll brief you, before the enemy does. . . . We handle everything from tics to 'uncooperative behavior' to 'combat fatigue.' We deal with sickness—the kind of sickness that doesn't show up on sphygmographs or fluoroscopes. A patient may run no fever, or hits 104 out of the blue. Don't think they all babble gibberish; most of them make sense —if you listen to their special vocabulary long enough and hard enough. They're using English but speaking a foreign language— the language of suffering, which requires special symbols. A man can have a pulse that suddenly beats like a trip hammer, or one that doesn't register much more than a corpse. There's a reason, there's always a reason. To call someone mad is meaningless." He got up abruptly, wiping his face with a handkerchief, to pace around the room or stare out of the window or lean against the wall or jab a finger into my shoulder as he held forth. "Some of our patients break into a sweat if a fly buzzes past their ear; others stay dead to the world with the retreat cannon exploding outside the window. Some will end their days in a veterans' hospital; others will walk out of here and go back to the shooting and deserve more medals than the President can ever give them. There's only one thing you can be absolutely sure of: every, repeat every, man who's in Ward Seven—no matter what he says or what you hear or what the textbooks say—is sick. Are you still with me?"

"Yes, sir."

"Have I said anything so far that doesn't make sense?"

"I don't think so."

"Is all this—uh—too elementary for a Harvard man?"

I shrugged. "I don't know much about—mental illness."

"Good. That's an honest answer. This is the only place I know where you can go around telling the truth all the time without being crucified. How much, by the way, *do* you know about psychiatry?"

"I've read some Freud."

"And? Were you impressed, outraged, converted?"

I cleared my throat. "I was—fascinated."

"Is that all?"

"Yes," I said stubbornly.

"What's the superego?"

"It's—like the conscience, isn't it?"

"What ideas of his struck you most? What do you think are the key concepts?"

"The whole idea of the unconscious," I said, trying to control my irritation. "The discovery that dreams have meaning. The idea of ambivalence . . . The fact that our behavior is determined—even random mistakes, slips of the tongue . . . The fact that sexuality is found even in infants."

"You left out the Oedipus complex," he sighed.

"I suppose that's terribly revealing." I did not try to tone down the sarcasm.

He grinned. "It shows you're a clean, wholesome, upstanding, one hundred per cent all-American boy. Are your parents alive?"

"Yes, sir."

"Then you'll have plenty of time to be reminded of Oedipus. Do you have any brothers?"

"No."

"Sisters?"

"One."

"Younger or older?"

"Younger."

"You're the oldest? You're lucky. . . . Why don't you take your tie off before you suffocate? It's okay. The C.O. doesn't wear a tie either—weather permitting."

I took my tie off gratefully and unbuttoned my collar. He picked up the report he had been reading. "How well do you write?"

"Reasonably well, I think."

"Here's some homework. It's a lousy job, but you might learn something. Tell me how it can be improved." The title read:

Fear versus Hostility in Combat
by
Josiah J. Newman, Captain, M.C.

"Don't spare the author's feelings," he said. "Do you want to hear more about Ward Seven?"

"Yes, sir."

"You'd be a fool to say no." He smiled.

I said nothing.

"The men call it 'Psycho Beach' or 'Flak Haven.' Banter reduces anxiety. Only the goons outside call it 'The Booby Hatch.' We get our cases from all over the hospital, the post, even the guardhouse—when it's clear to even the MPs that some disciplinary problems don't respond to punishment. We get them from overcrowded installations, from Fort Logan to Douglas. We get them from any transient outfit in the area—if we're the nearest Army hospital. And we get them from overseas, more and more of them, flown in from evacuation units, base hospitals, convalescent centers. There's a bigger shortage of psychiatrists in the Army than can be rectified if this war goes on for ten years, and the word has gotten around that I act like an M.D., not an officer, a psychiatrist, not a military man. We're on the side of the patients here. We try to give the same attention and concern to some miserable kid who's cracked up in a machine shop—not in the air, not under fire, not in a way that endows horror with nobility—as we do to a fifty-two-mission gunner from the C.B.I. Maybe that's unrealistic, but I don't know how else to do my job. When a man cracks up, be he a squadron commander with a Purple Heart or a radio apprentice in basic training, he's cracked up inside, within the world of his own conflict or fear—" He stopped, frowning, and stepped to the window, where he listened intently.

I heard the throb of engines in the sky, the staccato of gunfire, softened by distance. Then, far away somewhere, I heard a motor stuttering. That was what he had heard. We listened in silence until the coughing stopped and the motor went smooth and throttled full again.

Captain Newman relaxed and turned back to me. "When I first got here, the instructors used to make every trainee go up, even the plane-shy. Some of the men threw up every time they got in the air, or lost their sphincter control, or soiled their pants. Some did it after they landed. Some got nightmares; some shook so hard they couldn't hold a soup spoon. But—they had to go up. No molly-coddling around the Air Corps. No, siree. 'Snap out of it, buster! Quit goofing-off! You yellow? Where's your guts?' They sent acute anxiety cases into combat. The pilots flew; the gunners fought. Sure. They fought the enemy and they fought their terror. Only, they developed symptoms. Symptoms. Sooner or later they cracked up, or maybe tried to blow an officer's head off. Some were discharged from the service on a Section Eight count. Do you know for what? 'Lack of moral fiber.' God almighty! 'Lack of moral fiber!' The brass just couldn't get it through their heads that a symptom is a red flag with 'Danger' all over it. A symptom is the way anxiety breaks out. That's all. Symptoms are anxiety-equivalents. You wouldn't think it takes much brains to comprehend that, would you? It isn't only men like Colonel Pyser who think fear is optional. Some of my esteemed medical colleagues, who are descended from astrologists, can't understand that; they think panic a form of cowardice. . . . Tell me when I'm leaving you behind."

"I'm still with you."

"Hang on. The exercise will improve your mind. Well, what do you do with a man who's had it? Bust him? Court-martial? Send him back to civilian life? . . . The first thing I do, in a stroke of sheer genius, is remove the cause of the anxiety. Ground them. Yank them off flying service. You'll find some bona-fide war heroes around here—as ground instructors, in Communications, Weather, Tactics, Control Tower, but *not* flying officers. On the other hand, we get some dramatic results, therapeutically, and put men back in the air, too, back into combat." He drank some coffee, waving the mug to emphasize a point. "Where you come in, Lieutenant, is in helping us spot men who may break down in training or conk out under stress. It's not our job to care if a boy drinks, or is a wee bit paranoid, or is struggling with homo-sexual impulses. I have to concentrate on only two things: Can he fight? *Will* he fight? We're supposed to turn out killers, alas, not saints. You can also help me predict who will break down if we *don't* send them into combat. Oh, yes, some guys do. Who *needs* combat? They may be neurotic as hell, but they're worth their weight in gold. . . . We had a devoutly religious boy here who always fired his first burst at Jesus, in the clouds—because he felt Jesus wouldn't approve of killing. Only after he 'got rid of Our Lord first' could he fight—which he did in a way that racked up a record that would make your jaw drop. Strange are the ways of the psyche. . . . And don't think that because I make some cracks about tests I'm blind to their utility. I use them. Oh, I beef about their laboratory smell, but I'd be a damn fool not to know they can give me invaluable clues. Where I quarrel with the data-demons is this—"

I listened with the utmost fascination, of course, and more than a little flattered. Yet I could not help wondering whether Captain Newman talked this freely, this indiscreetly, to everyone. It occurred to me that he did a lot of his thinking in conversation, that he learned by hearing what he had to say. He tried to act cynical, but I wondered if he were not protecting himself against feelings to which he felt vulnerable. He had to be on guard, I suppose, against being seduced by his own empathy.

What I found most irritating about him was that he violated all my preconceptions of how a psychiatrist ought to act. Detachment, kindliness, wisdom—those are what I expected of one dedicated to the healing of perhaps the most painful and complex suffering of which man is capable. No three qualities seemed more unlike Captain Newman. Wisdom? He struck me as neither mellow nor moderate nor humble nor judicious; and if these are not the components of wisdom, then what is? Kindliness? "Kind" was one of the last adjectives I would have used to describe him. He was too direct, too blunt, too flippant, too frank for comfort.

As for detachment: his brusqueness, his offhand manner, his deflating remarks, his irony and petulance and shifts in mood were difficult to understand.

I do not know whether my expression, as all this went through my mind, betrayed me, but to my dismay he was saying, with an air that bordered on mockery, "If you're wondering why I'm sounding off to you this way, I'll tell you. First, I want to indoctrinate you—fast. Second, I'm bribing you. I'm trying to get you so interested in the ward that you'll identify with us and not the back-biting fraternity of the mediocre. Third, I know damn well you were only being polite, and lying through your teeth, when you said you hadn't heard any scuttlebutt about Ward Seven. You must have asked around before you got here; even if you were stupid enough not to, you must have heard some delicious cracks from Major Sibley."

Before I could demur, a stocky, bristle-haired master sergeant barged into the room. He did not salute. He cried, "What's holding you up, Captain?"

Captain Newman reached for a water carafe. "All right, Kopp. I'm sorry."

"We had to put Haskin in wet packs. But Perini wrote a letter home and Williamson made that telephone call to his old lady." Sergeant Kopp handed him some night reports and vanished.

Captain Newman scanned the pages absently, sipping out of the mug, and carrying on a conversation with me on the side. "Would you like to sit in on my staff conferences?"

"I'd like that very much," I said.

"Tuesdays and Thursdays, nine o'clock . . . Did you say you just arrived?"

"Yes, sir."

"Know anyone on the base?"

"No."

"Mmh . . . Busy for dinner?"

"No."

"Drop around." He tossed the reports into his tray and started out. "Six o'clock. Don't bring flowers."

I waited for him to go through the door first.

"My, my," he grinned. " 'Age does not wither, nor custom stale, his infinite charm.' "

As we stepped into the reception area, Captain Newman nodded toward the "Ward 7" sign on the wall. "That sign used to read 'Neuro-Psychiatric Ward.' What a hell of a thing to hit a kid with! The very first order I ever gave around here was to have that damn sign changed. Some of my patients drew up a petition; they wanted me to add a line: 'Officers Welcome.' " He laughed. "It hurt, but I had to turn the boys down."

"Thank you for the coffee," I said, starting to go.

"Hey, wait a minute." He studied me. "I just thought of something. I don't suppose you've ever been inside a psychiatric ward?"

"No."

"I can be pretty dense, as you'll learn. Are you going off to a Top Secret briefing, or tea with the General?"

"Oh, no. Just back to my new office—"

"Would you like to see what goes on?"

I tried to sound more casual than I felt. "Why, yes, Captain; if I won't be in the way."

"I won't *let* you get in the way," he growled. "Stay close to me, try to look as if it's all old stuff, and don't ask any questions." He motioned toward the iron door. "Let's get your feet wet, Barney."

III
WARD 7

We passed some private rooms. The doors were open. In one, a patient was sleeping. In another, two men in uniform were playing cards. A captain came out of a third room and waved at Newman. "How do you feel, Powell?" asked Newman.

Powell shrugged. "Those same damn tensions."

"Don't brag," said Captain Newman.

Powell laughed and went by us. He was carrying swim shorts.

We stepped to the big, iron-barred door. Captain Newman pressed the button. I heard a bell ring inside the ward somewhere and (it would be foolish to deny that I felt apprehensive) for a moment I hoped, idiotically, that no one would open the door to let us in. My heart was beating so loudly that I was sure Captain Newman could hear it. My mind, I suppose, was full of those grotesque images about "insane asylums" which are popular with cartoonists or night-club comedians: maniacal laughter, strait jackets, men foaming at the mouth or stalking about Napoleonically. But here—

The ward I saw through the ominous bars was pleasant, sunny, cheerful, a long row of beds—thirty or so on each side of a wide aisle, and more jutting off at an angle into a wing. Beyond the beds was a dining area, and beyond that a sun lounge with wicker furniture. Most of the patients were on their beds, reading, writing letters, chatting, drawing pictures; one was having his breakfast spooned off his tray by an orderly; several were wandering around the aisles or the sun lounge, from which I heard the pleasant, flat "clack . . . clack" of a ping-pong game and, from the radio, the drawl of the local announcer: "Temperature one-hundred-and-nine . . . no relief in sight . . ." Someone snapped the radio off and began to play a harmonica, some hymn, very sweet, beautifully phrased. (That, I learned later, was Stan Djuba playing. A Marine patrol had found him on Kolombangara, one of the lesser-known Solomon Islands, hanging in a banyan tree, trapped in his parachute, half-dead, half-blind, strangling amid shrieking white cockatoos.)

Captain Newman was saying something to me.

"I'm sorry, sir," I apologized. "I didn't hear you."

"I would never have guessed. . . . I was saying, don't let these damn bars throw you. Everyone feels a little uneasy, the first time."

"Oh. Thank you."

"What do you think the bars are for?"

"Why—to keep the patients in."

He eyed me with a sardonic twinkle. "They also keep the brass and the bastards *out*. That's a good thing to tell a patient when he first stands before this door."

An orderly came to the door, which he unlocked with a key he kept on a clip fastened to his belt; Captain Newman stepped in; I followed; the orderly locked the door behind us.

We were in a small bay, with three rooms on the right. "Treatment rooms," said Captain Newman. "We use them for Sodium Pentothal sessions—but never say that or the men will think you're a corn-ball. They call it 'flak-juice.'"

One of the treatment rooms was open. I saw mattress soundproofing on the ceiling and the inside of the door, a hospital cot.

"These are the only rooms in the ward that can be locked from the inside," said Captain Newman.

Suddenly, from somewhere outside but near, I heard the distinct, plaintive "Baaa" of a sheep.

"You're not hearing things—yet," grinned Newman. "We keep sheep in the back yard. For the laboratory. You need sheep's blood for tests: Wassermanns, agglutinations. I hope you have no negative transference to the source of our wool."

The ward was surprisingly cool. Several water tanks, with fans in the forward compartment, were set in the upper halves of windows. The windows were covered with heavy wire screens, padlocked. There were some private rooms ("for officers") along both walls, lettered from "A" to "H," each door with a shatter-proof observation window, about nine inches square.

And now, as we drew closer, I could no longer pretend that this was just another ward in a hospital. At the end of the aisle, an unshaved corporal was propelling a rocking chair furiously, back and forth, his jaw set, glowering at no one. A boy lay flat on his bed, staring at the ceiling; his hands were clasped; he was praying: "Hail Mary, full of grace, Mother of God . . ." On the floor between two beds crouched a young blond giant, superbly proportioned, naked to the waist, his head between his hunched-up knees, weeping, weeping with such anguish as I cannot describe.

Sergeant Kopp came down the aisle to us with a big, unattractive nurse, in her forties, who let her spectacles spin back into a small case pinned on her uniform.

Captain Newman started to introduce us: "Lieutenant Blodgett, my head nurse—" when, without the slightest warning, the ward exploded. A big Negro bolted up in bed. "Rise and shine, men, bat your guns! He's in!"

Cheers, whistles, hoots, cat-calls—not hostile, but amused, delighted, even affectionate—erupted all over the room.

"Boil the needles, Jasper!"

"Captain Flak-Juice rides again!"

"He's gonna goof off, fellows. Watch Doc goof off!"

"Hi, Doc, hi, Doc, how's the old hypo-jockey today?"

"Let's hear it for Newman!"

"Boo-oo. Boo-oooo!"

Stan Djuba's harmonica swung into "There'll Be a Hot Time in the Old Town Tonight." A man ran down the aisle imitating a siren, cranking his hand around and around, howling metallically, shaking with laughter.

"Hey, Doc," someone jeered, "who's the Boy Scout with you?"

One man put his hands to his mouth and imitated a bugle; another put his forefingers in his mouth and whistled "Dixie"; a third bellowed "Moooo—Moooo—" The door to one of the officers' rooms was flung open; a gray-haired Major stepped out, shouting, "Silence! I will not tolerate these manifestations any longer!" He wheeled around, slamming the door behind him.

"Man, oh, man, lookit Captain sweat!"

"Whaddaya say, Doc? Give us the poop!"

"How we doing, sir?"

Captain Newman made an elaborate show of surveying the ward. "You guys seem a bit depressed this morning," he said.

This brought down a new and appreciative wave of laughter.

"Let's have the theme song!" someone called, and a dozen men began to clap their hands in unison, chanting this ditty:

> Goody, goody gum-drops,
> Here's dear Cap-tain,
> Let's give a hand to
> Dear Doc New-man!
> Yeaaay, team!

Sergeant Kopp stepped into the middle of the aisle. "Okay, knock it off, knock it off." His voice was loud but his tone was perfunctory.

"What's the matter, Sarge, can't you take it?"

"We got Arkie, too."

"It's a double-header!"

"Double-header, my ass. It's a triple feature. Look at Blodgett!"

Nurse Blodgett sniffed her disapproval.

Now Captain Newman put both hands up, shaking his head
in a parody of despair. "One of these days you jokers are going
to drive me *nuts.*"

A rollicking cheer, greater than any before, went up.

"That's the idea, Doc."

"You said it!"

"Lay down, Ziggy; say everything comes to your mind!"

Sergeant Kopp caught my eye. "That's what they get the biggest charge out of—hearing him say they're going to drive *him*
nuts."

So this, I realized, was all part of an elaborate game Captain
Newman permitted them to play. He was their commanding
officer, their doctor, their warder, their judge. He could keep them
in Ward 7 or send them back to duty. He could put them under
restraint or get them out of the Army with a Certificate of Disability Discharge. He could put them to sleep with a hypo, or
dull their pain with sedation, or give them Sodium Pentothal to
reconstruct the horrors that had driven them here. He was, it suddenly struck me, the one man in the Army who would not punish
them, who was unaffected by their hostility, undismayed by
their misery, acceptant of their profanity or rebellion or rage.
To him they were patients—not soldiers, not "psychos," not
threats. He was their keeper, their confessor, their life line to
sanity. And in his head, they thought or hoped or prayed, lay
their hope of salvation: that miracle of insight and intercession
which could heal them.

What perverse delight, I wondered, did they get from baiting
him this way? Part of it, of course, was the pleasure of soldiers
deriding an officer with impunity. Part of it was the compen-
sation the ill get from provoking the healthy. But most of all, I

think, they reveled in the pretense, if only for a moment, that this was not a military installation governed by indifferent power and hateful disciplines; Newman let them treat him like a man coming into a roomful of irreverent friends. How on earth could he assert authority in this mocking congregation, I wondered, or regain respect after permitting such liberties? I soon found out.

As the men made their taunting noises, grinned their sarcasms, Captain Newman stood there, looking alternately amused and aggrieved, smiling at one remark, wincing at another, affecting difficulty in controlling his dismay.

"Give us the score, Doc!" someone called.

A hush fell on the ward.

Captain Newman pursed his lips reflectively. "Morale: excellent. Humor: improving. Manners: bro-*ther!*" He waited for the laughter to die down, and when it did said, with the utmost gravity, "Gentlemen, prepare for morning rounds," and turned his back to the ward.

Lieutenant Blodgett pushed a sort of tea-tray table toward him. The patients' charts, each on a metal clipboard, were neatly stacked in slots.

"What should I know?" asked Newman.

"Kolinski's refusing to bathe. . . . The Major in Room G got violent around 4 A.M. . . . Hillman wet his bed again. . . ."

Behind them, to my fascination, all the banter and noises faded now; the men in the aisles went back to their beds; some stretched out, others plumped up their pillows; an orderly helped a man from the sun lounge into his bed; the ward settled down. One boy had started a Bronx cheer when Captain Newman said, "Gentlemen," but stopped on a warning "Hey, jerk!" from his neighbor.

Captain Newman scanned the nurses' notes at the bottom of the first chart.

"Okay, Doc, they're ready," said Sergeant Kopp.

Captain Newman turned. "Thank you, men," he said. "May I

introduce Lieutenant Alderson, who will be working with us?"

I braced myself for heaven-only-knew what derision, but was greeted by nothing but polite "Hi!"'s and "Hello, Lieutenant"'s and casual waves of the hand.

Captain Newman slipped the first chart back into its slot and stepped to the first bed. The ward watched us, some men propped on their elbows, some leaning over the foot of their beds. The identification tape on the pajamas of the boy in Bed 1 read: "M. Cochrane." He had a snub nose and many freckles. Captain Newman rested his fingers on the boy's pulse. "How are you doing, Cokey?"

"Breathing."

"Congratulations. Don't stop."

A man across the aisle laughed.

"Breathing is the best I can say," Cochrane protested.

"Don't be greedy," said Captain Newman. "Some of your friends don't even know how to exhale."

He glanced at another chart and stepped to the next bed.

A burly, sweating patient, his skull shaved entirely bald, was playing solitaire on a lap-board.

"Who's winning?" asked Captain Newman.

Someone across the aisle relayed the remark down the line. "Did you hear that? Chattanooga's makin' with the solo cards and Doc asks him who's *winning!*"

Chattanooga glanced at me. "Don't let Doc con you, Lieutenant. He knows one guy ain't winning, that's for sure. Me! I'm the all-time eight-ball. The only time I ever copped anything was when I cheated. But you know what, Captain?"

"No. What?"

"I don't care! I don't care one lousy, friggin' bit—about nothing. I don't care about you or me or the friggin' Army or the friggin' war!"

"That's certainly covers a lot of ground, Chattanooga. I hate to tell you this, but I think you're getting better."

"Don't give me that jazz, Captain."

"I'm not giving you any jazz. What did your girl write you?"

Chattanooga shrugged. "The same old malarkey."

"Oh, my God," groaned Captain Newman. "You're never satisfied, are you? That girl's a hell of a lot nicer to you than you are to her. What's the matter with you, anyway? She loves you. Don't you ever give her a break?"

"The only break that broad ever gave me was right across the kisser, when she loosened two teeth. Right here!"

"How are you sleeping these nights?"

"Lousy."

"How come?"

"Who knows? Maybe it's my guilty conscience, like you think and I don't. Maybe it's all that dope you got me on. Chrissake, I don't know if you're trying to cure me or cream me!"

Captain Newman laughed. "I told you you were improving. You'll win one of those games yet."

We stepped to Bed 3. The patient had a white Navy hat perched on his head and, before Captain Newman could say a word, raised his hand imperiously, declaiming: "The patient slept fine. Appetite good. Urine clear. Stool like coffee-cake." He saluted. "Arthur Werbel, ready for discharge! But he ain't moving an inch out of this beautiful bed. He's got it made, Doc, *made!*"

"You can say that again, sailor," Captain Newman sighed. "But listen, you've got to develop some symptoms. How can I keep you here if you don't show some symptoms?"

Werbel grinned. "Symptoms? You describe 'em and I'll sure as hell develop 'em. I'm talented, Doc. Look." He twisted his face up and clutched his stomach. "Jeeze, Doc, it hurts, right in the gut. Oh, I'm dyin', dyin'! Gimme a kiss, Blodgie, before I kick off. Doc, tell her to give me a smooch. That alone shows I'm off my rocker, don't it? Hold my hand, nurse. I don't want to go out alone."

"That's awful," said Captain Newman.

Werbel threw his arms and legs out, spread-eagled on the bed, and began to shake violently. "My back! They got me in the back! I'm burnin' up!"

"That's worse," said Captain Newman with conspicuous disgust. "That wouldn't fool an interne in Ward Two, and you know how dumb they are." He glanced at me. "Werbel, tell Lieutenant Alderson something. Why do you wear that hat?"

Werbel's face transformed before my eyes. His hands flew to his Navy hat and jammed it down low on his forehead. "Drop dead, Lieutenant. No son-of-a-bitch alive is gonna get that hat off my head. I know all about the stinkin' Air Corps regulations and you know where you can shove them! You'll have to cut my head off first, see? I'm gonna get outa here, I'm gonna bust out, I'm gonna head right for the Navy, to be with Frank, Frank, my own brother. Who's taking care of him? You? President Roosevelt? General Arnold? Balls. They ketch me in the goddam draft and put me in the crappy Air Corpse. You heard me, corpse, corpse—they sure named it right. Murderers. That's what you all are—murderers, goddamn mother – – – – – – – murderers!"

"Take it easy, sailor," said Captain Newman quietly.

"Get me outa here, Doc! I tell you I *got* to go in the Navy, I'll do anything, I'll go in the boilers, I'll swab the heads, I'll take top-deck ack-ack, I'll stay down in a sub."

"You won't do Frank much good in a submarine."

"No, I guess I won't. I guess I don't make sense. I just hate the Air. Doc, tell me the truth, what's the *matter* with me? Can't you fix me up?"

"I'm trying. It takes time. . . . You might start by improving your manners, sailor. That wasn't nice, telling the Lieutenant to drop dead."

"Oh, that's true. You're right. I'm sorry, Lieutenant. I take it back. I don't want you to drop dead."

"Thank you," said Captain Newman. "You might apologize to Lieutenant Blodgett, too, for some of that juicy language."

"You're absolutely right. I'm sorry, Blodgie, I'm honest to God sorry. See? I'm apologizin', Doc. Only she's around here with that frozen puss so goddam much you forget she's for real; know what I mean? It ain't like she's a woman. Don't go yet, Doc. I want to tell you something—"

"Save it. This afternoon. I'll see you in my office." As Captain Newman stepped to Bed 4, Lieutenant Corum came down the aisle from the sun porch. She looked cool, clean, contained. A very thin boy was lying on his side in Bed 4. He had been watching us. He could not have been more than eighteen.

"Hello, Bobby," Captain Newman said. "What's the word this morning?"

The boy opened his mouth. His lips moved, but no word came out. He turned to Francie Corum, and I saw that his left arm was gone. She leaned over him. "Come on, Bobby. Let Captain Newman hear how nicely you can say it. You said 'Hello' to me this morning. Remember?"

"He did, Doc," called the man in the next bed. "I heard him say 'Hello' plain as anything."

Bobby's lips moved soundlessly.

Captain Newman put his hand on the boy's shoulder absently. He and Francie Corum exchanged glances.

We went to Bed 5. A swarthy fellow with ink-black hair was propped up, reading a comic book. He did not so much as look up. He had been staring at that comic book from the time we'd entered the ward.

"Good morning, Evjanian."

Evjanian gave not the slightest sign that he had heard.

Captain Newman shrugged. "It's up to you. You want to do it the hard way, do it the hard way."

Without taking his eyes off the comic book, Evjanian scowled, "You think you're a comic. Oh, yes, you do. You think you're a scream. You think you're the funniest guy ever set foot in this hole."

"That wouldn't be hard," said Newman.

"Oh, don't give me any of your booshwa. You know how I feel. Up to here, right up to here!" He passed the side of his hand across his throat, still not lifting his eyes from the page. "You're not fooling me. I'm wise to you. I'm on to all of you. What did you ever do in the war? Nothing. Sat right here on your can. But I got mine in combat. I'll give them an earful about you upstairs. Just wait. I'm going to tell them plenty about you."

"Mmh." Captain Newman was watching the comic book. It was trembling in Evjanian's hands.

"I know what you're thinking!" cried Evjanian. "It cuts no ice with me!"

"I'm sorry," said Captain Newman. "I wish it did. . . . When you're ready, let me know. You're just killing time. It's a damn pity."

Evjanian made no response. The comic book was shaking so hard in his hands now that I could hear the pages rustle.

"I wish you'd *turn* that page sometime," murmured Captain Newman.

"Tough titty," said Evjanian.

As we approached Bed 6, the Negro who occupied it lifted a paper bag.

"Hello, Smiley," said Newman.

"How do," said Smiley gravely. "They's in here nice an' snug, Cap'n." The paper bag contained nail parings. Ever since he had been wounded off New Guinea, Smiley was terribly concerned about what could happen to his nail parings. He was afraid someone would put them in the garbage and the ants would get at them, and if the ants got at them he would be able to feel it. The ants would get under his toenails and would eat their way up his body. Smiley would awaken the whole ward when the ants began eating away at him, screaming "Get them offa me!" During the day, the ants never attacked him. They hid somewhere. It was at night that they came out, at night when no one else could see them or help him. Smiley tried to stay up all night, clutching the paper bag, holding it in the air high out of the reach of the ants.

"Anything new, Smiley?"

Smiley shook his head. "They won't let ol' Smiley be. You gonna put the sign on 'em?"

"We'll lick them yet," said Captain Newman.

In Bed 7, Corporal Reggy Carrozzo—thick-necked, pock-marked—waited for us. "Morning, Doc!" he boomed. "How you feeling?"

"Fine," said Captain Newman.

"Sleep okay?"

"Sure."

"Any bad dreams, Captain?"

"The usual."

Carrozzo reached over, took Captain Newman's hand, and turned it palm up. "Dry. That's good. No sweat. That's the first thing to look for, right? You're handling your tensions better, boy." He winked at Francie Corum. "Nurse, give this patient twenty ccs. of flak and a high colonic. He's a good boy. Just a little wacky. Thinks he's a captain. Thinks he's a psychiatrist!"

The men across the aisle laughed. Carrozzo seemed pleased.

Captain Newman pushed open the door to one of the rooms on the side. Lieutenant Corum entered. I hesitated. He signaled me to follow him in.

In the bed, a gaunt, unshaved figure lay flat. His eyes were closed.

"Bernie," Newman whispered.

Sergeant Bernstein passed his hand across his brow. "They kept pouring water down the priest's throat, Captain, gallons of water, through that funnel they pushed in his mouth. He was the natives' priest, an old man, a nice man, and he didn't even scream. I could see it all from the bush, and I couldn't scream either, I couldn't lift a finger to help him, not a thing, nothing, oh, God, nothing at all. I saw—they had tied Dillon to a stake and used him for bayonet practice, one after another as if he was straw, but the straw ran red, red blood. Now—and when the priest's belly was full, from the water they poured into him, all bloated and standing up—Captain, oh, they jumped on it! Those Nips, those horrible little men, those devils jumped on it, like monkeys in a zoo, jumping up and down on the priest's belly, and he—" tears rolled down his cheeks—"oh, God, he split open, he burst open, the water gushed up and out like a geyser—"

"I know," said Newman quickly. "But it's over."

Bernstein shook his head. "No, I still see it, I still hear it, it never ends, and it's got to, but it doesn't, it isn't ever going to. Let me die, Captain. Please, give me something, put me away."

Lieutenant Corum whispered something to Captain Newman.

"Do you feel well enough to have a visitor, Bernie?" he asked.

Bernstein turned his face into the pillow.

Newman said, "Your father wants to come here. He's worried about you. . . . It's going to be all right, Bernie. Believe me. Try. Pretty soon, it's going to be all right."

Bernstein sobbed. Newman bent over him, his eyes sad, so sad, and whispered, "Bernie . . . Bernie . . . give yourself a break."

We went out.

A cheerful giant awaited us in Bed 9. He was eating an apple. His chest and shoulders were matted with reddish hair.

"How'd the Cubs do yesterday?" asked Captain Newman.

"Them cripples? They blew it again, in the ninth. They had two men on, so help me, none out, top half of the inning, the Phillies' pitcher strictly from hunger, and what do they do? Cavaretta hits into a double play, the next crud up walks, the pinch hitter runs it to three-and-two, and *fans*. Like a muff on some goddam bloomer team, he *fans*, and it's all over. I tell you, Captain, that Charley Grimm's got to go. He's just *got to go!* Know what I mean?"

"I certainly do, Baseball."

"He's for the birds! He don't know the fine points. That

cockamamy Dutchman—oh, Doc, I tell you it's a wonder I don't have ulcers. With a jerk like that managin' my club, I ought to have ulcers."

"Don't give up hope," said Captain Newman. "You'll get ulcers if you go on like this."

"Oh, no, I won't. A stroke, maybe, a heart attack—that I'll get. It's a miracle I'm normal. How do you figure Mr. Wrigley —*he's* no dope, a man like that, a rich millionaire, a college man that's for sure, built up that big chewing-gum business all over the world, not just in the States and Canada, you know, but all over the world—how come a sharp guy like that strings along with a bird-brain like Charley Grimm?"

"I don't know," Newman said mournfully. "It's pretty sad for anyone who loves the game."

"Loves the game?" Baseball echoed. "I *hate* the game!" His voice was shaking. "Doc, you think I can get out by Christmas? I promised my wife. I'd sure like to be home for Christmas. Gee, Doc . . ."

"Gee, Baseball, I'd sure like you to be home for Christmas. I'm rooting for you. You know that. But it's you who's up to bat, not me."

"No, Doc, honest, it's up to you."

"No, Baseball, honest, it's up to you," said Newman earnestly.

"I can't beat this."

"You can beat this. A lunkhead like Charley Grimm couldn't, but you can. You can hit a homer."

"If I hit a homer I get home! Isn't that right, Doc?"

"That's right, Baseball."

"I'll do anything you say to get out of here, Doc. Why don't you give me flak-juice? If you give me flak—"

"Flak isn't for everyone." Captain Newman frowned. "You know, your troubles started long before the war—"

"So what? You can fix it, Doc. You can make me go into it all—everything—"

"There are some things it's better to let alone."

"Oh, goddamit all to hell, Doc—give me a *chance!*"

"Listen, Baseball. Flak isn't magic; it's only a tool. Some guys get it and don't ever get home—"

"I'm not ending up in no state hospital!" Baseball clutched Captain Newman's sleeve. "Doc! Please. Give me the flak. I'm ready. I promise. I *want* it!"

Newman hesitated. "Come and see me this afternoon. We'll talk."

Lieutenant Blodgett made a note on her clipboard.

"Thanks, Doc. That fathead Grimm, we'll put him back in the Three-Eye League! Do you hear that, guys?" he shouted. "Doc and me'll send that son-of-a-bitch back to Shamokin!"

It went like that from bed to bed, Captain Newman's manner, his tone, his diction, his inflection, shifting from patient to patient. He was gruff with one, gentle with another, amused or ironic or concerned or impatient according to his appraisal of what a man needed, his sense of what lay behind the words or protestations or bravado with which they confronted him. Once he burst into anger; whether it was true or simulated, I could not tell.

As Captain Newman approached the bed of a boy they called "Chop-Chop" Maccarades, Gorkow, a tattooed bruiser across the aisle, raised his arm and rattled off a shattering imitation of machine-gun fire: "Eh-eh-eh-eh-eh-eh!"

Maccarades screamed, "Stop! Stop!" and leaped out of bed, clapping his hands over his ears.

Gorkow followed him with that imaginary gun, cackling, "Eh-eh-eh-eh-eh-eh!"

Maccarades dived under the bed, screaming.

The ward went wild. Men swore at Gorkow, shouted at Captain Newman, cried out. One began to giggle hysterically; another threw a pillow at Gorkow; the gray-haired Major came running out of his room, shouting, "Shut up, you punks, shut up!"

Lieutenant Blodgett and Francie Corum were kneeling on the floor, trying to soothe Maccarades, who was yelling: "Chop off his arms! Chop off his feet! Chop off his ears! Chop off his nose!"

Captain Newman stared at Gorkow without a word.

"Don't pick on me!" Gorkow cried. "Can't a guy have any fun around here any more?"

"No," said Captain Newman icily. "Not that kind of fun. This is my ward and these are my men. Either stop throwing your goddam weight around or I'll slap you into a veterans' hospital so fast it will make your head spin."

"Then get that little yellow bastard outa here," Gorkow cried. "He makes me puke. Just get that little yellow—"

"That 'little yellow bastard' racked up twenty-six missions!" Captain Newman burst out. "What the hell have you done, except beat up a noncom half your size? You heard me! I'm sick and tired of you. All you do is beef and bulldoze and feel sorry for yourself. When are you going to wise up? When are you going to start feeling ashamed?"

Gorkow muttered something hoarsely.

"Baloney," snapped Captain Newman. He turned to Sergeant Kopp. "The next time this character pulls something like this, bring him to my office."

"I can bust Arkie in two!" Gorkow sneered.

Captain Newman leaned forward. "You lay a hand on anyone, Gorkow, *anyone*, and you can start packing! If I didn't think there might be some decency behind all that bullying, smart-aleck stuff, I'd have shipped you out long ago. Only don't count on my sweet nature. I don't play the patsy forever."

"You don't like me!" cried Gorkow.

"You're damn right I don't," said Captain Newman, "not the way you are. But I'm stuck with you, and you're stuck with me. One of us has to change, and it's going to be you!"

Stan Djuba began to play a cowboy ballad on his harmonica. I could hear that harmonica long after morning rounds were completed, long after I followed Captain Newman out of the ward, long after I heard the iron door lock behind me, long into that first fitful, confused night in which I tossed in the hot darkness and dreamed of home and cool breezes and voices not twisted through suffering. All through my sleep, if sleep it was, my mind fumbled with a passage in which memory perversely persisted:

> O, now for ever
> Farewell the tranquil mind! farewell content!
> Farewell the plumed troop, and the big wars
> That make ambition virtue! O, farewell!

IV
TWO MEN
FOR THE WARD

The weeks came, the weeks passed. Just as the Major on the plane had warned me, we broiled by day and almost froze by night. The sun burned down and the sands burned up and we gasped for air between. At twilight, the colors showered down on the desert, clothing the ghostly yuccas in iridescence, and each night the stars, so brilliant, so indifferent, burned cold on the velvet sky.

I was working so hard that I lost track of time. I had no time to think or catch my breath or get my bearings. I was flooded by new patients, case histories, directives, interviews, conferences, staff meetings, red tape, bulletins, S. O. P., emergencies—above all, by the incessant and unremitting demands of Ward 7. One night a week I managed to break away to the Officers' Club, for a dinner better than they served at the Main Hospital mess, and once I even ventured into Colfax for a beer and movie, during which I promptly fell asleep. I never knew sleep could be so rare and so precious.

All day and night the brave, impudent planes climbed the

skies. They were beautiful to watch as they climbed and banked and rolled in defiant acrobatics. I grew accustomed to them buzzing the field, swarming in the heavens, celestial bees high above the blazing shield of the desert. My ears grew attuned, too, to listening another way. It was a rare stretch of time that passed without the sickening whine of a plane falling, the terrible sight of a plume of smoke-and-fire running down the sky, the distant thud of disaster. The sirens wailed as crash crews and ambulances tore out of our gates on their gruesome missions: somewhere, on some desolate place in the sands, in some dark canyon behind the far-off hills, on some godforsaken mesa or butte beyond the Jawbone Range, a boy we might have seen an hour earlier was dead or crying for help or sweating out entrapment. Each time someone crashed, we knew that someone else would weep.

Colfax kept growing. "Temporary" quarters sprouted all around us and mushroomed tin and tar paper. The stream of pilots and gunners and those who kept their ships in the air, the men we hammered into harmonious crews, to be joined by navigators and bombardiers from other bases, quickened and broadened and spread across our grounds. "Trainees," those peculiar students in a malevolent time, were transformed into pursuers, fighters, escorts, interceptors. Above all, they became killers. Most of them we "graduated" and never saw again. They were swallowed up in unit numbers: Eighth Air Force, Fifteenth Pursuit, Sixty-first Interceptor, Twentieth Bomber Command. Some we read about—in action over the thousand isles of the Pacific, or over China, Burma, England, France. The cocky kids who had sported those caps with the grommet removed became heroes, wash-outs, legends, cadavers.

The war threw its somber shadow over all of us. Those first alien names that had strangely held our destinies—Bataan, Singapore, the Macassar Straits—receded into a nightmare past, replaced by other names, no less strange or fateful: Guadalcanal, the Coral Sea, El Alamein, Tobruk. Slowly, slowly, incomprehensible disasters were replaced by fragments of hope and forerunners of victory—on the Bismarck Archipelago or North Africa, over an Oriental sea or the German heartland.

From all over the globe, the wounded and the dazed streamed home. Colfax was a pea beside a watermelon compared to Denver's Fort Logan or the great, posh hospitals at Atlantic City or Boca Raton. But even they were not large enough for war's casualties now, and planes touched our runways regularly to drop off men—shattered, silent, raving, stunned—from five thousand miles away.

Captain Newman pleaded with Lieutenant Colonel Larrabee to press the Air Surgeon's Office for two more psychiatrists, four more nurses, six more orderlies. We never did get the psychiatrists, and we only got one more nurse (a pleasant nincompoop named Iona Finch), but Area Command dug up two live orderlies and hustled them to Colfax. Within eight hours, the whole post was swapping yarns about them.

I was in Captain Newman's office, giving him a run-down on some tests I had administered to new admissions to Ward 7, when Lieutenant Corum came in. She seemed breathless. "Joe, two peculiar GI's checked in around seven-thirty this morning and have been wandering around the hospital ever since."

"What's peculiar about that?"

"They're alive, they're breathing, they can spell 'cat' and 'girl.' I think they're your new orderlies. And if you don't grab them, someone else will."

"Where the hell are they?" cried Newman.

"Outside Lost and Found—sleeping."

"Wake them up, wrap them in cellophane and show them the red carpet!"

"I deserve a free dinner for this."

"That's not all you deserve, Francie."

She blushed. "You'll be a witness to that, Barney, won't you?"

"If he doesn't take you to dinner, I will," I said.

Francie winked at me and saluted Newman. He groaned. She waved at us and disappeared.

In less than five minutes, we heard a diffident knock on the door.

"Come in," Captain Newman sang out. I had not seen him so buoyant for weeks.

The first of Ward 7's priceless reinforcements slouched into the room. He was a corporal, about five foot ten, well built, tanned, but he carried himself as if death were just around the corner.

"Good morning," said Captain Newman brightly.

The soldier touched a finger to his forehead, as if confirming its existence, and studied us through lugubrious eyes. He made no effort to conceal the fact that he did not approve of what he beheld.

"Sit down, Corporal."

The invitation proved belated: the Corporal had already deposited his weary coil in the chair across the desk.

"What's your name?" asked Captain Newman.

"Laibowitz."

"First name?"

"Jackson."

"How old are you?"

"Twenty-seven."

To my surprise, Captain Newman said frostily, "I believe it is customary for a soldier to address an officer as 'sir.' "

"Sir." Corporal Laibowitz shrugged. "What's customary for a soldier can be tough for a civilian."

"But you aren't a civilian," said Newman acidly.

"I *feel* like a civilian."

"Congratulations. Did you sign in at M.A.C.?"

"I was John Hancocked by that WAC at the front desk. Sir."

"Well, suppose you get your orders—"

"Okay." The Corporal started to rise.

"—later."

The Corporal sat down, in pain.

Captain Newman put a propitiatory smile on his lips and reached for his cigarettes. "Would you like to smoke?"

"Nicotine," announced Laibowitz, "is bad for the eyes."

"Oh. Do you have trouble with your eyes?"

"No, sir."

"Then why—"

"That's because I never touch nicotine," said Laibowitz.

Captain Newman looked startled. He leaned back in his chair to study the man before him with new interest. This did not present the slightest problem to Laibowitz, who suffered the scrutiny with the resignation of a man accustomed to the slow-witted. He was, all in all, rather good-looking—well-shaped features, a Grecian nose, a firm mouth, large, liquid eyes. It was only his manner —an amalgam of mourning and dyspepsia—which celebrated despair.

Captain Newman said, "I assume you've worked in a hospital before."

"Yes—sir."

Captain Newman waited. So did Laibowitz.

"Go on, Corporal."

"Go on where?"

"Tell me about your experience."

"What's to tell? The camp I just came from, I don't want to knock the government, isn't fit for a dog. Maybe a Nazi dog, not a U.S. citizen. They had me working the wards ten months steady, day and night. I didn't like it."

"You mustn't hide your feelings," said Captain Newman dryly.

"That's what I figured," said Laibowitz.

"What kinds of wards did you work in?"

"All kinds."

"Give me a hint."

"General, surgery, infectial diseases, where *I* caught everything, O.B.—that was for the officers' wives. The rate they're getting pregnant, we won't need a draft in twenty years. Also the V.D. department, which, to be frank about it, goes against my grains."

"Did you ever work in—an N.P. ward?" asked Captain Newman, rather too casually.

Laibowitz's eyes widened. "A *mental* ward?"

"I mean psychiatric cases—"

"*Nuts?*"

"They are not 'nuts,' " said Captain Newman firmly. "They're men who—"

"My God, Doc," cried Laibowitz, "you gonna put me in a loony bin?"

"It is *not*—"

"I'll drop dead!" Laibowitz struggled to his feet, wrestling with expressions worthy of Dante's doomed. "I give you my word, Doc, inside one hour—"

"Sit down."

"Better ask me to *lay* down! I'm already a patient."

"Now listen," said Captain Newman sharply. "I don't know where the hell you guys got all these cockeyed ideas. Most of the men in my ward are simply depressed—"

"So am I," proclaimed Laibowitz.

"—miserable—"

"*They're* miserable? Look at me!"

"Sit *down!*"

Corporal Laibowitz sank into the chair with noises suggestive of strangulation.

Captain Newman launched into a lecture explaining the functions of his ward, the nature of our tasks, the duties of a wardman. He was simple, direct and, I thought, remarkably reassuring. It made not the slightest dent on Laibowitz.

All the time his new chief held forth, Corporal Laibowitz kept uttering woeful lamentations and embittered asides. Captain Newman explained that we had a staff of excellent doctors ("For me alone you'll need one full-time," said Laibowitz), that the patients were not permitted razors, matches, blunt artifacts or sharp objects ("But *teeth* they've got?"), that an encouraging proportion of our cases responded favorably to therapy ("Don't spoil your record, Captain!") and were dismissed from Ward 7 to return to either army or civilian life ("I will gladly join them!"), that orderlies were pampered with frequent passes and off-post privileges ("You mean of their own free will they come *back?*"), and that when he was off duty, Corporal Laibowitz, along with the other wardman, would sleep in complete comfort and safety in the finest barracks on the base, a good five hundred yards away ("Who will drag me back and forth?" asked Laibowitz).

"That's about it," said Captain Newman efficiently. "Now, do you have any questions?"

Laibowitz raised his hand.

"You *don't* have to raise your hand."

"I'm as surprised as you to see I still got the strength."

"Ask your question."

Laibowitz rose. "Doc, I appreciate your trying to raise my morale. But let us face facts. You are putting me in a booby hatch! By Sunday I will be in a strait jacket."

Newman narrowed his eyes sternly. "That will be all. You will report to Sergeant Kopp."

"Who's he?"

"My wardmaster."

"Where does he keep his whip?"

"Laibowitz," snapped Captain Newman, "what the devil is the matter with you? You look like an intelligent—"

"Don't be fooled by my looks."

"You're making a mountain out of a molehill!"

"So I'm no good in geography."

"You'll get the best food on the post here."

"I already lost all my appetite."

"You have my deepest sympathy," said Captain Newman sarcastically.

"From plumbers I expect sympathy; from psychiatrists I expect understanding." Laibowitz looked aggrieved.

Captain Newman cleared his throat. "You may go now. Ring the bell outside the door. Sergeant Kopp will show you the ropes."

"He should only *give* me a rope; I'll hang myself."

"Dismissed!"

Corporal Laibowitz gave his captain one last, imploring look. "Doc—"

"Send the other man in!" said Captain Newman in his most military manner.

Laibowitz reaffirmed the location of his forehead and sagged out of the room. He might have been en route to the firing squad.

Captain Newman turned to me. His eyes were dancing. "He's going to make a good wardman."

"Do you really think so?" I exclaimed.

He gave me a pitying look. "He understands suffering."

Through the open door now clanked (I know no better word) a soldier who might have stepped right off a recruiting poster. His blouse, despite the heat, was absolutely crisp; a perfect knife edge ran along the forward edges of his sleeves; his tie was impeccably knotted; his belt buckle gleamed; his shoes glistened. This military paragon snapped to attention in a brace that would have done credit to a drill sergeant and, his eyes fixed straight ahead, barked: "Private Albert Lawrence reporting for duty, sir!"

"At ease."

Private Lawrence broke his salute and handed a slip of paper across the desk stiffly. His cheeks were as scrubbed as prize apples. His blond crew-cut was as even as a brush. His nose was thin, his lips straight, his jaw square. His bearing was so martial that he seemed to have been put together by an Army engineer: a bullet head, machine-gun eyes, teeth like cartridges.

"Sit down, Lawrence."

"Thank you, sir."

"Would you like a cigarette?"

"No, sir. I do not smoke while on duty."

"Well," said Captain Newman pleasantly, "let's say you're not on duty yet."

"In that case, sir, thank you, I will." Private Lawrence took a cigarette with a smart nod of the head and had a spotless Zippo burning under Captain Newman's nose before Newman had completed placing his cigarette between his lips.

"Thank you, Lawrence," smiled Captain Newman.

"Screw you, sir," said Private Lawrence.

I shall not even try to describe the expression on Newman's face, or the effect Lawrence's words had on me. I do not even remember how Captain Newman looked, because my eyes were riveted on Private Lawrence, who had clapped his hands across his mouth, his cheeks flaming, as he stammered: "Oh, God. Excuse me, sir. Please. I did not mean it. That dirty, filthy word. I cannot help it, sir. It just comes out!"

It would be banal to say that Captain Newman looked as if he could not believe his ears; it would also be inaccurate, for he looked as though he did. And before that stunned, incredulous expression, poor Lawrence became even more miserable and stuttered more abjectly. "I—can bite off my tongue, sir. You see—it only happens when I am with an officer, sir. It just comes *out*, sir!"

"How long," asked Captain Newman at last, "has this been going on?"

"Since—I was fifteen, sir, the first time. It started with one of my teachers. It doesn't happen every time. Oh, no! Days go by, weeks, and it's no problem, no problem at all. Then all of a sudden, like you saw, sir, bang!"

"How old are you, Lawrence?"

"Twenty-two, sir."

"And you've had this problem since you were fifteen?"

"Yes, sir."

"Only with teachers or officers?"

"N-no, sir. With any superior, like a boss."

Newman studied the ceiling. "Well, Lawrence, you've got quite an original problem there for a soldier, haven't you? Tell me, does it get any better, any worse?"

"That's hard to say, sir. Sometimes—sometimes I'm sure I've got it licked. Like this past month: I went eight days and never once used a filthy word! Then—" Lawrence bit his lip. "Son-of-a-bitch! Goddam it to hell and Hong Kong, plus a flying pass at Santa Claus—"

"Is your problem always the same 'filthy' word?" Newman cut in hastily.

Lawrence flushed. "No, sir."

"You mean sometimes it's *worse* than 'Screw you'?"

"Yes, sir. At first, when I was a kid, it was 'Go to hell.' That was bad—but it got worse. It began to be: 'Take a flying you-know-what for yourself, sir.' Then, lately, in the Army, where everyone uses bad words, it's—'Screw you, sir.' Sometimes worse. You know. The word that begins with 'f' . . ." Lawrence stared at the floor miserably. "You could gig me, sir. You could send me to the guardhouse."

"Sure. But they don't need my business. You have to make a reservation to get into our guardhouse." Newman rubbed his chin moodily. "Lawrence, tell me something. How the hell did they ever let you into the Army?"

"I was drafted, sir."

"But didn't your draft board know about your—compulsion?"

"No, sir. I was real good that day. I didn't have a single filthy thought."

"Weren't you worried about what might happen once you were in the Army?"

"Oh, yes, sir! But I thought the discipline might help me get over the—habit. That was wishful thinking, I guess."

"Did you ever see a doctor about this?" asked Newman.

"Yes, sir, about five years ago."

"What did he say?"

Lawrence knit his brow energetically. "He told me I had to decide who was going to be master and who was going to be slave —me or it. He said it was just a matter of will power."

"What did you think of that?"

"I thought he was a horse's ass. Excuse me."

Captain Newman glanced out of the window. I could see the heat rising off the parade ground like an evil vapor. "Who sent you here, Lawrence?"

"My lieutenant, at Santa Ana. He said you were just the man I ought to work for."

Newman reached for some water. "What was his name?"

"Kincaid, sir."

"Do you happen to remember his first name?"

"N-no, sir."

"Did he—uh—say *why* he thought I was just the man you ought to serve under?"

"He said—can I be frank, sir? Do I have your permission?"

"Please do, Lawrence. Be very frank."

"Well, sir, he said you have a natural talent for dealing with nuts and screws."

Captain Newman winced. "Do you think you're a nut or a screw?"

Lawrence's lower lip trembled. "No, sir. He said you were desperate—to get men with hospital experience."

"Good. When you write Lieutenant Kincaid, be sure to give him my regards. Have you had much hospital experience?"

"Yes, *sir!* Back home, sir."

"Where was that?"

"Buffalo General."

"Which wards?"

"Mostly mental wards, sir."

"Well," smiled Newman, "that's just fine. How long were you an orderly?"

"I never was an orderly, sir."

"I mean a wardman."

"I never was a wardman, either."

"Well, what jobs *did* you have?"

"No jobs, sir," said Lawrence earnestly. "I was a patient."

"What?"

"I was a patient, sir."

Captain Newman lunged forward. "You were a *patient?*"

"Five years, sir!"

"You were a patient in a psychiatric ward for five *years?*"

"Yes, sir. The doctors—I guess they didn't know what to do about my problem."

"And you were *drafted?*"

"Yes, sir."

"They *knew* you were a psychiatric case and still inducted you into—"

"Yes, sir," said Lawrence proudly. "You see, when I got out of the hospital I began looking around for a job. One day, the government wrote me about registering for selective service, so I did. I passed all the physicals easy, because I take tip-top care of myself, then I went in front of this special doctor who asked me how I slept and if I liked girls or had any emotional problems. I told him I liked girls a lot, because I do, and my most emotional problem was to get a job and amount to something. I would have mentioned—it, the swearing, but there was a real long line behind me, and the doctor looked sort of keyed-up, like people had their doubts about him. He waved me ahead to a sergeant, who was sitting at a table and filling forms out on a typewriter like a shot out of hell. The sergeant asked me, 'Occupation?' I answered, 'None.' He thought I was trying to be a wise guy, sir. He said, 'I suppose you are a retired millionaire?' real nasty. I said, 'No, my family are poor.' He said, 'You have to put *something* under Occupation, even if it's "Unemployed." ' So I said that was true, I was unemployed. So he said, 'That's better. And what did you do before you were unemployed, buster?' I answered, 'I was in the hospital.' So he said, 'Now we're getting somewhere,' and typed on my form, after where it said 'Occupation,' 'Hospital.' Then he asked me how long I'd been in the hospital. I said 'Five years.' So he typed in 'Five years.' Then he asked if it was any special kind of hospital, and I said, 'Yes. Mental.' So he said, 'Good for you,' and typed in 'Mental.' " Lawrence paused. "In a way, it was all very logical."

"Logical?" Captain Newman echoed. " 'Logical' doesn't begin to do it justice, Lawrence. It was wonderful! Standardized methods. Objective data. Foolproof. They took all those facts down and coded them and transferred them to punch cards." He turned to me with a wicked grin. "Isn't that what you systematic, scientific psychologists do?"

"Yes," I said unhappily.

"Then they filed all the punch cards in the central files in Washington, right? Everything neat, exact, in place. And when *I* asked for assistants with hospital experience they knew exactly how to get the answer. They just fed all those beautiful punched cards into a wonderful machine, set it for 'Hospital experience,' flipped a switch, and the machine whirred and buzzed and sorted and a bell rang—and presto! Out came: 'Lawrence, Albert, private; Experience: Hospital; How long? Five years; Specialty: Mental.' " He threw his head back and shook with laughter. "Oh, my aching back. Man, oh, man, in spades. Lawrence, I am indebted to you. Don't get worried. I'm not laughing at you. You have recharged my batteries. . . . Tell me, do you know what kind of ward I run here?"

"Yes, sir."

"Describe it."

"It's—like the one I was in."

"Very good. Now, do you want to work in a ward like that?"

"Yes, *sir!*"

"Why, boy?"

Lawrence hesitated. "I could help you, sir. I'll be a real good orderly. I know a lot about hospital routine. I can make beds, scrub floors, empty bedpans, keep everything spick-and-span. I am very neat and tidy, sir. I *hate* anything dirty. There's no excuse for it! It takes no more time to be clean than to be dirty and filthy!"

" 'Dirty and filthy,' " Captain Newman repeated.

Lawrence blushed. "I know what you're driving at."

"I'm sure you do. . . . Lawrence, you know I can get you out of the Army, don't you?"

"I—don't want to, sir."

"Why not?"

"I—think I'm better off in the Army, sir. Everything has to be clean. Everything happens on time."

"But what about your swearing?" asked Newman.

"I—well, I try to avoid certain officers, sir, the ones who make the bad words slip out."

"Like me?"

"Oh, no, sir," Lawrence protested. "I don't feel angry with you!"

"You swore at me. . . ."

"Because I was *nervous*, sir, not angry."

"You can be angry without knowing it."

"But I only get angry when I get scared. That's what one of the doctors told me. And I wasn't scared of you, sir."

"Maybe what you were afraid of was not me," ventured Newman, "but yourself."

"But I had nothing to get angry *about*, sir. I was just sitting out there on the bench, twiddling my thumbs, waiting for you. I waited all the time you were interviewing that creep J. Laibowitz."

"Exactly," smiled Newman. "You had to wait. Maybe that was what made you angry. At whom? Me—because I was the one who made you wait. I'm sorry I made you wait so long. I didn't know —about your special problem."

Lawrence's eyes widened. "I don't *blame* you, sir."

"Thank you, Lawrence. You're a fair-minded guy." Captain Newman rubbed his chin. "I'll make a deal with you. I'll try you out in the ward. Now don't get excited. We'll try it for two weeks. On probation. We'll see how it goes. Okay?"

"Yes, *sir!*"

"That's fine."

Lawrence rose and saluted, holding the salute magnificently.

"Dismissed," said Newman.

"Screw you," said Lawrence.

I don't think I have ever felt as sorry for anyone as I felt for Lawrence at that moment. He turned white as a sheet, almost breaking into tears, and began to beat his fist against his thigh furiously. "Oh, Jesus! God! God *damn* it! Sir—please, sir. Excuse me. Give me another chance. Don't hold it against me!"

Captain Newman waved a hand carelessly. "Probation—that's what threw you. No one likes to have a sword hanging over his head. The boner was mine, soldier. I'll have to think up something special for your kind of problem." He closed his eyes solemnly.

Poor Lawrence shot me an anxious glance, hoping, I suppose, for some sign of reassurance, but I could only smile idiotically. He swallowed, mumbling, "Thank you, sir."

I could not for the life of me figure out what Captain Newman would say or do now. When he opened his eyes he said, "Let's start all over. Private Lawrence, you will come to attention."

"Yes, sir." Lawrence sprang into a brace.

"Lawrence, I don't have to tell you, do I, that as a private in the United States Army you are under strict military discipline?"

"No, sir!"

"You understand, do you not, that when an officer gives you an order, that order must be obeyed?"

"Yes, sir."

"You understand that any order I, Captain Newman, give you must be obeyed to the letter, without qualification, evasion, ifs, ands or buts?"

Lawrence was beginning to turn pale. "Yes, sir."

"Very well, Lawrence. I am going to give you an order. Ready!"

Lawrence snapped his heels together sharply.

"Private Albert Lawrence, I hereby order you to swear at me, Captain Newman, twice a day! You will swear at me once in the morning, when I check in, and once in the evening, when I check out. *That is an order!* Do you understand?"

"Yes, sir."

"Repeat the order!"

"Yes, sir! The Captain has ordered me to swear at him twice a day, sir; in the morning, when he checks in, and at night, when he checks out."

"Right! And you are not to swear at me *at any other time!*"

"Right, sir!"

"Repeat that."

"I am not to swear at you at any other time!" cried Lawrence.

"And you are hereby ordered not to swear at any *other* officer, here or on leave, at any time whatsoever. Do you understand that?"

"Yes, sir! I am hereby ordered not to swear at any other of-ficer, here or on leave, at any time whatsoever."

Captain Newman rose formally. "That will be all."

Lawrence brought his hand down smartly, thought of some-thing, and brought his hand into a salute again. "Sir?"

"Yes?"

"May I ask the Captain a question?"

"You have my permission to ask a question."

"Thank you, sir. Should I stand at attention when I swear at you?"

Captain Newman's eyebrows arched in admiration. *"Ex*cellent point, Lawrence. That is terribly smart of you. . . . Yes, I think it would be best if you swore at me from a formal military stance."

"Thank you, sir!" Private Lawrence's hand whipped down, he made a right-about face and marched out of the room. He was walking on air. And why not? No one before had ever ordered him to swear. Men had chewed him out for swearing, or forbade him to swear, or punished him for swearing, or cajoled, threatened, chided or appeased him. But no one before had shouldered the burden of his need for him: no one had commanded him to do what he was driven to do, and dreaded. Reprimand, penalty, punishment—these were as useless as blood sacrifices after a hurricane. But an official *order*—! An order he could understand; an order he could execute; an order was someone else's will, with which Albert Lawrence could gratefully replace his own.

I caught myself wondering what Major Sibley would say had he witnessed this fantastic episode. ("Men like Sibley," Newman once sniffed nastily, "know more than they understand.") I even titillated my fantasies by trying to imagine the expression on Colonel Pyser's face had he heard a captain in the Army of the United States of America commanding a dog face to swear at him at officially designated intervals. It was a lovely thought.

It was quiet in the room now. Captain Newman went to the sink and splashed water on his face. He was drying himself with a towel, saying, "Barney, what odds will you take—?" when suddenly, from the ward beyond the iron door, we heard a hoarse, untutored voice sing out:

> Old MacDonald had a farm
> Eeyie ayie oh . . .

A few voices joined in:

> And on this farm he had some chicks
> Eeyie ayie oh . . .

More voices chimed in, including one high, sweet tenor:

With a chick-chick here
And a chick-chick there
And here-a-chick and there-a-chick
And every-other-where-a-chick. . . .

And as the bucolic catalogue of Old MacDonald's farm ascended, we heard the unmistakable voice of Corporal Jackson Laibowitz, who had not been in Ward 7 half an hour, boom out above all the rest: "Come on, you guys. Louder! Everybody! Come *on*, you crazy bums. Don't you want to get well? *Sing!*"

Captain Newman tossed the towel into the corner with a triumphant gesture.

The door burst open.

Lieutenant Corum came in. She was trying very hard to look serious. "Your new orderly is standing on a chair, conducting the Colfax Glee Club—continuous performances, nine to five, immediate seating on the mezzanine." She put both hands out helplessly. "You'd better get into the ward, Joe, before he starts passing out lollipops."

He laughed as they hurried out.

V

THE

INCREDIBLE LAIBOWITZ

Within an hour after Private Albert Lawrence arrived in Ward 7, he had a nickname. Corporal Laibowitz studied that punctilious military dress and manner with disgust, turned to Pepi Gavoni, one of the other orderlies, and announced, "This character is in the wrong army. He's a hammerhead."

From that moment on, Lawrence was known as "Hammerhead." He did not mind. He was, indeed, grateful for the affection any nickname implies. He took to his duties as if they had been especially designed to fit his needs. He worked like a slave, ate like a horse, and slept like a log. He scrubbed, scoured, mopped, wiped, aired. He made Ward 7 gleam with that purity for which his inner self yearned.

Lawrence followed Captain Newman's orders to a "T," swearing at him each morning, quite pleasantly, when Newman arrived, and swearing at him each evening, quite proudly, as Newman left. His compulsion seemed gratified by these fixed channels of discharge. His profanity indeed began to take on a certain note of affection—or, at least, inoffensiveness—just as that which is familiar always does; for even the foulest words lose their meaning if repeated over and over until they become only sounds to which anxious men assign anxious meanings.

Each morning, when Captain Newman called, "Good morning, Lawrence," Hammerhead would snap to attention and rejoin, "Screw you, sir!" Every night, when Captain Newman left, Hammerhead would be waiting outside his office. "Good night, Lawrence," Newman would say, and Hammerhead would fling his hand to his forehead and descant, "Screw you, sir!"

There was no alteration of this ritual, which soon assumed a certain sacerdotal quality. Lawrence sought neither variety nor originality in his symbolic defiance of authority. He was only at home with regularity.

The swearing caused a sensation in the ward, at first, albeit Hammerhead tried to swear at Captain Newman in a moderate and pleasant tone. The first time Laibowitz heard Hammerhead utter his fornicatory malediction, the startled Corporal spread his arms wide and cried, "The Japs must be in Kansas City!" But soon the swearing was accepted as part of that greater irrationality by which a military body is animated. Stranger, sadder, funnier things happened a dozen times a day in Ward 7. Laibowitz summed up the ward's consensus with that antiseptic disdain which was his métier: *"Nothing* in the Army makes sense."

Laibowitz became, as Captain Newman had predicted, a superb wardman. Newman had said: "He understands suffering." Laibowitz did more than understand it: he welcomed it, he encouraged it, he embraced it. He had been raised in an ancient and sapient tradition that regarded misery as normal, and contentment as neurotic.

After his initial horror over being condemned to "a loony bin," after those first violent protestations and apocalyptic prophecies, Jackson Laibowitz found himself in the one place in the Army, perhaps the world, which he truly understood: a place where everyone else was unhappy, too. This provided him with a sympathetic environment and such stout reinforcement for his own philosophy of gloom as life had heretofore denied him.

If Captain Newman automatically took the side of the enlisted men against the brass, Laibowitz went him one better: he became the champion of the patients against the doctors.

With that blithe extension of his ego which was his most disconcerting characteristic, Jackson Laibowitz began to refer to the men in Ward 7 as "my patients." He was only one of five orderlies assigned to Master Sergeant Kopp, but within a week he had altered his status from menial to co-director. With a benevolence that spurned the niceties of rank, custom or Standard Operating Procedure, Laibowitz set out to improve the diet, the regimen, the recreation and the therapy for those helpless souls whom, he took it as self-evident, fate had entrusted to his personal guardianship. In a hundred ingenious ways, some subtle, some blatant, and by a hundred artful stratagems, ranging from minor insubordination to brazen sabotage, he took it upon himself to reshape the world of the ward closer to his heart's desire. What Omar Khayyám had preached, Jackson Laibowitz put into practice.

Take, for instance, Laibowitz's method of dealing with orders. Written orders of which he approved, he executed with lightning dispatch; written orders of which he disapproved, he "mislaid," misread, misinterpreted or misrouted. His response to verbal instructions was even more exasperating: when he disagreed with an order, he simply pretended he had not heard it; when it was repeated to him, he concluded it had not been communicated correctly the first time, which made the second exposition no more reliable than the first; when it was driven home to him in an indisputable, peremptory manner that whatever his personal views, such-and-such a command *had* to be obeyed, he got "sick" and took to his quarters. Achilles had his tent; Laibowitz had his symptoms. Rarely has medical science been confronted with such symptoms as Jackson Laibowitz could summon to his cause

on a moment's notice. When that cause stood in need of reinforcement, camouflage, *blitzkrieg* or delaying maneuvers, Corporal
Laibowitz could conjure up such aches, wheezes, hoarseness or
vertigoes as stymied the most case-hardened diagnosticians on
sick call.

Laibowitz was not often forced to the extremity of malingering: *au naturel,* he displayed masterly skills in subversion and
staggering ingenuity in circumvention. He operated on the mar-
gins of insubordination with the guile of an Arab and the gall
of a moral commando. He never directly *disobeyed* Captain
Newman's will, for instance; he managed to modify it through
reinterpretation. He never contradicted Lieutenant Blodgett or
Francie Corum; he simply outflanked them. He simulated deaf-
ness with an innocence that defied exposure, and stupidity with
a poise that demanded admiration.

Laibowitz did not, of course, resort to high strategy when
simple buck-passing would suffice. When Sergeant Kopp, for
instance, told Laibowitz to perform some task which Laibowitz
considered beneath his talents (and his *amour propre* was such
that most routine duties failed to meet his elevated standards),
Jackson merely relayed the order instead of executing it. What always astonished me was how he got Pepi Gavoni or Albert Lawrence to do his bidding. He had the quintessential gift of leader-
ship: the knack of investing himself with that charismatic aura
which made others believe that here was a man whose talents
were so rare, whose soul so sensitive, whose spirit so precious
and so fragile, that it was their honored lot to reserve him for
responsibilities more exalted than the banal.

I have said that Corporal Laibowitz adopted an imperial role
vis-à-vis "his" patients. His intensely personal, protective concern for "his" cases grew by such leaps and bounds that he began
to resent the way our psychiatrists tossed the word "sick"
around. "Doc," he once asked Captain Mathieson, "why do you
call that boy from Texas 'sick'?"

"He *is* sick," said Mathieson.

"In my opinion, he is not sick; he is just miserable."

"He's miserable because he's in conflict."

"Who wouldn't be, going through what that poor guy went through?" Laibowitz cried. "Twenty-two days behind the Jap lines! In a stinking jungle, living like a rat, each minute dying a little, thinking they're going to catch him. Malaria, the trots, running sores on his feet, no food, no water, out of his head with fever. A Jap sentry clobbers him and is going to run a bayonet through his guts, Tex puts a switch-knife right in the Jap's heart. The blood squirts over Tex like it's coming out of a pump, and he throws up. From this you expect a man should come out singing 'I'm Looking at the World Through Rose-Colored Glasses'?"

"N-no," said Captain Mathieson, "but—"

"I'm glad you agree with my diagnosis," said Laibowitz, and promptly repaired to Captain Newman for "consultation" on the case of Tex Hovring. "Consider what he went through, Doc!"

Captain Newman nodded sagely. "I have considered it many times. But other men have gone through experiences as bad as Tex's, and didn't end up in Ward Seven."

"Them you can give medals; Tex, I give sympathy."

"He's getting more than sympathy; he's getting therapy."

"That he needs like a shark needs teeth. Send him back home to Dallas, to his wife and kids, and in a month, I give you five to one, he'll be as normal as me."

"Will he?" asked Newman with the boundless patience he seemed to show no one except Laibowitz, or a patient. "It was on his way back to Dallas that Tex broke down. He can't *face* his wife and kids, Jackson. He can't stop crying. He says he's not a man. He says he's a coward."

"That's because he's brave!" protested Laibowitz. "Brave enough to come right out and say what everyone feels but is afraid to admit."

"Everyone else doesn't try to jump out of a plane on his way home."

Laibowitz scowled. "So he flipped his lid maybe for a minute. From all the excitement! 'Sick' I call the odd-ball who *don't* know when to take a dive. Doc, honest to God, there are times I do not understand you!"

"When you're around, Florence Nightingale, I'm not sure I understand myself."

The irony was wasted on Laibowitz, who only remarked morosely, "That's what I figured."

The only men Laibowitz agreed to call "sick" were the psychotics—the men whom terror had driven beyond reality, beyond the now, the past, the future; the boys who lay in bed, staring into space, or sat in chairs in catatonic stupors; the ones who cowered in corners or hid under sheets; the men who saw nothing, sensed nothing, except the endless repetition of their nightmares; the ones who suddenly broke into howling fury, smashing at windows or walls with their fists, attacking anyone near them, running amok in terrible seizures. "Those guys," Laibowitz complained to Newman, "ought to be put in a nuthouse! They are destroying the peace and harmony of my ward."

Laibowitz disapproved of violence, violently. He saw no conceivable excuse for it. That very forbearance he showed any "unhappy guy" in the ward, he cut off with a kind of Puritan finality from those who resorted to physical self-expression. "They have no right to pamper themselves," he told Francie. "Rough stuff is for Nazis—and I don't mean only German Nazis, on account an Eskimo can act like a Nazi, too, to say nothing about our own type goons. *I* don't take a poke at a guy I don't like; they shouldn't take a poke at anyone either. A Joe who wants help should co-operate at least a minimum."

No one ever won an argument from Laibowitz. I never heard him confess error or recognize defeat. He was, like the prophets of old, absolutely convinced of his own righteousness. He held nondebatable opinions about everything from Doolittle's raid on Tokyo to disorders of the gastrointestinal tract. He was given to *ex cathedra* utterances and galloping *non sequiturs*. He rarely expressed an opinion without framing it as an axiom. He could not, indeed, conceive of having mere opinions, for he formulated his preferences as if they were steps in a larger, majestic philosophical system.

Take a matter as mundane as shaving, for instance. Laibowitz hated to shave. But he would never say—simply, directly—that he hated to shave. He wrapped his prejudice in the raiment of cosmology. "If God meant men should have clean cheeks, would He have invented hair?" Or, "What distinguishes male from female? Except for sex, nothing but beards." Or, "I read where the Chinese are the most civilized people in the world, and *Chinese men do not shave.*"

"Indians don't shave either," Francie once kidded him.

"That puts you in my corner," said Laibowitz, "because the Hindus could give us aces and spades in culture!"

"I meant the American Indians."

"You just dug your own grave, Lieutenant. The *American* Indians were the bravest men ever lived!"

Laibowitz's resistance to barbering was not made easier for him by the fact that patients in the ward were often permitted to go unshaved. One morning, when Laibowitz looked like the "before" version in an advertisement for razor blades, Captain Newman asked him testily, "Why didn't you shave this morning?"

"The Major in Room C didn't shave this morning either," said Laibowitz.

"You know perfectly well that the Major is forbidden to use a razor."

"So give me the same break; forbid I should use one."

"Major Slater is suicidal," said Newman.

"That's exactly what I'm becoming, with your fetish about hair."

"I asked you a question!" snapped Newman. "Why didn't you shave this morning?"

"Is this morning different from other mornings?"

"No. That's why you should shave!"

"Excuse me. There is a hole in your logic. That's why I shouldn't."

"Laibowitz—"

"A man can be born with very delicate skin!" cried Laibowitz. "Touch it with metal, it bleeds. Scratch it with steel, it gushes. Douse it with witch hazel, my whole body breaks out in a rash!"

"I'll report these original symptoms to the A.M.A."

"Put in that I also itch from the brush."

"Shave!" said Captain Newman.

"Why do you treat me like I was normal?" exclaimed Laibowitz. "If I was a patient, you'd call it a phobia and bring me breakfast in bed."

"But you're *not* a patient—"

"That, you can arrange in a second."

"—and you're not phobic!"

"So I'm *counter*phobic, like you said about Goo-Goo Gannon."

Captain Newman assumed his most forbidding expression. "That will be enough, Jackson. Shave!"

Laibowitz rolled his eyes around in anguish and glanced up toward the Almighty. "I think I'll lay down. I feel dizzy."

"That—is—an—order."

"It's against human nature," muttered Laibowitz.

This apothegm, "It's against human nature," was the last, unyielding bastion of Laibowitz's creed. Whatever he opposed, he transformed into an enemy of natural law. He believed that he knew more about "human nature" than any man on earth. He also seemed to think that *his* human nature was different from others' and required unquestioning acceptance. "Today I am depressed," he might announce, "so do not aggravate me with details. It is not advisable to get in God's way." Or: "Some men God gave big muscles; others He gave big brains. Don't ask me to move furniture."

I often heard him invoke the Deity—but in a most peculiar way. Whether he was devout or not I never really discovered; he called upon God the way a coach sends in a pinch hitter.

"I should of listened to my teachers," he once confided to me. "I should of gotten more education."

"How far did you get?" I asked.

"Second year high. Then I quit."

"Why?"

"Why?" he echoed bitterly. "Because of The System, that's why. The System gives the breaks to luck, not brains. My old man died, may he rest in peace, and someone had to go out and fight for a buck for my mother and kid sisters. So who's elected? Jackson Laibowitz." He waved his hand benignly, in a manner reminiscent of Captain Newman, from whom he picked up all sorts of mannerisms. "Go sue The System. I could write a book about it. It screws up Society. I could of gone for doctor, lawyer, even psychiatrist. With people, I was always good. Even in fifth grade, the kids opened up to me: 'Jackson, what should I do?' 'I feel lousy, I feel great, I feel funny, I'm mixed up—Jake, what's happening to me?' In my crowd, I was the unofficial couch. Before I ever heard of Sidney Freud. Before I heard even of Doc Newman."

Laibowitz's loyalty to Captain Newman was passionate, bottomless and unalterable. He would do anything for Newman—except change his behavior. This he defended with a certain pride and maintained with what I can only call a certain grandeur.

One day, I saw Captain Newman stalk out of the ward, his face a cloud, with Laibowitz in his wake. When they got to the office, Newman closed the door with a bang.

"Aha!" said Laibowitz. "A chewing-out is on the way."

"How can you tell?" asked Newman sarcastically.

"You look like a stand-in for Colonel Pyser."

Captain Newman sat down, very erect. "I suppose Sergeant Kopp is on leave."

"How did you guess?"

"I didn't have to guess; I smelled. The bedding in the ward."

"What's that got to do with Arkie?"

"When Arkie is on duty, the ward is as clean as a whistle!"

"Today it's 110 in the shade," observed Laibowitz, "so naturally, the bedding smells."

"If you *aired* it, Laibowitz, it wouldn't smell."

Laibowitz regarded his captain with solicitude. "I have been studying your behavior. When you're mad, you call me Laibowitz; when you're annoyed, you call me Jackson; when you're happy, you call me Jake."

"You're damn right I'm mad! That bedding is a disgrace."

"*Today* you think it smells?" cried Laibowitz. "You should of smelled it yesterday. It's a miracle my patients didn't faint like flies. I could of bottled that smell and sold it to Chemical Warfare."

"All sheets, mattresses and pillow cases are to be aired each morning," said Captain Newman firmly. "Do you understand?"

"Deaf, I'm not."

"That is an order!"

To a direct command, which Laibowitz regarded as the unfair advantage the Chiefs of Staff had given officers as against GIs who might best them in man-to-man combat, Laibowitz unfailingly responded with a surprise maneuver on the flanks. "I'm only human."

"So are the men who have to sleep in those beds!"

"I only have two hands."

"But you have four orderlies to help you!"

"They're human the same as me."

"That's enough!"

Now Corporal Laibowitz studied his captain with the utmost sympathy. "Doc, you look tired."

"Thank you very much. The condition of the bedding has tired me."

"If it tires you, imagine what it does to *me*."

"Stop playing ping-pong with my sentences! Get that bedding out of the ward and into the open air."

"That goddam sun could make the mattresses explode!"

"Then put them in the shade."

"By the time you get any shade around here it's time for my patients to go to sleep!"

"Don't talk like an idiot."

"That," Laibowitz grumbled darkly, "is what will lose us this war."

"Airing the mattresses?" exclaimed Captain Newman.

"Treating Americans like slaves."

The relationship between them never ceased to fascinate me. I often wondered how Captain Newman could permit Laibowitz to talk to him as he did. Francie told me that Newman once returned from the Administration Building in an angry mood: Colonel Pyser had dressed him down for a memo Newman had sent up through channels, via Lieutenant Colonel Larrabee, which was signed:

Josiah J. Newman
o-1-785-902
Captain: Chronic, severe.

"Chronic or acute?" and "Severe or mild?" were standard diagnostic categories which Army doctors were required to use. All of us knew that Lieutenant Colonel Larrabee had recommended Captain Newman for promotion, and that Colonel Pyser had sat on the recommendation with obdurate vengeance. The signature was funny, all right, but—"Colonel Pyser must have hit the ceiling," said Francie. "How dumb can you be?"

"I'm not trying to rack up points in a popularity contest," Captain Newman said sourly.

"You want to be popular?" asked Laibowitz, who happened to be tidying up the bookshelves. "I'll give you the formula, foolproof: Just ask people for advice."

"The one thing I don't need is advice," said Newman.

"I didn't say you should take it. I said just *ask* for it. Everyone will love you."

"You're a treasure house of wisdom today," said Francie.

"Today, I'm not even hitting on two cylinders."

"Express my thanks to the six that are out of commission," scowled Newman.

Laibowitz sighed. "So Corsets got you down, huh, Doc? Nuts to him. Don't let him bother you. Stick to your guns. You can't be a good doc and a diplomat."

"Baloney. Plenty of men around here don't get into the hassles I do."

"I don't trust that type," said Laibowitz.

"They're realists," said Francie. "Come on, Jackson, you of all people ought to know what a realist is."

"They're apple-polishers. To polish apples is to be a two-face. To finagle, you have to use up talent which is better to use in other ways."

"I get a fresh supply of talent each morning, Jackson," said Newman.

"By off-beam remarks, I'm not impressed."

"He was being sarcastic," said Francie.

"Sarcasm is for children; from psychiatrists I expect honestness."

" 'Hones*ty*,' Jake, not 'honestness.' "

"So flunk me on English! A frank friend is better than a Park Avenue Charley!"

I thought that it was Captain Newman's excessive indulgence that encouraged Laibowitz's unmilitary conduct, but I learned how wrong I was the day Laibowitz passed my office, on his way to Central Supplies, and asked if there was anything he could get me. "Yes, thank you," I said, and gave him a list. I needed P.P.S. forms, red pencils, and thumb tacks.

In an hour, Corporal Laibowitz returned—with P.P.S. forms, red pencils, and Scotch tape.

"Didn't they have thumb tacks?" I asked.

"You wanted *thumb* tacks?" he asked incredulously.

"Why, yes. That's why I wrote them down."

Laibowitz found fascination in the ceiling. "I can't read your writing."

"But I printed that list."

"Lieutenant, your printing is even worse than your writing."

Suddenly I saw a rare opportunity to achieve a miracle—make Laibowitz admit that he had made a mistake. "Did you by any chance keep that list, Jake?"

"Am I the type to destroy official documents?" He reached into his pocket and produced the list with an expression that warned me that where trust is stunted friendship will soon die.

"Read it," I suggested.

"I already strained two eyes trying."

"Read it aloud."

"With pleasure . . . Item number one," he read, "P.P.S. forms."

"Check."

"Item two: red pencils."

"I thought you said you can't read my printing," I smiled.

"This you call reading? I'm breaking a code."

"Try item three."

"Is that the one that says 'thumb tacks'?"

"Ah . . ." I sang out in triumph. "So you *did* understand."

"Scotch tape is better."

"Jackson, sometimes I wonder if you—"

"Put a thumb tack in deep, you need a crowbar to pry it out!" cried Laibowitz. "Stick your thumb, you can get blood poisoning. Be honest, Lieutenant; did you ever hear a man should get hurt from Scotch tape?"

"That's not the point. I *wanted* thumb tacks!"

Laibowitz bestowed a considerate expression upon me. "You got too much on your mind, Lieutenant. I don't blame you for not knowing what's best for your own welfare."

What Laibowitz was to Captain Newman, Pepi Gavoni, another orderly, was to Laibowitz—except that Gavoni was born to serve. Everyone liked Pepi. He was a short, jolly Italian with thickish glasses, a musical voice and an inextinguishable faith in men. Gavoni seemed to think that all human ailments could be cured with kindness and salami. He had an inexhaustible supply of both.

Every week a three- or four-pound Genoa salami, wrapped in brown butcher paper, arrived from Gavoni's patriotic sister in Passaic. He kept it under lock and key in his locker in the orderlies' bull pen. Gavoni dispensed salami as a reward, a bribe, a token, a sacrament. He would establish rapport with a new patient by offering him a mug of milk or coffee or a Coke—and salami. Whenever a man came out of a psychiatric hour with Captains Jarvis or Mathieson, or emerged from the treatment room after a Sodium Pentothal session with Captain Newman, Gavoni would approach him with an encouraging smile and a slice of his precious, garlic-laden solace.

Occasionally, someone would pick Pepi's lock and cut off a piece of salami on his own. Then Gavoni would fly into a terrible temper tantrum. He had an astonishing linear memory: he could tell down to the inch how much salami he had placed in his locker and how much should therefore be awaiting his dispensation. He was fanatically jealous of his right, as sole proprietor, to decide who deserved a slice and who did not.

Sometimes Laibowitz would play a trick on Pepi by removing the entire salami from the locker and hiding it somewhere in the ward. When Gavoni repaired to his cache for a slice of sustenance, or an emergency boon to some soul in distress, and realized that felony most foul had been committed, he would come bursting back into the ward in a rage, squinting through his glasses and shouting: "All right, you sons-of-bitches, who copped my Genoa? Speak up! Who did it? I'll kill you! Don't be afraid! Admit it!"

The patients, many of whom Laibowitz had apprised of the

trick beforehand, would promptly mimic Pepi's voice and fury, or offer him mock consolation. As Gavoni stormed up and down the aisle, hunting, threatening, accusing, demanding confession, Corporal Laibowitz would stroll in, a paradigm of innocence. "What is the matter, Pepi? What is going on?"

"Some bastard stole the Genoa!" Gavoni would fume. "Some sneaky, no-good son-of-a-bitch—"

"*Pe*pi!" Laibowitz would remonstrate with a look of pain. "Are you accusing one of our boys of being a *crook?*"

The men in the beds would groan, moan, whistle or applaud this defense of their characters.

"He's worse than a crook!" Gavoni would cry. "He's a low-down, yellow-belly thief!"

"Ah, Pepi, Pepi," Laibowitz would sigh, shaking his head. "Have you no faith in our fellow men?"

"To hell with my faith! Where is my salami?"

"Presto-chango! Watch, Four-eyes." Laibowitz would get the salami from wherever he had stashed it and would present it with a bow and a flourish, intoning, with a resonance a bishop might envy, "Laibowitz giveth, Laibowitz taketh away; oh, what a man is Laibowitz."

Now the ward would resound with cheers.

Once Gavoni got the salami back from Laibowitz, he found himself in an unnerving dilemma—for now he was torn between gratitude and anger: angry with Laibowitz for having filched the salami, but grateful to him for having returned it. (Laibowitz could, after all, have eaten, sold, bartered or donated it.) Gavoni would blink through his lenses and grin sheepishly, "Okay, Jake, I can take a joke. One thing about me, you have to give me, is I can take a joke. You want some salami? Go on, go on. Cut off a slice. Go *on.*"

Gavoni felt honor-bound to offer a slice of the salami to the very man who had purloined it. And Laibowitz, who possessed matchless insight into the dynamics of moral crisis, always rejected Pepi's offer. This made Gavoni prey to the most confused emotions: poor Pepi was not at home in a universe where good and evil had merged into a single firm.

It was all silly buffoonery, I suppose, but the patients in Ward 7 thought—in the strange, distorted, unpredictable way of men who live with agony—that it was the funniest thing in the world. And that, of course, is why Laibowitz did it. "My patients" were the only men on earth for whom Jackson Laibowitz would play the clown.

VI

THE

KNIFE

One morning, a courier from Colonel Pyser marched into my office, saluted, and presented me with a large sealed envelope for which I had to sign a receipt. A second envelope, inside the first, was stamped *"Restricted."* I opened it. It contained over 150 names; I was ordered to assemble all relevant hospital records for them. We were about to "graduate" another group of pilots and gunners—for combat.

None of us liked those medical inspections. The men were never told what they were being examined for, nor that they were to be flown overseas within forty-eight hours. They thought it only another routine medical check-up, another occasion for the innumerable shots which made their arms blue or their buttocks sore.

Breakfast, in the officers' mess, was always subdued on the morning of an overseas clearance. We knew that in a few hours the names on those sealed lists would materialize in a long line of naked men, naked except for their dog tags and a green card each man held in his hand. The cards would be marked, by one doctor after another; the men were already marked. They were marked for battle. They were marked for combat, for dog fights high above the seas or the earth, for strafing, killing, bombing, being hit, maimed, macerated, slain.

They would soon be warriors, these men. And then— Some would end up perched on open Cadillacs, moving down Main Street between cheering crowds; some would end in stinking P.O.W. camps—in Germany, Burma, Italy, an island pesthole under the Rising Sun. Some would paint rows of little Messerschmitts or Zeros or Vals or Isottas on their fuselages; and some would be transformed into similar symbols on an enemy's catalogue of death. Some would end up recounting tales of glory to breathless and adoring families—tales of Anzio or Tarawa, Bizerte, Nijmegen, Cassino, Berlin; and some would breathe their last alone—floundering in a rice paddy, or smashed against a volcanic peak, or babbling in a jungle infested with crocodiles and harvested by cannibals.

A plane would be their Pantheon or their pyre, their wings to fame or their aerial coffin. Some would get their pictures in the paper, some their names in books; and some would die on an alien coral reef, or hanging on a Norman hedgerow, or of thirst in a Sahara sandstorm, or raving under white orchids in Melanesia. Some would live to teach fresher, younger men how to trick the enemy into coming at them and into the blinding sun; and some would drown in the English Channel or the bitter North Sea or in some boiling slot between tropical islands that look like paradise. Some would cry on an operating table in a tent lighted by kerosene and bracketed by mortar; some would be spared for a cool, clean hospital in Devon or Ceylon; and some would hear barred doors shut behind them in a ward such as ours, in a dozen places around the globe.

Neither sense nor cause nor justice would influence the indiscriminate fate that Fate would soon apportion them. Some would end up giving speeches at Rotary Club luncheons; some would

only supply a name to a list ("Killed . . . Captured . . . Missing in Action . . ."). Some would end up in wheel chairs, rolled
out upon football fields before embarrassed crowds; and some
would know not even this dubious glory as they slept, anywhere
from Iwo Jima to Des Moines, under a shining white cross, or
a Star of David, or two rough slats nailed together over a pile
of stones.

I went through a dozen overseas inspections in the time I was
at Colfax, and I hated each. This one was my first. . . .

The officers were examined privately, in a conference room in
Main. The men were inspected in the Rec Hall.

They hung their uniforms on hooks all around the side. They
looked superb—muscled, lithe, bronzed from the sun. The long
line moved down a row of tables, where sergeants checked their
names off a master list, then passed before the array of medical
officers, this peculiar jury with stethoscopes, tongue depressors,
head mirrors, pen-lights, blood-pressure apparatus. Every part of
their bodies was scanned, thumped, poked, examined; every beat
and tremor was noted, every orifice studied; every eye was examined ("Look up . . . down . . . right at me. . . ."), every
ear and nostril scrutinized, every throat peered into ("Say
'Aahh,'"), every abdomen prodded, every heart attended, every
lung observed ("Say 'ninety-nine'"), every scrotum probed
("Cough, please").

Captains Newman and Mathieson were in a cubicle set up at
the far end of the Rec Hall. Their decision was the last. . . .

We processed 150 men in three hours.

I walked back to Ward 7 with Newman. He asked me to step
into his office, closed the door, and got a bottle of bourbon out
of the lower drawer of his desk.

I said, "No, thanks."

He gave me that exasperating, sardonic look. "This isn't for
your upper lip, kiddo, which is stiff enough to satisfy all the
Aldersons; it's for your lower lip, which is trembling."

I drank the whiskey.

It turned very cold that night. I wrote a long letter home:

Perhaps if I were a doctor, these inspections wouldn't hit me so hard. I suppose I feel thankful—selfishly thankful—that I was not standing in that line of naked men this morning, with only my dog tags and that green card that ought, more properly, to be red. I also feel guilty, I suppose, a little ashamed—because I'll sleep between clean sheets tonight, and can go to a movie, and am due for 5-day leave, and can eye the girls, and will have roast beef and pie-à-la-mode Saturday night.

Someone had started a rock garden beneath my window, and in the cold, ghostly moonlight the cactus we called "Spanish Bayonet," the cholla and creosote bush, looked like evil flowers on Mars.

I turned in early. I was exhausted and slept a heavy, troubled sleep, so I did not know what happened until the following morning.

Around eleven o'clock, the phone rang in Captain Newman's room in the B.O.Q. Newman, a deep and efficient sleeper, held extremely strong views about being awakened. As the phone rang again and again this night, arousing all sorts of hostile thoughts in Newman, shattering both his narcotic slumbers and his childish hope that if he thought of something else the operator would go away, he cursed, flung a hand around in the darkness and found the receiver. A worried voice called, "Hello! Captain? Hello?"

"Good-by," growled Newman.

"Doc?"

"No. Little Bo-Peep."

"It's *me*, Doc. Jake. I'm on night duty."

"So am I, apparently."

"Doc! We got trouble. Someone has gone berserk!"

Newman sat up. "Who? How?"

"Major Bullock. That squad commander you wouldn't check

out for combat this morning. He got into the ward with some cockamamy story Hammerhead fell for, and is turning the place upside down—looking for you! He's got a knife—six inches long, so help me—and ran in the shower room—waving that knife around, yelling he'll kill you something awful. Hammerhead and Four-eyes are holding the door to the showers closed, and Bullock's on the other side trying to bust out. If he gets out—"

"Get that knife away from him! I'll be right over."

"Get the *knife* away from him?" Laibowitz echoed in horror. "He might kill himself!"

"If I try to get that knife, he'll kill *me*."

"Listen, Laibowitz. You've got to get that knife away from him!"

"Doc, that's *dangerous*."

"I know it's dangerous. But you've got to do it!"

"I'm scared, Doc. Plain, goddam *scared*. That Bullock is built like a tank—"

"Damn it, Jake, there are three of you and only one of Bullock!"

"Don't let numbers fool you!" cried Laibowitz. "Hammerhead's chicken and Pepi's puss is like old liver."

"If Bullock keeps that knife he can cut up half the guys in the ward! You've *got to get that knife*—"

"Got to, got to! What do you think I been doing? I tried, Doc! I went in after him, he took a swing at me with that knife could of cut my goddam head off!"

Captain Newman was pulling his trousers over his pajamas. "All right, help Pepi and Hammerhead. *Keep that door closed.* I'm coming—"

"No, Doc! Wait! Hold the phone."

Newman heard the phone clatter against something. "Hello . . . hello, Jake?" Through the phone he could hear a blurred babble—shouts, screams, curses, then the slamming of a door. He dropped the phone, jammed his feet into his loafers and yanked a blouse off a hook as he went out of the door. He went down the B.O.Q. steps three at a time, working his way into the blouse, and ran down the path to the road that led to Main.

He kept hoping a jeep or a car would come along. The moon was going under some clouds and he heard the muffled voices of a crap game somewhere. When he turned the corner at the PX he sighted the hospital, all dark except for the night lights in the corridors and the O.D.'s window. The front door of Main opened; a figure, silhouetted against the inner lights, came out slowly and leaned against one of the posts on the portico. Steam was drifting off the figure's clothes weirdly. Newman cut across the driveway; the apparition straightened up; something glistened in its hand.

Captain Newman stopped short, then approached the front steps. It was Laibowitz waiting there and he was sopping wet, water running off his hair and uniform and out of his shoes. His shirt was slashed in several places and there was a bloody cut on his cheek. He was breathing hard. "Doc . . ." he gasped, holding his hand out. In his palm was a wet switch-knife with a long, ugly blade. "Look at—that goddam blade!"

"Come on."

Laibowitz hustled through the door after Captain Newman. "I went in—Pepi, Hammerhead—got ashamed—came after me. Good guys, Doc! You should put them up—for a medal."

"The hell with that! What happened?"

"Bullock—is yelling bloody murder. I tell him—real loud—'Hand over the knife!' He jumps me. I duck—he damn near gets Pepi, whose glasses are so steamed up he's blind as a bat and slips on a piece of soap. Bullock goes for Hammerhead. Hammerhead gets chicken—starts to run. A couple of patients bust in, screaming. Hammerhead yells, 'Get outa here! He'll kill you!' I make a dive for Bullock—knock him back in a shower. It goes on—I go after him—that water's running too *hot*, Doc, like the boys been complaining—it scalds your ass! I get Bullock down—

grab the hand's got the knife—beat his fist on the cement. That goddam water's blinding both of us. Hammerhead tries to kick Bullock in the head, but gets Pepi. I keep beating Bullock's fist on that cement—he drops the knife. . . . He cried, Doc. Bawled like a baby you stole from him a Tootsie roll."

They pushed through the swinging doors to the ramp.

"We wrestle him back to one of the rooms. Lieutenant Corum's just coming on—goes for a hypo—"

They could hear the uproar from the ward now. Pepi unlocked the door. He had a nasty bruise on his temple. Hammerhead and a crowd of patients were in front of Room B. Hammerhead and Butcher Gorkow were pulling at the knob to keep the door closed. Someone saw Captain Newman.

"Get that bastard out of here!"

"He's a killer!"

"Tie him down! Tape his mouth!"

"Oh, Jesus, oh, Mama, please take me home," a boy in one of the beds kept whimpering. "Oh, Jesus, oh, Mama, please take me home."

"Pipe down, knock it off!" Laibowitz shouted. "Doc's here!"

"Chop-Chop" Maccarades went into his hysterical singsong: "Chop off his head. Chop out his eyes. Chop off his arms. Chop—"

"Oh, Jesus, oh, Mama, please take me home."

Captain Newman raised both hands, calling in a loud, rather bored voice, "Okay, everyone. Back to bed. The show's over."

Hammerhead was addressing Bullock's door earnestly: "Screw you, Major Bullock. Screw you, sir." When he saw Captain Newman he turned red and stammered, "Excuse me, sir."

Captain Newman heard Bullock's screams through the door—not words or oaths or threats, just screaming.

"Hurry Lieutenant Corum along with that hypo, Hammerhead," Newman said. "Pepi, put an ice bag on that egg on your head. Let me look at that cut on your cheek, Jake."

"Bleeding to death I'm not."

"Put some Merthiolate on it; check out; hit the sack."

"In wet clothes a man can sleep?" asked Laibowitz.

"Change."

"I'm on *duty,* Doc."

"Get Ruskin to relieve you."

"I'm relieved enough already."

"Gorkow, get away from the door."

"I'll go in with you," said Laibowitz. "That Bullock's strong as an ox."

"You just wait here." Captain Newman started to open the door. "Jackson—well, thank you."

"What for?"

"You did a good job."

"You told me—I did it."

"It took guts. I appreciate it, Jake."

"Praise can go a long way," observed Laibowitz. "Also, I'm sorry."

"For what?"

"That I had to bust up your sleep."

"God," groaned Newman.

Lieutenant Corum came hurrying over with a hypo.

"You all right?" asked Newman.

She nodded, but she did not smile. Her eyes went past him uneasily to the door. "Be careful."

He sighed and took the hypo from her and entered the room.

Laibowitz put his face against the little observation window. He told me, the next day, that Bullock raised his fists, blood streaming all over his wet uniform from his nose, shouting, "I'll kill you, kill you, kill you!"

"You're not going to kill anyone!" Captain Newman shouted back. "Do you hear me?" He was shouting in a harsh, furious way Laibowitz had never heard. "Where the hell do you think you are? On Guado? In some goddam free-for-all? I ought to pin your ears back! Is *this* what you would have done overseas?"

"Don't get mad," Bullock cried. "Don't you get mad at me." His eyes went "furry" (that was the way Laibowitz described it) and he began to yell, "Just because I came here, saw you several times—did you have to wash me out for that?"

Captain Newman said something violent and Bullock backed away. "I've got to go over—my old man—he's with Halsey!"

Captain Newman said something earnestly and Bullock sank to the bed with a cry, flinging his left arm across his eyes.

Newman pushed the wet sleeve up Bullock's right arm. "Easy." He raised the hypo needle. "You need lots of sleep, Major."

Bullock was weeping, "Don't get mad at me, Captain. Please —don't *you* get mad at me, too."

The next morning, I heard five different versions of what had happened. The doctors in Main seemed to take special delight in ribbing me. They seized upon the Bullock episode as if it was a clear-cut demonstration of the inadequacies of psychotherapy, or Captain Newman's brutal use of it. I had a great deal of work piled up, but I could not get down to it. I found an excuse to bring some CI-206 tests into Captain Newman's office.

He wasn't there.

I was starting out, back to Main, when Lieutenant Corum came in. "Good morning," she said. "Have Captain Newman's esteemed medical colleagues been riding you about last night?"

"That's putting it mildly."

"How they love to gloat!" She flung herself into a chair, stretching her legs out and kicking off her shoes. "They get me so damn mad! Still, who am I to talk? When I first got here, I thought he was a fast-talking smoothie, too—too smart, too glib, and fresh. He's naïve, you know—for all his psychiatry, he's one of the least sophisticated men you'll ever meet. Did I ever tell you how he got me into Ward Seven?"

"No."

"I came here from Ellington. I was in post-op. I didn't know Newman from Adam—but every once in a while I caught him

staring at me as if I was a freak. I used to look up, and there
he was with those knowing, weary eyes pinned on me. He didn't
say anything, ask for a date, pitch me a line. Nothing. One day
he came up to me and said, 'How about your coming into Ward
Seven, Lieutenant?' 'No, thank you,' said I. 'I'm perfectly contented where I am.' He made a face as if he had swallowed a
pickle: 'I wasn't inquiring into your contentment. I can *use* you
in the ward.' Every damn day for a week, every time I turned
around or looked up, there were those steady, appraising, re-
proving eyes. . . .

"One night he asked me for a date. Big deal. He took me to
the Blue Cave—" she wrinkled her nose in distaste—"and what
do you think he talked about? My girlish charms? My fatal
capacity to attract wolves? My life or past or future? Oh, no.
He held me spellbound for three solid hours, talking about psychiatry. . . . The one personal comment he made, while we were
dancing, was to ask me why I was wearing a wedding ring. 'I
used to be married,' I said. 'I know that,' said Josiah J. Newman,
'but you're divorced, aren't you?' 'Yep—but the ring gives me a
certain amount of protection, which a nurse needs around here,'
I said. 'Not from me,' he said. . . . By the time he dropped me
at the barracks, I had agreed to try Ward Seven—strictly a
nine-day try-out, I insisted. . . ." She sighed, wriggling her toes.
"I've been here ever since."

"You like it?"

"I can't imagine working anywhere else."

"You must like Captain Newman," I smiled.

She gave me a tantalizing, sidelong glance. "Sometimes."

"I didn't know you had been married," I said.

She wriggled into her shoes and stood up. "It's something I
don't talk about. . . . When the genius comes in, tell him I had
to go over to O.T."

I was on my way back to Main when the door to the conference room opened. Captain Newman came out, followed by Cap-

tains Mathieson and Jarvis. Newman saw me and sang out, "Barney . . ."

"Yes, sir?"

"I want to talk to you. . . . Haven't you been around here long enough by now to drop those silly 'sir's?" he asked irritably. "Close the door. . . . What have they been gassing about to *you* over in Main?"

"They—well, they were talking about Bullock."

"That's peachy. What else?"

"That's about it."

"Like hell it is. They think I really goofed, don't they? They think no doctor, much less a psychiatrist, ought ever to blow his stack or talk to a patient the way I cursed out Bullock. Isn't that it?"

"Yes," I said.

He waved his hand derisively. "Don't let them get you down, Barney. I threw that fit with Bullock deliberately. What those proctologists can't understand is that I *had* to sound angry to get him to listen—really listen. I acted to Bullock the way Bullock acts when his defenses are overwhelmed by his hostilities. I confronted him with an image of—what? Of himself. I had to break through his rage to get to the fear behind the rage. That's what's always behind rage—fear, violent, unmanageable fear. Men like Bullock turn it against others; I turned it back on him. Above all, I had to show Bullock I wasn't afraid of him. Fear in others is intolerable to him. It triggers greater fear. Men like Bullock desperately want others not to be frightened by that in themselves which frightens themselves. I showed Bullock I wasn't afraid of him by acting angry with him: angry, but not hostile. Mark the difference. Never let off hostility against a guy like Bullock. It gives him a real reason to attack. Once Bullock saw that I was angry—not frightened, not hating him, just angry— he went into a reverse panic, a fear that *he'd* be killed, punished by me, abandoned, God knows what. Now he needed reassurance.

People who hate themselves need love—no matter how they distrust it. 'Don't you get mad at me, too,' he pleaded. I was the one who had to protect him from the very savagery he was running around trying to inflict on others." Captain Newman ran his hand through his hair impatiently. "Maybe I can get somewhere with him now. At least he'll be in the ward for a while."

I had lunch with Captain Mathieson that day. I liked Stacy Mathieson. He was a quiet, thoughtful, gangling man from Minnesota who always seemed to make sense. He wasn't easy to know, nor easy to get to, but when you did it was well worth the effort. Mathieson was at least ten years older than Captain Newman. He had a wife and two daughters. The Mathiesons lived in a pleasant house off the post. Captain Newman once told me that Mathieson had given up a thriving practice in dermatology because he was convinced that 90 per cent of his patients' skin diseases were psychogenic. I asked him about the episode with Bullock.

"Captain Newman would never have put on that riot act with Bullock in the open ward, in front of other patients." Mathieson struck one of the big kitchen matches he used to light his pipe. "The key to it was Newman's voice. Did you ever really notice his voice? There's a curious, warm quality in it, even when he's sarcastic. I'll bet that even while Newman was cursing Bullock out, shouting and ranting and swearing, his affect, his feeling, came through. They showed concern. Concern for Bullock, I mean. Newman *cared*. That got through to Bullock in a way nothing else could." Captain Mathieson paused. His honest, rugged features took on a quality of sadness. "How do you throw a fit of rage that's reassuring? . . . Do you know what Captain Newman answered, when I asked him just that in our meeting this morning? He looked flabbergasted, a little disappointed—in me, I guess—and exclaimed, 'I was shouting at the symptoms, not the patient.'"

VII

THE HAPPIEST
MAN IN THE WORLD

When things crowded in on us at Colfax, when the news from overseas was shattering or a crash on the desert took the life of a boy we liked, when the remorseless heat or the unremitting pressure or the endless, exacerbating Army routines began to get us down, someone would smile "How about Coby Clay?" and the grins would spread around the room. Coby's saga never failed to warm our hearts.

Coby was the happiest soldier on the post. For all I know, he was the happiest man in the United States Army, Navy or Marines. Captain Newman once told me that Coby was the only man he ever knew who was utterly impervious to life's vicissitudes. "He is consistently euphoric without being hypomanic." Coby baffled him, delighted him, and renewed his faith in the surpassing powers of a happy childhood. Coby baffled and delighted us all—all of us, that is, who did not have to contend with his one-man victory over the Army. It was his sergeant, his lieutenant and all the officers directly above them in the line of command whom Coby nearly drove out of their minds. As Laibowitz said, when the whole post was rocking with laughter over the *cul de sac* into which Coby had driven Colonel Pyser and the entire military establishment, "That Coby stepped out of some fairy tale or something. They ought to put up a monument. In my opinion, he is the happiest man in the world."

Coby was an Alabama lad, exactly six feet five inches in height. He had baby-blue eyes, curly hair and a cherubic spirit that spilled over from some inner reservoir of content. He walked around in a private cloud of delight, always grinning, chuckling, slapping his thigh in gratitude for his own inexhaustible good company. "Man, oh, man," he would chortle, "just you listen to that. Man, oh, man, that's mighty fine stuff." He was entirely at peace with the world and at home with himself—his body, his reveries, his Maker, his soul. His moods ran an exceptionally narrow gamut, being bounded at the lower end by pleasure and at the upper end by bliss. The only thing he was sensitive about was his height, which he reported, in rueful confession, as "five foot seventeen."

On the post we always knew when Coby was about to materialize; we could hear, in advance, the whistling or humming or chuckling which accompanied his running colloquy with his beatific self. Hear it? No; overhear it. For his contact with any of us, with the unhappy universe beyond his own fantasies, was fragmentary, and oddly compassionate. I think he felt sorry for everyone who could not join him in the idyllic past with which he chose to replace the irksome now.

Coby was an exceedingly amiable soldier, but he was most oddly co-ordinated. His long, far-flung limbs seemed to live a life independent of his torso. When Coby drew those six feet five inches to attention, for instance, he did it in sequence—as if his brain were sending messages to the outlying provinces of his bodily empire; naturally it took more time for a foot to respond than, say, a hand, since the one was so much farther from headquarters than the other.

Coby had immense biceps and looked strong, very strong, which I'm sure he was; but he did not feel strong. And a man who does not *feel* strong simply is not able to lift heavy loads, or move burdensome objects, or heave, haul, toss or carry things which much weaker men manage to do because they want to be strong. This was an illusion Coby did not entertain. He did not care a fig about physical strength; he wanted harmony, not power.

At an early age, he had found himself in a world where men competed—for jobs, for money, for women, for promotions—and he had long since come to the conclusion that he did not care to compete for anything. He was content with himself, encouraged himself, enjoyed himself and admired himself. "His ego," Captain Newman wrote in the confidential report on Coby Clay which Colonel Pyser requested, "appears to be inaccessible to conventional appeals."

It certainly was. For Coby was the only private in the United States Army who never made his bed; his sergeant made his bed for him, each and every morning. I think Coby was the only soldier in military history whom neither sergeants nor lieutenants nor captains nor majors nor colonels could prevail upon. They tried—all of them; Lord knows they tried. They tried command and cajolery, blandishment and bluster and threats of reprisal, but Coby would not make his bed. He would hear out the orders, the coaxings, the reasoning, the threats; he would gravely consider the appeals to sense, to teamwork, to *esprit de corps*. Then all he would say, with the utmost kindliness, was: " 'Tain't fit for a grown man to make his own bed."

All this broke upon our collective awareness the very first dawn after Coby was shipped to our unsuspecting installation, when his sergeant came into quarters to find Coby gazing out of the window happily, humming a roundelay. His bed was unmade.

Sergeant Pulaski, an uncomplicated Polish boy from Chicago, called, "Clay!"

"Yes, Sarge," Coby beamed.

"Clay," said Sergeant Pulaski sternly, "you didn't make your bed."

"That's right, Sarge."

Sergeant Pulaski wrinkled his brow. "Why not?"

Coby said, " 'Tain't fit for a grown man to make his own bed."

Sergeant Pulaski, who had a gift for unvarnished command, put his fists on his hips at once and barked, "What the hell kind of double-talk is that?"

"Back home," said Coby, "my maw always makes up my bed. Ever since I been born, my maw always made up that bed."

"In the Army," said Sergeant Pulaski slowly, "there ain't no ma's to make no beds. In the Army, soldier, everyone—everyone except officers—makes his own bed!"

Coby took thought and clucked his tongue.

"Inspection is in ten minutes."

"That's *nice*," said Coby.

"Now, boy, make that bed."

Coby sighed and shook his head with regret. "I ain't hankerin' to make no trouble for nobody, nohow; but I jest cain't do it."

"And why 'cain't you just do it'?"

"Why, I jest couldn't look my maw in the eye again if I made up my own bed."

Sergeant Pulaski stared at Coby in amazement, tightened his lips, declared, "A guy asks for trouble he's gonna get trouble!" and stalked out.

Coby lay down on his bed and sang himself a song. In less than five minutes, Sergeant Pulaski returned with Lieutenant Bienstock. I had briefly met Bienstock, a second lieutenant with fuzz on his cheek but not on his chin. He was an enthusiastic exponent of that Come-on-fellows-let's-all-put-our-shoulders-to-the-wheel attitude which never failed to puzzle military observers from abroad, who expect an army to be divided simply into those who command and those who obey.

Lieutenant Bienstock now hastened into the barracks with

shining eyes, alert ears and palpitating disbelief. "Which one? Where, Sergeant? Which one is it? That one? On your feet, soldier."

As Coby undulated himself upward, part after part, until all of his five foot seventeen assembled more or less at attention, Lieutenant Bienstock paled slightly.

"Mornin', suh," Coby smiled.

Lieutenant Bienstock glanced uneasily at Sergeant Pulaski and said, "Now listen, Clay. Sergeant Pulaski has been very patient with you, I must say. You don't want to get into any trouble, do you? And we certainly don't want to make you any trouble. Now, what's all this nonsense about your refusing to make your bed?"

Coby looked down at his superior from bland, unruffled heights. "Oh, I don't aim to make no trouble for nobody, nohow. I *like* it here, suh. But it jest ain't right, suh. I couldn't look my maw in the eye again if I made up my own bed."

Lieutenant Bienstock stared at the kind, forbearing face above him and, in a strained voice, asked, "Do you realize what you're *saying*, Clay? Do you know what this means? Why—you are deliberately refusing to obey an order from a superior officer!"

"Oh, no, suh," Coby drawled. "I ain't refusin' t'obey no one, nohow."

"Then you'll go ahead and make that bed!"

"Cain't," said Coby.

Lieutenant Bienstock glanced at Sergeant Pulaski nervously, wetting his lips, and said, "Sergeant, take this man to Captain Howard's office."

"Right." Sergeant Pulaski saluted and nodded to Coby, who regarded Lieutenant Bienstock in the kindest possible way before ambling out. Bienstock lighted a cigarette and inhaled deeply, organizing his thoughts. There were a great many of them. Then he hurried out and headed for Captain Howard's office in Building Two.

Coby was sitting on a long bench, one foot drawn up, his elbow on it, his hand dangling loosely, moving in lazy rhythm to his humming. Sergeant Pulaski was standing next to him in the correctest possible military fashion. Lieutenant Bienstock regarded Coby sententiously, giving him one last chance to reconsider or recant. Coby started to mobilize his bodily ingredients for ascent; Lieutenant Bienstock turned on his heel and strode into Captain Howard's office.

I disliked Captain Howard. He was a knuckle-cracker and a mint-sucker—efficient, crisp, hard-working and mean. An automobile salesman from Wichita, Herbert Howard was a stern believer in fair play, cold showers and clean thoughts. His thoughts were so clean that he spent most of his evenings at the Officers' Club boring us with his plans for a five-minute car-washing service he was going to open up as soon as the war was over. He was the kind of incomplete personality known as "a man's man." He had few friends and many doubts. When he thought no one was watching, he bit his nails. I am sure that when he slept, he looked puzzled.

He was tallying up some requisition forms when Lieutenant Bienstock entered. Bienstock saluted smartly, accepted Captain Howard's cursory "Proceed," and, while the latter continued to add and carry over, recited the details of Private Coby Clay's defiance of the simplest and most universal requirement of military life.

Captain Howard lifted his head with an expression of incipient outrage. "He won't make his *bed?*"

Lieutenant Bienstock cleared his throat. "Yes, sir."

Captain Howard scrutinized Bienstock as if at one who had just told him the sun had risen in the west that morning.

"He says it's against his principles, sir," Bienstock quickly added.

"His principles?" Captain Howard echoed. "What the hell is he, a Mo*ham*medan?"

"No, sir. He's from the South."

"So what? Halfa this little old installation is—"

"He says his maw always made his bed for him and 'tain't— it isn't fit for a grown man to make his own bed."

Captain Howard leaned forward, hunching his shoulders like a fullback plowing through the line, and cried, "His *'maw'*? What the hell's the *mat*ter with you, Bienstock?"

"Nothing, sir," said Lieutenant Bienstock with a pained expression. "I was just *quoting*."

"Well, stop quoting and talk sense! He calls his mother 'maw'?"

"Yes, sir."

"Is he a hillbilly or something?"

Bienstock hesitated. "I think he's from Alabama, sir."

"I don't care if he's a thirty-plus-three *de*gree Mason! Do you mean to stand there and tell me you let a damn dog face pull a cockeyed gag like *re*fusing to make his own bed on you?"

"Sir, I explained and insisted and argued with him. I even—"

Captain Howard's face assumed various variations of impatience as Lieutenant Bienstock proceeded. This made Lieutenant Bienstock more nervous, and he began to stammer. This made Captain Howard's lips thread themselves so that contempt replaced impatience. This made Lieutenant Bienstock blush. This made Captain Howard slap his desk with his open palm and snap, "You *argued* with him? What the hell's the *mat*ter with you anyway, Bienstock? You are an *of*ficer in the *Un*ited States *Ar*my! This isn't a debating *so*ciety. We're at war! Get the marbles out of your head and throw that no-good gold-bricker in the little old guardhouse!"

"Sir?"

"You heard me. Throw him in the can!"

"I thought—"

"That's not smart of you, thinking. Give him to the MPs, Bienstock, to the MPs. Twenty-four hours in the little old cooler will cool off that joker. It's as *sim*ple as that. Won't make his bed! 'It ain't fit for a grown man.'" Captain Howard's expres-

sion was a masterpiece of disgust. "Holy *Mo*ses, Bienstock, even
the *Com*munists make their own beds. Dismissed!"

Lieutenant Bienstock wiped his brow the minute he got outside the door, signaled to Sergeant Pulaski, and strode out as
Sergeant Pulaski told Coby, "Up!"

When they were fifty feet from Captain Howard's office, Lieutenant Bienstock took Coby under a tree and made a last earnest
effort to save him from his fate. Coby listened with the utmost
consideration. Anyone could see that he wouldn't want to hurt
Lieutenant Bienstock's feelings for the world. But what he said,
after Bienstock's moving appeal to reason, was, "Tain't fit for a
grown man to—"

"Sergeant," said Bienstock petulantly, "take this man to the
guardhouse! By order of Captain Howard."

Coby spent that day and night behind bars. He spent most of
the day singing and all of the night sleeping like a particularly
contented lamb.

When Coby returned to the barracks from the guardhouse the
next morning, Sergeant Pulaski was waiting at the entrance with
a superior smile.

Coby was delighted to see him. "Man, oh, man," he chuckled,
"I caught me up on plenty of snoozin'."

Pulaski said, "Okay, Clay. Let's us have no more trouble from
you, huh?"

Coby's eyes moved serenely around the barracks, coming to
rest on his own bed in the far corner. It looked as neat, tight
and oblong as a coffin.

"We got commended for neat quarters at inspection this
morning," growled Sergeant Pulaski defensively. "Okay, okay,
so *I* made up your bed. But no more trouble from you, huh,
Clay?"

"No, Sarge," said Coby. "I ain't aimin' to give nobody—"

"—no trouble nohow," Pulaski finished. "I heard you. Now get
the lead out of your tail and fall in with your squad."

Coby spent the day training with his company, went to sleep

that night, responded to reveille nobly the next morning, helped his comrades mop the floor and sweep the porch, lent a cheerful, helping hand to one and all—but he did not make his bed. Sergeant Pulaski looked hurt as he went out to find Lieutenant Bienstock.

Bienstock gave Coby a ten-minute lecture on military discipline, Captain Howard's cold heart, Major Forman's nasty temper, and the reputation of Colonel Pyser, an absolute Caligula in disciplinary matters. Coby could not have been more interested in these novel insights into the military organization of which he was so small a part. But he would not sacrifice his principles; he would not sully his mother's image of him; he would not make his bed. He returned to the guardhouse. And, back in the barracks, Sergeant Pulaski made his bed again, while Coby sang for his colleagues in the can.

The next day Coby was back with his fellows. That night he slept in the bed which Sergeant Pulaski had made that morning. The next morning he declined to make his bed, with genuine affection and regret, and went to the guardhouse again.

This went on for a week, Coby spending alternate nights at the guardhouse, sleeping alternate nights in the bed which Sergeant Pulaski, hamstrung and desperate, made for him. When it seemed clear that Coby Clay was willing to spend the rest of his days in this idyllic double life, Sergeant Pulaski appealed to Lieutenant Bienstock, and Lieutenant Bienstock reported to Captain Howard with an unmistakable note of panic in his voice.

Captain Howard cracked his knuckles, studied Lieutenant Bienstock with disgust diluted only with disbelief, and, between his fine, well-brushed teeth, said, "Bring that mother-loving soldier in to me." He had never laid eyes on Coby Clay.

When Coby presented himself, Captain Howard was on the telephone, tilted far back in his chair, his back to the door, reading aloud acidly from a report and bawling out a lieutenant in Quartermaster's. Captain Howard was feeling especially curt, concise and complete that day. He slammed the phone down, swiveled around to his desk, deliberately keeping his eyes on the report, and waited for the familiar: "Private ——— reporting, sir," from the soldier awaiting his dispensation. He did not get it, because Coby saw no reason to give it.

Captain Howard put his pencil down slowly, exactly parallel to the blotter pad, assumed an expression of icy foreboding, then slowly lifted his eyes up the height of the erect body before him. This calculated maneuver of the eyes had always before served Captain Howard's purposes; it effected a slow deflation of the other's ego; it smothered hope or illusion; it was a shrewd tactical gambit which made it crystal-clear who was standing and who was sitting, and who was going to continue standing at the sole pleasure of who was sitting.

But Lieutenant Bienstock had forgotten to tell Captain Howard that Coby Clay was six feet five. By the time Captain Howard's gaze reached the unexpected altitude of Coby's chin, Herbert Howard, who was only five feet eight, had his head far back in the socket of his neck and his eyes bugged in an involuntary bulge.

Coby blushed sheepishly, as he always did when people first comprehended his eminence. "I come right over, suh, like that there other fellow told me."

"Who?" asked Captain Howard.

"That there other fellow. The one brought me here before."

Captain Howard could feel his neck getting hot. "That 'other fellow' is an *of*ficer, an *of*ficer named Lieutenant Bienstock, and you will re-fer to him hereafter by name."

"He never told me his name," said Coby.

"Well, *I* am telling you his rank *and* name!" Captain Howard retorted, slamming his fist on the desk. "And even if you didn't know his name, you could call him 'lieutenant.' You understand *that* much, soldier, don't you?"

"Yes, suh!" Coby was always grateful for increment to his store of knowledge.

Captain Howard turned sideward and poured himself a glass of water, noting with approval that his hands were steady. He sipped the water slowly, lowered the glass, studied it, placed the glass back on the table, leaned forward, put his palms together, and said in an even voice, "Soldier, I want you to listen *care*-fully to what I am about to tell you. I'll say it slowly, so there is not the *slight*est chance you'll misunderstand. It involves your making a decision that may affect *your whole life!* Are you ready?"

Coby furrowed his brow, concentrating on every word Captain Howard had uttered, and nodded.

Captain Howard took a deep breath and let it out, word by word. "Either you make your bed, every morning, without *a* single beef, or I will throw you in the little old guardhouse for ten days." He fixed Coby with his deadliest I-take-no-nonsense-from-anyone stare. "Is that clear?"

Coby nodded.

"You understand it?"

Coby nodded again.

"Any question you want to ask?"

Coby shook his head.

"Fine. Now, boy, which will it be?"

"How's that again, suh?" asked Coby.

Captain Howard gritted his many teeth. "Which—will—it—be? Make your bed in the morning, *every* morning, or go to the cold, cold jug for ten days?"

Coby sighed, regarding the man seated before and below him with infinite compassion. "I don't want to make no trouble for no one nohow, suh, but 'tain't fit for a grown man to—"

The blood drained out of Captain Howard's face; all sorts of evil thoughts welled up in him and had to be denied. He placed a mint in his mouth and pressed a button on his desk. "Good-*by*, soldier!"

Coby spent the next ten days in the guardhouse. It was, according to the reports that Corporal Laibowitz brought to the hospital and that raced through all the wards with the speed of a forest fire, the happiest ten days of Coby's life.

The MPs and Captain Howard and Major Forman—to whom Captain Howard brought his problem, confessing defeat—simply could not believe it. They could understand it, but they could not believe it. Or perhaps it was the other way around.

For Coby Clay was behaving in such a way that the entire theory of punishment, as a deterrent, was endangered. Every day Coby spent happily in the guardhouse clearly demonstrated that the punitive could be made rather pleasant, and this challenged the very foundations of law enforcement. For the whole idea of a guardhouse, or any place of confinement, rests on the assumption that detention is hateful to man's free spirit and crippling to man's free soul. But now the American Army was confronted by a man for whom detention held no terrors, confinement meant no deprivation, discipline represented no threat. The awful truth, which was beginning to confound our brass, was this: Private Coby Clay *liked* the guardhouse. He slept like a king and sang like an angel. In fact, he preferred the guardhouse to the barracks. There was something about that bounded, ordered microcosm that appealed to Coby no end; there, life was reduced to its simplest form—devoid of conflict or the perplexities of choice.

The fact that Coby declined to make his bed in the guardhouse, too—politely, but definitively—presented its own special problem to the MPs: after all, there was no other guardhouse to which you could send a man to punish him for not making his bed in the guardhouse in which he was. "What in hell can I *do?*" Major Inglehart, commanding MP, often moaned to us. No one knew what to tell him.

Nor was this the worst of it. The other prisoners, who regarded Coby with the awe of apprentices to master, were beginning to be converted to Coby's unique philosophy of life; the insidious idea began to germinate in their delinquent brains that perhaps they could get away with not making their beds, too. To nip this frightful prospect in the bud, Major Inglehart swiftly transferred Coby to a cell with one Lacy Bucks, a young enlistee from Louisiana who could not endure Yankees but felt kin to anyone south of Tennessee. The major interviewed Private Bucks personally and, after a certain amount of shilly-shallying, bribed Bucks ("double rations") to make up Coby's bed every morning. "And don't tell anyone you're doing it!" Inglehart warned him darkly.

Bucks seemed contented to be silent for the Major, and the rations. Coby, of course, had no reason to tell anyone that Bucks was making his bed for him. He never felt the need of initiating any discussion of the bed problem; it was no problem to him: at home, his maw had made his bed; then Sergeant Pulaski had; now Lacy Bucks did. It was the most natural thing in the world to Coby Clay.

Things simply could not go on this way forever.

Besides, there was the problem of work details. Men suffering punishment in a guardhouse cannot, obviously, be permitted to spend their days in happy idleness while all around them their haggard comrades drill like furies, crawl through sand, contest barbed wire, run fiendish obstacle courses under a merciless sun, bivouac under a chilling moon. The Air Force could not be *that* naïve.

So Major Inglehart put Coby, Private Bucks and a barrel-chested boy named Tony Caralucciano into a detail to police the grounds. It seemed a safe enough assignment. But as it worked out, that threesome became the finest show at Colfax and nearly demoralized the installation. For Army regulations require that every prisoner must be accompanied by an armed guard whenever he (the prisoner) is allowed outside the guardhouse. This meant that as Coby, Bucks and Caralucciano ambled happily across the grounds, in a memorable formation which I shall describe forthwith, three MPs, carrying rifles and wearing battle helmets, marched stiffly behind them. When the heat was very great, clawing at the senses with fiery hands, the three prisoners in their loose and tieless fatigue garments were conspicuously more comfortable than their nominally freer custodians.

The formation of the detail added its own piquancy to the scene. Coby always took the middle spot, looming up above Lacy Bucks on his right and Tony Caralucciano on his left. Tony carried a long pole with a nail at the end; Lacy carried a burlap sack. As the three good men moved lazily across the ground they had been assigned to make bereft of trash, Tony would spear a piece of paper—a chewing-gum wrapper, an envelope, a crumpled ball of unrequited love—on the end of the nail that was on the end of his pole, and would bring the pole up horizontally toward Coby. Coby would remove the paper from the nail with the utmost delicacy, crooking his little finger, bring his hand across from left to right, where Lacy Bucks was holding the sack open, and let the piece of paper drop daintily into the sack. He hummed or sang during the entire operation. This did not help the morale of the guards.

Tony Caralucciano had a fine barbershop bass and, in the great tradition of his ancestors, loved grand opera. Lacy Bucks was strictly a hot-jazz type, the kind who tries to find in life the archaic excitations of the syncopated. Coby, a man of broad and generous interests, liked to sing anything. These three music lovers soon learned to float together on the sea of their common fantasies, singing or humming while they worked and as the spirit of the moment moved them. It was a thing beautiful to hear and, once heard, never to be forgotten. It particularly pleased the men in Ward 7. It went like this:

Each morning when "The Prison Warblers," as Francie dubbed them, moved into position ahead of their helmeted Cerberus, Coby would greet the day by humming a note—any note, whichever note best suited his mood. His mood was unfailingly happy. If Tony was feeling very operatic he would take off, using Coby's theme note as a springboard, into anything from *Tosca* to *Madame Butterfly*. If it was Lacy Bucks who was in touch with his private muses, he would give out with *Johnny One-*

Note or *Roll, Jordan, Roll.* And if Coby wanted to override his confrères, he would simply sing out his own immemorial hymns. There was no set pattern to it: whoever sang, the others accompanied; whatever one man finished, another would take up, on the last, long, expiring note, for his own. It was as close to true understanding as men can ever get. As one of the guards was heard to mutter, struggling with his confusion and dismay: "Them is the happiest goddam garbage collectors I ever did meet."

When Coby's term of punishment ended, he appeared, refreshed and forgiving, in my office. Major Forman had told Captain Howard to tell Lieutenant Bienstock to tell Sergeant Pulaski to deliver Coby to "the head-boys." Major Forman phoned me himself and said he wanted Coby Clay rigorously tested. "The works, Alderson!" he said. "I want you to give him every blasted test you ever gave anyone. Then take him over to Captain Newman and let Newman start where you left off. Send all the reports directly to me. I'm going to build up a file on this joker that buttons down every angle, then I'm going to take the case up directly with Colonel Pyser. If this guy is a nut, we'll get him out of the army on a C.D.D., and if he's faking we'll Section Eight him out. Either way, goddamit, we'll make him regret the day he ever decided to pull that gag about not making his bed. One way or another, Alderson, *this farce has got to end!*"

No one ever got as many tests as I administered to Coby Clay that day. I gave him the whole battery from simple IQs to the Cornell Selectee Index. I gave him Self-Idealization scales and Sentence Completions ("I faint at the sight of blood. . . . I avoid people who . . . I feel nervous when . . .") I gave him AGCTs and ACIOs. I tested him for mechanical aptitude, motor responses, minimum literacy, box counting, mental alertness, visual-motor skills. I gave him perception tests, emotional adjustment inventories, aptitude scales, visual classification series. I went through the manual put out by the Personnel Procedures Section of the Adjutant General's Office to make sure there wasn't a form I had missed.

It took me a good seventeen hours just to code, score and appraise my findings. The results were absolutely frustrating. As far as the accumulated diagnostic genius of our society could discern, Coby Clay was a healthy, responsible, wholesome, brave, reasonable, well-adjusted (though slowly co-ordinated) specimen of American manhood. His schooling was not all that might be desired; his vocabulary was far from impressive; his spelling was atrocious—but then, so was the spelling of most of our armed forces. Coby's IQ was 96—not high, to be sure, but you must remember that 50 per cent of the GIs in the Army ranked between 95 and 105.

"How," Captain Newman asked me, with rather bated breath, "would you summarize all this? If you had to describe Clay in one word, what would it be?"

"Delightful," I said.

Captain Newman put his head between his hands. "Okay, Barney, bring him around."

Captain Newman interviewed Coby Clay for an hour and returned him to the unhappy jurisdiction of Sergeant Pulaski.

The report which Captain Newman wrote on Coby for Major Forman and, through him, for Colonel Pyser, was something to treasure. There was not a note of irony in it, nor a smidgen of levity. It was precise, technical, thorough, and—to someone like Colonel Pyser—infuriating. Francie showed it to me, smiling. "If you want to see the great psychoanalyst at the top of his form, cast your youthful eyes on this." I copied parts of it for posterity:

Clay's reflexes are good, though not particularly rapid. He shows excellent psychological equilibrium. He has balance, proportion, and a good sense of humor. He sleeps well, eats well, and (aside from the particular problem for which he was referred to the undersigned) performs his duties in a responsible fashion. He may be classified as "Oral, passive." . . .

He discusses his convictions about bed-making (rather, about not-bed-making) without anxiety, ambivalence, or hostility. He appears to have deeply encapsulated opinions about the masculine and feminine roles, placing some things firmly in the former category and others (such as bed-making) in the latter. . . .

I do not believe his opinions on this subject can be altered by therapy. Clay may be described as having an unusual character structure. His aggressions are well in hand. His views about certain aspects of military discipline are unique, but not subversive. His ego appears to be inaccessible to conventional appeals.

(Signed) J. J. NEWMAN, *Captain, M.C.*

When Colonel Pyser called Captain Newman to his office, that report on Coby Clay lay on Colonel Pyser's desk. Major Forman and Captain Howard were present. They looked terribly serious: Pyser kept biting his mustache, Major Forman kept drumming his fingers, and Captain Howard kept sucking mints.

Colonel Pyser opened the conference bluntly: "Captain Newman, do you regard Clay as a mental defective?"

"No, sir."

"Do you regard him as a queer—I mean *as* queer, in any shape, manner or form?"

"No, sir."

"I take it, from your report, that you insist on considering Private Clay well adjusted?"

"Yes, sir."

"You couldn't find *any* signs of neurosis, psychosis or any other incapacitating factors?" asked Pyser almost plaintively.

"No, sir."

"What about moral turpitude—or *antisocial behavior?*"

Newman shook his head.

Colonel Pyser studied him hatefully. "So you won't recommend a Section Eight hearing for this son-of-a-bitch?"

"No, sir."

Pyser put his hands on the arms of his chair and looked as if he might spring at Captain Newman any moment. "Goddamit, Newman, you have recommended men for a Section Eight-ing who never gave us half the trouble this soldier has put the post through! And now, when we really need and can *use* an N.P. diagnosis you get more conservative than Herbert Hoover!"

"But apart from not making his bed, Colonel, Clay has created no difficulties—"

" '*Apart* from not making his bed'?" Pyser echoed, his cheeks going gray. " 'Apart from not making his *bed*'? What more do you want from a nut than refusing to make his bed and *enjoying* the guardhouse, for the love of Mike? I ask you again, Newman. Do you mean to sit there and tell me that you will not recommend this gold-brick or screwball or whatever-the-hell-he-is for a Section Eight?"

Newman met Colonel Pyser's glare steadily. "I *might* classify him as neurotic, phobic type—a bed-making phobia, but that would only go with a recommendation for a C.D.D."

"Medical discharge?" shouted Colonel Pyser. "Give that bastard a pension—on half-pay—for the rest of his life? Over my dead body, Newman!" He leaped to his feet and paced back and forth furiously, then wheeled on Newman. "The real test is—do you think this soldier is fit for combat?"

"Yes, sir."

"God," Pyser groaned. "Look; if we send him overseas, do you think he's going to change his opinion about making his bed?"

"No, sir."

"Right!" cried Pyser. "Then who the hell do you think *will* make his bed overseas?"

"Someone else," said Captain Newman.

Colonel Pyser stared at Newman bitterly. Newman said he could hear Major Forman's chair trembling, and Captain Howard sucking on a mint as if it were an oxygen tube.

"One final question, Newman. If Clay finishes his training, and if I send him overseas with his outfit, when the chips are down —is this joker going to fight or is he going to wash out?"

"This boy will never wash out," said Captain Newman.

"Oh, Christ," said Colonel Pyser.

And so when Coby Clay, that fine and delightful soldier, returned from his latest stretch in the guardhouse, rested and unruffled as of yore, and appeared before Sergeant Pulaski, smiling and considerate, that product of the West Side of Chicago studied him in silence for a long, long moment before inquiring, "Coby, you learned your lesson now? You want solitary and bread-and-water next? Or you gonna be a good boy and make your bed?"

Before Coby could even finish shaking his head, Sergeant Pulaski threw his head back, crying, "Oh, hell! Okay! All right, I give up! You win! A couple million guys in the whole screwy American Army, from North and South and East and West, and I have to draw you! So okay, soldier. That's the way God wants it, that's the way He's gonna have it! I'll make your goddam bed from now on."

And he did. Every morning. Every single morning, an American sergeant made a private's bed for him. It was the talk of the post—except at Headquarters, where no one dared mention it. Not a day passed but what Sergeant Pulaski got kidded and razzed and needled about this basic transmutation of the established order. Pulaski began to get mighty edgy.

Then one day Private Clay loomed over Sergeant Pulaski and said, "Say, Sarge, can I ask you somethin'?"

"Come on, come on," said Pulaski crossly. "Talk fast."

Coby scratched his head. "Well, I been thinkin' out about this bed-makin'. 'Tain't fit for a man to make his own bed, like my maw says. But I been thinkin' an' scratchin' aroun' an' all, an' I don't see no right reason why a man cain't make up someone *else's* bed. Like you been doin' for me. I figger my maw wouldn't hardly mind if I jest did that same little thing for you."

The kidding of Sergeant Pulaski stopped after that. For from then on, until that whole contingent of brave men was flown into action overseas, while Sergeant Pulaski made Coby's bed each morning, Coby—humming of dark glades and promised lands—made Pulaski's.

VIII

LITTLE

JIM

Corporal Laibowitz often made sojourns around the post as a self-appointed confidential agent. A careful and accomplished student of scuttlebutt, he had established grapevines to Headquarters, Hospital Administration, Colonel Pyser's office and Lieutenant Colonel Larrabee's staff conferences. He sometimes used Pepi Gavoni as a research assistant ("Make a pass at that typist who stencils the travel orders") or Hammerhead as a trial balloon ("Doc's giving a paper at the A.P.A. next Christmas. Spread the word. Start with the waiters").

Laibowitz's espionage network sometimes brought him quite rare nuggets of intelligence. He discovered that a lieutenant in Quartermaster's was meeting a WAC secretary every Friday night in a diner on the highway twelve miles from camp; they were shacking up in a motel named Fifty Palms. He found out that an imaginative bar boy at the Officers' Club was diverting the top three to four ounces on each bottle of gin to a container he kept handy under the counter, adding tap water to the original bottles and selling the diverted fire water at $2.50 per canteen. He knew, a week before Major Wickersham did, that Wickersham was being transferred to Alaska, and why—which Wickersham never did find out: He had been making too many passes at other officers' wives.

The product of Laibowitz's personal reconnaissances whom I shall never forget was Little Jim.

It was one of those afternoons when the sun was mercifully veiled by clouds. I was in Captain Newman's office, going over some case histories with him, when Corporal Laibowitz entered, carrying a tray. As he removed tea and Fig Newtons from the tray, he took the occasion to declaim without warning, as was his wont, "In Ward Four is a guy you should take into Ward Seven."

Captain Newman groaned. "Can't you ever find a man in Ward Seven who would be better off in Ward Four?"

"Games," said Laibowitz acidly, "are for children."

"So is sarcasm, you once said."

"Correction. On children, sarcasm is wasted altogether."

We sipped our tea. It was piping hot.

Captain Newman winced. "Dammit, Laibowitz, you know I prefer iced tea!"

"Ice freezes the muscles. Heat relaxes the same."

"Medicine will be indebted to you forever," said Newman. "But tomorrow, just to indulge the foolish whim of your rapidly aging Captain—"

"Do you want to hear about this guy from Ward Four?"

"I don't see how I can avoid it."

"I'm glad you brought up the subject," said Laibowitz. "Well, last night, late, maybe one, one-thirty, I happen to pass the Rec Hall and I hear something like music, very soft. It's dark, not a light on, but the moon is in business and I make out someone in one of the wicker chairs—near the windows. I go in and turn on a lamp and spot this guy huddled in the chair. He's holding a guitar and he's loaded: I can smell the booze a yard away. It's in a beer bottle on the floor. I tell him he's got to get back in the sack or he's in for trouble. He begins to mumble, 'Okay, Big Jim, let's cream them tonight.' I get him up on his feet and he blubbers, 'Okay, Big Jim . . . Little Jim's comin'. . . . Let's kill us some Germans. . . .' I get him back to Ward Four, where the nurse on duty is plenty ticked off. It's the third night in a row this guy snuck out and got plastered. I tell her she's got a disturbed personality on her hands, not an ordinary lush, and advise her to send the guy down to see you. His name is Tompkins. James Bowie Tompkins."

Captain Newman nodded wearily. "That's fine. That's just dandy."

"I'm not *done*."

"Excuse me."

"I checked on this boy this morning. The doc on duty up there is some chiropractor named Beshar. I told him, in my opinion Tompkins ought to see a psychiatrist—you. An hour later Tompkins came down."

"I didn't see him," said Captain Newman.

"How could you? You were giving Lissner a Pentothal. I asked Tompkins to wait. He gave me a 'What-do-you-think-I-am-a-patsy?' look and said he's got to get some chow. So I start shooting the breeze with him to keep him there—casual, like you do, but watching him, like a hawk. He made a dirty crack about you and said no one is going to slip a needle into him, and pfft!—he's up and gone!" Laibowitz pursed his lips sagely. "This boy is in a bad way, Doc. Cocky, but tense. He didn't fool me. My diagnosis is 'Depression: Agitated. Troublemaker.' "

Captain Newman rubbed his forehead. "I hope you didn't tell him that."

"Fresh, maybe I am; stupid, no. A patient I treat like he's made of eggshells. All I told this kid was for his own good he should positively come back to see you and take the load off his emotions, which are ready to pop."

"Jackson," Captain Newman sighed, "may I remind you for the hundredth time that it is *not* part of an orderly's duties to go around the hospital drumming up business?"

"From such business, who except the sick can profit?" Laibowitz left with a look that suggested what a prophet has to go through in his own country.

Captain Newman resumed his comments about the new cases. As I got up to leave, he said, rather apologetically, "Oh, if you happen to be around Ward Four—see what the story is on that boy."

The head nurse in Four told me Tompkins was a waist gunner who had flown into Colfax from North Africa two weeks earlier, with thirty-four missions behind him, a Purple Heart, a citation for courage, and a battered guitar. He had been grounded for insomnia and severe gastrointestinal pains. He was a quiet, cooperative patient—except for the times he slipped out of the ward and got drunk. No one knew where he was getting liquor, or where he kept hiding it.

I wandered into Ward 4.

Corporal Tompkins was stretched out on his bed, fully and neatly dressed, puffing on a long, thin cigar. He could not have been more than twenty-one or twenty-two, but he had an old man's face. His guitar was on the chair next to his bed.

"Hello, Corporal."

He sat up. He was short—just over five feet five—wiry and compact. He eyed me craftily. "Howdy."

"How are you?"

He smirked and tapped his cigar ash into a waste basket.

"Mind if I sit down?" I asked.

He shrugged. "The chairs ain't reserved."

I sat down. "Where are you from, Corporal?"

"Kaintucky."

"Whereabouts?"

"You wouldn't know, Lieutenant. Right from the hill people an' sour mash. Brung up with mud on m' feet an' rot-gut in m' belly an' now I'm a heero for Uncle Sam."

I could not tell whether he was pulling my leg. He kept a sly grin on his lips.

"I see you play the guitar," I said.

"You see, but you ain't heard," he snickered. "That there ol' gee-tar scared more guys in m' outfit than all the Jerries an' the JUs an' MEs put t'gether."

"How are you getting along here?" I asked.

He shrugged. "I been in worse places."

"Is there anything you need?"

"Sure. Cheaper booze an' juicy broads . . . Don't knock yourself out, Lieutenant. I'll git me outa here afore you do." He touched his forehead with one finger, picked up his guitar, and walked away. He walked with a swagger, a bantam cock's bravado.

I spoke to Captain Beshar about Tompkins. He made no effort to pretend that he liked him. "Cocky little bastard," he said. "He wouldn't help a blind man cross a street. He's just another one of those hot-shots from combat who hates all us feather-merchants."

Tompkins neither liked nor disliked the pleasant, unhurried world of the convalescent ward. He had won no friends, made no enemies, shared no secrets, offered no portion of his self or his past to the others. Several nights a week he would steal out of the ward with his knowing, insolent smile and would cat-foot it into the Recreation Hall or behind the PX, where he would strum on his guitar and drink whiskey from a long-necked beer bottle until he slid into insensibility. Once Captain Beshar had seen him pull a bottle out of the water tank in one of the toilets, and confiscated the bottle. Tompkins simply made new arrangements with his bootlegger, whoever he was.

"I hear he got a citation," I said.

"Sure," said Beshar. "He's probably a brave little punk. They usually are."

"May I see his chart?"

"Go ahead."

I made some notes out of Tompkins' history and left—to find Tompkins leaning against the wall just outside Captain Beshar's

door. He gave me an ironic glance and walked away. I wondered
if he had been eavesdropping.

When Captain Newman entered his office next morning, Corporal Tompkins was waiting for him—sitting in his chair, tilted
far back, his feet on the desk, a panatela at a cocky angle in his
mouth. "Come on in, Captain. I been waitin' for you."

"You've been doing more than that," said Captain Newman.

Tompkins grinned. "I jest like to put m' feet up." He got up
abruptly. "I ain't stayin'. You want me to talk, you don't need
no flak-juice. Jest come to Rec Hall. At night. When I'm swacked.
I ain't promisin' nothin'. No one is gonna slip me no needle and
shoot me full of flak-juice. I'm wise to the way you hook 'em—
git 'em talkin', then slip 'em the needle. Right?"

"No," said Newman. "No man ever gets flak-juice unless he's
willing to—"

"Well, Little Jim ain't askin' for it! The way I hear it, that
flak-juice gives you a jag an' you start gabbin' an' gabbin', an'
when you git up you don't remember a thing. Right?"

"Something like that."

"I knew I had you taped."

"That isn't hard. If you really want to know, flak-juice puts
you to sleep, in a kind of twilight sleep. It helps you remember."

"Remember? Remember what?"

"What you can't forget," said Newman.

Tompkins scowled. "Nuts. That's for psychos. I ain't one of
your goof-balls, y'know."

"Who said you were? Hold out your hands, please. . . . Come
on, I won't touch you."

Tompkins put his hands out slowly, smiling. "Stiddy as rocks!"

"Sure. Now turn them over."

Tompkins turned his palms up. They were glistening with
sweat.

Captain Newman said, "Thanks, Jim," and turned away.

Tompkins studied his hands thoughtfully, then wiped them

on his shirt. "Some things ain't purty, Doc. Some things jest ain't purty!" He broke the cigar in two and flung the parts on the floor and hurried out.

In a moment, Laibowitz materialized in the doorway. "What's your diagnosis, Doc?"

"It is customary," said Captain Newman, "to greet an officer by saying, 'Good morning, sir.' "

"I said 'Good morning, sir,' yesterday."

"How time flies."

"You don't have to hide your emotions from me, Doc," said Laibowitz cryptically and left.

"Between Dr. Laibowitz and myself," Captain Newman told me at lunch, "Tompkins is going to ask for Pentothal."

"Are you going to see him? In the Rec Hall, I mean?"

He gazed at his plate abstractedly. "I don't know. He loads himself up with booze. He's getting barbiturates upstairs. I can control the Pentothal dosage, but the combination of flak and alcohol and barbiturates—hell, no. He might go wild. He might die."

Captain Newman returned to his office after dinner that night and left the door wide open. He waited until long after "Lights Out," but Tompkins did not appear. He did not appear the next morning either, nor the next night, nor the next.

But three nights later, at eleven, just as Newman was about to leave for his barracks, Tompkins appeared in the doorway. He looked unsteady. He was clutching his guitar.

"Hello, Jim," said Captain Newman.

"I guess—you don't want to hear me talk, huh, Doc?"

"Why do you say that?"

" 'Cuz you don't come! To Rec Hall."

"This is my office, Jim, not the Rec Hall. It's better to talk here."

"Not for Little Jim, it ain't. You come like I said, alone, an' if I'm swacked enough—" Suddenly the boy dropped the proud, sly mask of his deception, his face gaunt, and cried, "It ain't purty, Doc! Jeeze, it ain't purty!"

"I know it ain't, Little Jim."

"I ain't beggin', see? You want me to talk, you know where you can find me. Goddam you, Doc! *Why* didn't you come? Why *don't* you?" He swung his guitar into the air wildly and lunged out of the door.

The next morning, Laibowitz asked, with a professional air, "What's holding up Tompkins' treatment, Doc? He's waiting for you to make the move."

Captain Newman turned on his underling brusquely. "It is *not* the function of an orderly to advise the chief of the neuropsychiatric service—"

"From peasants, I expect pride. From psychiatrists, I expect imagination."

"Jackson—!"

"You say that like in front someone wrote 'Stonewall.' "

"Can you conceivably get it through your head," said Captain Newman firmly, "that I know what I'm doing?"

"How can I know what you don't tell me?"

"Tompkins is *not* ready. He keeps angling for me to come to him. And the minute I do, he'll interpret it as a triumph—"

"So let him! All his life a loser, this once throw him a hand."

"Laibowitz, *will* you listen?"

"What am I doing," cried Laibowitz, "skiing?"

Captain Newman sank into his chair, wondering for the thousandth time what it was about Jackson Laibowitz that drove one to despair: intransigence? arrogance? pride? a compulsion to dissent? an egomania so vast, so impenetrable that—whatever it was, it was a force that was unyielding, unreachable, unswayable. "Now you listen to me, Jake," said Newman irritably. "Tompkins is sick, sicker than you suspect and than I at the moment completely understand. I can't help him as long as he makes a game out of this, a contest of wills. When a boy protects himself this strongly, protests so violently about flak-juice

—maybe he knows better than I how dangerous it can be for him. Maybe he shouldn't be forced to remember. Some men can't take treatment. . . . I just don't know *why* he's thrashing around this way. Maybe all his drinking is an effort to get caught and punished for that—and not for the real guilt he's harboring. . . . It's wrong for me to give in to him too easily. He might like me—and feel like a worse heel then, and maybe hurt himself. For me to help him may require that he hate me a little. Kindness can kill a man who must punish himself." He got up impatiently and ran his hand through his hair. "Dammit, Jake, the easiest thing in the world is for me to go to him! I'd sleep a helluva lot better tonight. But what's best for me may not be best for him. He'll come to me when he's really ready: when his defenses yield, when his suffering surmounts his hostility, when his need is greater than his fear. Then—perhaps—I can help him. *Can* you get that through your head?"

Laibowitz had listened to all this, his head cocked to one side, with the air of a savant grading a precocious student. "Okay, Doc. You have changed my whole opinion of the case."

"That pleases me no end," said Newman dryly.

"You don't look it."

"Laibowitz, sometimes I think you've got the hide of an elephant!"

"Around here," cried Laibowitz, "an elephant would have a nervous breakdown!"

When Captain Newman returned from staff meeting, there was a sealed envelope on his desk. It was addressed in a crabbed, childlike hand:

Big Shot
Cu-koo Squad

He opened it. On the back of a prescription blank was printed:

Rec-hall. Tonight.
Jim T.
Pleas, come—Doc

After the lights went out in the wards that night, Captain Newman went up the ramp that led from Ward 7 to Main. The Recreation Hall was deserted. Several table lamps were burning dimly, but no one was there. Captain Newman turned the lights off and went to the farthest corner and sat down in a wicker chair. He turned that lamp on, picked up several magazines, selected the *Sportsman,* and waited.

It seemed like a long time before he heard a shuffle near the side door and a whisper: "Douse the light?"

Newman looked up. "Don't worry. Come in."

Tompkins moved into the doorway. The guitar hung at his side. "They'll gig me if they find me."

"I'll take care of that."

Tompkins dropped into a wicker rocker, putting the guitar across his knees. "You like to hear me massage the gee-tar, Doc?"

"I'd rather we talked."

"I ain't even drunk. Wait." Tompkins began to strum some chords on the guitar. "Hell, Doc, that's a lie. Little Jim's tanked up good—afore I come in. That's a fact. Oh, Jeeze. Oh, Jeeze, Doc. I feel it acomin' on. IT'S GONNA COME OUT! An' it ain't purty. I want to fergit it. I jest got to fergit it!"

"But you can't, Jim. Not really. It's like I told you: Some things you can't forget, until you've remembered them."

"Hey, that's purty good. Man, that's purty damn good. Well, I ain't gonna tell you, see—not the whole thing. Only . . . About Jim de Silva; that was his name. Big Jim everyone called him, an' one hell of a flyer. Man, could he handle that crate! Only guy in the whole goddam squadron knew how to bounce a B-24 around real good." He gave the foolish, vacant laugh of inebriation. "I'd git me loaded every damn night, hidin' in different places, every night afore we had to go up. Know what it means if you don't show up for a mission, Doc? Court-martial. No foolin' around neither . . . But Little Jim Tompkins here always showed. Yup. You know why? 'Cause *he'd* make me. That's right.

Big Jim. He'd find me. No matter where I'd hide, I'd feel this big paw shakin' me an' hear that big bastard's voice saying, 'Come on, buddy boy, time to go. This is Big Jim. Come on, Little Jim, we got to take us a ride. We got to kill us some nice, rosy-cheek Jerries.' An' I'd open my eyes and see that big Portagee bastard grinnin' at me, an' I'd say, 'Yeah, man. You're Big Jim an' I'm Little Jim an' no one's ever gonna kill us two!' An' he'd pull me to my feet like I was a bag o' hay an' hustle me out that field an' get me in that goddam crate. . . . Only buddy I ever had, Doc. Only guy ever took care of Little Jim real good. An' I—I—" The tears began to course down his cheeks. "Don't let me talk no more, Doc. Please. Stop me. If I remember, I'll blow my top. I'm tellin' you, I'll *blow-my-top!* Stop me, Doc. Please stop me—'fore I smash up that lamp an' throw around them chairs an' push m' fists through all the goddam glass in the friggin' windows!"

"Sure," Captain Newman cut in harshly. "You'll smash up the lamp and throw around them chairs and push your fists through all the goddam glass in the friggin' windows—and it won't help one bit, boy. Not one damn bit! And you know it. You've done it before, and it didn't help, and it won't help now."

Tompkins looked at Captain Newman with bleary and imploring eyes. "That's where the flak-juice comes in, don't it?"

"Yes."

Tompkins moaned. "I'm in a sweat. I don't want to think of it. I got to stop thinkin'—"

"But you *are* thinking of it—all the time, day and night, week after week, month after month after month. You play the guitar —to use up your thoughts. You fight off sleep—so you won't dream. You get swacked—to run away from memory." Newman changed the timbre of his voice abruptly. "What a stupid way to live, boy. What a goddam stupid way to *live!*"

Tompkins' body was racked by terrible sobs.

Captain Newman turned away, letting the boy cry unobserved,

and when he heard the weeping soften and the sniffing begin, he said quietly, "When did it happen? Come on, Little Jim. Why don't you spill it? Why don't you get it off your chest, once and for all? What happened? When?"

"November 17. We take off, 18:05. Me an' Buck in the waist, an' Lieutenant Bates with Big Jim—" He caught himself and cried, "Yeah! Like hell! I'm no good. I'm a yellow-belly who let— Oh, Jeeze, Doc, gimme the flak-juice. You win. *I'm askin' for it.* Give it t' me! Please. Now, right *now!*"

Captain Newman got to his feet slowly and stretched. "Okay, Little Jim. If you lay off the booze for two days, not a *drop*, understand, and I tell them to stop medication—no pills to help you sleep—I'll give you the flak. Thursday morning. In my office. Ten o'clock." He forced a yawn.

"Not now?" cried Tompkins in consternation. "You ain't gonna do it now? When I'm askin' for it?"

"Nope," Newman yawned. "It'll hold, boy. Jeeze, I'm bushed. I'll see you tomorrow. Why don't you hit the hay?"

Tompkins wiped his eyes with the back of his hand. "Sure, Doc. Anything you say, Doc."

Captain Newman started for the door. Tompkins was not following him. He was nestling down in the chair, working his shoulders like a cat. Newman paused, frowning, then he pushed his voice into a shout. "Tompkins, what the hell's the matter with you? Haven't you beaten yourself up enough for one night? *Don't you have any pity?*"

Corporal Tompkins gave a cry, leaping out of the chair. "Okay, okay, don't blow a gasket! Jeeze, they sure picked the right guy to boss the loony squad!" He staggered past Captain Newman with a clutter of elbows and knees and unguarded emotion.

He was halfway to Ward 4 when he reeled, retching, stumbling, trying to use the guitar as a crutch, sinking at last to the floor.

Captain Newman hurried to the boy and kneeled beside him. "Little Jim . . . Get up. . . ." But Little Jim could make no more than foolish, vacant sounds. Captain Newman lifted his head and slapped his cheeks gently. "Come on, boy. You've got to make the sack. . . ."

Little Jim began to whimper. "I don' wan' go up . . . not this one . . . please . . . scairt, I'm so scairt . . ."

Captain Newman raised his voice, calling: "Wardman! Orderly! Here!"

But no one answered his call.

So Captain Newman put one arm under Corporal James Bowie Tompkins' shoulder and the other under his knees and lifted the boy, who still clutched the guitar, and carried him down the corridor.

As he lowered the limp, surprisingly light body on a cot in the emergency cubicle, Captain Newman heard the boy mumble: "Knew you'd come back . . . Big Jim . . . Thanks . . ."

Early Thursday morning, while I was getting dressed, I heard a low, insistent whistle, and some gravel hitting my screen. I went to the window. Tompkins was standing below my room, signaling. He put his hands to his mouth, not to shout but to whisper, "You got a minute?"

"Come in," I said.

He shook his head. "I ain't no officer."

"Wait. I'll be down."

He was sitting on the stairs of the porch when I came out, chewing on one of his long, thin cigars.

"Good morning. What's on your mind, Little Jim?"

He got up gravely. "I got to ask you somethin', Lieutenant. Ain't had chow yet, have you?"

"No."

"I'll walk you a piece." He came around to my left side obediently, and as we went down the path toward the PX and the hospital beyond, he said, "I ain't fergittin' you come up to Four an' talk t' me that first time. Well, I got no kin folk—none livin', I mean—an' I was wonderin', well, I'd like for you t' be there this mornin', when I git the flak-juice first time—if you want to, a course. I ast the nurse, Lieutenant Corum, if it's allowed. She says Doc Newman has to decide, but I figger it's okay so long as it's okay with me. If you want to, a course."

"I'd like to very much, Jim. But—maybe you ought to think it over." I did not tell him I had never seen Sodium Pentothal administered. "Under flak a man says a lot of things he might not like anyone except the doctor to know."

"No kiddin'?" he said sarcastically. "I been all through that in m' head. *I* know what I'm liable to gab about. I got mine in a ding-do near Kasserine Pass, I guess you heard about. Next thing, I'm in a Red Cross wagon or somethin' with some Ayrab puttin' towels on m' head. What happened—between the crash an' the Ayrab—I disremember. That's what the flak-juice got to git me to spill. Doc'll slip me the needle, but I'd sorta like some-one in my corner, like they say. A course, if you don't want to—"

"I do, Jim. I'm pleased that you want me there."

He tossed his cigar away. "I'll put it to Doc," he said.

At 8:30 Captain Newman telephoned me. "Tompkins left me another note. I suppose you know what it's about?"

"Yes, sir."

"This is a new one on me. Damned if I know what's best. It can't harm, I suppose, and it might help. It seems to mean a lot to him. . . . Do *you* want to sit in?"

"Yes, sir."

" 'Sir,' " he echoed sardonically. "I'll save some flak-juice for you, too."

From 9:50 on, while Captain Newman finished his morning rounds, Laibowitz kept clearing his throat, looking at his watch, hinting at the passage of time, announcing at last, in a bell-like tone: "It is nine fifty-eight on the nose. All your needles are boilin'. Do you want me to help you?"

"No, Dr. Laibowitz, I'll try to muddle through on my own."

"Progress does not come from turning down talent," said Laibowitz darkly.

"Get Tompkins and Lieutenant Alderson. Bring them to Treatment One."

I was waiting in Captain Newman's office. Tompkins was standing outside. He would not enter or sit down. He was very pale; his shoulders were turned inward.

The moment Laibowitz came along, Tompkins straightened up and said, "Let's git goin'."

"Okay, okay," said Laibowitz. "Don't get jumpy, pal. Doc's got the touch with the needle. He's no dentist, you know."

When we came to the big, barred iron door, Tompkins looked at me nervously.

"The treatment rooms are just inside," I said.

"They ain't gonna keep me in there, are they? After?"

"No, Jim."

"You sure? I'll come right out again after the flak?"

"Get a load of that!" exclaimed Laibowitz. "Guys are *begging* to stay in the ward. We got a full house and a waiting list as long as your arm."

"My arm ain't so long. That's why I ast m' friend, the Lieutenant, to stick around."

Pepi unlocked the door and saluted me.

Captain Newman was waiting for us in Room 1. He was talking to Francie earnestly. She nodded to us and left.

"What do you say, Doc?" Furtively, Tompkins' eyes took in the sink, the cot, the medical cabinet, the one chair.

"Barney, you'll have to sit on the floor," said Newman.

"That's a hot one," said Little Jim. "I git the bed an' he gits the dog part."

Captain Newman laughed. "You can tell all your buddies up in Four the kind of service we give around here." He stepped to the window and put it down. "Okay, Jim. On the cot."

"You—gonna squirt the stuff in me?"

"Yep." Captain Newman picked a syringe out of the tank with a forceps.

Little Jim sat down on the bed. "Kin I take off m' shoes?"

"Sure."

"I sleep better without. That's what I'm gonna do, right? Jest sleep?"

"Uh-huh. Roll up your sleeve."

"Man. Ten in the mornin' an' I got me two officers puttin' me t' bed!" His heavy shoes dropped to the floor. He rolled up his left sleeve and stretched out on the cot. "You want me t' think of somethin' special?"

"Nope. Just relax. This shot won't hurt. It's just like all the others you guys get."

"I'll bet. Will it knock me right out?"

"Practically. You'll get drowsy. When I tell you to count, start counting—but backward, from one hundred. Got that?"

"Hey, that's sharp."

Captain Newman got two tiny, sealed ampules out of the cabinet and set them on the night table. One was labeled "Sterile Water." The other label read: "Pentothal Sodium (Sodium Ethyl—1 Methyl-Butyl—Thiobarbiturate—0.5 Gm. With 30 mg. Anhydrous Sodium Carbonate)." He took a nail file and cut a ring just below the tip of each ampule. He put a tourniquet on Tompkins' arm, to make the cubital vein larger. Then he got a large hypodermic syringe. He knocked the tip off the ampule which contained sterile water, sucked about ten ccs. into the syringe, knocked the tip off the Sodium Pentothal ampule, sucked the white powder into the syringe, went back to the sterile water ampule, filling the syringe up to the twenty-cc. mark.

Tompkins watched all this. "Holy Jesus, that's big enough for a horse!"

"All right, boy," said Newman gently. "Here we go." He rubbed a swab of alcohol on Tompkins' arm.

It was hot in the room. The small clock on the cabinet said 10:04.

Tompkins waved to me like a kid going on a trip. There was a ring of sweat on his neck.

Captain Newman sat down in the chair and jabbed the needle into the vein, depressing the plunger with his left thumb, very slowly. He had a pencil in his right hand, poised over a notebook. "Okay, Jim. Count. Backward . . . one hundred, ninety-nine . . ."

Tompkins emitted a brief "Oh!" then a sigh, "Mm . . . feels good . . ."

"One hundred, ninety-nine . . ." Newman whispered.

"Hunderd . . . ninedy-nine . . . ninedy-eight . . . seven . . . six . . ." His voice fell away, roused. "Hey, where am I? . . . nine . . . ten . . . How about—havin' drink—on me? . . . oh . . . good . . . fordy-seven . . . Ma . . ." His breathing was getting slower and slower. By the time the calibrated plunger showed sixteen ccs. had gone into Tompkins' vein, the boy's eyes were closed and he was tossing his head and making faint sucking sounds. His mouth opened; his breathing changed, deepening, devoid of apprehension. "Ooooh," he moaned, then was silent.

Overhead, far away, far, far above us, I heard the planes throbbing in the sky.

Captain Newman leaned over, his mouth close to Tompkins' ear, and began to talk, softly, gently, his voice infinitely reassuring, imitating the accent and inflection of the boy on the cot: "Okay, Jim . . . we're goin' up now . . . gonna take us a ride. . . . It's Tuesday, November seventeenth—eighteen-oh-five. Come on, Little Jim. Got to kill us some Jerries. We got to cream them. . . . Man, that crate's all warmed up . . . climb in . . . that's it . . . motors' revving. . . . Let's go, boy . . . come on . . . come on. . . ."

His tone was coaxing, wooing, and it seemed to promise, in its very hushed ease, that all would be well, that this was not an end of days nor a floodgate to punishment and horror, that though pain was agonizing it was not fatal, that it was safe to enter the past again.

Tompkins began to mumble: "Ok, Jeeze . . . no . . . Don'

wanna . . . This's a sweat-job. . . . This one's a piss-cutter. . . .
Sonvabitch, okay, Big Jim! Here we go. . . . Hot . . . friggin'
hot. Hey, Buck, we get us swacko minute we get back, huh? . . .
Goddam them motors. . . . Up—up—*up*. Go—Jim—*up!* Jeeze,
pull this goddam coffin off the groun'—*up*—yih! We're up! . . .
This is a cinch, sure. Hey, Buck, Buck, hommeny fingers up? An'
pig's-ass t' you. Nothin' comin' at us, nothin' shootin'. Give 'em a
bust. 'Waist gunner to pilot; waist to pilot: Okay I take a practice blast? . . . Roger.' "

Tompkins' hands came up as if he were clutching a machine
gun, and his voice imitated a burst of gunfire. "Pr-r-r-! P-r-r-r-!
. . . 'Waist workin'. Over . . .' Shoot the breeze. Hey, Pete . . .
Cinchy . . . Hey, Buck, let's get us some broads when we get
back—a tomato with a big bazoom. . . . Like hell y' will. Remember the dame with the big knockers? Ha, ha. Let's— *What's
that?* Down there, Buck! Four o'clock! Oh, Jeeze, comin' at us,
from four—three! Go back! Jim, please, get away. *Flak!* Two
o'clock! M.E. 109! Dirty—German—" His whole body shook as,
holding the imaginary gun, he rattled off a burst of fire at the
Messerschmitt that was once more coming in at two o'clock.
"Prr! Prr! Got him! Look't 'im bust open! Fry! He's goin'
down! Burn! Yellow bastard! Burn! Fry—Jeeze, three more—
oh—" He screamed. "Us—*hit!* . . . Oh, no! Omigod! Oh, Jesus!
The *oil!* Dear Jesus, save me, please, holy God, I'll be good. I
promise—Ma, I'll be a good boy. . . . Number-three eng— We're
goin' down! *Paw!* Oh, Paw, please, help me! *Gonna crash!* Big
Jim, you sunvabitchin' crud—*up!* Pull 'er up, *up*, please— Ooooh
—Look *out!*"

A long, attenuated "Aaaah!" of terror came from him, the
sound pulled out like taffy, then a wailing ululation. His face was
pasty, dripping sweat; his head was tossing, turning, a bubble of
foam trickling out of the corner of his mouth.

Captain Newman depressed the plunger he had never removed
from the boy's vein, sending another cc. into the vein, whisper-

ing: "C'mon. Okay. C'mon. You're down. It crashed. You're in that plane." He withdrew the needle. "Tell it—spill it."

"Yeah . . . plane . . . smoke . . ." Tompkins' hands flew up over his head and grabbed the iron rung of the cot. *"Smoke!* Lemme out! Oh, Christ. We're *burnin'!* Out—*out!"* He pulled himself against the frame of the cot furiously, his arms bulging, his whole body quivering, trying to repeat an earlier escape through a hatch. "Oh, Buck. *Buck!* Oh, no, no, no, *no!* Mother o' God, where's his *head?* He got no head! Buck! Oh, God, *put back his head.* Please—someone—he don't look right. . . . *Fire!* The tanks. Out . . . Pull . . . up . . . *up.* . . ." He began to sob, the tears pouring down his cheeks now, his teeth rattling. "Out—*out!* I'm out! Yay! Jump! Bang! Run, run! Hey, Big Ji— . . . What? Yell?! *Who's yellin'?"*

His face and arms and body froze, just as a voice from the burning plane had frozen him that morning as he had run away. "Big Jim—where—in *there*—callin' me. 'Little Ji-i-m!'" Tompkins' voice shrilled out in a thin, high wail. "'Help. Save me. Little Ji-i-m.' *Go back!* No! Run! I got to go back! I got to pull him out! No! *Run!* The hell. Get away! No! Pull him out, you yellow bast— The *gas!* . . ." From the boy's mouth came a whoosh and a hollow roar, like the roar of a plane catching fire. "Run, run, run, run, run, ru—"

His head fell to one side; a groan rattled in his throat and died away, and he lost the consciousness he had lost once before.

I heard Newman's heavy breathing. Perspiration ran down his face. He was watching Tompkins. I glanced at the clock. It was 10:18.

I remembered something Newman had told me one night in his quarters, when we were having a drink together after working very late. He was a little high. He had been sounding off on insulin shock therapy. "Now, take Pentothal. It's dangerous. Not for the patient, who won't remember a thing you don't remind him he said; but for the doctor. It plays into your omnipotence fantasies. It feeds your illusion you've got magic. Oh, it's easy to feel omnipotent; what's hard is to know what's right. . . . You inject twenty ccs. of a hypnotic drug and you're behind all the symptoms, all the resistances, all the defenses. You're face to face with all the soft spots, the weakness, the doubt, the guilt, the undifferentiated rage. . . . Sometimes, when I hear the things these boys say when they go under, when I really let myself know what they've gone through, I wonder how much we expect a man to endure. God! . . . No, not God." He had gotten up to pace back and forth in the small room. "God won't give you a clue. For a moment, you're that boy's god. I hate that—part of me hates it, at least, the part that knows you can be corrupted by so much power. That's one reason I don't use hypnosis. I hate having someone put his will at the mercy of mine. Still— I use Pentothal, the agency of a drug, for access to the trauma, to what men can't tell you or can't bear to face. . . . They all feel good after flak-juice; they think they've had a wonderful sleep. . . . Then *your* problems begin. How much do you tell them? How much do you hint? How fast can they take how much? What do you never let on they said? When do you get tough? How long do you hold their hand? When do you confront them with the rough stuff? What role do you play? Above all, what's *right*—not for you, but for him? What's right *for the rest of his whole life?* And who has the right to decide? The Army? Pyser? I have no one to turn to. *I* have to decide. . . . I give myself a hard time. Maybe I don't have to. But what am I supposed to be, anyway? A judge? A priest? A miracle man? Am I the one to decide between good and evil? Do I set boundaries for guilt, or administer dosages of pain and penance? . . . Hell. I'm a doctor —that's all. I'm supposed to heal, not judge. But they *want* you to judge. They want you to punish them, absolve them, sentence them, release them. . . . Consider what the patient projects onto me: hope, faith, infantile trust. But you're alone, all alone. You're his last straw, his last hope. He turns you into his loving mother, his feared or forgiven father, his final court of appeal.

You're all he's got to cling to—a raft in the sea in which he's drowning. He thinks you can save him—from death, from hell, from madness. The books don't help you—this is all too new. You're in some damned, dark arena—another man's unconscious—where unimaginable horrors roam." He had refilled his glass. "These boys have to go up and hang in the air and get shot at. We ask too much of them; they ask too much of me. I think of all these things beforehand, sure, one way or another, and I try to balance them out before I give flak-juice. . . . And when it's over they lie there, peaceful, sleeping like a child, and I feel like an empty bag—dry, drained out—no, that's not right. I feel weighted down, tired, carrying a goddam mountain on my back. And a little scared. I'm safe—hell, no one ever got shot down in a psychiatric ward. You don't crash behind a desk. But the boy on the cot? Should you send him back? . . . Well, the Pentothal begins to wear off, and the boy on that cot begins to come around. And now I'm the one who has to stand between his sanity and the merciless forces—panic, guilt, conscience—that put him there. Do you still wonder why I keep a bottle of whiskey in the bottom drawer of my desk?"

All this came back to me as I saw Captain Newman bending over the cot, staring at the sleeping Tompkins. I still heard that frightful wail: " 'Help . . . Save me . . . Little Ji-i-m . . .' "

I shall never forget the expression on Newman's face. He passed his hand across his mouth, like a man emerging from shock, then sighed and straightened up, turning away from Tompkins, and unbuttoned his collar absently. I don't think he remembered that I was there. His shirt, under his arms, was dark with sweat. He opened the window. A hot breeze drifted across me. The sun was hammering on the drum of the sky. Captain Newman stood at the window, gazing blankly into something that was not there. He looked haggard. After a moment, he roused himself and opened his mouth wide and took some long, deep breaths. It was 10:20.

Captain Newman wiped his throat with his handkerchief,

glanced at Little Jim, turned to the sink and turned on the fau-
cet. He splashed water on his face and got a towel and dried
himself. He fumbled for a cigarette and was about to light it,
but put it down, frowning, when he saw me. It took him a moment to realize I had been hunched up on the floor all the time.

Tompkins began to mumble something. Captain Newman
tossed the towel into a bin. Tompkins gave a massive, arching
yawn, stretched his arms, rubbed his eyes. "Doc . . . Musta
dozed off."

Captain Newman leaned against the wall.

"Jeeze, feel good. Best I slept in months." He sat up, yawning, scratching his head, and put his feet on the floor. He noticed
stains on his trousers. "Christ, I'm leakin', sweatin'. Like a pig.
That's what I'm sweatin' like—a knocked-up pig . . . Hey,
Lieutenant. Whaddaya know? You been here all night?"

Captain Newman held the pack out and Tompkins took a
cigarette. "Man, musta got me ten, twelve hours hushaby." He
rubbed his eyes again. "Hey, Doc, d' I gab a lot in m' sleep?"

"Uh-huh." Newman struck a match.

Little Jim hesitated. "What d' I say?"

"Omigod!" Newman affected disgust. "Every one of you
jokers thinks he blabbed out the secret that's going to lose the
war or something! Every one of you thinks he's the worst. I'm
not passing out any prizes for suffering, boy. And if I did, you
wouldn't have a chance! Hell, I was expecting stuff would blow
me right out of that chair. You're not even in the running. I've
got guys in the ward make you look like Little Orphan Annie."

"But I—Big Jim—"

"I know, I know, I know all about it." Captain Newman dismissed it with an impatient gesture. "It will hold. Tomorrow,
same time, same station. Up, boy, off your can. Get some coffee
from Laibowitz, run around the track, play some volley ball.
I've got *work* to do."

Little Jim grinned with his old impudence. "So that was flak-juice? Big deal!" He winked at me and waved a finger toward Newman cockily. "Best shot I ever did git from ol' Uncle Sam. Beats booze." As he left, he was whistling. But he walked unsteadily, not yet returned from Pentothal's euphoric haze.

I struggled to my feet.

"Wait," said Captain Newman. "Give him time to get out."

After a few minutes, during which he stared at the floor and did not utter a word, Captain Newman said, "All right," and we left the treatment room.

Francie unlocked the iron door to let us out. Her eyes searched Captain Newman's countenance. "Oh, Joe! . . . That boy. It wasn't 'pretty,' was it?"

Captain Newman handed her his cigarette to stub out. "No, Francie. It wasn't pretty."

The next day, Corporal Tompkins came strutting into Captain Newman's office five minutes late, a thin cigar stuck in his mouth. "Howdy, Doc!" He plumped himself on a chair, tilted far back, braced his feet against the desk, blew a smoke ring into the air, and grinned, "Man, I feel perky this mornin'. You talk, I'll jest listen. I got nothin' more t' say—nothin'! Gimme the gospel."

Captain Newman surveyed him frostily. "Take your feet off my desk, soldier."

Little Jim looked flabbergasted.

"You heard me!"

Tompkins slammed his feet down to the floor.

"Sit straight up in that chair!"

The front legs of the chair hit the floor.

"Take that cheap cigar out of your mouth!"

Tompkins' chin began to tremble.

"Go on! Put it out!" said Newman harshly.

Tompkins broke the cigar between his fingers and ground the pieces into an ash tray.

"Don't you ever pull that kind of crap on me again, Tompkins.

When you're in this room, you'll show respect—for me, and for yourself. . . . I'm not going to let you cheapen any guy who did thirty-four missions and wears all that spinach on his chest. Do you understand?"

Tompkins glared at him, his lips white.

"Okay, buster. Act tough. Clam up. Sure, I'll do all the talking. You just listen. I'm going to help you—even if you fight me every inch of the way. I can be just as rough on you as you are on yourself. So let's take the gloves off and give James Bowie Tompkins a real good shellacking."

Tompkins' eyes burned, hard as beads.

"Attaboy," said Captain Newman. "Be real stubborn. Keep it up. Keep torturing yourself. Keep blaming yourself. Rub your face in it. . . . For what? Because you ran away when you heard Big Jim yelling—"

"Stop!"

"Stop?" Captain Newman echoed in astonishment. "What for? Are you the only guy in the world has a right to treat you like a dog?"

"You said I ran away!"

"Sure. So what?"

"I ran *out*—that's what I did. Ran out on him—like a rat!" Tompkins' face was ashen. *"I let him die.* There warn't a piece of him left, even to put in a grave—and that's what I did, see? And I ain't never gonna fergit it!" He pounded the desk with his fist. "Never, never, never!"

Captain Newman nodded. "Now we're getting somewhere."

"I'm no good!"

"You sure ain't."

"I'm a goddam, low-down yellow-belly."

"Right. You're not worth the ammo to blow your brains out. You never did a decent thing in your life. *You* never flew no thirty-four missions. *You* never got no Purple Heart. *You* never won a combat citation."

"Lay off—"

"You were scared when that crate crashed—so what? Who wouldn't be? But Jim Tompkins isn't *allowed* to get scared, is he? You panicked, ran for your life—like any other guy would. But Little Jim—oh, no, he isn't allowed to be human, is he?"

"I shoulda gone back!" cried Tompkins. "Holy mother o' God! It was Big Jim in there! My own buddy. I shoulda pulled him out!"

"Right. You shoulda *tried*. . . . But what makes you so damn sure you'd been able to pull him out?"

"Huh?"

Newman shrugged. "The plane would still have exploded— and blown you, too, into all those little pieces no one ever found. So the Nazis would have chalked up another guy—a pretty sharp gunner, over thirty missions. *That* would have been smart, wouldn't it? Handing the bastards who shot down Big Jim another guy on a platter, for dessert!"

"But—"

"Don't interrupt!" Captain Newman banged the desk with his fist just as Tompkins had done. "You heard Big Jim's voice. You turned. You saw the plane and the flames and you froze—exactly like any guy who isn't off his rocker would. That was being a rat, wasn't it, a yellow-belly? You never helped a buddy, I suppose. . . ."

"Sure I did. But every guy did—"

"I don't suppose you can think of one single time you were brave—"

"No! I once dove in a burnin' cockpit—dug out two guys—"

"Oh, let's not put *that* on the score card," said Newman dryly. "Let's not let Little Jim off the hook, boy. We've got to punish that Tompkins real hard. After all, he personally shot down the B-24 himself—"

"Me? You're bats!" cried Tompkins. "It was flak—the Messerschmitts—"

"Shucks. I thought we could hang the whole crash on you."

"That don't make sense!"

"Neither does what you've been doing to yourself." Captain Newman leaned back now, expressionless, and let the silence hang in the air for a while. "You feel guilty? . . . You should. You need to suffer? . . . Go ahead. Only try to be fair about it, man. Let's figure out a reasonable amount of misery to pay off that guilt. . . . I got me an idea, Jim. A real beaut of an idea. Why don't you chop off your foot?"

Tompkins' eyes widened.

"You heard me, Jim. Why don't you go out and get an ax and have an 'accident' and come back without a foot?"

"I don't git it."

"No? How about your hand, then? Lots of guys pay off like that. You can, too. Go out, get careless—"

"Don't talk crazy!"

Newman shrugged. "Is a hand too much? Okay. Then how about some toes? Or a finger? One lousy little finger—"

"You're nuts!" cried Tompkins. "You're batty! None of that'll bring Big Jim back!"

Captain Newman nodded sadly. "Neither will what you've been doing to yourself."

Tompkins made a whimpering sound and buried his face in his hands.

Captain Newman let him weep and weep, saying nothing, gazing out of the window, wondering at the boundless dimensions of anguish, wondering how the enemy ministered to pain magnified a hundredfold by guilt, hearing vagrant and irrelevant resonances within the inner chambers of recall, until he heard Tompkins moan, "Oh, Jeeze. Look at me. Me—crying like a kid!"

"It's about time. You're crying for Big Jim. You ought to. You loved him. And he's dead." Captain Newman sighed. "Now you can let yourself feel, Jim. . . . Well, have we beat you up enough for one day? Wash your face and get some coffee. . . . See you tomorrow. We've got a lot of work ahead of us. Next time, you don't have to prove anything by being late."

Every day, Tompkins reported to Captain Newman. And every day—in varied ways, with varied intensities—Newman acted out the role of Little Jim's relentless conscience. He knew that only by taking over the harshest features of the harshest self could he reach the boy whose self had closed itself off to mercy.

Francie Corum told me not to be surprised if Captain Newman was short of temper. She did not have to tell any of us that. We had never seen him so irritable and we stayed out of his way.

Francie began to go in and out of Newman's office more often. Sometimes she sent Laibowitz or Pepi in with coffee and Lorna Doones, even though Newman had not phoned out for anything. She seemed to be waiting outside his door each night, and when they went to the Officers' Club she made him leave early. I sometimes saw them walking around the pool together, around and around, he gesticulating or stopping short with some wild, impulsive gesture, and she listening, always listening, grave and calm. Once he flopped into a beach chair wearily, and she took her shoes and stockings off and sat down, not far from him, her feet playing in the water. The moonlight ran down her hair like quicksilver. After a while she stood up and went toward the club, barefooted, and called to one of the Filipino boys to bring Captain Newman a drink.

Each night, as he lay in bed, Captain Newman told me months later, he went over the next day's requirements: he would have to present Tompkins with the naked image of his own self-hatred, his own unreasoning harshness. And when punishment had run its course, when pain cried out for surcease, Captain Newman had to offer the boy a chastened conscience, a conscience which could diminish its unyielding and symbolic demands.

What was harassing Captain Newman, I think, was the knowledge that if Little Jim stayed sick, he could live on in the hospital until the war was over. But if Newman succeeded, Little Jim would be sent back into combat. And then—?

"We protect the sick ones," Newman blurted. "We feed them

and love them and keep them safe. But the healthy, the strong, the brave—those we send out to be killed. Our job is to make men well—well enough to go out and kill. All right. But, well enough to go out and *be* killed—oh, God, that's where it's hell."

One morning, Little Jim came in to Captain Newman's office and said, straight off: "Think I can git back overseas, Doc?"

Captain Newman searched for some matches. "Why?"

"It figgers, that's all. I been doin' lots of figgerin'. I didn't kill Big Jim. The Nazzies did. So I want me another crack at 'em, Doc. To kinda even up the score. Whaddaya say? You goin' to fix it for me to git back to some shootin'?"

That, I think, was the moment Captain Newman had hoped for, and dreaded.

"I hear the missions are getting rougher and rougher over there," he said gruffly.

"Bound to."

"A lot of our guys are getting shot up."

"Sure are."

"There are no more milk runs, boy! You can get your head blown off in one of those raids."

"You sure can, Doc."

Captain Newman took a moment to pour himself some water. "You know you can stick around here a little longer."

"Nope, Doc. I got to git me out of here. A couple more missions, Doc, that's all I want."

"You sure?"

Tompkins hesitated. "If I ain't sure of that, I won't never be sure of nothin'. I jest *owe* it, I guess. I let Big Jim down. I guess I owe it to him, an' to them other guys went down with us, too."

Ten days later, Corporal James Bowie Tompkins, USAAF, gunner, was shipped out, out of the hospital, off our post on a desert palpable with heat, to an Eighth Air Force squadron somewhere in the green and mist of England.

He came to see me before he left. His hair was pasted flat, slick and stiff and wet. He was loaded down with a duffel bag, a B-4 bag, and that ungainly guitar. "Got a minute, Lieutenant?"

"Certainly."

"I jest come to say good-by."

I stood up and put my hand out. He wiped his hand on his trousers, like a country boy, and pumped my hand three times. "I thank you for what y' done, Lieutenant."

"I didn't do anything," I said awkwardly.

"Oh, yes, you did. That first time you come to see me, up in Four, you talked to me jest like I was edjicated. An' when I took the needle, you was in my corner, like they say."

"I think you deserve all the credit, Jim. You and Captain Newman."

"That ol' Doc," he grinned, shaking his head. "Say, could you leave this on his desk sometime?" He unbuttoned the left pocket of his blouse and pulled out a letter. "I ain't got time to go battin' m' gums around with him, bein' m' plane's about due to take off. . . . Good-by, Lieutenant. Say good-by to ol' Laibowitz—and that there salami boy, Gavoni. Tell 'em I'll see you all in church."

I watched him go down the hall, the duffel bag on his shoulder, the B-4 bag bouncing against his shank, the guitar hanging down his back from the cord he had slipped over his head. I had forgotten how short he was. I thought of his Purple Heart and his citation. He had the special courage of the small or the weak: the courage of necessity.

The letter he had left with me was addressed:

DOC NEMAN
Pers.

When I gave Captain Newman the letter, he opened it, read it, turned scarlet, glanced up quickly, read it again, folded it, and put it into his pocket without a word. He turned away, reaching for his clipboard. "How about running some tests for me on the kid in Bed Nine?" he said. "He's just simple-minded enough to be up your alley."

The war in the Pacific took a turn for the better—Tarawa, Kwajalein, Eniwetok—and the victories of MacArthur's island-hopping began to lighten our hearts. Tokyo Rose sounded hollow for a change. The Russians held at Stalingrad and encircled two German armies. Everyone was talking about a second front in Europe. Churchill glowered more jauntily. The President seemed strong—stronger than De Gaulle or Chiang Kai-shek or Stalin himself. Our Navy swept across the seven seas. Day and night, our armadas smashed at Germany from the air, and England became the assembly point for an invasion such as the world had never seen before.

Easter came to Colfax, the nights cool and sweet now, and our desert burst into color, blazing with wildflowers I had never dreamed could grow in the barren sand. In the sometime river beds, the smoke trees flamed purple.

I went home on furlough. Was there ever such a time? I slept until no one believed it, gorged on Ella Mae's cooking, dated Lucy Bainbridge every night, and toured more teas, cocktail parties, receptions and dinners than anyone has a right to expect. My mother was older, grayer, but so happy to have me home again that the house was lighted up by her pleasure. My sister was off in Washington, working for the cloak-and-dagger geniuses in O.S.S., and we drove down from Philadelphia to visit her. Father was working too hard, grumbling about the manpower shortage, but he was full of vinegar and that vast, imperturbable optimism I had seen fail him only twice: when my younger brother died, and the night after Pearl Harbor.

And then, like the snuff of a candle, the furlough was over and I was back at Colfax.

Corporal Laibowitz met me at the field, which was very nice of him. He gave me the news in the jeep ride to Main. The runways had been lengthened and added to; two huge new barracks had gone up overnight; Major Castle had been sent over to General LeMay's hot outfit; Colonel Pyser was hassling with some new executive officer in Area Command. "How's the war going with the poor, gas-starved, tire-hungry civilians?" Laibowitz asked me. "My heart bleeds for the patriotic public."

"They're scratching along," I said. "What else is new?"

"It's Lieutenant Corum's birthday. We're all giving her a present. You know, I think Doc's getting a case on her." He eyed me sententiously.

"I'm surprised it took you so long to notice," I said.

"Noticing a symptom is one thing," he cried. "Diagnosing the disease is another."

"Since when is love a disease?"

"Since *when?*" he echoed. "Lieutenant, excuse me, you are young and full of naïve ideas. Give me the choice between the Oriental fevers and the bug of romance, and I will gladly start taking quinine."

Captain Newman threw a party for Francie at the Officers' Club. It was a good, gay party, with lots of laughter. There were seven of us in all. Captain Newman was in fine form, reminiscing about his intern days at Cook County Hospital in Chicago. Francie was radiant that night. She was wearing a charm bracelet on which a golden circle gleamed. Engraved on it was:

F. C.

1*st* place

—The Boys

We were swapping jokes, some old, some new, waiting for the birthday cake to be brought in, when a courier from the Message Center came into the club and handed Captain Newman a telegram. He signed for it, excused himself, read it—and reached for the Scotch. His hand was trembling.

"What's the matter, Joe?" asked Francie from the head of the table.

"Nothing. Where the hell is that cake?"

Francie stood up without a word and came around the table and took the telegram out of Newman's hand. She read it.

"Oh, Joe," she said, and handed the telegram to Captain Jarvis.

He read it and said, "Oh, Christ," and passed it across the table—not to his date, a pneumatic nymph from town, but to Captain Mathieson, who read it and put his pipe down.

"Bad news?" his wife whispered.

Mathieson handed the telegram to me. I read:

THE SECRETARY OF WAR DEEPLY REGRETS TO INFORM YOU THAT JAMES BOWIE TOMPKINS . . .

I suddenly heard Little Jim's voice again, as clearly as if he were standing beside me: "I got no kin folk: none livin', I mean—" and I realized what he had put into that letter to "Dr. Neman" he had asked me to deliver that last time I saw him, the last time any of us would ever see him: "Inform next of kin . . ."

We never had Francie's birthday cake. She excused herself, and took Captain Newman under the arm. He mumbled some vague apology as she led him out. I saw the Pysers and the Larrabees at a big table near the door. Colonel Pyser's eyebrows went up as Captain Newman and Francie passed him; he watched them through the glass doors until they disappeared into the darkness.

In a moment, Stacy Mathieson said there was a patient he had to look in on before midnight, and Bill Jarvis' blonde said she had had "a blast," but a rough day coming up, and I was alone at the table.

I tried to finish my coffee, but it was cold and sour.

When the Filipino boy brought the birthday cake in, I told him to take it over to Ward 7, and I went to the bar. . . .

The next morning the staff seemed singularly quiet, and Ward 7 somewhat subdued. Then Laibowitz burst into Captain Newman's office. "My God, Doc, you *saved* that kid!"

Newman turned away.

We learned the details a week or so later, in a letter Captain Newman got from a friend, an air surgeon with the Eighth Air Force: Corporal James Bowie Tompkins, of Boonefort, Kentucky, waist gunner in the lead plane on a massive blockbuster raid on Berlin, had shot down two Folke-Wulfes, they thought, and was last seen going down with nine comrades, in the doomed, riddled, flaming pyre of his Flying Fortress.

I thought of the terrible lines in *Paradise Lost:*

> Him the Almighty Power
> Hurled headlong flaming from the ethereal sky
> With hideous ruin and combustion, down . . . down . . .

IX

HOW TO
STEAL A JEEP

It was inevitable, I suppose, that Laibowitz, Gavoni and Lawrence would be nicknamed the Three Horsemen. Not the Three Musketeers—the Three Horsemen: even the most pedestrian minds in the Air arm felt honor-bound to do things differently from the lesser Army or the cocky Marines.

Our Three Horsemen were fiercely loyal—not to the Air Corps, not even to the hospital, but to the Ward. For the sake of the Ward, these three peculiar men became unabashed thieves, finaglers, scavengers, con men. They conducted nightly raids on kitchens and commissaries all over the post on behalf of their ailing constituents, for whom they stole butter, cheese, eggs, cream, O. Henry bars, jams, marmalades, pretzels, pastries, potato chips. Nor did they confine their depredations to food. They invaded "enemy territory" (officers' quarters) in daring liberations of sheets, pillow cases, soaps, unguents. They regarded no place as sacred, no objects as taboo, for they considered themselves no more than good Samaritans, engaged in the equitable relocation of government property.

What the Three Horsemen could not steal, they swapped; what they could not swap, they "borrowed"; what they could not borrow, they sequestered. They were given to unique interpretations of what lawyers call the right of eminent domain.

Their blithe banditry drove certain mess sergeants and supply officers into thinking they were beginning to come down with hallucinations. Ward 7's three benefactors kept taking cases of olives out of the Pilots' Snack Bar, replacing them with the nutritious but widely loathed Spam, until the pilots' mess lieutenant was on the edge of a nervous breakdown. They even substituted rotten for fresh peaches in the C.O.'s mess so often that our General's bewildered steward began to carry a .45 on his hip.

Newman's Raiders filled the ward's supply rooms to bursting, then used secret caches in the Recreation Hall, Main Hospital, and heaven alone knew where else for the overflow loot. Sometimes, despite their many depots, the cartons and boxes and crates overflowed their coffers and threatened to betray them. To solve these periodic *embarras des richesses* Jackson Laibowitz would load the surplus boodle into a jeep, covering the incriminating contents with a tarpaulin, and drive around the post to engage in barter. Laibowitz always took Gavoni, never Lawrence, on these delicate errands. "You don't know how far to trust Hammerhead's neuroses," he warned me, apropos another matter.

Now, barter is part of the lifeblood of any military economy, but the form of barter which the firm of Laibowitz & Gavoni practiced raised that primitive custom to the level of a fine art. First, Corporal Laibowitz would soften up his victims by the most brazen flattery, lies or hints of personal reward. He would congratulate the gunnery chef on his spaghetti, the navigators' on his sexual prowess, a Transport WAC on her coiffure. Then Gavoni would remark that through a typical snafu in Area Command, or Supply, or Quartermaster's (all roundly hated by men of good sense) the hospital had just received an absurd superfluity of certain precious wares. The fact that Pepi blinked through his glasses seemed to invest his prevarications with an aura of veracity; for some reason I have never understood, the nearsighted always seem honest.

Laibowitz would then proceed to gull his clients, trading them tapioca for cocoa, peanut butter for fresh eggs, crackers for Canadian bacon. He derived special satisfaction out of bartering items back to the very quarters from which he had but recently liberated them.

I knew nothing about all this at the time, of course. Neither did Captain Newman nor Francie. What is more remarkable, neither did Master Sergeant Arkie Kopp. The first inkling any of us, indeed, had that something peculiar was happening vis-à-vis supplies came one Monday morning. "Captain," said Arkie with a puzzled air, "the storeroom is jammed, absolutely *jammed*, with oatmeal I never even ordered."

Captain Newman, who loathed detail, suggested that Arkie check his records more carefully.

The next morning, Sergeant Kopp said, "About the oatmeal, Captain, I guess it's okay. Laibowitz said the boys been swapping with some of the other commissaries."

"Is the ward *that* fond of oatmeal?" asked Captain Newman in surprise.

"No, but we need an awful lot of it. On account of Oatmeal McKee."

"Roger," said Newman cheerfully.

We all knew the special needs of "Oatmeal" McKee. He was a favorite of everyone in the hospital, an ex-football star from Wisconsin with an engaging wink, a swashbuckling style, and an astonishing repertoire of risqué stories. A hot pilot from the original Eagle Squadron, Ramsey McKee had flown fifty-two missions, sported a chestful of decorations and had been shot down twice over Hitler's *Festung Europa*. He had escaped from two P.O.W. camps: beating his way across occupied France with the aid of the underground once; and reaching an escape point on the Hook of Holland from a *stalag* near Regensburg by a fire-bucket-brigade sequence of seducing Aryan maidens. He told them, in the flawless German he had learned from his governess in Milwaukee, that he was a *Luftwaffe* inspector for Field Marshal Göring.

Several days after Captain McKee was assigned to Ward 7 for observation he broke out in angry welts and blotches. He complained bitterly about their itching.

As Laibowitz brought his breakfast to Room B one morning, McKee saw a bowl of oatmeal on the tray. He grabbed the bowl and turned it upside down, shouting that no one was going to make him eat baby food.

Laibowitz began scolding McKee. "You should be ashamed, Captain. You have to eat. You need to build up your strength."

"This stuff isn't fit for a pig!" roared McKee.

"Pigs are fat, so they don't need it. You're skinny, so you do."

"Go to hell." McKee picked up a glob of the cereal. "This is what this is good for!" He plastered it on his arms. "Mud, mud—" McKee stopped short. "Say, that's good." He rubbed some on his chest. "Holy MacArthur!"

"You nuts?" cried Laibowitz. "You think this is a beauty parlor?"

Ramsey Williston McKee had discovered that his skin could be de-itched by oatmeal.

And oatmeal he got from that day on—whole baths full of it. The Three Horsemen began cooking oatmeal in a ten-gallon vat on one of the big stoves in Main, and each night carried it down the ramp and into Ward 7. It took two men to do it, each man holding one end of a long khaki webbing they ran through the handles. They poured the oatmeal into one of the hydrotherapy tubs just off the ward, and stirred the goo around with wooden paddles. "Oatmeal" McKee would test the temperature with his elbow, then lower himself into the soggy stew.

What the river Ganges is to Hindus, oatmeal baths became to

McKee. For hours on end he lolled in his cereal blissfully, passing the time by singing risqué songs in a loud and pleasing bari-
tone. His repertoire ranged from an impure edition of "Willie
the Weeper" to a ribald rendition of "The Bastard King of England." He celebrated the erotic, the profane and the salacious in
a remarkable variety of rhymes. He even translated the enemy's
anthems into lurid chorales, so that *Horst Wessel*'s virtues turned
into an affinity for males, and the goal of *Wir fahren gegen England* was not 10 Downing Street but the compliant ladies who
line Piccadilly at night. Even Head Nurse Blodgett, whom we
all thought hardened beyond prudery, would hurry out of the
ward with rosy cheeks when McKee got into the swing of things;
Francie Corum only smiled, making neither comment nor objection, and went about her duties. I never ceased to admire her
transcendent poise.

The patients voted "Oatmeal McKee's Evening Hour for
Young and Old," which is what they named his nightly ablu-
tions, their Number One choice in entertainment. But Jackson
Laibowitz, oddly enough, did not approve. Laibowitz was a Puritan. Whenever McKee let fly with song, Laibowitz would im-
plore him to use less picturesque material. "Captain, *please*.
Didn't you ever go to church, for God's sake?"

"I don't do anything for God's sake!"

"Don't you know a single song without dirty words?"

"I know one about a soprano and a sexton will put hair on
your chest!" roared McKee.

"Weren't you ever in 4H or the Boy Scouts? Don't you know
something *clean?* Come on, Oatmeal; try 'My Bonnie Lies Over
the Ocean.' "

McKee was only too glad to try "My Bonnie Lies Over the
Ocean." But his bonnie lay under a sailor.

In any case, you can see why Sergeant Kopp and Captain Newman were not surprised by the vast quantities of oatmeal which
appeared and disappeared in Ward 7. . . .

One day, Sergeant Kopp came to Captain Newman troubled by a new mystery. "I just can't figure it *out*, Captain! Something's so fishy it stinks to high heaven."

"What is it now?" growled Newman.

"That's what I'd like to know. Every day it's something different. This morning it's fruit salad! I just counted eleven cartons in the storeroom—but on Friday we were down to eight. Yesterday it was Jello—four cases more than we had a week ago, even though we've been serving Jello like crazy! Look at the figures yourself, Doc. Take 'Relishes and Condiments.' That should be a pretty solid, steady item, wouldn't you say?"

"I always considered 'Relishes and Condiments' as solid and steady an item as you could find anywhere," said Newman.

"Well, Doc, consider again. 'Relishes and Condiments' are having growing pains! Look: ketchup, olives, pickles; the numbers on the left show stock-on-hand, Monday morning; those on the right show Tuesday night. Them numbers jump up, Captain, even though *there hasn't been a new shipment in a week!*"

Captain Newman examined Kopp's columns unhappily.

"I hate to put the finger on my own guys, Captain, but I have to say it! I'm getting *pre*-tty suspicious of three certain parties."

Captain Newman shot his sergeant a reprimanding glance.

"What *else* can I think, Cap? You don't believe in spooks, do you?"

"N-no, I don't believe in spooks, but that doesn't mean you should accuse my orderlies of being burglars."

"I didn't *accuse;* I just expressed suspicion. *Somebody's* got to be behind this snafu, and those three choirboys are just hopped up enough—maybe with the best intentions . . ."

"All right, Arkie. Let me have these figures. And send in those three jokers."

Captain Newman brooded over the inventory pages until the Three Horsemen filed into the room. They were so suspicious of

Captain Newman's motives, even before they knew his agenda, that they left the door open.

"It is customary," Captain Newman began acidly, "to close a door after one has opened it."

Laibowitz jabbed Gavoni; Gavoni nudged Lawrence; Lawrence cursed and closed the door.

"Men," Captain Newman said weightily, "I am going to ask you some simple questions, and I want straight answers. It's about—certain supplies."

"Supplies?" echoed Laibowitz innocently.

"What type supplies?" blinked Gavoni.

Hammerhead riveted his gaze on the ceiling.

"Sergeant Kopp informs me that certain supplies keep increasing when they ought to be decreasing."

"Doc," said Laibowitz, "Arkie's been very jumpy lately! Overwork."

"I hadn't noticed," said Newman dryly.

"That's because you been overworking, too."

Captain Newman tapped the inventory sheets sententiously. "Take pickles. We have two cases more in stock today than we had yesterday."

"Arkie forgets to count the cases in the back of the shelves," said Laibowitz promptly. "When we tidy up, we put the cases from the back up in front, so naturally—"

"Naturally," echoed Newman caustically. "Then how about chicken soup?"

"Chicken soup?"

"Chicken soup! With noodles! There were only six cases in stock on Monday; today there are eight."

"It's those jerks in central commissary!" exclaimed Gavoni. "They could foul up a roll of dimes!"

"Then what about coffee? Ten cartons on the first, fourteen today!"

"*That* I can explain," announced Laibowitz. "I made a trade."

"With whom?" asked Newman.

"With Reilly."

"Who's Reilly?"

"A mess corporal."

"Where?"

"Grounds Maintenance."

"What did you trade him?"

"For what?"

"For the coffee!"

"Oh." Laibowitz pursed his lips thoughtfully. "Applesauce."

"But I thought our patients *love* applesauce," said Newman.

"That was last month. They're in a new phase."

"We got rid of that applesauce in the nick of time," opined Gavoni. "The boys were planning a hunger strike."

Captain Newman stared out of the window for a moment. "Laibowitz, what if I asked this Corporal Reilly from Grounds Maintenance to corroborate your story?"

Laibowitz's face turned dark as a cloud. "I'll bring him over gladly, on the double! Put him on the grill yourself."

"What will he *say*, Jackson?"

"What will he *say?*" cried Laibowitz. "What do you expect him to say? He'll deny everything I said!"

"Ah, then you admit—"

"I admit Reilly is the worst liar you ever laid your eyes on! He swaps me coffee for applesauce and his mess sergeant is chewin' him out for it ever since—so naturally he'll double-talk. Test me. Let me bring him over. It will take maybe five minutes."

"Skip it," sighed Captain Newman. He knew that in maybe five minutes Laibowitz could bamboozle, bribe, flatter or finesse anyone below the rank of lieutenant to repeat any story he wanted. (Captain Newman could have phoned Reilly directly, of course, but he didn't; I think he did not want to catch Laibowitz in a lie.) He turned to Private Lawrence. "Is there anything you want to say about the changing mystery of our supply closet?"

"No, sir!" barked Hammerhead.

Captain Newman proceeded to lecture his orderlies on the

perils of crime. He warned them that they were playing with fire, that they would land in the guardhouse if caught in misguided philanthropy, that the misappropriation of government property was a court-martial offense. "I hope this is the last anyone in Ward Seven will hear about this kind of thing!"

It wasn't.

One morning, I learned from a cutie in Administration, Major Hornaday, one of Colonel Pyser's aides, hurried into his superior's office with an expression of acute dismay.

"Who crashed?" cried Colonel Pyser.

"No one, sir. It's a confidential report—from Major Leuthardt, Security. He says that jeeps are in the process of disappearing!"

"What?"

"Major Leuthardt says that some man, or group of men, appears to be engaged in the process of stealing jeeps."

"What the hell do you mean, Hornaday, 'appears to be in the *process'?* Is or is not a jeep missing?"

"That's just the point, sir," said Hornaday nervously. "As of this moment, no single complete jeep is missing, sir; but different *parts* have disappeared from a good *many* jeeps. Major Leuthardt believes that someone is stealing these parts, one by one, and will soon have a complete jeep, ready to assemble—"

"Goddamit, Hornaday, let me see that report!"

Colonel Pyser read the report, biting his mustache and muttering. Hornaday had reported accurately. The Captain in charge of the motor pool, one Alfred B. Koverman, was going crazy because every morning one or another of his jeeps turned up with a part missing—a magneto, a spark plug, a windshield, even a wheel. Captain Koverman had tightened the guard detail on all repair and garage sheds, but still the parts kept vanishing. Captain Koverman had appealed to the Security Officer.

Major Leuthardt had gone into action with gusto. His investigators had searched the grounds and the barracks with a fine-tooth comb. He had called spot checks all over the base without notice. He had put gumshoes on two jeep drivers notorious for their practical jokes. But not a single part of a single jeep was found.

Leuthardt then figured that the parts were probably being smuggled off the post, so he ordered the sentries at the four gates to double-check every car and truck that left. This was done. Nothing turned up. And still parts of jeeps kept vanishing.

We knew something serious was afoot when Colonel Pyser himself, attended by Majors Leuthardt and Hornaday and a pimply-faced A.D.C., stalked into the hospital. In a few minutes Captain Newman was summoned to the office of Lieutenant Colonel Larrabee. They were closeted there for quite a while.

Francie told me that Colonel Pyser could be heard storming up and down Larrabee's office, never directly accusing anyone, but declaiming that he had inside information that Newman's orderlies had been up to some pretty shady dealings around the post and Captain Newman had to goddam well crack down on his sharpshooters or take the consequences.

Captain Newman returned to the ward in an ominous mood and called the Three Horsemen into his office. "This time some-one has gone too far," he said sternly. "It may interest you to know that Security is hot on the tail of someone who is stealing— a jeep!"

"A *jeep?*" echoed Gavoni.

"Who in our ward could use a jeep?" asked Laibowitz.

"I want a straight answer," said Captain Newman, "a simple 'yes' or 'no.' . . ."

Never were answers more indignant and negative.

For days, extravagant rumors swept the post. Then Major Leuthardt's minions were put to shame when Pfc. Robert E. Randolph, a postal clerk, caught the criminal red-handed. It was a Sergeant Hrdlicka, from Flight Operations. (Newman was immensely relieved.) It seems that Hrdlicka, whose hobby was kleptomania, had been collecting a jeep, part by part. He simply wrapped each part in a laundry case or a duffel bag, brought it to the post P.O., and mailed it to a friend in Klamath Falls, Oregon. It was an exquisite scheme, worthy of the admiration it elicited. The admiration only increased when we learned that although Hrdlicka had the greatest faith in the U.S. mails he insured each shipment.

Hrdlicka was caught because one package slipped out of his hands, just as he was handing it to Pfc. Randolph, and made a faintly metallic sound, quite unlike the sound of falling laundry, as it hit the floor. Randolph jiggled the package around and, hearing noises that could hardly be made by mobile linen or cotton, took the parcel to his superiors.

They called Hrdlicka into a back room and asked him to open the package for postal inspection. He refused. So they took him to Major Leuthardt, before whom he invoked his constitutional rights. Leuthardt took him to Colonel Pyser, who opened the package: a carburetor clattered out onto Colonel Pyser's desk.

"I have been framed," said Hrdlicka at once.

"By whom?" asked Colonel Pyser in his barbed-wire voice.

"Oh, hell," said Hrdlicka.

He was shipped out of Colfax in handcuffs. For all I know, he is still in Leavenworth. Hrdlicka was the subject of informal seminars in the enlisted men's quarters for months. We all relaxed.

Then, out of the blue, Lieutenant Colonel Larrabee called an emergency meeting of all the officers in the hospital. Behind closed doors, he informed us of a crisis which, he prayed to God, would never reach the ears of Colonel Pyser: The player piano—the big, brown, old-fashioned player piano in the Recreation Hall—had disappeared! I was sitting next to Captain Newman, otherwise I might never have heard his groan.

"Gentlemen, ladies," said our hospital chief, wiping his brow, "we've *got* to find that player piano."

For the next week we all made discreet inquiries, but no one unearthed a single clue as to (a) where the missing player piano might be hidden, (b) if it was still intact, (c) how it had been removed from the Rec Hall, (d) by whom, (e) for what purpose.

Our hearts were momentarily lifted by the discovery (by an anesthetist) of forty player-piano music rolls in an oil drum behind one of the machine shops. But no trace was found of the instrument itself.

Lieutenant Colonel Larrabee called another meeting in his office, at which Corporal Ethel Widenour, his administrative assistant, came up with a solution so ingenious that she was the toast of the Officers' Club for a month. "Why not just wait until the next cargo plane crashes?"

Lieutenant Colonel Larrabee stared at Corporal Widenour distastefully. He had never approved of admitting women into the armed services. "And what good, may I ask, will *that* do?"

"We could just add one player piano to the cargo manifest," said Corporal Widenour, "and that will make the loss hunky-dory, because the player piano will go into the official records as smashed or burned along with the rest of the cargo."

"Ethel," exclaimed Larrabee, "that's a stroke of genius!"

Captain Ubell cut in waspishly: "And what if someone in G-2 asks what the hell we were doing shipping out a player piano— *by air?*"

Without a moment's hesitation, Corporal Widenour replied, "We'll say we were lending it to another installation—for the Fourth of July."

And that was how the player piano was accounted for. One of our freight planes, headed for Scott Field in Illinois, crashed on take-off. The crew got out alive, but the C-47, fortunately, burned to a crisp. Five minutes after the sirens sounded, Corporal Widenour had the cargo manifest out of Transport's files, recalled all six copies from the distributees, and calmly typed this addition onto the fatal cargo list: "One (1) Player Piano."

How Jackson Laibowitz ever found out what was going on I

shall never know. What I do know is that he said to Captain Newman, "What about those forty rolls of punched paper, Doc? They're piled up in a corner of the Rec Hall like a sore thumb. Someone will get wise."

"Mmh," said Captain Newman coolly.

Laibowitz shrugged. "It's not my funeral. Still and all, someone better take care of them forty rolls before Colonel Pyser's snoopers smell a rat. . . . That Corporal Widenour!" He clucked his tongue in homage. "That kind of talent we could use in the ward."

That afternoon the forty rolls of music for the defunct player piano disappeared from the Recreation Hall.

And that night Arkie Kopp ran into Captain Newman's office with a haggard cry: "Pineapples! Eleven cases of sliced Grade A pineapple—and this morning, so help me, Doc, we had only seven!"

X

GINO

McGRAW

Winter came to Colfax.

The radio told us that blizzards were raging from Buffalo to Boise. Minneapolis was freezing at fourteen below and Denver lay under two feet of snow. For sixty miles around New York, ice broke the power lines and lights went out, heat went off, water pipes burst. A Greyhound bus broke down in Pennsylvania and thirty-four passengers, including the inevitable pregnant woman, had to trek two miles through fearful snowdrifts to shelter at the inevitable roadside diner.

But on our desert it was the golden time of year. Each night a million stars danced in the cobalt firmament. Each dawn the sun came up like the mouth of a red cannon, baking us, toasting us all day long. And at sunset the sky became a vast orchard, and peach, lemon, cherry, plum rioted over our heads.

Captain Newman often worked late these nights, long after Captain Mathieson had gone home to his wife and his music, long after Captain Jarvis set off for the town bars or the nurses' barracks in what Newman called "the quest for the holy quail"—

"quail" being females whom Jarvis could romance, seduce and replace.

This was a quiet night. A dusty moon was powdering the desert with silver. The air, sweet with jasmine and mock orange, swelled with the hum and rasp of night insects.

Captain Newman was hunched over his desk, his goose-neck lamp bent low over the clinical report he was finishing on Gilbert Rennick. Rennick had never recovered his powers of speech after being trapped for two hours in the ball-turret of a bomber that was limping back toward its island base in the Admiralties, badly shot up, smoking, flopping crazily from side to side. Rennick was pinned down in a crouch, his left arm smashed, his collarbone cracked, unable to move. The escape hatch was jammed. Oil kept seeping into Rennick's prison from a punctured line, slowly rising to his waist, his chest, his armpits. The oil could turn into fire, from a spark or a flash of flame from the burning engines, or it could just go on rising until it passed his mouth, filled his ears and nostrils, seeped into his lungs to smother his life out. Rennick kept passing out from the pain and screamed for help whenever he recovered consciousness, but when the foul oil passed his chin and reached his lower lip he had to keep silent. The pilot ditched the plane in the sea and the impact split the ball-turret open, but the horror did not leave Rennick's eyes for weeks. . . .

Captain Newman glanced at his watch. It was past ten. "Lights out" had sounded in the ward, which was uncommonly quiet tonight. Francie Corum was on five-day leave to San Francisco to visit her brother, who was home on Navy furlough. Laibowitz had left Captain Newman some hot chocolate and Nabisco wafers half an hour earlier and had gone off to town with Pepi Gavoni. Except for the oval scoop of light from the goose-neck lamp, the office was in darkness.

Newman was reaching for a blotter when he became aware of the low sibilance of breathing, very regular, very controlled.

Someone was in the doorway. He glanced along the shadow on the floor and saw a pair of highly polished GI boots on the threshold, pointed toward him but set rather far apart. He looked up. A soldier was outlined against the night light in the corridor, his face lost in the shadow, his body short, compact, powerful. His hands were held slightly away from his sides, like a wrestler poised for attack. The strained breathing turned into a voice, huskily: "Doc . . ."

"Yes."

"Busy?"

"Not too," said Newman.

"Okay if a guy comes in?"

"Sure. Come in."

The soldier took a step into the room.

Captain Newman reached over to switch on the overhead light, but the soldier said quickly, "No, no, Doc. Please. This is okay by me," and lowered himself into the chair, bracing his elbows against the back. "I just was passin', seen the light, I peek in and spot you, so I say to myself, 'What the hell, Gino, you got nothin' to do; why not take a load off your feet, shoot the breeze with Doc?' That okay?"

"Sure, that's okay," said Captain Newman.

The soldier was about thirty. Three chevrons, above three arcs, were on his sleeve. An overseas cap was tucked inside his belt. His hair was black and close-cropped. He had bad teeth and a long upper lip, disfigured by a scar. His eyes were deep-set, black, burning, and they were fixed on Captain Newman.

A waltz, from a radio in Main, drifted lazily into the room. Captain Newman put a smile on his lips and pushed his cigarettes across the desk.

The soldier shook his head. "Not me, I give them up five-six years back. I used to go through three-four packs a day; specially when the heat was on, I'm like a chimney or somethin'. No more. I don't need no smokes, no booze, no broads. Not me."

"What do you mean 'when the heat was on'?"

The soldier laced his fingers together. "I got nothin' to hide—well, maybe nothin'. Before I get in this soldier suit, Doc, I used to be—well, a hood, is what. In Detroit, where I come from . . . By the way, the name is McGraw, Gino McGraw. Yeah, I know: how come the screwy name? My old man was a Mick, my old lady is a Guinea, so it's Gino for Angelino, for my ma, and McGraw for my old man. Look, Doc, don't look at me like I'm a rummy! I'm fine, just *fine*. I ain't buckin' for no phony discharge, either, know what I mean? Not me. Could be I'm bustin' in on somethin' important?" He started to rise.

"Who said I was doing anything important?" asked Newman.

"I thought maybe on account I didn't go through them nurses, no appointment . . ."

"Forget it, Sergeant."

Sergeant McGraw dropped back into the chair. "Thanks . . ." He looked around the office nervously, then slumped low. "What do you do when you done something bad, Doc? Something real, real *bad!* Oh, Doc. Oh, Doc. I been to confession maybe fifty times—and I truly confess, and do penance just like Father Callahan dishes it out, but it don't do no good, Doc, no *good*, because I'm still tied in knots, and it's burnin' a hole in my guts. Oh, Doc. I done lots of bad things in my life, but nothin' like this!"

Captain Newman waited. When Sergeant McGraw said no more, he asked, "Do you want to tell me what you did, Gino?"

"Want to? No; I don't want to; but I *got* to. I got to, or I'll blow my stack for good! Doc, can you help me?"

"I'll do my best. What did you do that was real, real bad, Gino?"

"I—killed a baby."

The night sounds, the insects, the waltz were annihilated. Gino McGraw closed his eyes and began to rock from side to side. After a while, Newman asked, "How?"

"She don't tell me for months, Doc. She don't write me, she

don't answer me, not once, not one letter, not one lousy line for all the times I write her, from every place I been." He raised his head. "Any of the guys upstairs tell you about me?"

"No, Gino."

"Not even Frankie Lucas, my buddy, he came around to see you coupla weeks back, when he was throwin' up every morning? Not even Frankie?"

"Frankie never talked to me about you."

"He's a good Joe, that Frankie; he don't pop off, like lots of creeps around here. Well, okay, I guess I can trust you. I done time, Doc; I was in prison. When I was a kid, I started stealin' from newsies, bustin' into the grocery, small stuff like that; then I hook up with these guys and we hold up a gas station, a coupla drugstores, then trucks. Booze trucks. That was the jackpot. We made a pile." He hesitated. "Well, what the hell, that's a long time back, right? Since then I'm a good soldier and got shot up, you can see." He jabbed his thumb against his blouse where a purple bar and a theater-of-war emblem with two battle stars were pinned. "I'm shootin' my mouth off, I know. It's rough, Doc, it's real rough."

"What are you in the hospital for?"

"Ulcer; a bleeder, they call it. It was murder over there, for a while. You see your own blood when you go to the can, it scares the be-Jesus out of you. That scared me more than them slanty-eye Japs. Let me tell you somethin', Doc; all this belly-achin' about the Army, it's a lot of bull, is what it is. The Army is kid stuff. Take it from me, plain *kid* stuff. Why, they give you free guns, free ammo, and you get up there and you can knock down whatever you see. Why, you can even shoot on Sundays!"

"You like that?"

"I ain't denyin' it. On account me bein' a good Catholic, and some of the guys we went up against in Detroit, they respect Sundays, too, so none of us did no shootin' on the Sabbath." He stopped. "I guess I'm double-talkin', huh?"

"That's okay."

"Naw, I'm just crappin' around. I know. Give me a fix, Doc."

"You said something about a girl," said Newman. "The girl who won't write you."

"Yeah. Well, I met her in a diner, the White Rail. You ever been to Detroit, Doc?"

"No."

"Well, this diner is way the hell out on Highway 112, where it crosses Barrington. Me and Solly went in, my side-kick, one night. And there was this dame behind the counter. She won't cop no beauty prize, you understan', but she looks nice, and stacked—*man*, is she stacked! Even under that white uniform, you can see. Well, Solly moves right in, sayin', 'Sister, they oughta fire you outa this joint on account you take a guy's mind off what's to eat.' An' she comes right back at him: 'The only time your mind is on food is when you sleep on a crate of tomatoes.' So Solly asks if there are any other tomatoes in her family like her, and one crack leads to another, her givin' Solly better than she gets, and I'm laughin', and she says it's extra for the floor show. Well, I like her and I date her up, to take her home, it being so far out and everything. Solly blows and I just hang around, watchin' her work. Oh, she's got it, all right, like a pin-up you go to sleep dreamin' about. Then I talk her out of goin' right home, and take her to a dive I know down the road— good steaks and *vino*. . . .

"Well, we kick it around. Talk, Doc, did we yak that first time! Before I know it, I'm givin' her a line about bein' in the used-car business, with two-three places of my own, and how I figure I can make close to fifty grand before long. And she's tellin' me her old man died a year ago and her mother and sister are in St. Joe, that's in Missouri, and she sends money home, her old lady bein' laid up with artharitis. . . . Oh, she's a good kid, I tell you; nice, no tramp, no push-over like the others I been runnin' around with. So I take her home and, Doc, I can't even lay a hand on her! Not a finger, she's so strick. . . .

"I begin hangin' around the diner each night and take her home, or to a pizza place or a beer joint, or dancin'—always tryin' to connect, sure, but she don't let me get to first base. It takes me three-four weeks even to get a good-night kiss outa her! I tell you, Doc, I'm on the ropes so I don't know if I'm comin' or goin'. And I don't mind, that's the kicker. She's the nicest dame I ever seen. I feel for her like I never felt for no *broad,* know what I mean? And she begins to go for me, too, I can see, and she don't play it cute and tease around.

"Pretty soon, she says okay she'll be my girl, and we—well, you know, Doc. We—did. I was her first—that way. That, I'm sure. . . . Well, we shack up six-seven months, really in love, and I give her a diamond ring. She bawls when she takes it, and we're engaged. Was I happy! I bring her home to my old lady and my old lady says, 'Gino, this is a nice girl. Gino, you be a good boy and be nice to this girl. Gino, this is a girl I like for you to marry and start a nice family of your own with.' " Gino shook his head. "So it's a week before the weddin', and I get picked up. On a stolen-car rap, no foolin', it being nothin' I even know about! But that don't cut no ice, oh, no; they throw me in the can like they caught me drivin' into City Hall in a hot car and they slap me around. But I got nothin' to tell them. Solly gets me his own lawyer, a sharp Irish politician with plenty of pull. I tell him to tell Vera I'm out of town on a big deal, somethin' I can knock off five-six grand. . . .

"And I look up the next mornin', in the jail where I'm sweatin' it out—and it's like the whole world caved in on me! Because there's Vera, standin' there, lookin' at me like I never seen no one look in my life. She's burning, she's ice, like a statue, white, cold. 'Your mother told me where you were,' she says, the freeze on every word. 'Honey,' I say, 'you oughtn't come here.' 'You never told me you done time, Gino!' she says. Oh, Jesus. You could of knocked me over with a Sen-Sen. 'Honey,' I say, 'it was before I even met you; and it won't happen again! I'll stay out

of trouble from now on, so help me; I got a line on a job—'
'You punk,' she says; not yellin', not even mad, like you'd think,
but real quiet, and it's like a knife goin' in my heart. 'You cheap
little punk. You two-timer. They ought to beat your brains out.
You and all the rest like you, and I pray to God they do.' And
she takes off the ring I gave her and throws it at me like I'm
dirt and walks out.

"I tell you, Doc—I yell after her, 'Please, wait, *listen.*' I rattle
that door till I think I'll pull the whole cooler down, but she
don't even turn around. One of the dicks hears me. I beg him to
bring her back and make her listen, but he says, 'You're up the
creek this time, Gino. I know that girl. I knew her old man, too.'
And what do you think he tells me? He tells me her old man was
a cop! A cop who got three slugs in his back one night in an
alley and they never know who done it, and ever since then
Vera—well, you can imagine how she hates anyone who— Oh,
Jesus.

"I send her word, right away, through Solly. I tell her I understan' how she feels, she's got a right to, but still and all I *love*
her—and that's the most important thing, isn't it? I promise her
I'll change right down the line, I'll get a job, drivin' a hack, layin'
pipe, anything. . . . Not a word from her. Not *one—lousy—
little—word!* Nothin' . . .

"My case don't go through like my lawyer tries to fix it, and
it looks like I have to take the rap. But he knows a big shot on
my draft board, who calls the judge—so whaddaya know? The
bench gives me a quick pick—either go to the can for six
months or sign up for the Army. *That* angle I never doped out.
I choose the Army.

"And I make a good soldier, Doc, ask anyone you want! I
mind my own business and knock myself out and get promoted
and all. So what? All this time, I'm writin' Vera. Every day.
Maybe only a page, sometimes three-four-five. And all this time,
not a word or answer from her. Not a letter, not a line, not a

lousy single word! Till one day at mail call, no warnin', I get this letter. I'm jumpin', I'm so glad. I open it. . . .

"There's not even a 'Dear Gino' in it, or a 'Love, Vera,' or anything. Just one piece paper, on it fourteen words, I know, I counted a million times, sayin': 'I have to get an abortion. *And the sin is on your head forever!*' Oh, Doc. Oh, Doc . . ." McGraw began to rock from side to side again. "I never hurt a kid in my life! I'm *nuts* about kids! Even in the rackets, I never done nothing that bad. I got principles, same as anyone. When we hold up a truck, I never shoot at the poor slob behind the wheel. I just try and keep him from gettin' his head blown off.

"But this kid, this baby I put in her, it was my kid, too! And she has to go and get rid of it! Because of me. Because she don't want it should have an old man who's no good. And it's like I done it with my own two hands, Doc! I killed that baby." The black, deep eyes filled with tears. "I killed him."

"Why do you say that?" asked Captain Newman.

"Because I killed him."

"But you didn't."

"Yeah, sure, phony baloney."

"Look, Gino. You didn't ask her to get an abortion, did you? You didn't make her do it. You didn't agree to it. You wanted to marry her. How can you say—"

"Sure, I know, I think like that, too, sometimes, but it don't take with me. Doc, right after I get that letter, I write her. I tell her I still love her, everything will be okay. I tell her I *love* babies, we can have four-five kids if that's what she wants. I get the letter back—not even it was opened. That hurt. She just mailed my letter right back! So I write her again, and same thing. It comes back, not even opened up!

"I get emergency leave, sayin' my old lady is dyin', and beat it home and right out to the diner. How she knew I was comin', I never know; maybe from my old lady. Anyway, Vera ain't in the diner. She ain't in her flat. She's sick, the landlady tells me, visitin' her mother in Missouri. Well, I'm ready to hop a plane out there—I'm at the airport, tryin' for a seat to Kansas City, and boomin' out of a radio on the ticket counter comes—Pearl Harbor! . . . People are runnin' around like chickens without a head. The radio says we all got to hustle back to our outfit, even before a telegram comes to my old lady's place, ordering me to report.

"I never made St. Joe. They fly my outfit out to San D., and before I know what hit me we're flyin' out further and go into action. Midway, no less, me in the 431st Bombard Squadron, I'm at the top gun, and when that ding-do is over we see more action, twenny-nine nights runnin', Doc, near the end not knowin' if I'm comin' or goin' or shootin' at Japs or boxcars, so they ground me.

"But I write her. Any chance I get, from any place they put me, every goddam *day* I write! An' I never get no answer; not one single word. Nothin'—nothin'—every letter of mine back, every friggin' letter, not even opened . . . What the *hell*, Doc! How much can a guy take? Maybe I don't write so good, never goin' past seventh grade, but I put nice words down for her, every day, every single, goddam day. . . . Oh . . . Oh . . ." He bit his lip.

Captain Newman tried not to look at him. He half-turned in his chair. "How long did that go on, Gino?"

"Five-six months. Some fun, huh? . . . Okay, Doc, I know—you can't do nothin', no one can, I just got to wise up, right? I just got to take it. Okay. But—how would *you* feel, Doc? If the girl you love done that to you?"

"I'd feel like dirt," said Captain Newman. "I couldn't take it."

"No kiddin'?"

"I'd hate her."

"Yeah?"

"Sure I would. A girl I wrote to so much, so often, so desperately—"

"It sure got me no place."

"In spades."

"You can say that again, Doc."

"God almighty, Gino, how long do you expect to go through all this misery?" cried Newman. "I said I'd hate anyone who did that to me—but by now, I wouldn't let her kill me. I'd make myself forget her. I'd get another girl. You loved that girl so *much*, Gino—it hurt just to listen to you."

"No kiddin'?"

"No kiddin'. Do you still, after all this, do you still love her?"

Gino lowered his head. "I'd crawl on my hands and knees for her. I'd cut out my heart."

"Oh," said Newman. "Listen. Hundreds of guys have sat in that chair. They've poured their guts out to me by the hour. I've heard things that can make you ashamed of the human race. But I've heard things that can make you proud, too. I've heard men talk about their mothers, their wives, their sweethearts in a way that—well, I want to tell you, Gino, I don't think I ever heard anyone talk about a girl the way you just did. I don't think anyone ever loved a girl more."

"*No* foolin'?"

"No foolin'. Do you happen to have a picture of her?"

"Are you kiddin'?" Gino smiled and unbuttoned his breast pocket and removed a folded cardboard about the size of a playing card. He folded the cardboard back carefully and removed a snapshot, which he placed on the desk before Captain Newman.

The snapshot was not very good. It showed a girl in front of a sign on which the words said "White Rail." She was wearing a white uniform and a waitress' starched cap. She seemed young, pleasant, well formed—that was about all one could tell.

"A nice girl," said Captain Newman. "That's a *nice* girl, Gino."

"Thanks, Doc."

"What did you say her name was?"

"I told you, din I? Vera."

"I mean her last name?"

"Oh." Gino grinned. "Smith. Can you tie that?" He pushed his cuff back quickly and looked at his watch. "Past eleven! I better get back before I get slapped with an AWOL." He got up. "Maybe I'll come in again, Doc, huh? When you got nothin' to do?"

"You don't have to go now, Gino—"

"I better."

"I'll call upstairs if you want to go on talking."

"No, Doc. Frankie'll worry. Some other time, huh?"

"Any time you say, Gino."

"Thanks, Doc." Gino pulled the overseas cap out of his belt. "Thanks. Don't worry about me, Doc." His shoulders blotted out the light from the hall.

The next morning, Captain Newman dictated to one of the WACs from the hospital's stenographic pool. He dictated his report on Gilbert Rennick. He also dictated a letter. I found the carbon attached to a page of notes, headed "Gino McG.," in a pile of folders he asked me to file for him. I was surprised by the English, which was rather stilted and did not sound like Captain Newman:

Miss Vera Smith
White Rail Diner
Highway 112 and Barrington
Detroit, Michigan
DEAR MISS SMITH:

Sgt. Angelino McGraw is a patient in the hospital here. He is very unhappy, Miss Smith. He has endured much suffering and has done heroic things for our country.

I hope you will not mind my writing to you (he has told me much about you) but if you could merely write him a letter, it would mean very much to him. It would be a kind thing to do.

You can address him at the hospital above, or in my care. Please write him as soon as you can. He still loves you, very much, and is sick.

Sincerely yours,
JOSIAH J. NEWMAN
Captain, M.C.

Captain Newman and Francie were leaving the ward, several

nights later, when Sergeant McGraw came down the ramp from Main. When he saw them, he stopped.

"Hello, Gino," smiled Newman. "Where've you been?"

Gino shrugged. "Just thought if you had a coupla minutes to kill—"

"I can be back around nine."

"No, Doc, skip it."

"Why not at nine, Gino? I'll clear the decks."

Francie started to say something, giving Gino her sunniest smile, but he said quickly, "It's okay, Doc. Some other time."

"Then how about the morning? First thing."

"Sure, Doc. Maybe. I'll see you." He cocked a finger and waved as he disappeared.

Every day, from then on, Gino would drop in to pass a few minutes with Captain Newman. Sometimes it would be in the morning, after mail call, sometimes at night, when he saw the light from the goose-neck lamp and knew Captain Newman was working past hours. But Gino never said very much any more, nor did he stay very long. He only seemed to be checking in. His eyes kept questioning Captain Newman, as if he were waiting for Newman to tell him something. He would take his leave abruptly, saying something like, "Fine, okay, don't worry about me, Doc."

"But I do worry about you," Captain Newman once said.

"Yeah? How come? You ain't got enough screwballs in the joint?"

"How about you coming into my ward, Gino?"

Gino's jaw dropped. *"Me?* Hey, Doc, you flip your lid or somethin'?"

"Just for a couple of weeks, Gino. You could take it easy, and we'd have more time to talk. . . ."

"Oh, no. I'm getting *outa* here, Doc—the minute they give me the high-sign upstairs. Any day, now. Five'll get you ten if I'm not outa here by Feb one!"

"I wish you'd think about it."

"You're talkin' to *Gino,* Doc, Gino McGraw! I'm a bull, strong, I don't cut out no paper dolls, not me. I can take it."

"That's what worries me, Gino. You're always telling me you can take it, not to worry about you. But all the time you're worrying about yourself. That's fine, worrying, when you've got a problem. It's the *way* you're worrying that bothers me. . . . No man ought to keep taking it and taking it—"

Gino snorted, "I'll be outa here by Feb one. Wait and see."

"I hope so, Gino."

"Say, Doc, you got anything to *tell* me?"

Newman hesitated. "What do you mean?"

"You know what I mean. You heard anything—to tell me?"

"No, Gino."

It was almost three weeks before Captain Newman got an answer to his letter. The envelope was postmarked "St. Joseph, Missouri." There was no return address on the envelope, nor on the sheet of stationery on which, in green ink and an absurdly ornate hand, was written:

DEAR CAPT. NEWMAN:

You should be commanded for taking such big interest in patients.

I do not wish to ever hear a single thing from Mr. A. McGraw or about him.

Your truly,

MISS VERA SMITH

That night Gino drifted into Captain Newman's office, saying, "Say, Doc, did I just take Frankie Lucas and two meat-balls in blackjack. Thirty-eight bucks and goin' strong when the game busts up!"

Newman laughed. "Good going, Gino."

"You on your way out, Doc?"

"Not really. Sit down."

"Not tonight, Doc. I come around because—to tell you about clobberin' them jokers, but good. . . . You been workin' hard, Doc?"

"Not too. How about you?"

"I feel great. . . . You looked pooped, Doc."

"I was born looking pooped. It's the rings under—"

Gino put his hand out and touched Captain Newman on the sleeve. His voice was harsh. "Let's stop stalling. It's no good, huh, Doc?"

"What do you mean, Gino?"

Their eyes met.

"You know what I mean, Doc. You wrote to her—right? You wrote her, and you been waitin' all this time, and now she answered. . . ."

Captain Newman turned away and poured some water into his glass from the carafe. He had resolved not to tell Gino, if he could avoid it; not to tell him for a while, at least; or if he had to, to temper it somehow, some way; or if he could get him into Ward 7, to tell him then. "Gino—"

"Her answer," Gino rasped. "It's no good, huh, Doc?"

"Listen—"

"For Chrissake, Doc!" Gino exploded. "Why don't you level with me? Stop treatin' me like I'm a goddam baby or somethin'. I got a right to know! Well, you don't have to tell me now, because I can read it off your face. She answered, didn't she? *Didn't she?*"

"Yes—"

"And *it's no good,* huh, Doc?"

"No, Gino," said Newman slowly. "It's no good. . . . But listen—"

There was no one there to hear the rest of it, the supportive words, the phrases of consolation, the balm of hope clutched from the future. There was no one there. . . .

And when Francie pushed the half-open door back, a few minutes later, Captain Newman leaped out of his chair. "Gino! I'm glad—" He stopped and struck the desk with his knuckles.

"It's time to knock off for the day, sir," she said.

"Okay, Mother," he muttered, and picked up the phone.

Francie sat on the edge of the desk and watched him.

Into the phone, Newman said, "Major Callahan, please."

Francie frowned. Major Callahan was the Catholic chaplain. "Is it that bad, Joe?"

"Hell, how should I know? How does anyone know?"

She leaned over and kissed him on the cheek.

Gino stopped coming to Captain Newman's office.

Newman went to see him in the ward upstairs every morning, and every night before checking out. But Gino would not talk much. Major Callahan went to see Gino, at Newman's urging, and Gino would be grateful and humble, listening to the chaplain obediently, nodding, "Yes, Padre . . . I know, Father. . . . Sure, anything you say. It's nice you come here. . . . Sure, I'll come to Mass." But he didn't.

Whenever Captain Newman tried to focus Gino's mind on the future—the girls he would meet, the one he might love, the children she could bear him, the joy his mother could know—Gino would snort, "You're breaking my heart, Captain." Whenever Newman suggested he come into the ward, Gino would grin derisively: "I'll be outa here by Feb one, Doc. Wait and see."

It was two days before "Feb one" that Gino was discharged from the hospital. He did not come to Captain Newman's office to say good-by. Frankie Lucas said he had gone to Detroit to see his mother before reporting back to his outfit overseas.

It was not until a month or so later that we heard, quite accidentally, that in the early hours of a Sunday, after morning Mass, Angelino McGraw, Sergeant, USA, holder of the Purple Heart, wearer of a good-conduct badge and service ribbons with two battle stars pinned on them, was found in the men's room of the Greyhound Bus Station in St. Joseph, Missouri, hanging from a beam, with his belt around his neck. Not even his feet were swaying.

XI

COLONEL CROWTHER
AND THE GODDAM DUCKS

One of the things for which Colonel Pyser never forgave Captain Newman was the scandal involving Colonel Crowther. It was, to be sure, one of the wackier things that happened at Colfax. But it was silly to blame Captain Newman for it. Colonel Pyser might just as well have blamed the heat and the sirocco winds, or Colonel Crowther (who made a jackass of himself), or the traveling carnival that came to town with the baby ducks.

It all began when General Armstrong and Colonel Pyser flew to Washington for Top Secret briefings. That left Colonel Crowther as our acting C.O. Let me tell you about Eiley Crowther. He was a bombastic martinet from the National Guard whom no one liked. He was addicted to Southern Comfort, Coca-Cola and huge cigars. He was a lecher and a hypochondriac. He ogled every female who had the misfortune to cross his path and, when he thought no one was watching, doused himself with an idiotic assortment of pills, elixirs, laxatives and febrifuges. He had hands like hams; perhaps that was why he sweated like a pig.

He did have a phenomenal capacity for work, most of which he created, and a genius for creating administrative snafus, which only he could then unravel. I never could figure out exactly what functions he performed in the service of our country, but there was no denying that he always *acted* busy. He was reputed to be a crackerjack administrator, and that may have been so: it is difficult to know whether a man is a good administrator because he is so busy, or a bad one for the same reason.

Colonel Crowther became acting C.O. around 12:25 on a Thursday. Power does strange things to men: some it ennobles; some it corrupts; some it intoxicates; some it destroys. All that the heady draught of Command did for Eiley Crowther was make him silly. By 16:30 he had invited seventy officers to a party at the Officers' Club, for Mrs. Crowther, on Saturday. It was some anniversary of theirs—meeting, kissing, betrothing or heaven knows what. To my surprise, I was invited (perhaps because of my promotion to the dizzy rank of first lieutenant).

That party was a corker. The Colonel bought up most of the New York champagne in town, and dispatched two command cars across the Mexican border, forty miles away, to bring back cases of gin, Carta Blanca beer and Puerto Rican rum. I'm afraid we all got royally stoned. The fire waters flowed, as they say, like water. A kind of hysterical conviviality soon reigned over us, abetted by the boisterous Colonel himself, who went around waving his cigar and his drink in the air, slapping the male officers on the back and the females on the rump.

Our voices got louder and louder, our laughter shriller, our spirits more and more giddy. Many toasts were offered, many corsages crushed. Hilarity reigned in the lounge, and furtivity on the terrace. Several officers waxed too mellow and several wives waned too soon. During the mounting daffiness, one *amour* was consummated in a hammock and one liaison attempted in the pool. It was a night the post did not soon forget.

Perhaps it was all the booze and champagne. Perhaps it was the example of a C.O. acting like a sailor on shore leave in

Marseilles. And perhaps what happened was no more than a climax to that silliness which possesses us after too-long frustration, when the soul yearns for the catharsis of folly. In any case, after we had replaced the water in our systems with alcohol, the influence of which is considerably more startling, Major Cy Watts was suddenly inspired to mount a chair, crow "Cock-a-doodle-doo," and challenge anyone in the club to try and Indian-pull him across a line he had made on the floor with adhesive tape from the bartender's first-aid kit. Watts, a big bruiser from cattle country, was a whiz at the Indian wrestling game—as officer after officer soon learned. They tried in vain to push, yank, pull or jerk Watts out of position. He met all challengers *seriatim*, with a superior grin and bulging forearms.

"Fifty dollars says *no* one can throw Cy off balance!" cried his wife proudly.

"Oh, is she loaded!" someone observed. I could not tell whether the comment referred to Mrs. Watts' wealth or condition.

But no one accepted the challenge.

"I will make it easier," crooned Mrs. Watts. "Twenty will get you thirty!"

"I will take that bet," announced Captain Hedderich. We were all amazed, because Hedderich was a smallish and rather thin officer. "On condition," he added.

"You are out of your mind!" screamed a lady.

"Yeah?" smiled Hedderich mysteriously.

"What do you mean 'on condition'?" demanded Major Watts.

"On condition Captain Newman hypnotizes me first, so's I can use my hidden psychological powers to the fullest."

Major Watts laughed so hard I thought he would collapse.

"I don't care if Newman feeds you spinach and makes you think you're Popeye the Sailor Man," retorted Mrs. Watts.

"*Just* a minute," cried Mrs. Hedderich, pushing her way to the fore. "My husband was hypnotized once with his head on one chair and his feet on another, and two men stood on his stomach in between!"

"I don't care if they jumped up and down on his appendix," sneered Major Watts.

"Okay, will you agree to let Captain Newman hypnotize me first?" demanded Captain Hedderich.

"Sure! Let him hypnotize your wife, too, for all I care."

As Captain Hedderich began to count out twenty dollars, Mrs. Hedderich grabbed Captain Newman by the arm. "Hypnotize Skinny and we'll split the thirty!"

"I never hypnotize anyone with less than two heads," said Captain Newman.

"Ha, ha, ha," laughed Mrs. Watts sarcastically. "Go ahead. Make him dopey-eyed. Why, Cy will pull Skinny's arm right out of its socket."

"Says who?" cried Mrs. Hedderich.

"Says me!" trilled Mrs. Watts.

Friends of the contesting ladies now bombarded Newman with partisan pleas. "Hypnotize him, Doctor!"

"Call their bluff!"

"Do it for science."

"Hold your horses," said Francie, stepping between Newman and the Amazons, who promptly outflanked her.

"Lover boy," cried the wife of Major Rinehart, throwing her arms around Newman's neck, "hypnotize me, too!"

"Margie!" exclaimed her husband. He was her third edition.

The crowd now produced such idiot sounds that Colonel and Mrs. Crowther came over from the bar to see what was going on. Mrs. Crowther was a pink-cheeked matron who was constructed along the lines of a Florentine *palazzo,* her upper story considerably overhanging the lower. She was, like many Southern belles, a barrel of charm on the surface and a pillar of concrete beneath. "Why, Captain," she purred, "can you rilly just hypnotize any pretty little thing you set your mind to?"

Newman, who was trying to disengage himself from Mrs. Rinehart's embrace, said, "No, but I had a professor once who hypnotized dogs."

"Bow wow wow," cried Mrs. Rinehart, puckering up her lips.

"Let little old Captain Newman tell you about that little old professor," said Francie diplomatically, unlocking Mrs. Rinehart's arm from Newman's neck. To him, she hissed, "Sex fiend."

"It was in Vienna," said Newman hastily. "The professor's name was Pflaum, Waldemar Pflaum. He was seventy-one, near-sighted and absent-minded. He bought a car—and began running into walls, lamp posts, café tables. He was such a crazy driver that his children began to pray the minute they saw him put on his goggles."

"Stop stalling!" cried Mrs. Rinehart.

"Now, Marge," said Francie, disengaging her arms again.

"Professor Pflaum was terrified he would run over a dog," Newman proclaimed loudly, "because he drove so slowly that packs of dogs kept running alongside his car for blocks, snapping at the tires. The professor got so worried that he gave up driving and began to brood over his problem—and he came to the conclusion that the dogs were trying to commit suicide under his wheels. 'Zey vait aroundt corners, hidink,' he told me, 'and soon zey see Professor Pflaum approaches, zey make "Arf! Arf!" undt *jomp onder mine vheels!*' "

I happened to glance at Colonel Crowther. He was staring at Newman with an expression that was at once rapt, beguiled, incredulous and suspicious.

"Obsessed with the idea that the dogs of Vienna were obsessed with him," Newman continued, still eyeing Mrs. Rinehart skittishly, "Professor Pflaum decided to see whether he could hypnotize a dog out of its death wishes. Like this." Captain Newman began to swing an imaginary watch on an imaginary chain before an imaginary dog, mimicking Professor Pflaum in a musical monotone: " 'Ze little eyes get tired, no? Ze little head feels havvy, yes?' "

Francie nudged me.

Colonel Crowther's head was moving in rhythm to Newman's hand, his natural ruddiness seeping out of his cheeks.

"Ze eyes so tired . . . Ze head so *schwer* . . ." intoned Newman hollowly, swinging that imaginary watch, moving his head like a metronome—and Colonel Crowther's florid face, which Newman, like a ham actor carried away by his own performance, scarcely noticed, bobbed right along.

"Oh, God," breathed Francie. "Grab him."

"Colonel—"

It was too late. With a peculiarly pleasant whimper, his eyes rolling upward so that they looked like hard-boiled eggs, our Colonel suddenly went limp, moaning, and sank to the floor.

"Colonel!"

"What happened?"

"Stand back!"

"Give him air!"

"Gracious," said Mrs. Crowther crossly, "he has fainted."

"Open his collar."

"Get some water!"

But before anyone could get to him, Mrs. Crowther was kneeling beside her recumbent spouse with an expression of disgust. "Eiley! Get up!"

Eiley did not bat an eye, whereupon Mrs. Crowther began to slap his face with a regularity that showed an exceptionally keen ear for rhythm. "Eiley, you goose. Get *up!*"

Our acting C.O. lay inert.

"Eiley! Don't be stubborn!"

Eiley was out like a sun-struck bear.

Now Captain Newman, jolted out of self-admiration and into a queasy awareness of his handiwork, was loosening the Colonel's tie and collar. "Come on, Colonel." He patted the waxen cheeks briskly. "You're okay. Wake up."

Colonel Crowther opened his eyes blearily.

"*That's* it, Colonel," cooed Francie. "Upsy-daisy."

There was no upsy-daisy or anything vaguely like it, because when Colonel Crowther began to collect his senses, blinking his eyes, his vision focussed in on Newman's foolish (it was meant to be reassuring) grin. "Take your eyes off me!" he cried, wrenching his head to one side. "You hypnotized me! That's what he did—hypnotized me!"

"Eiley!"

"Tell that head shrinker to take his goddam eyes off me!"

"Don't put your eyes on *him*, you fool!" snapped his wife.

Francie and Newman were helping Crowther to his feet with soothing sounds, but the Colonel kept trying to push Newman away. "You hypnotized me!"

"No, sir," said Newman earnestly. "It's just very hot in here—"

"Don't give *me* any of that crap, Newman!"

"—and we all had too much to drink—"

"Take your goddam eyes off me!" cried the Colonel, yanking his head as far from Newman's satanic orbs as he could. "Someone get me a drink! No damn hypnotist is going to foul up this party—"

"The ducks!" Major Busrick yelled, at this critical juncture. "They're in the pool!"

There was a rush to the French doors. In the huge officers' swimming pool, made magical by the moon, a platoon of ducks was paddling about sedately.

A lusty cheer went up from the corybants, because—but first I must tell you about those ducks.

A month earlier, during a nerve-frazzling stretch of heat, training crack-ups, and bad news from the war fronts, the gaudy wagons of a traveling carnival passed Gate 3 on the road that led to town. A flutter of handbills, thrown to the sentries by "a Gypsy lady who looked hotter than Lana Turner," announced that Valmore's Carnival and Mardi Gras would make a five-day stand in Colfax, fresh from its triumphs in Nogales and Tucson.

Valmore's Carnival and Mardi Gras was, despite the elegance of its name, about as seamy a caravanserai as ever wandered across the wasteland. Its Ferris wheel was wobbly; its merry-go-round was warped—its orbit off-center, its music off-key, its horses off-color. The "glamorous Midway" which a barker in a purple vest ballyhooed through a megaphone was not more than a dusty lane lighted by unshaded Mazda bulbs.

And yet, the carnival served us well. We enjoyed it out of necessity. The officers' children, of course, adored it. And it was the children who discovered that one game of chance, which involved throwing darts at balloons on a velveteen wall, offered unique prizes—baby ducks. Whoever broke three balloons in a row won a "real, live, delightful Peking duck, perfect pet for young and old alike."

When Valmore's Carnival and Mardi Gras pulled up its stakes and departed from our desert eyrie, no less than seventeen ducklings were ensconced in seventeen separate bungalows on the post to gladden eighteen childish hearts. (Lieutenant and Mrs. Braunfeld had twins.)

The children treasured the ducks who, in the manner of fowl everywhere, despised the children. The children showered food and love on their feathered pets. The ducks, a peevish lot, bit friend and foe alike with unbiased beaks. As time passed, the children grew irritated; the ducklings just grew.

At this point, Lieutenant Colonel Larrabee asked Captain Newman to drop into his office. It was unfortunate that some sadist had concealed ocellated sand lizards in several of the patients' beds that morning, and all hell had broken loose in Ward 7, so Newman was in a somewhat misanthropic mood.

Colonel Larrabee was tilted far back in his chair, his hands crossed over his stomach, his lips simulating a smile. "Joe," he began lightly, "how do you like ducks?"

"Roasted," said Newman.

Larrabee laughed much louder and longer than this chestnut deserved. "Joe, you slay me. Absolutely slay me! Knew you'd come up with something good." He finished off a few tardy chuckles. "Say, did I—uh—tell you my kid has a duck?"

"You did."

"Oh . . . Well, she—that is, *we* won the duck. At that carnival, you know."

"I know," said Newman stonily.

Lieutenant Colonel Larrabee made a temple of his hands. "That damn duck is driving us batty. . . . My wife, Yolanda, was wondering—can't we just put the duck in the yard behind your ward —with the sheep?"

"With the *sheep?*" echoed Newman. "The sheep are not pets, Mike. They are used by the lab—"

"It wasn't *my* idea, for heaven's sake! The kid threw a fit when I suggested she give the duck away."

"You have my heartfelt sympathy."

"She calls the duck Peter Pan."

"Obviously a child of culture."

"Joe, you've got to help me!"

"Roast him."

"You can't eat someone called Peter Pan!"

"I will gladly eat him," said Newman.

"Oh, no. No, Joe. The kid would find out." Colonel Larrabee waved his hands in the air. "I've *got* to do something about that goddam duck!"

"What did you have in mind?"

"I told you what *I* had in mind," said Colonel Larrabee caustically. "Now suppose you put your fertile cells to work and suggest an alternative."

"I wonder what the Japanese officers are doing at this very moment," said Newman.

"That's *not* funny. If they had an epidemic of Peking ducks on an air base—"

"Peking is in China, not Japan."

"And Colfax is in America, not Siam!" exploded Larrabee. "Stop being a comedian and tell me what the hell to tell Yolanda."

Newman knit his brow.

Larrabee wiped his forehead.

"He could disappear," Newman ventured.

"How do you mean?"

"Say he's been kidnaped. Tell your kid there's a crime wave of ducknapers—"

"This is nothing to joke about," said Colonel Larrabee testily. "The kid says we've got to put Peter Pan someplace where she can say hello to him every day, to and from school. That's why I thought of your enclosure, Joe. It's right on her way to the school bus. Besides, a duck in your yard might take your patients' minds off their troubles! We might even buy a few rabbits—"

"I am running a psychiatric ward, not a farmyard."

"Ducks can do wonders for morale!"

"Ducks also quack."

"This duck is just a *baby*."

"Baby ducks are the worst quackers of all. They arouse pity."

"Then what the *hell* am I going to do?"

"Give the duck away."

"No go. We tried. People are trying to palm off their ducks on us!"

Captain Newman looked astounded. "Do you mean to say you can't find a single set of doting parents on this post—"

"I mean that what with rations, this gruesome heat, and everyone going stir-crazy, no woman in her right mind wants to add the care and feeding of ducks to her troubles!" Lieutenant Colonel Larrabee locked his thumbs together bitterly. "Any other bright ideas?"

"Just shoo it out of the house."

"My kid will throw a fit! The duck might starve."

"It'll be fed by every softhearted GI on the post."

"It might get run over."

"Did you ever try to run over a duck?"

"My brat will run from one end of the post to the other to make sure that damn duck is alive!"

"Good," Captain Newman smiled. "She's way overweight."

The next morning, the Larrabees banished Peter Pan from their premises. He appeared in front of the PX, waddling around with a sort of sneer on his visage. The example spread like wildfire. By noon, eight more ducks were out on the streets; by nightfall, fourteen relics of the carnival were marching around the post with inane dignity. Marching, not waddling: these ducks were sensitive to their environment.

Their marching was not, of course, all that it might be, since some ducks were taller than others, and some went up when others went down. Seen broadside, they appeared to be attached to a crank shaft. But considering their peculiar construction and limited cerebration, the ducks maintained a distinctly military air. This made a favorable impression on all who spied them.

The ducks soon became an accustomed part of our lives, wandering all over the grounds as if they had always been among us, like relatives. Occasionally, they bit each other, instead of a passing child; sometimes they sent jeeps screeching off the road, or halted convoys at moments of high military purpose; but for the most part, they enlivened our existence by arousing foolish whims in foolish men. That is just what they did the night of Colonel Crowther's party, after Major Oliver Busrick spied them gliding across the surface of the officers' swimming pool.

"They're *dar*ling," said Mrs. Rinehart.

"Let's feed them!"

"Aren't they a*dora*ble?"

But Mrs. Crowther exclaimed, "They will befoul the water! Eiley . . ."

Colonel Crowther, who was just recovering from his "hypnotic" trance, turned redder than usual. Someone handed him a drink, which he downed swiftly, then gave his wife an imploring glance; but she only pulled her upper story higher, sternly.

The Colonel muttered something under his breath and strode out on the terrace.

We followed.

He stared at the ducks gloomily. One of them began to quack. "*Eiley* . . ."

"Oh, hell. Someone get those goddam ducks out of the pool."

"Yes, *sir!*" cried Major Busrick, who was both plastered and bucking for promotion, as he jumped into the pool, uniform and all. He began to thrash around after a duck. The ducks, baffled by Busrick, quacked fiercely and skimmed away—whereupon a Lieutenant from Analysis and Review leaped into the water. The cheer which now went up inspired a dental WAC to scamper up the springboard, from which she stepped like a parachutist. Her entry into the water elicited hearty whistles and wolf calls —which sent Miss Lena Desplaines, the town belle with whom Captain Jarvis was madly in love that night, into the pool in a run-off dive and a flash of chiffon.

Nothing begets lunacy like lunacy. Now a captain from Comptroller plunged into the pool at the deep end and a secretary from Travel Orders plopped in at the shallow. I heard a whoop from a major as he pushed his wife into the pool, and a "Geronimo!" from a wife who evened the score. All around that delirious oblong, men and women began to shove each other into the water. This drove the ducks crazy: they flapped their wings, squawking like furies, and as they churned up the water, some officers grabbed at them from above the surface and others tried to snatch them from beneath. Feathers flew in the air and drifted on the water. Some ladies trailed diaphanous wings as they swam; others turned into diaphanous cocoons as they treaded. Mrs. Rinehart was so carried away that she stripped off her gown and plunged into the water in nothing but brassière and panties.

To Mrs. Crowther, whose face was the color of old paste, this was the last straw. "Eiley!" she shouted. "*Are you not going to do anything about this?*"

"I certainly am," replied Eiley, and pushed into the pool the nearest object in uniform, which happened to be Major Callahan, our Catholic chaplain.

"Eiley!" gasped Mrs. Crowther. "Have you gone *mad?*"

"Yup," he said, and transferred a female captain from a dry to a wet milieu.

"Eiley! Your rank! Your uniform!"

Our acting C.O. turned on the woman he had once promised to love, honor and obey. "Amelia, why don't you just shut your trap?"

"Bingo!" cried Ollie Busrick.

"I—want—to—go—home!" Mrs. Crowther announced.

"Bon voyage," replied the Colonel.

She barged toward the club, a vessel of wrath steered by rectitude, and her mate glanced after her evilly. As Captain Newman opened one of the French doors for her, Colonel Crowther narrowed his eyes. "Newman . . ."

"Yes, sir."

"Come here." Colonel Crowther drew himself erect, but turned his head away from Captain Newman. "Push me into the pool!"

"My God," said Lena Desplaines, treading water.

"Our Lord had nothing to do with it," said Father Callahan, beside her.

"The Colonel has snapped his cap!"

"I think Newman's hypnotizing him again."

"Colonel—" Newman faltered.

"Push," Colonel Crowther commanded him.

"I think—"

"Don't!"

"But—"

"Who the hell's in charge of this post, me or you?"

"You, sir, but if I may—"

"Goddamit, Newman," roared Crowther, "don't you understand an *order?*"

Captain Newman pushed.

That scene will be etched on my mind forever. Never had Colonel Crowther looked so likable, so imposing, a leader of men at last, as when he fell, hands anchored at his sides like a man paralyzed while standing at attention, to make a resounding and, all things considered, quite magnificent splash.

Colonel Pyser returned on Monday morning. Within half an hour, the fur began to fly. Colonel Crowther was in Pyser's office for forty-five minutes and came out looking like a ghost.

Colonel Pyser next summoned Captain Newman. He tried to get Newman to admit that he had hypnotized Colonel Crowther. Newman denied this.

"How do you explain the push?" demanded Pyser.

Captain Newman said he was obeying an order.

"Even a private can refuse to obey an unreasonable order!" said Pyser.

Newman said Colonel Crowther was in no mood to be reasoned with.

Colonel Pyser said it wasn't a matter of reason but sense.

Newman said he was as sorry as Colonel Pyser that the whole thing had happened.

Pyser said that no one could be as sorry as he was that Newman had enlisted in the first place and that if he had had to enlist why couldn't it have been in the goddam Marines or Coast Guard?

Newman said he was coming to the same conclusion for a different reason.

Pyser turned green and said that such insolence bordered on insubordination.

Newman asked, "Is that all, sir?"

Pyser banged his fist on the desk. *"I'm* the one who decides when 'that is all, sir'!"

"Very well," shrugged Newman.

"It's not very well by a long shot!" barked Pyser. "This is going to cost you your goddam promotion!"

"One reason is as good as another," said Newman angrily.

"*No* reason's as good as this one!" raged Colonel Pyser.

It went on like that until Colonel Pyser began to get hoarse.

Officers wove in and out of Colonel Pyser's office all morning. They entered crestfallen and departed craven. There had not been so many red faces in the Administration Building since the day Fishhook Matrobe, a gunner in training, had shot down two of our own planes. (Fishhook would have brought down two more had not his instructor, in the cockpit behind him, knocked him unconscious with a Thermos jug. Fishhook, who insisted that the ATs looked exactly like Zeros, was court-martialed. After Captain Newman testified that Matrobe was subject to paranoid seizures of "irresistible impulse," Fishhook was put on the train to a veterans' hospital, though he kept protesting he was more of a Methodist than a veteran.)

Colonel Pyser got on the phone to General Armstrong, who was still in Washington. Before the sun went down, Colonel Crowther was ordered to overseas duty. The official announcement said he had requested assignment to a combat zone, but that fooled no one.

All day, penalties blew out of Pyser's office like a tornado. Weekend leaves for any officer who had jumped into the pool were canceled.

As if all this was not enough, an epidemic of dysentery decimated our ranks; our movie projector broke down; General Armstrong returned in so irascible a temper that calisthenics and marching drills were reinstituted even for medical officers; our volley-ball team was massacred, before two thousand spectators, by our arch-rivals from Yuma; and a series of crash calls ruined our sleep and depressed our spirits four nights in a row.

Yet we bore these misfortunes with fortitude, as men do under adversity if they can but draw sustenance from memory. For we could always lean back and smile, recalling how Colonel Crowther had been "hypnotized" by Captain Newman, how he had shouted, "Amelia, why don't you just shut your trap?," how

Ollie Busrick had dived in after the ducks, how Colonel Crowther had thundered, "Goddamit, Newman, don't you understand an *order?*"

On the bulletin board of Ward 7 there mysteriously appeared, one morning, a hand-lettered scroll:

TO

JOSIAH J. NEWMAN

Captain, M.C., A.U.S.

For curage above and beyond call of duty

We never did find out who put the scroll there, but when Francie asked Jackson Laibowitz how he would spell "courage," he eyed her critically and replied, "Lieutenant, with that type mentality it's a miracle you're not in the F.B.I."

XII

MEDAL

IN THE SKY

Reuben Todd was a soft boy, with a dulcet voice and eyes like glowing candles. He had a magnificent body and could lift three hundred pounds with ease, but his nature was as gentle as a child's. His head was beautifully formed, though too small for his powerful neck and shoulders; his skin—blue-black—shone with a marvelous luster. No one had a sweeter smile.

Ruby spent most of his time sitting on the edge of his bed, putting on his bathrobe, taking it off. Sometimes he would do this all day long. When I first asked him why he was doing this, he told me, "Might git me home this very day, might git me off real fur away." His sentences often turned out in rhyme.

Ruby was brought to the hospital on one of those days when the sun was so hot that the grease-monkeys on the flying field lined up Coke bottles on the cement outside the hangars and watched the glass droop out of shape. Ruby had gone AWOL. The MPs found him sitting barefooted under a chaparral in an *arroyo* some six miles from the post, smiling and nodding his

head; all he said to them was something about a medal in the
sky. It sounded like jabberwocky and Ruby had such a strange
smile that they took him to Ward 7.

The first thing Ruby said when he entered Captain Newman's
office was, "Cap'n, you please lind me some money?"

"Officers aren't allowed to lend money to soldiers," Captain
Newman said.

"Oh, Ah knows that. But 'tain't much."

"How much were you thinking of?"

"Three-foh cent."

"What do you want all that money for?"

Ruby scratched his head. "Thass funny, ain't it? Ah disremember. Don' tell me, Cap'n!" His face lighted up and he snapped
his fingers. "Ah wants t' go shoppin'!"

Ruby's unit was part of a flight maintenance crew. He loved
to hose the planes down and polish them, but he would often
"disremember" and wander off. He usually ended up in the precious shade somewhere, sitting against a shed or a wall or a tree.
He would take off his shoes and socks and give himself a good
talking-to. "Now, Ruby," he would say, "put yo' head t' work
and try an' 'member what that white gennuman tole you. C'mon,
Ruby. Ain't gonna move them feet one speck till you do. What
that nice white gennuman tole you, Ruby? What he say?"

Sometimes he would sit under a cottonwood all day long, his
shoes off, his toes wriggling in the earth; and when an MP patrol
would find him—sometimes on the edge of the field, sometimes
miles from our installation—and would ask what in hell had
happened, Ruby would sigh, "Ah got thinkin' o' m' Aunt Sooky."

He often talked about a "medal in the sky." When asked what
medal, or what he was talking about, Ruby would screw up his
face and give no answer.

Captain Newman sent Ruby into my office for primary intelligence and literacy tests. Ruby stood before my desk, fiddling
with his bathrobe, scuffing his slippers on the floor like an em-

barrassed schoolboy who had been sent to the principal's office
for some infraction of rules he did not understand.

"Ruby," I said, "I'm going to ask you some questions—quite
simple questions. Think carefully before you answer. I'll write
your answers on these sheets of paper."

"Oh, my," he sighed.

"What's your name?"

"Ruby."

"I mean your whole name."

"Reuben Todd Blessby God."

"I beg your pardon?"

"Thass all right. Thass what Aunt Sooky call me, ever sense
Ah was a babe in the ohrange crate. Ah'll say it easy-like, so's you
can write it down good: Reuben Todd, blessed by God."

"You must have been a happy baby," I said.

"Oh, Ah still is," said Ruby solemnly.

"Where were you born?"

"Miss'sippi."

"What town?"

"Oh, 'tain't no *town*, suh."

"Well, what was the name of the nearest post office?"

"Oh, my," Ruby sighed, "now Ah *is* sad. Ah never git no letter; who gonna write Reuben Todd?"

"What's your father's name, Ruby?"

"He ain't got no name."

"I beg your pardon?"

"Daid folk got no name."

"Oh . . . What *was* his name?" I asked.

"Oh, he was name o' Ebenezer. But no use writin' that down;
no one ever call him that. People called him Pokey."

"And your mother?"

"Mammy?" Ruby brought a sigh up from his deepest depths.
"Mah po' Mammy. Me an' three mo' chillun she had, then she
die, too."

"I'm sorry."

"No need bein' *sorry*—'twas eighteen year back."

"What was her name?"

"Rachel. God bless Rachel Todd!" Ruby's face darkened. "Them three! Them others. Them was the wild ones. Hated them an' they hated me. Them was the ones sent mah Mammy to a early grave."

"Which three?"

"Them three." He pressed his lips together.

"Your brothers and sisters?"

He nodded.

"Who raised you, Ruby?"

"Ah done raise m'self."

"Well, before you got into the Army, whom did you live with?"

"M' Aunt Sooky."

"Where does she live?"

"Where she *live?* Why, Lootenan', Ah got to laugh. She live where she al'ays live."

"Where's that?"

"Back home."

A trainer far off began to sputter in the sky. I hoped the boy would make it.

"Did you have a job before you got into the Army?" I asked.

"Oh, no, suh. Ah was a cowboy."

"A what?"

"A cowboy."

"In Mississippi?"

He nodded, pleased. "That was by Mistah Fairabee. My, they was gennul folk. House like God's mansion, and chillun white as snow. Ruby was happy fo' all them days." He laughed, his mouth pink and coral. "Ah done the dishes an' mop the floh, Ah clean the silver an' wax the doahs. Then, when m' work is folded, Ah take me out in the pasture an' pat them cows. Yes, suh, Ah was a right good cowboy."

We discussed Ruby's case in staff meeting next morning. Ward 7 was entirely filled, said Captain Jarvis, and Main was pressing us to admit patients they were having trouble with.

"This boy ought to be washed out," said Captain Mathieson.

"On what ground?" asked Jarvis.

"He sounds like a mental defective."

"Try and get him out—past Colonel Pyser," said Jarvis.

"Then he ought to get a medical discharge of disability," said Mathieson. "A C.D.D., Section Two count."

"And go on a pension?"

"No. He's not entitled to a pension if the disability wasn't incurred in the line of duty."

"L.O.D. or no L.O.D.," said Jarvis, "old Corsets will raise hell if you bring up a man who's strong as an ox and presents no serious problem to anyone—except a psychiatrist."

"Or the MPs," said Francie.

"Let's return him to his unit for a trial period," said Jarvis. "They can put him on a routine that's no strain on his intelligence."

Captain Newman thought for a moment. "We haven't much choice. But tell him to report back once a week, Bill. Keep an eye on him."

Ruby was assigned to latrine duty. It did not interfere with either his euphoria or his meanderings. He kept wandering around the grounds or, despite the most explicit instructions, off the post. If the MPs didn't find him he would fall asleep wherever he was and slumber through the night and start wandering again the next day.

One Saturday night, a half-breed who lived in a shack on the edge of town found Ruby sleeping in his chicken coop, with the chickens all around him. He called the local police. They called the MPs, who put Ruby on an open truck with three drunken soldiers they had picked up in an off-limits saloon, and started back to camp. Two MPs were in the back of the truck with the men. One of the drunks, a North Dakotan named Stoker, began an altercation with the guards and, as the truck tore down the road, tried to grab a truncheon from one of them. The MP began to beat Stoker on the head.

Ruby cried, "Oh, no, please don', please don' hit that white boy!"

A second drunk leaped up and attacked the MP, and the second MP opened his scalp so that the blood gushed forth.

"No, no, please, no!" Ruby cried, and burst into tears. When the third drunk jumped into the fracas, the MPs laid about them. Suddenly Ruby grabbed an MP in each of his powerful hands and began to knock their heads together, pounding them like coconuts. He beat one guard unconscious and broke the jaw of the other before the driver stopped the truck. The driver and the sergeant who had been riding in the cab clobbered Ruby into insensibility.

They treated Ruby's wounds in Emergency, then threw him into the guardhouse, where he began to babble. The next day they marched him to Ward 7.

Ruby stood before Captain Newman's desk with his bandaged head hung low. He had a frightful bruise across his right cheek; his eyes were bloodshot and puffed up; his nose was swollen. The MPs had told Captain Newman that Ruby had gone berserk.

"Ruby, you look awful."

"Ah don' feel so good, neither."

"Are you in much pain?"

"Oh, 'tain't the hurtin'. I *done* bad, is what."

"Did you know that one of the MPs you beat up is still in the hospital?"

"Oh, my. Oh, my. Ruby's so 'shamed. Ah ain't mad at that soldier. Ah ain't riled with no one."

Newman sighed. "Sit down, Ruby. Why did you do it?"

"They was beatin' that white boy. Ah beg 'em t' stop, but they keep right on makin' the blood go, so Ah pick 'em up an' knock their haids t'gether like Aunt Sooky teach me. T' make 'em *stop,* thas all. Ah jist knocked and knocked—" He stopped. "Ah guess Ah fergot to stop. Ah knocked and knocked—an' *they* stopped."

Captain Newman shook his head. "Ruby, how do you like being in the Army?"

"Oh, it's *nice.* Ah's lonesome when Ah hanker fo' home an' all, but the eatin's big an' the sleepin's good. Only one thing upset me—make me shake."

"What's that?"

"They's teachin' shootin' an' killin'. Ah *hates* killin'!"

Captain Newman hesitated. "How would you like to come into Ward Seven for a while?"

Ruby cast an apprehensive eye toward the big, barred door. "On t' other side dat doah?"

"If you don't come in with us, you'll have to go back to the guardhouse. . . ."

Ruby touched the patch on his head and meditated. "Why you want Ruby?"

"So we can take care of you."

"*You* take care o' me? Why thass fine, suh, thass fine!"

So Ruby came into Ward 7. At first he loved it. He loved the clean white sheets and the cooling fans, the lazy living and indulgent regimen. Pepi Gavoni gave him a slice of salami the morning he was admitted; Ruby loved it. He took to following Corporal Laibowitz around the ward and began to help Hammerhead mop the floors and empty the trash baskets.

But bit by bit the luster left Ruby's eyes, and his spirits sank and he grieved. He missed the open fields and the healing sun, the cottonwood trees and their dancing shade, the sand between his naked toes. He missed the touch of the planes' wings and the drone of grasshoppers. He worried about who would feed "them Paisano cocks"—the road runners with the scampering gait, excessive neck and ludicrous beak who scurried across the desert, leaving tracks shaped like the Maltese Cross.

All day long now, Ruby would sit on the edge of his bed,

taking off his bathrobe and putting it on, saying, "Any time now Ruby goin' home; got to be home an' not alone." Even Francie Corum, whom he adored, could not restore his elfin smile.

Captain Newman concluded that there was nothing we could do for Ruby Todd, except get him a discharge. He went to Colonel Pyser, to sound him out—and Pyser hit the ceiling, just as Captain Jarvis had predicted. "I won't stand for another C.D.D. this month, Newman!"

"This boy shouldn't be in the Army."

"Too goddam bad! I've got a duty to the taxpayer, too. Even if you get him out on an E.P.T.S.—*assuming,* mind you, there's anything wrong with him that existed prior to service—he might get free hospital care for the rest of his life!"

"Then I request a Section Eight hearing," said Newman.

"Oh?" Colonel Pyser glared. "On what grounds?"

"For the good of the service."

"I know what a Section Eight means!"

"He beat up some MPs."

"Then court-martial him!"

"No, sir. He's not responsible. He's mentally retarded."

Pyser bit his mustache. "You think you're pretty damn smart, don't you, Newman?"

Newman said nothing.

"Okay, Captain. Go ahead. Just you go ahead with a request for a Section Eight hearing—and we'll see."

When Ruby heard he might be getting out of the Army soon, and on his way home, he began to sing and smile again.

Every morning now, when Captain Newman entered the ward, Ruby would hail him with a cry: "Who'll git that medal, that medal in the sky?"

Captain Newman thought up a new name every day: Joe Louis, Elijah, Satchel Paige. No matter what name he gave, so long as it was unexpected, Ruby would shake his head in admiration and chortle: "Man, oh, man, lissun t' ol Doc today."

One afternoon, Captain Newman answered, "Ruby."

"*Who'll* git that medal?" repeated Ruby in amazement.

"You," said Captain Newman. "Reuben Todd, blessed by God."

Ruby fell back on his bed, laughing and hugging himself.

As soon as he awakened the next morning, Ruby asked Francie if he could see Captain Newman.

"What's wrong, Ruby? You look so sad."

"Oh, nurse Lootenan'—Ah's got the miseries."

When Captain Newman came by, in morning rounds, Ruby said, "A man keeps follerin' me 'round. He's follerin' me every place."

Newman hesitated. "Which man, Ruby?"

"We ain't been introduce."

"What does he look like?"

"He's a officer. Sometime he send a fraind. They's three in all—"

"Three?"

Ruby scowled. "Ah don't want *no* one follerin' me every place!"

"Why are they following you, Ruby?"

"They want to shake mah hand. They want forgivin'."

"Forgiving for what?"

"Fo' what they done."

"What did they do?"

"Oh, thass secret."

Captain Newman pondered glumly. "Would you let them shake your hand, Ruby?"

"No, suh!" Ruby scowled. "Them three is bad, real bad in the eyes of the Lawd."

The section Eight Board met in Room 100 of Main. Laibowitz escorted Ruby over. I met them while I was on my way.

Ruby kept chortling cheerfully, "T'morrow come, Ruby be on his way home. No mo' sorrow, come t'morrow. Ain't that right, Lootenan'?"

"I hope so," I said cautiously. "But maybe not tomorrow, Ruby; maybe you'll have to wait a little."

He laughed. "Ah'll be free's a mockin' bird, right soon! Ain't that right, Jake?"

"Don't count your chickens before they're hatched," Laibowitz growled.

"Ah ain't *got* no chickens."

"I mean, don't start goofing off. Like the Lieutenant says, they can send you home, and they can put you behind the eight-ball, too."

Ruby slapped his thigh and laughed. "You don' *know* somethin' Ruby got on his side."

"Sure," said Laibowitz. "You've got a basketful of luck, on account of you're an Irishman."

"No, *no*. The good Lawd, Jake! Ah got me the Lawd!"

"He's not on the Section Eight Board," said Laibowitz.

We were at the door.

Laibowitz stopped and inspected Ruby's appearance critically. "Tuck in your tie. Stop grinning like you're going on a picnic. Listen, kid: you be real polite now, do you hear? There'll be lots of brass in there, but don't get cute or nervous or anything."

"Cap'n Newman inside, t' help ole Ruby?" asked Ruby anxiously.

"Yeah," said Laibowitz. "Be polite, now. You call everyone 'sir.'"

Ruby nodded. His eyes were very bright.

Laibowitz stuck his hand out. "Good luck, you crazy bastard."

Ruby laughed. "Ah ain't crazy. Ain't *you* comin' in?"

"Naw. Me and Colonel Pyser ain't buddies lately. I don't invite him to Ward Seven, so he don't invite me to a Section Eight."

The Section Eight Board sat at a long trestle table covered with green felt, under a big clock. On the table before each officer lay a copy of Captain Newman's clinical report and recommendation. There was an American flag in a gleaming brass standard in one corner of the room, and a War Department flag in a standard in the other.

From left to right the Board consisted, on this occasion, of Captain Howard, Lieutenant Colonel Frick, Colonel Pyser, presiding, Captain Goldmark, and Major Eckers, who was the best bridge player on the post.

There was a much smaller table about ten feet in front of the trestle table. At one end of this table sat a stenotypist, Tech. 4 Art McKlosky. At the other end sat Captain Newman. I saluted the officers at the trestle table. I could not help thinking how vast a distance ten feet could be. Colonel Pyser nodded. I sat down in a straight-backed chair behind Newman. He whispered to Ruby, "Stand there, please."

Ruby shuffled past us, smiling sheepishly.

Colonel Pyser trained those gimlet eyes of his on Ruby and rapped his gavel on the wooden block. "Recommendation for discharge from the service. Captain Newman."

Captain Newman rose. "Newman, Josiah J. Captain. Serial number: zero one—seven eight five—nine oh two."

From the corner of my eye I could see Ruby grin at him, but the gravity of Captain Newman's expression must have impressed him, because the grin turned sickly. Newman turned to face him. "Private Todd, state your name, rank and serial number, please."

"Reuben Todd Blessby God." That was all Ruby said. He looked frightened.

"The patient's name," Newman addressed the board, "is Reuben Todd. An aunt taught him to add 'blessed by God.'" He referred to his notes. "His serial number, which he can't entirely remember, is four dash six six one dash three five nine. . . . Private Todd, how long have you been at Camp Colfax?"

Ruby screwed up his eyes. "My, it's a long, *long* time."

"About seven months?"

"Lessee now. Ah come to that big soldier-place back home fust—"

Colonel Pyser tapped the table with his finger. "You can skip all that, soldier. Get to the evidence, Captain."

"Private Todd, how many times have the MPs picked you up since you came to this base?"

"Who?"

"The Military Police. The men who bring you back to camp whenever you wander off."

"Oh, them. Some of them's *bad,* but some of them's nice."

"He's been picked up by the MPs, off grounds, five times," Captain Newman told the board.

"Ah don' mean no trouble. They jist—"

Colonel Pyser tapped the table.

"Private Todd, who is the President of the United States?"

Ruby looked at Captain Newman in surprise. "Howzat agin?"

"I asked, who is our President? What is his name?"

"Oh, him," Ruby chuckled. He put his right forefinger under his nose and closed his eyes and thought. "Now *nobody* tell me, 'cuz Ah knows 't fine; Ah'll git that name, jist give me time." He shook his head and snapped his fingers four or five times, then opened his eyes. "Ah don' rightly recolleck."

I glanced at the officers behind the table. Lieutenant Colonel Frick was frowning. Captain Howard was slipping a mint into his mouth. Captain Goldmark was looking at Ruby with pity. Major Eckers glanced toward Colonel Pyser. Colonel Pyser's face was blank.

"What does the President do?" asked Captain Newman.

Ruby snapped his fingers. "Is zat what you stretchin' fo'? Why, that fellow—he got him a big bookkeepin' job in Washington."

Captain Goldmark smiled. Captain Howard frowned. No expression altered Colonel Pyser's glacial mien.

"Ruby, where is Washington?"

"Oh, a *long* way. Yes, suh. You cain't put on yo' walkin' shoes an' mosey over."

"Ruby, what is the capital of the United States?"

"The what?"

"The capital. The seat of our government."

Ruby scratched his neck. "No one tole me. Downtown?"

"Ruby, tell these officers about the men who keep following you."

Ruby turned his head to one side. "Ah don' *like* that queshun!"

"I know you don't, Ruby. But—"

"You *know* it upset me!"

"I know. But I want you to tell this board of officers. How many men are there?"

"You *know*, Cap'n. Ah tole you."

"Yes, Ruby, but you must tell these gentlemen yourself. It's important."

"They's three," said Ruby sullenly.

"And what are these men doing?" asked Newman.

"Oh, oh. They tryin' t' put a cuss on me. Follerin' me an' makin' signs, breathin' hard t' give me the miseries. Them's bad men, Doc, the Devil's kin', tryin' t' fix Ruby like they fix m' Mammy. Tell 'em to stop thair follerin' an' cuss-puttin'! They gives me bad feelin's, bad, *bad* feelin's!"

"What do you mean by 'bad feelings,' Ruby?"

Ruby began to quiver. He did not answer.

"Where are those three men now?" asked Newman quietly.

Ruby turned slowly, surveying the room. "Oh, they's good at hidin', they is. They's not here. They's outside, waitin', waitin'."

"Do you know who those three men—"

"Captain Newman," Colonel Pyser cut in, "you may proceed to another area."

"Ah 'preciate all you doin', Doc!" exclaimed Ruby. "You tryin' t' git me sen' home, like Ah want."

Captain Newman flushed. "Ruby, what work do you do here?"

Ruby bobbed his head around and laughed. "Thass funny, Ah swear—"

"I see nothing funny about it," Colonel Pyser interrupted.

Ruby's face fell.

"Just answer the question! Captain Newman asked what work you do here?"

"*No* work. Why, *nobody* work in the Army!"

Colonel Pyser struck the table sharply with his gavel. "Recess. Five minutes. Newman, may I see you for a moment?"

We all rose. Captain Newman followed Colonel Pyser into the hall.

The room was very quiet. Captain Howard and Lieutenant Colonel Frick drifted toward a corner and went into a huddle. Every once in a while Howard slipped a mint into his mouth. Captain Goldmark stepped to the window and stared out across the grounds, toward that one patch of green, before the Officers' Club, which reminded us that there were places where grass was green and thick and grew without daily watering. Major Eckers did not leave his chair; he hunched over the green felt and scribbled in a notebook. I wondered whether he was making notes on Reuben Todd or on some game of bridge.

"Somethin' wrong, Lootenan'?" Ruby whispered.

"N-no," I lied. "It's just a recess."

Ruby sighed. Then he put his hand around to the small of his back and scratched himself.

In a few minutes, the door opened. We all came to attention. Colonel Pyser strode into the room. There were times when Pyser looked like a mummy: this was one of them. Captain Newman's face was flushed.

Colonel Pyser rapped his gavel. "The hearing is resumed."

We all sat down.

"Lieutenant Alderson."

I rose and gave my name, rank and serial number.

"You administered certain intelligence and personality tests to Private Todd?" asked Colonel Pyser.

"Yes, sir."

"And the comments recorded in the record before us, were they made by you?"

"Yes, sir."

"Are these your findings? Step up here, Lieutenant. Do you certify them to be accurate?"

I stepped to the table and scanned the page Colonel Pyser was holding up before me.

"Yes, sir," I said.

"That will be all, Lieutenant. . . . Captain Newman, you will conclude now."

Captain Newman rose. "My diagnosis and clinical comments are before the board, sir. As a medical officer, and as chief of the neuropsychiatric service, I recommend without reservation that Private Reuben Todd be discharged from the service, under the provision of Section Eight which . . ."

The hearing was over.

That night, I learned what had happened in the hall between Colonel Pyser and Captain Newman. As soon as they left the hearing room, Colonel Pyser turned on Newman and said, with a clammy smile, "When you came to my office to sound me out about a C.D.D., you didn't tell me your boy was a dinge."

"A what?" asked Newman deliberately.

"You know goddam well what. He isn't exactly brilliant, is he?"

"No, sir."

"But you wouldn't want to insist that the ranks of an army, especially in the middle of a war, ought to be filled exclusively by—geniuses?"

"Not exclusively," said Newman.

"Dumb clucks perform plenty of useful functions in civilian life, don't they? It doesn't take a helluva high IQ to collect garbage or haul sand bags, does it?"

"No, but I'm not asking a Section Eight on Todd because he's dumb—"

"I'm perfectly aware of that, Newman. You're going to testify that he's 'sick,' aren't you?"

"Yes."

"Just how 'sick'? A little? A lot?"

"Sick enough to be discharged from the service."

"Ah . . . Just sick enough, eh? What the hell's the matter with you anyway, Newman? Do you fall for every sob story you hear? Can't you spot a malingerer when you see one?"

"Todd's not malingering," said Newman. "His unit is due to go overseas soon—and that boy gets violent; he says he hates killing, he's afraid of bloodshed—"

"He's in a goddam *ground* maintenance crew. He's not going to fly—"

"He shouldn't be in uniform!" said Newman.

"No?" Colonel Pyser's eyes bored into Newman. "I'm not a psy-chi-a-trist, Captain, but I know a thing or two about men. I can spot an odd-ball as fast as anyone else, and I sure as hell can spot a man who'll make a good soldier. Maybe not Grade A and maybe not Grade B, but in my book C is still a passing grade. All that crap this coon spills out about men following him! He's smart enough to know what'll get him out on an N.P. count. And those questions of yours played right into his hands. 'Who's the President?' 'Where's Washington?' The hell with that! We're not running a seminar on current events. That soldier is built like a Mack truck. He's stronger than you or me or half the men out on the field this very minute! With all the boon-doggle in 4Fs and turnover do you want me to wash out a soldier who's a first-class work hand because he can't do quadratic equations?"

"That's not the reason—"

"That joker's putting on the cleverest snow job I ever saw!"

"It is *not* a snow job," said Captain Newman sharply. "That boy can't follow an order—"

"He can swing a pick and shovel!"

"He can't observe discipline—"

"Oh, yes, he goddam well will, if you stop teaching him to act like a screwball."

"No one taught him to become paranoid, Colonel."

Colonel Pyser's eyes glittered. "Pa-ra-noid. That's what you say! I can get plenty of medical officers who'll testify otherwise." Colonel Pyser gave Newman his death's-head grin. "Get one thing through your head, Newman. I'm from the North. I've got no more use for race prejudice than you have. Any man can win my respect. But there are only two kinds of soldiers: good soldiers and bad soldiers. White, black, yellow, brown—I still divide them up that way. There are only two kinds of niggers, too: good niggers and bad niggers. That black buck in there is a bad nigger. And I intend to see to it that he turns into either a good nigger or a corpse!" He turned on his heel.

"Colonel!"

Colonel Pyser turned. "Yes?"

"May I quote you on that?"

Colonel Pyser's skin turned the color of dust. "Do that, Newman. You just go ahead and do that, and I'll ship you out to the worst hellhole I can find on the face of the earth."

Ruby cried that night. Francie Corum fussed over him, Pepi Gavoni brought him a huge slice of cake and milk, Laibowitz tried to teach him how to play casino; but Ruby only moaned and sobbed.

The next day he was very quiet. He would talk to no one. He just sat on his bed, taking his bathrobe off and putting it on. Occasionally, he talked to himself. No one could make any sense out of what he mumbled. I went into the ward after lunch, and tried to cheer Ruby up by telling him that we did not know what the board would rule, that his chances for a discharge were still good, that even if the count went against him this time Captain Newman would surely bring him up again soon. I don't think he heard a word I said.

Just before retreat, a courier from headquarters appeared in

Captain Newman's office with a sealed official envelope: the Section Eight Board had voted, four to one, to reject the request for discharge in the case of Private Reuben Todd. He was recommended for hospitalization and "further observation. . . ."

It may only have been coincidence, but within three days Captain Goldmark, who had voted for Ruby's discharge, was sent to "Death Valley," which is what the men called the special training base, some twenty miles from the post, which was used for desert maneuvers.

The days grew shorter, the nights longer and colder. We "graduated" 80 pilots and 250 gunners. We conjured up space for twelve more beds in Ward 7 by cutting down the size of the orderlies' bull pen and the nurses' rest room.

Several days before Ruby Todd was due to come up for his second hearing for a discharge, Corporal Laibowitz hurried into Captain Newman's office, white as a sheet. "Doc! The back yard. Quick!"

We followed Laibowitz through the iron doors, onto the sun lounge, out of the back door which Hammerhead was holding open with an expression of dismay, down the back stairs to the enclosure where the hospital sheep were huddled in a corner, baaing and bleating in shallow fright. Not all the sheep, though. In the center of the enclosure, three lay dead. Their throats had been cut. The blood around their heads was like a dark red mounting.

I felt queasy. Laibowitz tugged at my sleeve. In a corner of the yard, against one of the cement posts that supported Ward 7, Ruby Todd was seated, hunched up, his arms hugging his knees, his face turned to the twilight moon.

Captain Newman went over to him. In the silvery light, a spoon, wet with blood, gleamed in Ruby's hand. He had rubbed and honed that spoon across the cement post until its edge was thin and sharp.

"I asked him why he did it," Laibowitz blurted, "and he said something about them being the three wild ones, the ones who drove his Ma to an early grave."

Captain Newman removed the spoon gently from Ruby's hand. "Come on, boy. Let's get to bed. You don't have to worry any more."

From then on, Ruby was very quiet. He would not talk, even to Francie. He sat on the edge of his bed, putting his bathrobe on and taking it off. When anyone tried to talk to him, he turned away.

How Captain Newman finally got him to talk I do not know, and what they talked about each morning, day after day, I can only surmise. But one night, just as Captain Newman was about to leave the ward, Ruby threw his head back, laughing, *"Who'll* git that medal in the sky? Ah'll tell you good!" He leaped into the aisle, pulling his bathrobe tight, bowed to Francie and, with his old, bright, enchanted grin, announced: "Ruby made 'im up a pome!" Then he chanted this:

> Ah seen that medal
> An' Ah tetched 't hard,
> Meant for good boys
> An' come from God.
>
> No medal fo' them three,
> No medal fo' two,
> No medal fo' shephe'd-boy
> Or L'il Boy Blue.
>
> *Ah* got that medal
> Fo' Reuben Todd,
> An' thass th' medal,
> Thass th' medal,
> *Thass* th' medal from **God.**

XIII

THE

CELLAR

I was trying to score some AGCT-7s, one beautiful morning when cloud galleons sailed across the sky, all saffron and gold, and verbena and primrose were beginning to blossom on the distant dunes. Captain Newman came into my office. I started to rise, but he motioned me down gruffly: "Stop setting a shining example. No one's watching, except me." He tossed a folder on my desk. "Here's a new case for you to process. A scopophobe."

"A what?"

"A scop-o-phobe." He grinned maliciously. "I thought that would deflate you. Didn't they teach you any Greek when you were with the Harvards? A scopophobe, son; one who has a terror of being seen. Covers his eyes, buries his face. It should tax your ingenuity to interview him. . . . Farewell." He seemed immensely pleased with himself, too pleased, I thought, and wondered why until, his hand on the doorknob, he added, as a rather too-casual afterthought, "Oh, by the way, I have news for you. You'll have to give up this office. We're replacing you here—with a real psychologist, from Mather. A Lieutenant Osterman, very smart, trained at the institute at Yale." I could feel myself turning red, and not a little angry. "From now on, he'll handle all the routine hospital stuff—so you can concentrate on Ward Seven. We're moving you into the office right across the hall from me."

Through my surprise (I felt terribly pleased, of course) I managed: "Oh. Thank you."

He winced. "Don't. Thanks make me feel either noble or guilty; I don't deserve the first and I'm tired of contending with the second. I'll tell you the truth: I'm selfish. I'm also fed up with hiking all the way over here every time I want you to sharpen a pencil. I'm putting you where you'll jump when I holler. Move in any time—like at once."

Within five minutes, Corporal Laibowitz appeared in my doorway, elaborately matter-of-fact. "You need a hand moving?"

"That would be fine. How did you know?"

"Not from Captain dear Captain. Lately, Doc has the Indian sign out. I got it from the song of a little bird—five feet two, redhead, upstairs." He stuck his head into the corridor. "Okay, you guys, on the double."

Into my office rolled a hospital bed guided by Pepi Gavoni, fore, and propelled by Hammerhead Lawrence, aft.

"Detail, halt!" called Laibowitz. "Our country needs you. . . . Lieutenant, tell my assistants what goes, what stays. They're bucking for promotion."

While his "assistants" loaded the contents of my desk and files onto their unorthodox moving van, Corporal Laibowitz directed their labors with sage instructions. "Easy on the water jug, Pepi . . . Not the *drawers*, fathead; they've got drawers where he's going." To me, he observed, "The way I see it, this is a step up the ladder for you. A lot of things go on in the ward you missed from here. Now, you're smack in the middle. Keep your door open and it's the information booth in Penn Station."

Laibowitz was correct about my new office, as he was about so many other things. I could see everyone who entered or left the ward, everyone who waited on the bench outside Captain Newman's door. That was where I first saw Captain Vinson.

It was several days after my "step up the ladder." I was giving one of the revised Air Crew tests to a Sergeant Fawcett, a sawtooth apprentice from Radio who had never stopped complaining about his classification, when I heard Francie Corum's voice in the corridor: "Easy. This way . . . That's *fine*, Captain."

The slow clack of her heels was followed by a hesitant shuffle. I glanced across Fawcett's shoulder. Captain Newman's door was closed. Francie's white uniform came into view; she was helping a tall, terribly thin captain whose Eisenhower battle jacket hung on him as on a skeleton. His tie was loosely knotted and hung askew, the way a tie hangs when someone else has fixed it for you. His head was lowered; his arms hung at his sides; his shoulders sagged. He might have been an automaton. No matter how many times I saw that posture, that stance not of weariness or despair but of utter, hopeless defeat, I could feel my heart sink.

"I'll wait right here with you," Francie smiled. It wasn't a very persuasive smile. She had to take the captain by the arms and turn him, guiding him down to the bench. He sank onto it with an effort and moved his head up slowly; his eyes—dull, gray, very light—drifted across the corridor; they lighted on me, but they were eyes that did not see me, or anything else; they were vacant, unfocused, devoid of curiosity or will or desire. They were even devoid of grief.

I heard Sergeant Fawcett clear his throat and resumed the testing, but I could not keep my eyes off the captain who occupied that bench like a shell from which all spirit has departed.

At five minutes to the hour, Captain Newman's door opened. A patient in pajamas came out. Newman said, "Okay, Fireball. You've got it made."

The patient grinned and made an "O" with his fingers.

Francie rose. "This is Captain Vinson," she said, handing Newman a manila folder.

"Hi," said Captain Newman.

The man on the bench gave no indication that he had heard. Captain Newman touched him on the shoulder. "Captain . . ."

Francie helped Vinson to his feet, and then an astonishing thing happened. He lifted his head mechanically, blinked, and, in a monotone, without the slightest expression or feeling, recited: "Vinson, Paul . . . Captain, A.C. . . . I have—no desire —to live."

Newman and Francie exchanged glances. He read the name on the folder. "Come into my office, Paul."

As Francie tried to steer him, Vinson took a clumsy, shuffling step forward.

"No, Paul, to your left," said Newman.

"Left."

"Yes."

"Which." He did not ask it, he pronounced it: "Which."

Newman tapped Vinson's left arm. "That's your left. This—" he touched the other arm—"is your right. Left—right . . . Right —left." He touched the arms alternately. "Remember?"

Vinson blinked gravely and tilted his head to one side, like a boy putting a seashell to his ear, listening, waiting—for an echo, a clue, some chord from the past, some divination of the known. "Remember." He frowned; memory did not serve him. "Remem-ber. No."

Captain Newman led him into the office. The door closed.

Sergeant Fawcett departed, begging me to give him a break on the tests: "How about it, sir? Can I get a switch—to gunnery, anything, just so I get a chance to *shoot* at something, not sweat it out in a hot-seat with my number on it. I hate them goddam earphones!"

"Let's see how it goes," I said.

In half an hour, I saw Captain Newman's door open. He came out, but Vinson remained standing near the desk.

"Come on, Paul," Newman called over his shoulder.

I watched the new patient shuffle across the hall to my office. It seemed to take forever, he took such small, clumsy steps.

"This is Lieutenant Alderson," Newman said. "You two ought to hit it off. I'll see you tomorrow. At two-three, Paul. Not two—two-oh-three. Latch on to that. Okay?" He handed me Vinson's case folder. I saw that he had affixed a note:

Try to make contact with him. Anything. Especially about—a cellar.

He left.

Vinson was standing before my desk, those gray, empty eyes fixed on nothing.

"Do sit down, Captain."

He did not move.

"In the chair."

He lifted his head. "Chair. Oh." He lowered himself very slowly. Even in his haggard, wasted condition, he was remarkably handsome: a long, narrow head, high forehead, a patrician nose, a firm mouth. His hands were beautifully formed, his fingers the longest I have ever seen.

I did not know where to begin; it seemed wrong to start with the conventional "How are you? How do you feel?" Instead, I tried: "How did you get along with Captain Newman?"

He considered this, I think, quite dutifully, but did not answer.

"Captain Newman," I repeated. "You were just in his office."

"New-man. Oh. Yes. A new man." His eyes floated around the room aimlessly. They came to rest on the calendar on the wall behind me. He looked puzzled. "Numbers . . . Dates. Yes, old. How old—I."

I opened the folder. "You are twenty-six—no, sorry; you're twenty-seven."

"Oh." He ran a finger down his cheek. "Father. Do I. Have."

I examined his biographical sheet. "He is not living, I'm afraid."

"Minister. He. Arms—strong. Voice—like God . . . God." He cocked his head to the side again, courting recollection, and when he spoke again it was as if he were dreaming. "God . . . Father. Since I—since I . . ." He stopped.

"Since you what, Captain?"

He blinked. "God—Father. Merciful Father. Amen . . ."

"Since you blacked out?" I asked.

He turned away.

"Since you—were hurt?"

No answer.

"Since you—last remember?"

He licked his lips. "Born. Where."

I referred to the record again. "Framingham."

"Fram-ing-ton."

"No, Framingham. In Massachusetts."

"Middle name. What."

I held the page up before him, leaning forward so he could read it for himself. "Your middle name is Cabot. Paul Cabot Vinson."

"Cabot. Yes. Mother. She—dead. I. Die. Died. I did. They—did they tell. Whom. Do they tell. When you die."

"They tell your next of kin." I scanned the last page of his admittance record. "Your wife's name is down here."

"Wife."

"Yes."

"Marry. Many came—father, to marry. Church. Our parlor. Parlor—book—saints and beasts—top shelf. Aunt. Ella. *She* hid book. Hated—her. She—" He stopped. "Wife. Name."

"Her name is Elinor."

"Elinor. No more."

"Elinor Carsons Vinson," I said.

"Carsons. Vinson. Oh. Her name. Same—as mine . . . Tired. Hungry. Is it time—for me to be hungry. It was a long trip."

"From where?" I asked cautiously.

He paused. "There."

"I don't know where that is, Captain. Could you tell me?"

He looked blank.

"Could you try to remember?"

"Yes. Vinson. Paul. *Cabot*. See. I remember. I—twenty-six—no, sorry, seven. There is—wife. I—must sleep. Tired. Very." He started to work his way out of the chair, fumbling, mumbling something. It sounded like ". . . rank . . . serial . . ." but I could not be sure. He sank back, dropping his head. The effort of getting up—of trying to get up—seemed to have exhausted him. His breathing was low and shallow.

"You're seeing Captain Newman tomorrow," I said quickly. "You won't forget the time?" He had not heard me. "You won't forget the *time*," I repeated, "tomorrow—Newman's office?"

"Time. Time to—two. No, three. Three after two. Yes. Two-oh-three."

"That's very good, Captain," I said. "You—" I stopped.

His eyes were closed.

"Captain . . ."

His breathing was slow and steady.

"Captain!" I called.

He seemed to have fallen asleep.

I came around the desk. "Captain Vinson! Wake up." I shook him gently, then vigorously, but I could not rouse him. I had read about narcolepsy somewhere, but I had never seen a man drop into sleep so quickly, so deeply. I was afraid he might have had a stroke. I did not know what to do. I slapped his shoulder lightly, calling his name, "Get up. . . . Captain Vinson . . . you must get up. . . ." He did not move. His breathing was very deep and even. "Captain!" I shouted . . . I put my mouth close to his ear. "Captain! Wake up. Wake up! *Wake up!*" It was no use. He might have been drugged. I was scared.

I hurried across the hall and knocked on Newman's door. He

was with another patient but he came out, and when he saw the expression on my face his eyes widened and he went right past me and into my office. Vinson was still in that strange, comatose state.

"Captain . . ." Newman called.

Vinson did not respond.

Captain Newman looked at me. "What happened?"

"We were talking about his appointment with you. He remembered the time. He repeated it—and just seemed to pass out. I couldn't awaken him. I tried, but he won't get up."

Newman studied the sleeping figure for a moment, then leaned against the desk, frowning, his eyes taking in every aspect of the slumped, unconscious form in the chair. Then he bent down, putting his lips close to Vinson's ear, and, in a very soft, caressing singsong, murmured, "Paul . . . Paulie, boy . . . get up. . . . Time to get up, Paulie . . ."

Vinson stirred.

"That's a good boy, Paulie. . . . Time to get dressed . . . go to school . . . *Good* boy, Paulie . . . That's nice. . . . Open your eyes. . . ."

Vinson raised his head, yawning.

"Time for school, Paulie," Newman crooned in that lilting cadence. *"That's* better. . . . *Good* boy, Paulie . . . Eyes open— nice and wide."

Vinson sighed—sadly, so reluctant—then blinked and opened his eyes.

Captain Newman straightened up, giving Vinson his biggest smile. "Feel better, Paul? . . . Took a little nap, didn't you? But now you're up and wide-awake, aren't you?" His eyes never left Vinson's, and that even smile was fixed on his lips. "That's the stuff, Paul. You go with Lieutenant Alderson, now. And don't fall asleep again, not until you get into bed. Okay? . . . Stand up. . . . I'll see you in the morning." Newman rested his hand on Vinson's shoulder for a moment, and left. When he got to his door he turned. Vinson could not see him. He pointed to the ward.

Vinson was standing beside the chair. He made not the slightest sound or movement.

"I'll take you to your room," I said. Had he heard me? "Captain . . ."

Vinson said, "Will you—see me again."

"Certainly," I said.

"Certainly. When."

"Oh, tomorrow morning, if you like."

"Morning . . . Trouble. I have trouble—getting up."

"What do you mean?"

"I—open my eyes. Wait. Think. Hand. Which hand—pulls back cover. Foot. Which—goes on floor. Until one figures it out—you can't get up."

"I understand," I said, and wished I didn't. "Don't worry about it, sir. I'll have one of the orderlies help you."

I could hardly bear to be with him now. I remembered something Captain Newman had said, so many months ago: "We ask too much of them; they ask too much of me." I walked ahead of Captain Vinson and as soon as I reached the iron door, I rang the bell. I wondered if he had any notion of where he was going. I heard him sniff uneasily. It was the smell of Lysol he had gotten; Hammerhead had been cleaning up again. I glanced at him out of the corner of my eye.

Some of the sounds and sights of the ward broke through to his awareness, I think, because a reflex of distress touched his features. On the other side of the bars, Sunshine Young was chuckling over a Sunday comic supplement. I heard someone whistling, "Me and My Shadow." Homer Bittner, who cried out if anyone touched him, was glaring at a sheet of paper, puffing his cheeks out, then spit on the paper and flung to the floor the whole box of crayons with which he scrawled the graffiti of the deranged. Suddenly Sergeant Milo Nevers sat upright in Bed 14, holding his Bible aloft, his eyes fierce, intoning in a cavernous voice, "I will show unto thee the judgment of the great whore that sitteth upon many waters! Mystery, Babylon the Great, MOTHER OF HARLOTS AND ABOMINATIONS OF THE EARTH!" Nevers, who claimed he was an evangelist, was always accusing someone of evil thoughts, evil glances, evil intentions. Sometimes he would slam the Bible shut, shouting petitions to "the one and only God Jehovah" to strike his enemies blind, pour fire on their heads, burn their bowels, rend them limb from limb, commit them to everlasting hell and perdition. "All this I ask in the name of sweet Jesus," he would thunder, "who is our Saviour and our Salvation!" The men in the ward hated him. They called him "Nasty" Nevers. He closed his eyes now and recited from memory, booming out the words: "Raging waves of the sea, *foaming out their own shame;* wandering stars to whom is reserved *the blackness of darkness forever—*"

"Pipe down!" someone yelled. "You friggin' fag!"

"Pee-oo, pee-oo, peeoo!"

"Shut up, you psalm-singing son-of-a-bitch!"

Captain Vinson began to tremble.

"You'll be in a room by yourself, sir," I said quickly. "Don't mind all this. It's not always that way." And while I uttered the ineffectual phrases of reassurance, I suddenly realized that I had totally forgotten the one thing Captain Newman had asked me to try to get Vinson to talk about: "the cellar."

"Captain, if you want to go back to my office—"

But Gavoni was unlocking the door.

Late that afternoon, Jackson Laibowitz brought Captain Newman a tray with tea and marshmallows, taking the occasion to make the following announcement: "Finnigan is getting better. He wants to be moved to another bed, Doc."

"But you just moved him yesterday, didn't you?"

"So? Every second day, I move that guy. I used to think he was a social climber. But that ain't it. He just wants to hate a new location, because he's fed up with hating the old one. . . . About the new patient, this Captain Vinson: you want to tell me anything?"

"No."

"*No?*" Laibowitz looked incredulous. "That's a man with class, Doc; educated, refined, but sick in the *heart,* not just the head, which has some marbles missing. My diagnosis is: Depression, acute and severe. Right, Doc?"

"Wrong," said Captain Newman.

"I never *saw* a patient look more sad," protested Laibowitz.

"Don't confuse sadness with depression, Professor."

"Is there a difference?"

"You bet there is, a helluva difference. It's healthy to feel sad. Sadness is a form of longing. But depression always contains an element of hostility—yes, hostility, which has turned inward. Looks, Laibowitz, can be deceiving."

"Can a man look sad and still be happy?" exclaimed the Corporal.

"Yes."

"Example?"

"You."

Laibowitz made a moue in which the love of learning wrestled with the deflation of ego. "Good point, Doc. I admit it. So what's *your* diagnosis of Captain V.?"

"I don't make off-the-cuff diagnoses, Jackson. *I* like to study the patient."

"You are better when you follow your instincts."

"You flatter me," said Newman dryly.

"Never. An actor I flatter; a psychiatrist I give it straight from the shoulder."

Captain Newman groaned. "God."

"Religion is not your strong point."

"Jackson, you're impertinent!"

"There you go!" exclaimed Laibowitz. "Why do you always climb on a high horse when I give you a piece of truth?"

"It must bring up memories of my unhappy childhood," Newman said tartly.

"That's no excuse. *Everyone* has an unhappy childhood; but not everyone gets sarcastic the minute you level with them. How should I handle Captain Vinson?"

"Gently."

"A brute I'm not!" cried Laibowitz.

"I didn't say you were."

"You hinted! A case like Vinson, I handle with kid gloves. Should I treat him like a neuro or a psycho?"

Captain Newman made an impatient gesture. "Neither. Treat him like a child. He'll have to learn the simplest things all over again—how to brush his teeth, tie a knot, lace his shoes."

Laibowitz made clucking noises of sympathy. "Poor bastard. How'd he get it?"

"Dr. Laibowitz," said Newman, "it's always a pleasure to have you come in on a case. Your fees are high, but you're certainly worth it. I regret to inform you, therefore, that we don't know a thing about Captain Vinson. We do not know how he 'got it.' We are trying to run down his history, which is lost—somewhere between England, Washington and here. And *don't* you try to dig the traumatic facts out of him!"

"A man isn't trusted, it does something to his morale."

"A captain isn't respected, it does something to his digestion!"

Laibowitz ignored this. "He's skinny as a toothpick. Should I con Captain V. into eating?"

"By all means."

"Now you're talking turkey, which is what I'll put on the menu."

"Comments like that certainly brighten the day of a superior officer."

"Doc, be honest: how many officers in this army can you call superior?"

"You may leave, Corporal!"

"Captain," said Laibowitz, "there is a Chinese proverb describes how you make a man feel: 'In a barrel of rice with my lips sewed up'!"

They had first diagnosed Vinson's case as encephalitis, in Ward 3—because of his strange, sudden, uncontrollable spells of sleep. Once he had gone into a narcoleptic state for three days and nights. They had not been able to awaken him—not with slappings, or noise, or even toothpicks inserted under his nails. His stomach had gotten more and more bloated, distended, because he neither urinated nor emptied his bowels. When he did awaken at last, thinking he had taken a nap, he went to the toilet at once. When he came back to his bed, Major Parrish, who was treating him, began to ask him some questions. Vinson lowered his head. . . . They could not rouse him again.

The thing that had baffled the doctors upstairs was that all the lab tests they had run on him—the spinal puncture and X-rays of the head and neurological examinations—turned out negative. They could find nothing wrong organically—no lesions, no brain tumor. They decided to send him down to Ward 7.

The first thing Captain Newman said, after studying Vinson's charts, was: "We've got to give him a reason to stay awake."

Captain Newman spent most of his first sessions with Vinson simply trying to keep him interested: encouraging him, reassuring him, coaxing him. He made little effort to tell Vincent anything except what Vinson wanted to know, or what, through the eloquent nuances of the unsaid, he surmised Vinson wanted to know but could not ask. Occasionally, he tried to bring the conversation around to "the cellar," but whenever he did that, a curtain seemed to fall before Vinson's eyes.

Once Francie found Vinson slumped over, in the middle of the sun lounge, listening to a broadcast by Elmer Davis, head of O.W.I. Davis was describing a massive bomber raid over Germany, in that flat, astringent voice we all had come to respect. When he said something about the Eighth Air Force, Vinson turned his back to the radio like a petulant boy punishing an adult who has not been nice to him.

"The Eighth was your outfit, Captain, wasn't it?" Francie asked. Vinson left the sun porch. He went by me without a word, his face flushed, his lip trembling.

I passed his door a minute later. He was stretched out on his bed. I still could not believe that anyone could fall asleep so swiftly, so deeply. But Vinson was not pretending. He was sleeping as if he had been drugged. Or was it sleep? Had it overtaken him, or had he embraced it? Was it sleep or coma?

And his eating. He ate with his fingers. It was only after weeks of cajoling by Laibowitz, that Vinson began to use a fork and spoon. . . . I would have thought that a man so thin, so haggard, would now be ravenous, or would devour the delicacies that Laibowitz and Gavoni set before him. But Vinson ate no delicacies at all—no ice cream, no cake, no sweets, no dessert. He did not even butter his bread, and often—absently, as if in response to some secret, inner compact—he would pour water into his milk or soup to thin them out. "He eats like a prisoner!" Francie exclaimed.

Captain Newman looked up quickly. "Yes," he said. "That's it. That's what he is. Maybe that's what he wants to be."

Occasionally, Laibowitz would lure Vinson into a game of checkers or parcheesi, but after a few minutes his interest would die away and he would doze off. He simply could not concentrate for long.

Once a week, a letter arrived for Vinson from his wife. He showed no interest in them. Laibowitz chided him about this until Vinson agreed to let Laibowitz read the letters aloud to him. Laibowitz read the letters as if he were the finalist in an elocution tournament, but even his orotund phrasings failed to affect Vinson. For the most part, the letters described things Mrs. Vinson had done since last writing: relatives she had visited, books she had read, flowers she was planting. They had no children. She sometimes sent pictures, cut out of a seed catalogue, of peonies and azaleas. She seemed to think her husband had been sent to our hospital because of the climate: she often inquired about his lungs. Several times she wrote that she wanted to visit him, "but as you made me promise, before you went overseas, I shan't come until you approve." Once she added:

Please do not think you must wait until you are entirely recovered. I have always known how you wished to protect and spare

Your loving wife,
E.C.V.

She always signed herself "E.C.V.," which made Laibowitz snort, "Does she think she's in the secret service? Dames. Dames."

Bit by bit, under Captain Newman's tutelage, Vinson began to rediscover what the rest of us have never lost—the known. He relearned the numberless aspects of the ordinary: how to turn a knob, button his blouse, butter his bread. Soon names, dates, places, mostly from his boyhood, came back to him. He began to gain weight and he walked better. He came to my office, every so often, to talk—pleasantly, but aimlessly. He seemed to be waiting, waiting for tiny increments of strength or confidence or courage. It was as if each day another door swung open in the corridors of his memory. When this happened—a recollection of his mother or a playmate on Nantucket, the spaniel that belonged to the girl next door or a box of stereopticon pictures in the attic—he was like a boy stepping with wonder into a dusty, unremembered room. But whenever Captain Newman mentioned "the cellar," Vinson withdrew, and in that silent, affectless state, that unseeing, unhearing, unresponding limbo, nothing seemed to break through, or to matter.

Now Captain Newman became irritable and impatient—with himself as much as with Vinson. He reminded me of a guide who has, through infinite patience, coaxed a panic-ridden man up to some mountaintop from which the world can be seen anew —only to discover that the man is blind. But Vinson was not blind. No faculties were dead. It was only his feelings which were throttled, denied, imprisoned in some deep and inaccessible well of terror.

Several months earlier, at Lieutenant Colonel Larrabee's suggestion, Captain Newman had begun a weekly seminar for the doctors from Main. He had wanted to announce the subject as "What Doctors Don't Know about Human Behavior," but we talked him out of it. His second choice was "With Gun and Camera through the Unholy Land," but we talked him out of that, too. Francie persuaded him to use "The War Neuroses." He growled that she was beginning to treat him as if they were married, but he used the title.

His seminars were jammed, from the beginning, and they were about as lively, unorthodox and illuminating as any I ever heard of. Newman loved to teach. He also loved to perform. He pretended he was ad libbing, but I know that he prepared himself for each session many nights in advance. The give-and-take of discussion exhilarated him. Some of the medical officers thought he was arrogant, and some made patronizing comments about his "free-wheeling verbosity," but none, I think, failed to learn something.

The case of Captain Vinson came up at one of the seminars when Major Parrish, who had treated Vinson before referring him to Ward 7, asked, "Can't you use Scopolamine or one of the other truth drugs for amnesia?"

"Vinson isn't suffering from amnesia," said Captain Newman. "Amnesia is what he *wants*. . . . Memory is dangerous; it can reopen feeling, pain; to remember one thing, however innocuous, is to open the gates to remembering a lot of others—things he does not want to live over again. . . . Remember how Vinson acted when we first saw him. All of his reflexes were slowed down. He showed no startle reaction, no choreiform movements. He didn't tremble. He didn't sweat. But he didn't complain; he made no demands; and he showed no guilt. . . . Whenever a name, a phrase, a recollection signaled danger to him—wham! His ego promptly blocked it out. And all that suggested something other than amnesia. In an odd way, the whole peculiar clinical picture shows residues of health. Yes, health. Because Vinson's ego *is* strong enough to mobilize itself for defensive functions. And that's what I'm pinning my hopes on."

"What about Sodium Pentothal?" asked an endocrinologist.

"Not in a case like this. Such a patient conks out under flak-juice. He doesn't talk out or act out a trauma. He doesn't abreact —through the explosive release of violent impulses—the way others do. I used Pentothal once on a fighter pilot who went right under, even though I didn't have the needle in him more than a second. He'd gotten only one or two ccs. I tried to cue him, in my inimitable manner, slapping his cheek, talking into his ear, and finally he began to respond. But how? All he did was chant, 'Wanna go home, wanna go home, wanna go home.' That was all he would say for twenty minutes."

"Couldn't you increase the dosage?"

"I did—but five more ccs. put him to sleep like a lamb."

"What are these fellows anyway—zombies?" asked a cardiologist.

"That," said Newman distastefully, "is what they act like."

Now questions were fired at Captain Newman from all over the room.

"Is Vinson schizophrenic?"

"Nope."

"Is he in a severe depression?"

Newman shrugged. "Perhaps."

"Is it combat fatigue?"

"Let's put that one in cold storage. PWs go into this same state, repressing affect, even after they've been away from combat or any danger for years."

"Is he catatonic?"

"Certainly not."

"*Was* he, when he first came here?"

Newman hesitated. "I think he tried to be, but couldn't make it."

"Okay, Svengali," came Major Copeland's wry voice, "we're all panting to know. What's your diagnosis?"

The doctors laughed.

"My first diagnosis was—apathetic state, of unknown origin."

The doctors leaped on this. "Apathy?"

"That's not a diagnosis."

"That's a symptom!"

"I'm convinced apathy *is* a distinct syndrome with a specific etiology. Look at it. Apathy follows a long stretch of deprivation; not danger, mind you, but deprivation: bad food, rotten climate, harsh treatment and loneliness—terrible, prolonged loneliness. Apathy is a defense against surrender to utter hopelessness. Above all, it follows the godawful feeling of having been abandoned. What do I mean by apathy? I mean the state in which all the instinctual drives diminish. Apathetic cases aren't interested in women; they don't even masturbate. Why? Because of the range and intensity of regression—across the entire libidinal front, all the way back to the most primitive state of ego development . . . Vinson fled from the unbearable by embracing emptiness, gentlemen." He hesitated. "He is becoming coherent. He learns. He is beginning to remember. There's nothing really *bizarre* about him. It's just that—pieces are missing. . . . But there's something else—something that puzzles and bothers me. I have a suspicion that his 'amnesia' is not really amnesia: it's too selective. I have an odd, persistent hunch that Vinson knows what he's trying to forget."

Several men cut in, but I doubt that Newman heard them. "I *don't* mean that Vinson is faking. And I *don't* mean that he's enjoying this. And I *don't* mean that he hasn't gone through hell, or isn't still going through it. . . . I just think he is trying to shut out whatever might be pleasurable. Why? I think that **he** wants *not* to get well. . . . If I could find out what *happened* to him, I'd have a peg, a hook, a lever to work with. As it is, I'm shooting in the dark. I've got only one clue: something pretty damn rough happened to him overseas—in a cellar."

The next morning, Captain Newman told Laibowitz, "I want you to take Captain Vinson to the Rec Hall movie tonight—and tomorrow and the next night."

"To the same picture?" asked Laibowitz, in some horror.

"That's right."

"What are they playing—the Bible?"

"No. It's a tear-jerker."

"I'll hate it," said Laibowitz.

"But you're not my patient."

"He'll need new therapy after he sees the same picture three nights in a row. Why do you choose me for this cockamamy mission? I'm no fan-mag dope."

"I want you," said Captain Newman sweetly, "because you're the corniest pigeon on the post."

Laibowitz tried to look indignant, but there was no concealing his pride. "So what's this cinematic masterpiece about?"

"It's about Love."

"That Hollywood," smirked Laibowitz. "Always coming up with something new."

Laibowitz's opening comment the following day was, "You called that movie a soap opera, Doc? That picture is a Niagara of *schmaltz*. It is for birds and bees who don't know about birds and bees."

"How did Captain Vinson like it?" asked Newman.

"Like a boy at his first ball game, but no one told him the rules. He keeps asking me questions till I am blue in the face. '*Why* does he love her? . . . How can he tell? . . . Does she believe those words?' Doc, it's like I'm an Advice-to-the-Love-lorn column!"

"And how," Newman asked, "did you answer his questions?"

"Listen, Doc, I got the pitch from you. You want goo, I deliver molasses. 'Why does he love her?' the Captain asks me. I answer, 'With love, you don't ask why.' 'How does she *know?*' he asks. I say, 'Look at her face.' 'Does she *believe* those words?' he throws me, like a curve. I say, 'It ain't the words, but how he says them.' 'Are they in love?' he pops up. 'In love?' I yell. 'You ask if those two are in *love?* Listen, Captain, if they're not in love, good-by human race!' . . . Say, Doc, you're not even listening."

"Oh. Sorry." Strangely enough, Captain Newman had not been listening. "It was a real, juicy tear-jerker, wasn't it?"

"Oy," moaned Laibowitz.

"Did you cry?"

"Me? Cry? My God, Doc, you could of floated a destroyer from my bawling alone!"

"Did he cry?"

Laibowitz frowned. "You sure ask the right questions. It was the goddamdest thing, Doc. When that picture was kind of slow, even boring, Captain Vinson is wide-awake. When I'm laughing or bawling or on the edge of my seat, believe it or not, Doc, he's taking a nap!"

Captain Newman sighed. "I believe it."

"Yeah? How come?"

"He won't let anything touch him; sleep—that's his defense. . . . He just won't allow himself pleasure, any pleasure, even the pleasure of feeling again."

"He didn't once laugh or cry!" Laibowitz blurted.

"The day he cries," said Newman, "you'll know he's getting better."

Laibowitz mopped his brow. "Doc, I tell you I had such a steam bath with all that *schmaltz* and smooch, I had to take a cold shower."

"That's good for your circulation."

"If my circulation gets any better," cried Laibowitz, "I'll join the frog men!"

A few days later, Captain Newman called me out of a briefing session on "Stanines" with some P. R. and T. brass who had converged on us from Santa Ana. ("Stanines" was a contraction for "standard nines," the predictive scores, ranging from one to nine, on certain aptitude tests.) Newman's voice had that slight rasp which showed he was trying to be official. "Mrs. Vinson is here."

"What!"

"Don't look so damn flabbergasted. She flew into Phoenix, rented a car and drove down."

"But what brought her—"

"I did. Telephoned her over the weekend." He made a sour face. "Okay, so I'm reaching! What have I got to lose? Vinson may respond to her; he certainly doesn't turn cartwheels for me. She has the most beautiful voice you ever heard, by the way. If she's half as gorgeous as she sounds—! I hope she's been so frustrated so long that she needs him. Love, Junior, Sex. Dr. Newman's Magic Liver Pill. It has been known to work miracles."

I wondered what he was going to ask me to do.

"I tried to prepare her for what kind of a husband she's going to find," he scowled. "What a fiasco. Funny thing about people: they can accept a man's being shot up, minus a leg, dying—but try to get it through their heads that it's psychiatric and they throw a fit. And yet, it's not so surprising. Everyone knows how thin is the ice of his own reason. . . . She just didn't hear what I said. So—uh—you talk to her first. Then bring her in to me. Got it?"

It was an assignment I didn't relish.

"It's right up your alley," he said. "You went to the right schools, Belden; you've got the right accent. She talks like she

went to a finishing school for concupiscent debutantes. . . . It'll
be tough enough for Mrs. Vinson to have to see her husband.
To ask her to put up with me, too, cold . . . I wouldn't wish that
on any Junior Leaguer. . . . You're the bridge, son, between Society and Psychiatry."

"Right up my alley," I said sarcastically.

"Is *that* where you used to take girls?" he grinned.

A WAC brought Mrs. Vinson to my office. I had left the door
wide-open, but she knocked politely. I greeted her, rising—and
I can only hope that my face did not reflect my utter discom-
bobulation. Captain Vinson was tall, handsome, distinguished,
even in despair; his wife—I have rarely seen so unprepossessing
a woman. Not ugly, I hasten to add; she was not ugly; she was
drab, colorless, lacking the slightest semblance of charm or grace
or femininity. She could not have been higher than his elbow,
she was so small; and she looked at least ten years older than
he. She had the body of a girl of twelve. She wore neither rouge
nor lipstick. Her mousy hair was pulled back straight and wound
in a bun. She was wearing a "sensible" little hat with a visor, a
cotton blouse under a pale green suit, low-heeled shoes. She reminded me of a Girl Scout leader come to be briefed on her
duties for a cook-out. "How do you do, Lieutenant?" She extended her hand; it was a long time since I had seen a woman
wear white gloves in the morning.

We shook hands. I held her chair for her.

"Thank you," she smiled. "It's a lovely day out, isn't it?"

Captain Newman was right: her voice was throaty and marvelous. If one closed one's eyes, she would be alluring.

"Mrs. Vinson," I began, "Captain Newman thought that you
and I might have a little chat—first."

"Oh. I know I shall enjoy that." She took a pair of glasses out
of her purse and put them on, the better to appraise me. The
lenses magnified her washy eyes. "Yes, Lieutenant?"

"Captain Newman has been working with your husband intensively, and will give you the—clinical picture. Perhaps I can sketch in the background, the rules of the ward—"

"Excuse me, Lieutenant. When shall I see my husband?"

"Oh, I imagine that Captain Newman will have someone bring him to you after—"

" 'Bring'?" She sat up. Her feet barely touched the floor. "Is he injured?"

"Oh, no."

"Then why did you say 'bring,' Lieutenant? Did you mean in a wheel chair?"

"No, I—"

"Is he on crutches? Is he incapacitated?"

"No, no. It's nothing of that sort. He's— Mrs. Vinson, I'm afraid you will find your husband very different from—when you last saw him. His speech, his movements, his whole manner and appearance . . ."

"I do not understand."

I hated what I had to say. I hated Newman for making me the one to say it. I cleared my throat. "He will seem strange, listless, remote, not in—contact. Mrs. Vinson, your husband had a terrible shock overseas, some severely traumatic—a deeply disturbing experience."

She might have been one of the Gray Ladies, a volunteer for hospital work, receiving instructions about a patient she was to help with occupational therapy, as she sighed, quite pleasantly, "Naturally, I have wondered what my husband's precise ailment is, Lieutenant. He has not written me for a very long time. He was listed as missing in action for over a year, you know. I wrote to the International Red Cross, of course, convinced that he had been captured, believing him to be in a prisoner-of-war camp, in Germany or France. They had no record of him, but that has happened to other wives; I never lost courage. I had every faith he was alive. I prayed. Then I was informed that he had been liberated—in France. My, what a day that was! I cried with joy. He was taken to a convalescent home, I believe. I wrote to him at once, through his new APO number, of course; so many letters. It troubled me that he did not answer. But I could understand: a wound, no doubt, or the dreadful mails. . . . I heard, occasionally, from the hospital authorities, or a kind nurse. Because of my persistent inquiries, I was informed that his incapacitation was 'psychological.'" She smiled, more to herself than to me. "Knowing my husband, I was sure it was only transient. He is basically sound and well, I'm sure. Don't you agree? In his mind, I mean, his faculties?"

"Mrs. Vinson," I said carefully, "this is a psychiatric ward."

"Oh, I know, Lieutenant, I am aware of that. I am sure that many men's emotional reverses require—this kind of medical attention. But my husband— No. We are not people who pamper ourselves. War requires fortitude. We are proud that we can draw on our inner strength—our faith in God. . . . You said he had gone through some terrible experiences. Do be frank, Lieutenant; please; tell me exactly what they were." She was as bright and blithe and pert as a sparrow.

"We don't know," I said.

"I beg your pardon?"

"We have not been able to find out."

"But surely you have *asked* Cabot to recount what those experiences were!"

"Of course we have. But—your husband just does not talk about some things, Mrs. Vinson. He will not even answer simple questions—"

"How like him," she smiled. "Perhaps you and Captain Newman do not understand him. Cabot always was given to—reticence. He probably does not wish to confide matters which are invested with special—emotion. You must not think he is some vulgar, self-dramatizing hypochondriac."

I tried not to let annoyance get the better of me. Yet how long could I be patient? How long could one remain indifferent to such prim, superior obtuseness? "Mrs. Vinson, it isn't 'reticence,' nor a reluctance to 'confide' in us. When we admitted your husband, he was a ghost, a shell, a man who recalled no more than his name and rank. He did not even know how old he was!"

"Surely you exaggerate—"

"Mrs. Vinson," I exclaimed, "you *must* try to understand. I— I'm afraid that you must prepare yourself for the possibility that your husband—I hope I'm wrong—may not recognize you."

What faint, thin semblance of color had ever animated those dismal cheeks drained away. Her eyes, which had flared up for an instant, with hate or anger or loathing, went dazed, moist. "Oh, my God," she whispered. "Oh, dear God." She ripped off her glasses and placed her palms over her eyes and wept. That thin, pitiful body shook as the tears poured down her cheeks. She was moaning, "Our Father who art in heaven, hallowed be thy name . . ." It was terrible to see, terrible to hear. She clasped her hands before her, rocking back and forth, praying, "Dear God, be merciful . . . thy servant . . . thine . . . the power . . ."

I came around the desk. "Mrs. Vinson . . . please . . ." I touched her shoulder.

She was fumbling in her purse. "Sorry. I—have not been well. It is all right now. Forgive me." She was wiping her eyes and nose. "You must think me a fool."

I bent down and found her glasses and handed them to her.

"Thank you, Lieutenant. You are kind. I shall be better now." She fussed with her hairpins, fixed her hat, then placed both hands in her lap with the utmost sedateness. "There! He will not see me cry. You may rest assured of that. . . . And now, I wish to see my husband."

"Is there—anything you want?" I asked awkwardly.

"No, thank you . . . Lieutenant, my husband will recover." I led her across the hall.

When Captain Newman got a good look at her, his smile froze, then transformed itself into a glassy grin. "I'm glad to see you, Mrs. Vinson."

I left them.

I watched Captain Newman's door for a long time—half an hour, longer. I wondered what he was telling her. I wondered how much that strange, stubborn slip of a woman would understand.

Francie Corum escorted Captain Vinson to Newman's door. He looked like a movie star cast in a glamorous role. His hair was combed, his uniform freshly pressed. Francie knocked and opened the door. I saw Captain Newman behind his desk, and Mrs. Vinson rise before it. Francie nudged Vinson.

Vinson stepped into the room. He turned slightly, at an angle to me. His eyes rested on his wife for a moment, then passed across her to Newman. "Wife?" I heard him ask.

"Yes, Paul."

"Wife." He did not move.

Mrs. Vinson lifted her thin, little-girl arms stiffly. "This is Elinor, dear."

Captain Newman walked out.

Mrs. Vinson took a cottage in Papago Springs, a trailer camp and motel about five miles south of Gate 2. Each morning, at eleven o'clock, she came to the hospital to see her husband. Captain Newman let them use one of our treatment rooms (one outside the locked ward), instead of the visitors' room in Main, which he called "the mourners' pit."

I saw her virtually every day, but I could not for the life of me figure out what she was thinking or feeling. She was always composed, correct, formal, dropping her "Good morning"s or "Good day"s as if we were neighbors passing in some town square. I wondered what she did with herself during the long days and nights when she was not at the hospital. She carried a tapestry reticule, and whenever she waited on the bench outside Newman's office, her tiny, bony fingers were busy with a tatting shuttle.

I sat down to chat with her once, to ask her how she thought her husband was coming along ("Oh, *splen*didly," she said in that exquisite voice), and I saw she was making a doily. She must have completed a dozen of them while she was at Colfax.

One day, after her hour with her husband, she went by me without a word, her face set and strained. Francie, who was just entering the ward, looked after her. "What upset her?" she asked.

"Search me."

Francie went into Vinson's room. "How did it go today, Captain?"

He tilted his head in that odd, sideward way, rummaging through the past, pleased to find, rather than remember, something there. "Well, thank you."

"You must be very glad your wife came to Colfax."

Vinson considered this gravely. "I believe—I make her unhappy."

"Why do you say that?"

"She—always asks me if I love her. I wish she would not."

"Is that what she asked you this morning?"

He nodded, then yawned and yawned.

"And what did you answer?"

"I said, 'I like—many people. You, my nurse, Mr. Laibowitz, Mr. Gavoni.' I believe—she wanted to cry. She did not, but wanted to. Why? Doesn't she want me to like people?"

Francie made a helpless gesture. "A woman wants a man to love her in a special way, a way he loves no one else in the world."

"That is selfish."

"No, it's natural. The love of a man for a woman isn't like any other kind of love."

"I—am not sure what that means. Some things—sound simple —but I do not understand them. I will—sleep now."

The next day, Vinson told Captain Newman, "I had a dream last night." It was the first dream he had ever reported. "The dream was about you, saying one name, over and over: 'Descartes.' I wrote—a thesis on Descartes, you know. For my M.A. In the dream there was writing—on the clouds. I could not understand—words, on clouds; they burned, clear: *'Cogito ergo sum.'* " He made a faint, scornful sound. " 'I think, therefore I am.' Silly. As well say, 'I *think* I think—therefore, I think—I am.' Would you begin that way? The very beginning? *'Cogito ergo sum'*?"

Captain Newman did not answer.

"Please. Would you?"

"No."

"What would you make—the first axiom?"

Captain Newman hesitated. "I think I'd say, 'I feel, therefore, I am.' "

"Oh. Not reason, but feeling. Neat. But why?"

"Feeling precedes thinking, doesn't it?"

Vinson studied his palm. "That's—my problem, isn't it? To feel." He yawned.

"To let yourself feel," said Newman. "Paul . . . *Paul!*"

Vinson had dozed off. . . .

That night Captain Newman took Francie dancing, to La Cucaracha, a roadhouse thirty miles from camp. He was a bad dancer. He claimed he was indifferent to "ritualistic sublimations of eroticism." I was dating Sheila Devereux, a pretty girl from Pasadena who was visiting her sister and brother-in-law, Captain Binyon, one of our orthopedists. We were all at one table.

Captain Newman was in an abrasive mood that night. He kept wise-cracking Captain Binyon, who passed the ribs off with lame retorts and nervous giggles. Mrs. Binyon kept quoting T. S. Eliot, which did not help things at all. Captain Newman had no prejudice against poetry, so far as I know: he just did not like it appearing out of people's mouths. Twice he asked Mrs. Binyon, a ripe, sponge-rubber blonde, why she didn't have any children.

"I *don't* think that's any affair of yours," she snapped.

"If it was, lady, you'd be pregnant!"

Francie groaned. "You must forgive Captain Newman, Mrs. Binyon. He had a hard day at the jute mill: no one laughed at his jokes."

"Envy!" declaimed Newman. "An open-and-shut case of—"

"Don't name it," Francie cut in quickly. "I'm sure Mrs. Binyon is not interested in the type of envy—"

"Mrs. Binyon should be interested in all subjects beginning with 'p': pediatrics, pregnancy—"

"Oh, goody!" Francie cried out like the Sweetheart of Sigma Chi. "Here's the waiter with some nice, hot *tacos*." The *tacos* were nice and heavy.

Newman took one bite and growled, "Instead of eating them, why don't the Mexicans walk in them? It would solve the barefoot problem."

"There is a poem by Yeats—" Mrs. Binyon began formidably.

"I'm sure there is," said Newman. "Let it live."

The Binyons left soon after. Sheila laughed. She was not fond of her brother-in-law. She was also vastly amused by Captain Newman. We ordered a fourth round of drinks.

Sheila said, "For a brilliant and omniscient psychiatrist, Captain, you certainly take the cake."

"Oh, my aching back," he said. "Binyon bores me!"

"He bores me, too. He is a drip. What's the *matter* with him?"

"What's more important," cut in Francie, "is what's eating you, Joe?"

"Therapy, dear child. Therapy. It comes in a hundred disguises. What do you think of Mrs.—" he noticed Sheila lean forward eagerly and made a face—"Mrs. V.?"

"Who?"

"Paul's wife."

"I feel sorry for her," said Francie carefully. "But I respect her. She's well bred; she's a lady."

"I wish Katy Wolchewski was still around," he said abruptly. "Now there was a lusty, *zaftig* piece of woman."

Francie put her glass down. "Now *what* made you think of Katy?"

"I've been thinking of her for a week."

"You'd better start taking cold showers."

"Don't be silly. I just wish it was Katy who had Captain V. in a private room for an hour a day!"

"Oh," said Francie. "I see. I see, indeed. Yes, Joe, you might have a point there."

"Is this a secret," asked Sheila, "or can any number play?"

"Go ahead, tell her," he said. "She's nubile, and Barney's out of knee pants."

Francie smiled. "Katy was one of our nurses, a Polish peasant type, broad of beam, buxom of—where buxom counts. Everyone liked Katy. Especially the men."

"She was *not* a nymph," said Newman.

"Heavens to Betsy, who said she was? She was just generous and all-giving. She went to Mass every day. What she did about confession, I'm not sure. . . . Katy always volunteered for night shift. The funny thing is, Blodgett and I had no idea what was going on. We never heard the slightest gossip to make us prick up our dainty little ears. Every man in the ward knew, but not one of them snitched. That was before the Reverend Nasty came into the ward, of course. . . . Katy just felt sorry for men, Barney, and for their—primitive needs. She gave her all for her country, whenever it was asked of her."

"And when it wasn't asked for," said Newman, "she created the demand."

"Right in the *ward?*" asked Sheila.

Francie laughed. "Katy was resourceful. I suppose I ought to be blushing, but I look terrible in pink. She also gave the men the admirable illusion that they were seducing her. You never saw so many proud, strutting Lotharios in your life. Dear Katy."

Francie sighed. "But the inevitable snake invaded this Garden of Eden: a trigger-happy major we had in Room D. He had the poor taste to allege that Katy was being unfaithful to him—unfaithful, if you please. He went up and down the ward, pulling rank, until a Pfc. from Palestine, Texas, hauled off and knocked him half through the wall. The next thing we knew, Colonel Pyser had Joe on the carpet. Brief pause for station announcement."

"Captain, take it away," said Sheila.

"I have seen our worthy colonel in many a mood," said Newman, "from the vitriolic to the homicidal, but never have I seen him as apoplectic as he was that historic day. His outrage was galloping. 'Goddamit to hell and gone, Newman,' he bellowed, 'are you running a ward or a bordello?' . . . He laid it on the line, and I had to do something about Katy. Sin can thrive and blossom and do whatever else sin does, so long as official cognizance is absent. But now, alas, Colonel Galahad, whose strength is as the strength of ten because his heart is pure detergent, put the finger on Katy. . . . I called her into my office. She was an angel. She made no fuss, offered no explanations. She only said, 'I don't want to cause you or the boys in the ward any trouble, Captain. I'll take a separation from the service. But I don't want anything *dirty* on my record.' So we got her out, on a 'personal hardship' count."

"Is that all?" cried Sheila. "Is that the end?"

"No," said Francie. "The men gave Katy a farewell party—well, maybe half of the men, the ones not too sick to have been indifferent to Katy's charms. The party was right in the ward. A beautiful party. You'd have thought she was getting the Congressional Medal of Honor. They gave her a present, too: an elegant, lacy nightgown with a big, red heart embroidered on it. Katy cried. The boys yelled, 'Speech, speech!' Katy wiped her nose and said, 'All I can say is, I love you, *I loved you all.*' And she did. She had. . . ."

"How beautiful." Sheila began to cry.

We drove back to camp in Newman's car. We were drowsy and quiet. It was a night such as only the desert can provide: soft, mystic, unearthly in the utter deadness of its silence. The air was unbearably sweet. The scarlet-tipped ocotillo, the gray-green palo verde, the white-speared yucca some call Our Lord's Candle, were outlined in the pearly light, forms on a moonscape. As we came through Small Horn Pass, a soft wind played across that vast, inviolable world, rippling the sand, sending powdery puffs of it swirling, drifting, vagrant pieces of veiling. Once tumbleweed rolled across the glistening road.

Francie was driving. Captain Newman was slouched in the front seat, his cap pushed down on his forehead. I thought he was asleep, but the smoke from his cigarette kept curling up.

"It's been a wonderful night," said Sheila, kissing me on the ear.

The beacon from our control tower swept the arching velvet of the sky.

As we turned off the main road toward Gate 3, Captain Newman suddenly blurted: "He married her. He *chose* her!"

"Who?" asked Sheila.

"One of my patients," he growled.

"You're unfair," said Francie. "She may not be beautiful, nor your idea of something sexy, but—she's *honest,* Joe."

" 'Honest!' " he snorted in disgust. "He needs a woman, sweetheart, not a notary public."

At long last, after Lieutenant Colonel Larrabee enlisted General Armstrong's personal intervention, after an exchange of telegrams to the Air Surgeon's Office in Washington, who cabled SHAEF in London, we received the report for which Captain Newman had been waiting. It had been lost in a bombing raid that had gutted a hospital in Chelsea, then recovered but mysteriously routed to an evacuation unit in the Midlands.

It set forth the following story:

Captain Paul C. Vinson had been the navigator on a Flying Fortress that was demolished, by either flak or JU88s, over France. Several parachutes were seen opening before the ship blew apart. Parts of the plane were scattered across a mile of fallow fields outside a village near Saint-Quentin. Six bodies were found and identified by the enemy. Vinson was listed as missing in action. A year went by . . .

After D-Day, after the breakout at Saint-Lô, a squad from one of General Patton's advance columns swarmed over a house on the main square of a village, directly across from an abandoned Gestapo station. The house had gotten a direct hit. In the smoking rubble, an old Frenchman staggered around, carrying the bloody body of a girl in his arms. Our Major in command shouted to the old man to get out. The old man shoved aside a big coal scuttle with his feet and stamped on the floor wildly. The Major saw a trap door. "Who the hell's down there?"

The old man only made hoarse, animal sounds like a wild man.

The Major banged on the trap door, shouting: "Come out of there, whoever you are, or I'll blow you out!"

There was no answer.

The Major signaled a corporal to lift the trap door and stood back. The corporal yelled something.

From the cellar emerged a gaunt, unshaved apparition in a rough sweater and filthy corduroys, dazed, blinking, shielding his eyes from the light.

The Major pointed his gun at the specter, barking: "Maquis? Kraut? *Deutsch? Français?*"

The man tried to salute, but he couldn't straighten up, he was shaking so. When he saw the old Frenchman and the body of the girl he began to howl.

"Come on, you son-of-a-bitch! *Qui êtes-vous?*"

" 'Merican. 'Merican."

"Name! Rank! Serial number! Goddam it, *talk!*"

"Vinson," the man gasped. "Captain. O-four-nine-three-dash . . . one . . . one . . ." and collapsed.

They flew him to England with a planeload of stretcher cases. He was in a state of shock. He did not utter a word for weeks. He ate with his hands, like a child, smearing food on his face. To one psychiatrist who tried to talk to him, a month later, Captain Vinson only muttered, "No—desire—to live."

The rest of the report was taken up with someone's diagnosis (wrong), comments (banal) and recommendations for therapy (innocuous).

I thought that now that Captain Newman had his clue, now that he knew what "the cellar" signified, Vinson's recovery would be rapid. But I was wrong. We knew, by comparing the dates (from the time his plane had gone down to the time he had been rescued), that Vinson had been in enemy territory for thirteen months. That was about all we did know: Vinson would not talk. Would not? Could not? We did not know.

One afternoon, Captain Newman asked Vinson, "Don't you get fed up sitting here day after day? Don't you ever want to get out of the ward, take a look at the world again?"

Vinson pondered listlessly. "Where?"

"Anywhere! Take a walk, go over to the ball field, browse in the library, watch retreat—" He did not finish the sentence. Something—alarm? recognition? some subversion of vigilance?—had flickered in those distant eyes.

"I—would like music," Vinson murmured. "Yes—music—"

"You must have been quite a reader," said Newman deliberately.

"I like Brahms—"

"Haven't you missed books?"

"My—eyes are bad, and—"

"We'll get you glasses."

"I—read in the ward. Papers, maga—" Vinson recovered quickly. "I mean, if you send in books—I'll try—"

Captain Newman got up. "Let's take a look at the library."

"I'm tired." Vinson swallowed hard.

"It won't take long."

"I don't *want*—"

But Captain Newman had opened the door. "Come on, Paul."

He went out. After a moment, he heard Vinson's hospital slippers padding behind him. Newman led the way up the ramp— through the swinging doors, down the "B" corridor of Main, past the Recreation Hall to the library.

Captain Newman entered the library. The padding stopped— beyond the doorway.

Newman signaled the WAC on duty to leave, and went to the shelves. "Come in, Paul." He heard Vinson cross the threshold. "Close the door." He heard the door creak. "I'm a sucker for travel books, Paul. What's your secret vice?" He heard a strange suspiration.

Vinson was leaning against the door, breathing hard, sweat on his forehead, his eyes fixed glassily, but not on the books or the room or Newman.

"What's your name?" Captain Newman barked.

"Vinson! Captain! O-four-nine-three-dash-one-one-one . . ." Pressed against the door, his arms spread out, his head turning from side to side, Vinson slid down, slowly, down to the floor, chattering, "one-one-one . . ." before he fainted.

"Were you captured by the Germans?" Newman asked, later.

Vinson mumbled, "I don't—remember."

"Your panic in the library—"

"I don't know!"

"There's only one situation in which a man recites only his name, rank, serial number!"

"Is—that what I did?"

"Yes."

Vinson moved his hands in distress. "I have a headache. I—would like to lie down."

"How many missions did you fly?"

Vinson licked his lips. "One. That's all. One."

"You had to bail out?"

"I—feel bad."

"What happened?"

"Why do you nag me?" cried Vinson. "Let me alone! Let—me —*alone!*"

"And if I do? Do you think that will help you? Is that all you want? Do you want to spend the rest of your life this way?" Captain Newman hesitated. "Listen, Paul. I can't keep you in the ward forever. If you don't get well—I don't want to commit you, but I'll have to. It's up to you. Do you understand? I know it's hell to relive what happened. But you've got to. You've got to choose: fear or pain. And pain is easier. Do you know why? Because fear never ends; pain—however excruciating—does. You have to choose, Paul: pain, for a while, I'll help you; or fear —forever."

"Damn you," said Vinson bitterly. "Damn you."

Captain Newman waited until the Vinsons spent their hour together the following morning, then, after Vinson left, entered the treatment room. Mrs. Vinson was surprised to see him.

"How do you think Paul's coming along?" he asked.

"Oh, he's improving," she said brightly. "I think he's ever so much stronger and—less depressed. Don't you?"

"I'm not jumping with joy. Frankly, I had hoped for more, with you here."

"I am a patient woman, Captain," she smiled.

"Maybe too patient."

"I beg your pardon?"

He shrugged and sat on the cot. "Tell me, how do you spend your time with him? What do you talk about?"

"Well, I try to be pleasant, naturally, and cheerful. I—oh, talk about our home, the garden, trips we can take when he comes home. Sometimes I read him letters I've received, from his aunt, my mother. . . ."

"How does he respond? Is he interested?"

"Oh, yes. I am *sure* he is. He may not say so, but I know my husband very well, Captain. Sometimes we pray together."

"Pray?" Newman looked up. "How do you pray?"

"Well, we thank God that Cabot is still alive, that God in His mercy sought fit to spare him."

"Do you kneel?"

"Sometimes—I kneel."

"Does he?"

"No," she said shortly.

"Does he often fall asleep?"

"Oh, yes. He is very tired."

Some men passed outside the window, laughing, and a loud voice said, "She had headlights you could read by! Man, she was stacked for action—"

Captain Newman said, "How old are you, Mrs. Vinson?"

She flushed. "I was thirty-three in November."

"How long have you and Paul been married?"

"Six years."

"Had Paul ever been in love with anyone else?"

"He—was scarcely a flighty boy, Captain."

"Most boys have a romance or two before they settle down. So do most girls—"

"Cabot and I do not fall into that category," she said primly. "You find it hard, apparently, to accept my husband and me— as a combination."

He hesitated. "I wonder about it."

"Because I am—plain?" she blurted. "Because I am older?

Oh, I know full well I am no beauty. I know that he is so hand-some, and I— But there are more important things than appear-ance, Captain, or an accidental discrepancy in age. I love him. I always did, from the very first, as few women, I think, can love. And he loves me! He has always loved me—that I know in my heart. We are—we were the happiest couple in the world, Captain! Simply because we do not wear our feelings on our sleeve, or carry on in public, or dramatize our emotions— is that so strange to you? Does that occasion your—your prob-ings, your skepticism?"

"No," he said gently. "That's not what I wonder about."

"Then what *are* you driving at?" she cried, a note of harshness for the first time in that incongruous, wonderful, melodious voice.

"I wonder about something you will hate me for mentioning," he said. "I hope you will understand: I don't want to embarrass you. But if it helps me understand, it can help Paul. . . ."

"What do you wish to ask me, Captain?"

Their eyes met.

"This room, Mrs. Vinson. It contains only one chair—and a cot, a bed. It also has a lock. I was not unaware of that when I arranged for you and Paul to meet here and not in the visitors' room. . . . Mrs. Vinson, have you ever locked that door?"

Those ashen cheeks turned scarlet. "I did not realize, Captain, that you are one of those who reads sex into everything!"

"Not 'everything.' But you're his wife. He's a man."

"Not just now, is he?"

"That's the point. What have you done to change that?"

She turned away angrily. "This is most embarrassing!"

"I'm not surprised."

"There are more important things in life than—that!"

"Than sex, you mean."

Her lips pressed together. "You were right. You do offend me."

"How long has it been, Mrs. Vinson, since you and Paul slept together?"

"Obviously, since he last was home, before he went overseas." She was twisting her handkerchief with a violence one would not have expected in her.

"Two years?"

"Almost. I hope that answers your question."

"No, not entirely. What about you, Mrs. Vinson? Don't *you* feel any desire—"

"A decent woman has control over such feelings!"

"Why?"

Her lips parted in astonishment. *"Why?* Really, Captain! Must you be vulgar? Because she is *decent."*

"There are times when a decent woman permits herself to lose control. Women who show their love, who make love freely, with joy, giving pleasure—do you think they are not 'decent'?"

She rose abruptly. "This is disgusting. We shall never agree."

"Wait."

"There is no point in continuing this conversation!"

Gruffly, he said, "I think there is—if you love him, really love him; if you want to help him."

"There is nothing in the world I want more!"

"Then act like a woman to him—not a choir companion."

She wheeled on him bitterly. "And how do you propose that I—"

"If you don't know, after all these years, ask any woman—or any man. Put on some lipstick, rouge, perfume. You might even wear something the Salvation Army doesn't approve of—something soft, flattering, feminine."

"You mean erotic, don't you?"

"Why not? Erotic comes from Eros. Cupid. Love."

"I am hardly the kind of woman who can be expected to act like a prostitute! Good day, Captain." She stormed out of the room. Her cheeks were flaming with rage.

That was on a Friday. On Saturday, Mrs. Vinson appeared at the hospital as if nothing had happened, unchanged in her dowdiness.

On Sunday she asked permission to take Captain Vinson to chapel. After she brought him back to the ward, she went over to the chaplain's bungalow. She and Major Sherrington, the Protestant chaplain, were in his study for an hour.

On Monday morning, Mrs. Vinson telephoned me and asked if she could see her husband not at eleven, as usual, but in the late afternoon. She said she had an appointment in town. I checked with Lieutenant Blodgett. No treatment room was available until six o'clock. I told that to Mrs. Vinson.

"That is perfectly acceptable," she said.

She appeared at the hospital as Captain Newman and I were going into the officers' mess. I am sure she saw us, but she pretended she had not. She was wearing a new dress—a rather silly, gaudy dress, I am afraid, but it was new and bright. Her hair was done up; the bun was gone; she had cut her hair and gotten a "permanent." She was wearing lipstick and there was color on her cheeks.

I returned to my office after seven, to work up some case histories for our next staff conference. It must have been an hour later that I heard someone running down the corridor, sobbing, crying in choked, terrible sounds.

I leaped out of my chair. Someone was pounding on Newman's door. I yanked my door open just as he came out and grabbed Mrs. Vinson by both arms. She was hysterical. "Stop him—someone—*stop* him!" she screamed.

Newman ran toward the treatment room. I followed him. Halfway down the hall, we could hear Vinson's voice, shouting: "No, no, no, no, no, no!"

Newman stopped before the open door of the treatment room. He did not go in.

I saw Vinson. He was beating the cot frantically with the rung or leg of a chair, his eyes wild, sweat pouring down his face, ranting: "No, no, no, no, no!" Shattered pieces of the chair were scattered on the floor. He kept hitting the cot and raving, "No, no, no, no, no!"

Mrs. Vinson tried to push past me. "*Stop* him," she gasped. I caught her. She tried to force her way past me, past Newman, into the room, but I held her back.

Vinson neither saw us nor heard us. He kept pounding on the bed, shouting those violent negations, "No, no, no, no, no!"

Newman did not move.

Faces appeared behind the barred iron door—masks, astonished, fearful, gaping out at us, bobbing up and down like puppets in some horrid Mardi Gras.

Mrs. Vinson began to scream and beat me on the chest. I fought her back to the wall. She went limp.

Vinson's desperate beatings began to slow down; his voice broke; he began to falter, "No—no—" until, exhausted, he dropped his club and fell to his knees. "God," he gasped, clasping his hands together, and bowed his head. "Dear Father—I beg—thy forgiveness—help me—" The rest was lost in sobs.

There was a jug of coffee on Captain Newman's desk, and two cups. Mrs. Vinson's eyes were red from weeping. She held her cup in both her hands, perhaps to warm them, perhaps to still their trembling.

"It was my fault," said Newman miserably. "I wish I could tell you how sorry I am. It must have been awful."

She shook her head dully. "I told you, but you wouldn't believe me. I knew it was wrong, wrong. . . . I was smiling at him, holding him by the hands, talking to him. He looked puzzled. I pulled him toward me, trying to—to show him how to put his arms around me. His expression—it was terrible, terrible. He pushed me aside and picked up a chair. I thought he was going to—" Her voice broke. "I disgusted him, revolted him!"

"No," said Newman quickly. "What you did was *tempt* him. That's quite different. . . . He was 'disgusted,' if that's the word you prefer, with himself, his 'weakness,' the feelings you stirred up in him. And he was angry, very angry, because he almost lost control. Angry with himself, not you." He sipped some coffee. "I'm sorry that it was you I had to put through this. But I'm not sorry it happened. On the contrary. I hope you'll comfort yourself with the knowledge that you have helped your husband enormously."

She looked up in bewilderment.

"Yes, Mrs. Vinson. This time, for the first time, you really broke through his defenses. His outburst tells us something, something very important. He feels guilty, terribly, remorselessly, about—well, about something I'm at last beginning to understand. He's punishing himself. Ever since France, ever since he was liberated, he has been torturing himself. He is making himself atone—"

"For *what?*" she cried out. "He did nothing wrong! He *couldn't* do wrong! Hasn't he gone through enough? Hasn't he suffered enough?"

Newman hesitated. "Not by his standards. That's the point."

The *dénouement* came soon after.

Vinson was seated in the chair in Captain Newman's office. He was very quiet, oddly sullen.

"I've canceled all my appointments for this afternoon," Newman began. "We're going to work, and we're going to get somewhere. Today. It doesn't matter how long it takes. Do you know what I mean?"

Vinson said nothing for a moment, then sighed, "I feel—tired."

Newman nodded. "And soon your eyes will feel tired, won't they? Then you'll feel sleepy, so sleepy, won't you, and you'll just drop off."

Vinson glanced away.

"You'll fall asleep whenever you don't want to talk—or remember. But I'll awaken you, Paul. I'll awaken you and bring you back every time. Do you understand?"

Vinson yawned.

"Stop that!" said Newman. "First, some simple questions, Paul, easy to answer . . . Where did you spend your summers, when you were a boy?"

Vinson hesitated, blinking. "What?"

Newman repeated the question.

"Oh. Nan-tucket."

"With whom?"

"Mother. Father."

"When did your mother die?"

"Uh—I was young—nine." He yawned.

"Stop yawning. How did you get along with your father?"

"I—admired him."

"Did he ever punish you?"

Vinson's eyes dropped. "Y-yes."

"How?"

"He—struck me."

"Why?"

Vinson's eyes closed.

"Paul!"

"Mmh?"

"Open your eyes!"

"I don't want to—" The words went indistinguishable. Vinson lowered his head.

"No, Paul." Newman came around the desk quickly. "Wake up. Come on." He tapped Vinson on the shoulder. "Come on, Paulie. Come on, boy. Why did your father strike you?"

Vinson roused himself. "What? Oh. I laughed—during prayers."

"Was that the only time?"

"Yes."

"Did your mother ever strike you?"

"No."

"Anyone else, ever?"

Vinson shook his head.

"What did you do before you enlisted?"

"Taught."

"Where?"

"A—boys' school."

"Where was it?"

"Tor-Torrington."

"Your father—did he want you to go into teaching?"

"He—hoped I'd—go into the ministry."

"The way he did?"

"Y-yes."

"Why didn't you?"

"I—didn't believe . . ."

"In God?"

"I didn't believe—in God."

"Do you now?"

Vinson hesitated. "No. Yes." He wiped his mouth. "I'm thirsty. May I have—"

"Later. But you talk to God sometimes, don't you? You pray. For God to help you, to give you strength."

Vinson said nothing.

"Your wife is religious, isn't she?"

"Yes."

"Do you think she loves you?"

Vinson nodded.

"Can you conceive of her ever doing anything to hurt you?"

Vinson frowned, cocking his head to one side, and yawned.

Newman raised his voice. "You're not sleepy! When you were at college, Paul, which teacher did you like most?"

"Merri—Professor—Merrifield."

"And in high school?"

"Miss—Carpenter."

"In grammar school?"

"I'm—not sure." Vinson ran his finger across his brow. "Tired. I'm so tired—"

Newman cut in, "No, Paul. Come on. You can remember. You know you can."

"What?"

"Who was your favorite teacher, in grammar school?"

"Oh. Mayhew—Miss Mayhew."

"Who was the first girl you ever had a crush on?"

"Why—are you asking—"

"You'll see. Come on. Your first girl—the first girl you can remember. Her name."

"B. It began with 'B.' Betty? Bea—no—Barbara. Yes. Barbara."

"Her last name?"

Vinson mumbled, "S. Sloan. Yes. Sloan."

"Barbara Sloan?"

"Yes."

"Who piloted your B-17?"

"Meredith. Rob—" Vinson went very pale. He caught himself, starting to rise. "No—that's wrong! I mean—I don't know—can't remem—"

"But you did. Meredith. Robert. When did you take off?"

"I—don't remember."

"Like hell you don't."

"I'm not sure," Vinson burst out. "Can't you see? Don't hound me! All these questions—"

"You answered them!"

"I'm sick."

"No."

"Let me go!"

"No, Paul."

"I can't—"

"You can! You've got to. You will. You know I'm right, Paul. You know that now *I* know—"

"No! You don't! You're wrong! I won't!" Again Vinson started to get up, but Newman put his hand on his shoulder. Vinson cried, "You said *choose:* pain or fear. I tried. I can't. It's both, *both.* I'm afraid! Can't you see?" He beat his fists on the arms of the chair frantically and began to shout, "Afraid, afraid, afraid—"

"But *not of the cellar!*" shot Newman.

The fist froze in mid-air. "What? What did you say?"

"I said, 'But not of the cellar.'"

Vinson's eyes were burning. His cheeks turned paler and paler.

"It's not the cellar you're afraid to remember, Paul, is it? It never was!"

"You—don't—understand," Vinson whispered.

"You mean there's something beside fear and pain, don't you? Something else is tearing you apart."

"What?"

"Guilt."

"No!" Vinson began to tremble. "Guilt? Me? Why?"

"Because you *liked* it there, in the cellar."

"No!"

"It was dark, deep, safe—"

"No!"

"—a refuge, a blessing."

"That's a lie—"

"No more war, no flights, no flak, no danger. You wanted to stay there forever, didn't you?"

"Stop!" Vinson leaped to his feet. "No! No!"

"You never tried to escape."

"I *couldn't*—"

"How do you know, Paul?" sighed Newman. "You never tried."

Vinson was breathing hard, staring at Newman, sweat breaking out around his mouth, and he sank back into the chair, his hands now clutching the arms of the chair so hard that the knuckles were white. "I hate you. I want you to know how much I hate you!"

"I'm sorry you do. But I don't blame you. You'll get over it. . . . Now listen." Newman put a hand on each of Vinson's and leaned over him, resting his weight on Vinson's hands on the arms of the chair, putting his face close to Vinson's. "The pilot was Meredith. Robert Meredith. You told me that, remember? Let's go from there. Who was the co-pilot?"

Vinson closed his eyes.

"Come on. The co-pilot. You remember. His name!"

"Oh," Vinson moaned.

"Paul!"

"Let me sleep—"

"Soon."

"Please . . ."

"Talk, Paul!"

Vinson's head drooped and he began to breathe deeply.

"Paul!" Newman shouted.

Vinson began to snore.

Newman whispered into his ear, "Paulie . . . Paulie boy . . . Wake up. You're going to wake up now. . . ." His tone was very soft, reassuring and musical. "That's a good boy, Paulie. . . . Little Paulie is a *good* boy. . . . That's right. . . . He's *all* done sleeping. . . . He's getting up now. . . . His eyes are opening. . . ."

Vinson opened his eyes, yawning.

"Co-pilot," said Newman. "Your co-pilot. His name!"

"Lashley."

"First name?"

"Chip."

"Did you make target? Come on. Fast."

"Yes."

"Drop your load?"

"*Yes!*"

"On target? Dead? Off?"

"Zero." Vinson's eyes began to roll. "Oh—"

"Paul!"

Vinson bolted up. "Yes? What?"

"Was there a moon?"

"No."

"Stars?"

"Some."

"The Jerries came?"

"Y-yes."

"JUs?"

Vinson's chin was quivering.

"Come on! Were they JUs? MEs? What were they? You can do it!"

"Eighty-eights!" Vinson blurted.

"How many?"

"Lots."

"And flak?"

"Oh, God," Vinson began to whimper.

"No, Paul. Come on. Don't stop. There was flak, flak, lots of flak—"

"Flak!" Vinson cried hoarsely. "Filling the sky. Red, white, puffs, hell, hell, opening, up. Tearing the squadron—to pieces. *Caroline Belle:* exploding. *Bomb Boy:* corkscrewed. Slaughter-house! Wings—props—bodies—sailing, falling, broken, dolls, oh, God, stop, help. Tail fin—door—big door—on *fire,* floating by. Smash! Smoke—in ship. Gas. Reeking. Smell. Body—a body—one boot, ripped off—foot—blood—the parachute, snarled—he smashed our fuselage. Retched. Puked. Awful. Sick." Vinson shuddered, moaning, his face gray. "Shells. Voom, *voom!* Blast—air, freezing. Plane—our plane—hit, lurched, spun, spinning, nose down, upside down, falling, turning, falling, screaming, choking. I—there—flung out, shot out, falling, *falling.* Cord! The cord. *Had to rip* the cord! My gloves—thick— Oh, God, *pull*—the *cord!*"

"You did." Newman kept his weight on Vinson's hands. "You ripped the cord."

"Yes. Ripped it. Yank! Whoosh! Tore—back—my back. Un-

conscious. A second. Another. Floating. Black, strange. Big pillow, soft, dropping, falling, floating . . . Dark. No moon. No
stars. Fires in the sky. Puffs—white. Searchlights—stabbing.
Motors—beating—whining—further, distant, gone. Chatter—guns
—fading, fading. Quiet. Floating, drifting, cotton. Gust of wind
—downdraft—angling, falling, helpless. Pray. Praying. 'Don't
leave me! Please, dear God, dear father, father. Father, don't
hit me!' Oh. Oh . . . Trees—looming, rising. 'Oh—please—God
—*Dad!*' Crackle, rip, wrench, down, *down*. I—I—was down."
Vinson's chest was heaving. Then, frowning, he opened his eyes,
and said quietly, "So—I'm talking. All right. You are heavy. My
hands, please."

Newman straightened up. "You're doing fine."

Vinson glanced at him. "Am I?"

"Trust me, Paul. Go on. You were down. . . ."

"Yes—I was down." Vinson made a bitter grimace. "All right.
I *can* be coherent, you know. . . . My ankle was twisted—fierce.
I think—no, I know, what's the use—I passed out. . . . Terrible
dream—nightmares: falling, burning, the Germans . . . I felt
—the sun on my face. An old man was standing over me. Beret.
He—put his finger to his lips. I got up. He took his coat off, motioned me—put it on, over my uniform. He rolled up my trousers.
Never a word. He never spoke a word or made a sound. . . . He
made a bundle of branches, tied them with a vine, put the bundle
on my back, signaled me—to stay close. He kept putting his
finger to his lips, and pointing, beyond a hedgerow. I saw a
steeple, heard a rooster—a motorcycle. We hit the ground. The
old man grunted. Through the bush I saw a flag, going up. It
caught the wind. The swastika, black, in a white circle, on
red . . .

"We circled the village, came to the back of a house—his house,
the old man's, across the square from their headquarters, from
the Nazi flag. . . . He tapped the door. A voice inside, whispering, French. The old man scratched on the door, a signal. A bolt,

slid back; the door swung, open. A girl. Fifteen? She saw me. The old man covered her mouth, pushed me in. The kitchen. A big coal scuttle, near fireplace. He shoved it aside. Beneath, a trap door. He heaved it up. Down there—it was dark. . . . The old man—he was a mute—made signs, to the girl. She told me, whispering, in French. My French is good. 'You must stay down there,' she said. 'We must not talk. The Boche. If they hear a man's voice . . . I will bring food. . . . We must burn your uniform. . . .' She gave me a candle, matches. The old man—pumped my hand. *'Ne désespérez pas, m'sieur!'* she whispered. . . . I went down, down, alone, out of the light, down— into the cellar."

The drone of trainers in the sky, the strains of Sousa from the parade ground where the band was rehearsing—none of these Vinson heard. He was lost, but well lost now, in remembrance.

"The trap door closed, the lid of a casket. All sound smothered. I sank to the ground. But it was not ground. It was flooring. I lit the candle. In the pale, yellow flicker—I saw the cellar. . . . It was no cellar. Books—everywhere I looked—books, books, every inch of wall covered with shelves, books, books. . . . Her father had done it before the war, she told me later. The Boche —took her father to the house across the street. They did terrible things to him. . . . They put his body on a scaffold and hung it by the neck. But everyone knew he had been dead before they strung him up. . . . The old man vowed he would kill those who had killed his son. The girl said he wanted me to promise I would help him, when the time was right. . . ." Vinson shuddered. "They were not allowed to lock the doors, or the windows. The Germans kept snooping around. They took the curtains away, forbade them to cover the panes. They were allowed no light after curfew. . . . But—he was a man, that old man. Seventy-two, the heart of a lion. He stole out of the house each night. He put sugar in their gas tanks, sand in their motors, shorted their motorcycles. He tore down roadmarkers. He strung wires across the road, decapitated patrolmen. Once—he strangled a sentry. Everywhere, even on their occupation posters, their H.Q. walls, he painted the Cross of Lorraine. Oh, that was a man." Vinson stopped. "I was no man." He buried his face in his hands. "He came down once and took me out. The girl was scared. 'You will kill a Boche,' she said. We started out. . . . There was a German—a soldier—dozing in a car. The German—he looked like Lashley. He couldn't have been more than twenty. He was so young, fresh, nice-looking as he slept. I raised the garrote, started to drop it, around his neck—and dropped it and ran and ran. I was sick. I threw up. I cried. Running, wildly, I prayed and cried. I ran back. All the way. Into the house. Into the cellar. I pulled the door shut over me. I fell—fainted. . . . The cellar—I never left it again. . . .

"The cellar. No windows, no door. A lamp, gallons of kerosene, stolen from 'the beasts of occupation.' A table, a chair, a pallet. A black pot, which that girl emptied each morning. Every morning, every night, she rapped on the trap door—two slow, three fast—and handed down food. Sometimes a whispered word, but Grandpa did not approve. A ray of light, morning, evening, that was all. The rest of the time I was alone. . . . Alone. With the books. Oh, God, those books." His voice broke. "Molière, Comte, Plato—how beautiful in French. Montaigne, Voltaire, Lucretius. I read. How I read! . . . I was trapped, a prisoner, in a cave; I saw no sun, no sky, no stars, no bird in flight—but I was free, free!

"I hated the Army!" he cried. "From the first, yes, I hated it. From the moment I had to strip and join a line of naked men with a card in my hand. I hated the drills, orders, discipline, commands, the stupidity, the arrogance, the fatuous faces. I did my duty. Yes. I knew I had to fight and I knew we had to win. But I hated it. I had no will, no soul. Where was God, to permit war?

"In that cellar, for thirteen blessed months, I was free. A cel-

lar, no sound, a room, a womb. Cared for, sheltered, safe, alone.
'Liked it there?' I loved it! I loved every single moment of it!
Get out, escape, I said. Escape—! I knew it was my duty—but
I couldn't, I didn't want to, I was afraid, afraid to try. I read
and read and read! To hell with the world, the war. I did not
care. I did not miss anything or anyone. Not letters or voices or
word from home. Home? I *was* home. My father—'Fear the
Lord!' he bellowed. 'Purge the heart! Be manly! Don't be weak.'
I heard his voice, in my mind, day and night—until I closed my
mind to it. I taught myself not to hear. I taught myself to forget him, her, everyone, everything! I would live for me, me
alone. No one could hurt me there, in the cellar." Vinson hung
his head. "Months and months and months. They—the old man,
the girl, they were risking their lives for me; and I was afraid to
risk mine for them. The war—was roaring on—the men on foot,
in the air, my friends, companions, old outfit, fighting, dying—
and I— Yes. You're right, safe, safe, ashamed, but safe in my
cellar. I would not let myself think of that. I could not bear the
—knowledge of what I was doing. I made a promise: Someday I
would make it all up—to everyone. Someday—somehow—I would
pay. Each day, I got on my knees and prayed. Prayed? No, I
promised. I promised God that if He would keep me safe and let
me live—when it was all over, I would make it all up. Someday
—somehow—I would pay—pay for this thing I was doing.

"And then—barely, faintly, I heard the muffled thunder, distant cannon. Day by day, closer. I tried not to hear. One day,
heavy fire, closer, terrible, smashing. The house tumbled overhead.
Trucks, rumbling. Then stomping, clattering, above me, and the
door opened. Light poured down. A man's rasp, in English:
'Come out of there or I'll blow you out!'

"I went up. The old man—holding her body, her body, broken,
dead. Oh, God, dear God. Soldiers—four—with guns. Americans,
my comrades, my liberators. A major, red eyes, bleary, barking,
'Okay, you son-of-a-bitch, who are you?' My heart froze, my

blood, my tongue, my mind." Vinson faltered, covering his face.
"Oh. Oh . . . Inside me, deep in the cellar inside myself—I began to cry. I could hear it—the crying—for me, to me, alone. 'Go
back. Go down. Paul boy, go home.' Everything was going dark,
darker, in that rubble, in the daylight, darker than it had ever
been underneath. And I wanted it! I wanted it darker, darker,
so I could hide! I heard, somewhere, the major shouting. I
couldn't see his face. Shouting—I couldn't bear it—again to be
barked at, ordered, to go up, planes, flak, bombs. I—gave my
name, I think, and rank, I think, and serial—the blackness fell
everywhere. . . .

"They flew me out, with dying men, praying men, crippled men,
to hospitals. Nurses, doctors, questions—I don't know, I didn't
care. I was back, in my cellar. . . .

"Then, long after, holding a paper and someone, Nurse Corum,
at my elbow, and you were there. I said, didn't I: 'Vinson, Paul.
Captain, Air. I have—no desire—to live.' "

Four days later, Captain Vinson said, "I think I ought to go
back now."

"Where?" asked Newman.

"To my outfit. They're fighting over Italy now."

Captain Newman paused. " 'Ought.' How about 'want'? Do
you *want* to go back?"

"Yes."

"To fly again?"

"Yes."

"On some bomb runs?"

"Yes."

"Aren't you afraid?"

"No."

"Then you're not ready," said Newman.

Vinson looked startled, then smiled. "I should know better by
now than to try to fool you. Afraid? Yes, of course I'm afraid.

I'm not a very brave man, I suppose. There's little of the hero in me."

"Then why do you want to go back?"

"Because I ought to. Yes—'ought to.' Because I believe in duty, what one owes one's country, one's friends and comrades. Don't you?"

"Civilization isn't much more than a catalogue of 'oughts,'" said Newman. "But 'ought' has many enemies: want, need, fear. That's what conflict is all about. That's why men break down."

"I don't think I'll break down again, Captain."

"You might. Any man might. Any man will, if the pressure is long enough, terrible enough."

"We'll see," said Vinson.

"But I'm the one who has to decide—now," said Newman shortly. "I have to be sure you can take it."

"You can never be sure, any more than I can, Captain, until I try."

Newman stood up. "No. You've been through too much. You just should *not* go back to combat. Overseas—yes. I'll certify you for overseas duty."

"I want to go up again," said Vinson.

"You can go into flight operations, ground duty, lots of things. You'd make a helluva good man in a dozen jobs that need to be done—"

"I'd rather not. Let me get my missions behind me first."

Newman rubbed his chin irritably. "You want to be a hero. You're determined to prove how brave you are."

"No," said Vinson. "Often, during my time here, Captain, you asked me to trust you. Now I'm asking you to trust me."

Newman turned away. "Have you talked this over with your wife?"

Vinson paused. "No."

"Don't you think you should?"

Vinson shook his head. "I started to tell her, yesterday. It frightened her. . . . Anyway, I'd like, for her sake, to have it look as though I had been ordered back to combat. I'd rather she didn't think the choice was mine. She thinks I've done enough. But I don't. And that's what counts, isn't it?"

"Yes," said Newman. "That's what counts. . . . Tell me something, Paul. Do you love her?"

"Love her?" Vinson echoed in amazement. "What a strange question for you to ask. Love her? I worship her! She's the loveliest woman any man could be blessed with—the kindest, the dearest, the most loving. And in these past few weeks—I can never be grateful enough to Elinor," he said awkwardly. "She's different. She—I—we're both more mature, I think. We've come to know each other in a new way. . . . Captain, will you let me go back to combat?"

Newman wiped his neck and turned to the window glumly.

Vinson lighted a cigarette. He had begun to smoke again.

"There was a boy in this ward once," Newman said, "a tail gunner who had been in a bomber that was knocked to hell. The pilot shouted to the crew to bail out. The boy started to—and saw his buddy, unconscious, covered with so much blood he was hardly recognizable. The boy pulled his buddy to the bomb bay. Half his buddy's face was shot away, and the other eye, the remaining eye, had fallen out of its socket. The boy cried and crawled to a first-aid kit. He put his buddy's eye back in the socket and covered it with a piece of tape. The pilot was yelling, 'Bail out! Bail out!' The boy jumped with his buddy in his arms. His parachute opened, all right, and they both got down. After they hit the ground, the boy saw that his buddy's eye had fallen out of the socket again. He began to cry again and put it back. He thought he should have put that eye back better. He thought he had put the eye back badly because he was so scared, because he was in such a hurry to get out of the plane, to jump. At the evacuation hospital they told the boy his buddy would never see again. The boy collapsed. He wept for days. He could not forgive himself. He couldn't sleep. He said he could not sleep because in his dreams he saw his buddy's eye staring at him, accusing him. He tried to kill himself. . . . They sent him here and I worked with him. I tried. I tried everything I knew. But it was no use. It was no use telling him that you can't restore sight in an eye, no matter how carefully you put it back and tape it up, when all the nerves have been destroyed. It was no use, because—" Newman paused. "There were other things he was punishing himself for, too. His brother . . . Oh, what the hell! I can tell you about a hundred cases—worse."

Vinson said nothing.

"It's not just you I'm thinking of!" said Newman. "There will be eight or nine other men in a Fortress."

"I know. That's why I want to go up again, Captain."

Newman sighed.

"Thank you." Vinson rose. "I won't try to thank you for everything else—I mean, for all you've done."

"It was a pleasure," said Newman wryly.

"You—well, you know."

They shook hands.

And now Captain Newman smiled. "You're quite a man, Paul."

Vinson turned red as a beet. "I have yet to prove that."

"You will," said Newman.

The Vinsons said good-by to me the morning they flew back to Boston. He had ten days of home leave. It was hard to believe he was the same man who had shuffled into my office so many weeks ago. ("Old. How old am I.") And Mrs. Vinson—she looked no different, except for her short hair. She was wearing the same little hat with a visor, the same "sensible" suit and shoes, the same white gloves. The only difference was in her eyes: they were sparkling.

I noticed that she was wearing a corsage, a sprig of lilies-of-the-valley.

"Aren't they pretty?" she murmured in that marvelous, incongruous richness of a voice. "And wasn't it sweet of Captain Newman to send them to me?"

XIV

THE

SHEEP

Those sheep in the yard below our sun porch, so indispensable to the hospital laboratories, had sedulous eyes and foolish noses. They were, like sheep everywhere, given to prolonged immobility and bucolic "Baas." They bothered no one, pursuing their shallow ways in composure—undemanding, uncomplaining, mutely inglorious. Their stoic stance and intermittent bleatings even seemed to soothe some of our agitated patients, and certainly endowed Ward 7, from the rear, with a distinctly pastoral aura. They would also have supplied a distinctly pastoral aroma, had not Private Albert Lawrence ministered to their dunging thrice daily. Other men would have shoveled with resignation; Hammerhead shoveled and trundled with joy. For where other men are devout, Hammerhead was clean; where others know religion, he knew compulsion; while millions kneeled down, he tidied up. Immaculacy was his God, dirt his Devil. I think that in his secret heart Hammerhead believed in salvation through sanitation.

Occasionally a harmless snake or an anything-but-harmless

Horned rattler, that deadly night hunter which hibernated all winter (a few minutes in the hot sun killed them), would get into the pen—and the sheep would go wild with panic. Hammerhead would run out with a shovel and pound at the snake furiously; he would stay with the sheep, soothing them with baby talk and stroking their noses. The relationship between Hammerhead and the sheep was emphatically symbiotic.

We rarely discussed the sheep, because there is little about sheep worth discussing—unless you are a herder. Once a sarcastic colleague from Main asked Captain Newman how he liked being the custodian of sheep as well as men, and Newman replied: "I'm the only psychoanalyzed shepherd in the world." Another time he got off an outrageous pun: "When you have sheep, your problems are just offal."

One day, Corporal Laibowitz popped his head inside my door, to say, "You want to see something funny?"

I certainly did, so I followed him through the ward and onto the sun lounge, from which we looked down upon two sullen orderlies from Main who were taking orders from a lab technician in a white coat. The lab man was brandishing a large syringe. The orderlies kept advancing on the sheep in the most resolute manner, prepared to seize one or another by flinging themselves upon a woolly body—but each time they flung themselves upon a neck they found themselves embracing a void. Corporal Laibowitz enjoyed this very much.

The lab man, annoyed, jammed his syringe in his vast pocket and told the orderlies *he* would show them how to corral a sheep. "We will advance side by side, arms out, and nail that little bastard in the corner," he said. They marched forward side by side, swooped down upon their target, and, since there were three of them, succeeded in getting quite frustrated.

The lab man cursed profusely.

Laibowitz smiled. "Sheep," he mused. "They are devils in sheep's clothing. Lambs one minute, greased blankets the next."

Below us, the technician brushed off his white coat, studying the sheep hatefully, then looked up. "Hey, Corporal!" he called. "How about giving us a hand?"

"What do you need a hand for?" asked Laibowitz.

"To catch some lousy mutton!"

"There's no one here with only one hand."

The technician, who had never before tangled with the Aristotle of Ward 7, snapped, "Don't be a wise guy, soldier!"

"I will send you a gaucho." Laibowitz turned and sang out: "Nevada! Idaho!"

Two patients approached us: Vasquez leaving his bed, Doland his coma.

"Go down in the pit and show those grease-balls how to fake out some baa-baa." Laibowitz unlocked the back door for them.

In pajamas and hospital slippers, the two men trooped down the stairs. They appraised the flock with practiced eye, snared a lachrymose tup with dispatch, and held him down, a bleating banshee, while the technician got his blood. Then the sons of Nevada and Idaho filed back into the ward. As Vasquez passed us, he sneered.

"Them dudes need a good snappin' dawg," said Doland.

"We just sold our last snapping dog to the border patrol," said Laibowitz. "Hey, Pepi, how about some salami for these boys?"

The sheep. They were nothing more than that: sheep, until—

One morning, General Armstrong sent out a flash bulletin: Colfax was to be honored by a visit from Assistant Under Secretary of War for Air H. B. Hollingshead, from Washington, and Major General Claude O. Fessel, our area commander. Since we rarely saw V.I.P.s of such stature at Colfax, the whole post went into a tizzy of preparation. Not a nook or cranny escaped scrubbing, paint or refurbishment. The steps in front of Administration were given three coats of paint, the flagpole two; a parabolic arch of welcome, bristling with the flags of all our allies, soared over Gate 1; jeeps equipped with lime markers traced fresh lines on the parade ground.

Our guard of honor drilled like fiends. Our cannon squad rehearsed with dummy loads (since an Under Secretary was saluted by seventeen guns and four ruffles and flourishes, an Assistant Under Secretary deserved no less). Our band marched back and forth, playing "Up We Go, Into the Wild Blue Yonder" until heads ached for a radius of a mile in every direction.

The PX ran out of saddle soap and boot polish. The drycleaners in Colfax were deluged with officers' uniforms. The slavies in our laundry sweated; the cooks in our kitchens cursed; the sergeants barked and snapped like men possessed.

From dawn to dusk, Colonel Pyser poked into corners and chivied his subalterns. Some officers began to look haggard and their children began to grow restive. The children nagged their mothers, who nagged their fathers, who nagged the children. Each night, in every barracks and officer's abode, the paths of sleep were strewn with broken glass.

Colonel Pyser summoned Lieutenant Colonel Larrabee and Captain Newman to his office for a confidential briefing: a friend in G-2, Washington, had tipped him off that the Assistant Under Secretary was especially interested in N.P. wards. (His son, it was said, had cracked up in commando operations with Carlson's Raiders.) "For Chrissake, Newman, keep your prize nuts under wraps!"

Captain Newman lectured Wardmaster Kopp and the orderlies on things to be done, avoided, watched, anticipated. "Now, is everything clear?"

Corporal Laibowitz raised his hand. "Doc, what do we do about Hammerhead? With all that brass in the ward, he'll go crazy not swearing."

Private Lawrence turned scarlet.

Captain Newman rubbed his chin. "I can give you a pass."

Lawrence looked miserable. "I don't want to go to town alone, sir. I would miss the whole show."

"Put him in a bed, Doc," suggested Laibowitz. "Then, if he starts swearing, they'd figure he's a psycho—"

"No!" said Captain Newman severely.

"Maybe if you just assigned me to the yard, with the sheep," said Lawrence. "I could see the show, and the brass won't get near me."

"That is a wonderful idea," said Captain Newman. "Thank you, Albert. I appreciate your co-operation. Just stay down in the pen."

Hammerhead was so happy that he cried, "Screw you, sir."

The great day broke like sea foam, fresh and joyous. Couriers whizzed from H.Q. to flying field to parade ground. The band was mustered out early, polishing their bugles and horns and drums.

At 8:50 A.M. a bulletin from Control Tower announced that the plane had radioed its E.T.A. as 10:05.

At 9:15 the guard of honor drove out to the landing strip in 6x6s. Their white leggings and white gloves, burnished helmets and parachute-silk scarves, their ramrod posture on the truck benches drew admiring glances from GIs I would have thought inured to pomp and circumstance.

At 9:35, Lieutenant Colonel Larrabee telephoned Captain Newman. "Everything okay down your way, Joe?"

"Yes, Mike."

"You've got no patients cutting up or anything; I mean nothing that might embarrass—"

"Don't be silly," said Captain Newman.

At 9:50 the great silver bird that carried our august visitors was sighted skirting Jawbone Range to come in from the northeast, through Cuyuga Pass.

At 10:02 Captain Newman's phone rang. He picked it up, saying, "Captain New—"

A hysterical voice from Control Tower exploded: "Get the hell over here! The sheep!"

"The what?"

"Your sheep! Your goddam sheep are running wild all over the field and the goddam plane can't come in!"

Over the airfield, several moments earlier, General Fessel's ship had lowered its wheels, starting into its glide path, when the pilot heard a panicky voice in his earset: "Tower to pilot, tower to pilot! Do *not*, repeat *not*, come in! Over!"

"Pilot to tower, Roger. I will not, repeat not, come in. What's cooking? Over."

"Sheep, over!"

"Sheep? Over."

"Yeah, sheep! On the field! You'll have to futz around up there till we get them rounded up!"

The pilot went into a climb and bank. On the field below, pudgy forms could be seen bounding about, with soldiers running after them, waving caps and arms. The honor guard could also be seen, lined up, flag waving, and the band at attention, brass trumpets shining in the sun, and the band leader, baton frozen in mid-air, glancing over his shoulder in astonishment.

"Sheep?" the Assistant Under Secretary of War for Air asked Major General Fessel.

"Sheep?" General Fessel echoed of the co-pilot, who had been sent back from the cockpit to convey the strange tidings.

"They'll be rounded up in a minute, sir." But the co-pilot, a lad from Cohasset, knew not sheep. And these sheep were running wild: intoxicated by freedom, stampeded by pursuers, blinded by light flashes from bass bugles and tuba and cymbals.

On the ground, General Armstrong bit a few words out of the side of his mouth to Colonel Pyser. There was no doubt that he was violent. Colonel Pyser spat an order to a Major, who responded like the soldier who got that message through to Garcia. In a jiffy, plane-jockeys and grease-monkeys poured out on the

field, shouting, whooping, whistling, waving arms, rags and as-
sorted objects at the sheep. But no sooner were the frantic crea-
tures harried toward a hangar at one end of the field, which they
must have thought an abattoir, than they reversed course and
streaked back in panic.

At this point, the Assistant Under Secretary of War asked his
pilot to come down lower, so that he could get a better view of
what was going on. As the plane buzzed the field, the sheep, half-
crazed, thought they were being attacked by some leviathan from
above; they went entirely amok, and all around them uniforms
sawed the air and men flopped to the ground.

Captain Newman, meanwhile, had hastened out of his office
with a heavy heart, calling for Sergeant Kopp or Corporal Laibowitz or Pepi Gavoni. They were not in the ward. They were on
the portico of Main, waiting for the parade.

"*Our* sheep?" blanched Sergeant Kopp.

"They will get hurt," exclaimed Gavoni.

"Hammerhead!" cried Laibowitz. "I should never of trusted
him!"

As they leaped into a jeep, fun-loving GIs piled into two
others. The convoy raced toward the field. They passed Private
Albert Lawrence midway, running after two prancing sheep and
raging, red-faced, cursing as he had never cursed before.

"You ought to be court-martialed!" Laibowitz shouted.

"Boiled in oil!" howled Gavoni.

"Drop dead!" screamed Hammerhead. "Some son-of-a-bitch
left the gate unlocked! Screw you! Screw him! Screw everyone!"

The jeeps tore right out on the field. Kopp and Laibowitz
stood up. Pepi crouched, peering through his lenses manfully.

In the plane, overhead, the co-pilot exclaimed, "They seem to
be herding the sheep with *jeeps,* sir!"

"How resourceful," said the Assistant Under Secretary of War.

From the first jeep, racing alongside one maddened quarry,
Sergeant Kopp leaped bravely. Sergeant and sheep rolled over
and over, a blur of wool and khaki. From the second jeep, a

soldier fell, rather than jumped, on a howling target; from the third, a corporal plopped down to straddle a ewe who bounded off like a mustang.

A truck from a hangar, commandeered by Major Waggoner, who was almost as batty as the sheep, zoomed out on the field from another quadrant, its running boards crowded with mechanics. Some irreverent souls cheered the way they cheered at a movie when the U.S. Cavalry thunders to the rescue.

Never, I think, were sheep pursued with such novel equipment or caught by such unorthodox methods. What with the plane swooping low, the sheep bounding high, the men wrangling in motorized rodeo, and the band idiotically striking up "The Stars and Stripes Forever," that landing field, as Major Shellenback observed later, "looked like a Walt Disney cartoon gone nuts."

"Tower to pilot, tower to pilot. All clear. You may, repeat may, come in. Over."

"Pilot to tower, pilot to tower. Am landing, repeat landing— but keep your eyes peeled, goddamit!"

And so the plane landed. The band struck up again. The guard presented arms. Our C.O., *et alia,* froze in salute.

Out came the Assistant Under Secretary of War for Air. Forward stepped General Armstrong. Off went the cannon. Down the ramp came Major General Fessel, two majors, one A.D.C., two P.R.O.s.

Forward stepped General Armstrong. "Welcome to Colfax!"

Salutes flurried. Eyes locked. Hands clasped.

"Sir," said General Armstrong, "I must apologize for those sheep—"

"Sheep?" The Assistant Under Secretary of War blinked blandly. "What sheep?"

"Thank you, sir," said General Armstrong, with feeling.

The cannon shattered the skies. (Back in Ward 7, patients dived for cover and bedlam reigned.)

Our C.O. introduced his staff. The formal review began, Assistant Under Secretary in the van: past the guard of honor, down the line of officers, up the row of pilots, down the crews before their glistening craft.

Ten shiny staff cars crawled on field. Visitors ascended, hosts followed. The procession wound around to Gate 1's festooned arch and moved down Victory Drive, lined with the flags of seventeen major powers and twenty-eight co-belligerents. (It should have been twenty-nine, but someone had snafued on Guatemala.) Down the proud dog-face ranks—presenting arms, eyes front, cataleptic—the cavalcade sedately crawled, to Administration, where Headquarters' contingent braced bravely.

Staff officers were introduced, lesser personnel bemumbled en masse. Began inspection: buildings toured, mess halls scanned, kitchens sniffed. Praise from on high was uttered, gratitude from below returned.

Only eleven minutes behind schedule, so well had the groundwork been laid, the dignitaries broke bread in our C.O.'s private dining room.

High matters of state were no doubt discussed over the victuals, for the Assistant Under Secretary of War for Air looked no less dour when he emerged than when he had entered. The grapevine reported that the discussion embraced new planes and enemy interceptors, fire power and lead time, digressing only over coffee to praise the postprandial naps of War Secretary Stimson as against the preprandial pep talks of Navy Secretary Knox.

At 2:18, Lieutenant Colonel Larrabee greeted the visiting delegation on the hospital's portico. By 2:20, they were launched on the rounds of morale-building in Main. At 3:25 they strode down the ramp to Ward 7, where Captain Newman and the rest of us waited. Salutes. Introductions. "How do you do"s. A shaking of hands, an exchange of grimaces. The hand of the Assistant Under Secretary of War, in mine, seemed limply noble. His nods to the nurses were benign, his greeting to Francie more appreciative.

"Our neuropsychiatric section is a locked ward, of course," said our C.O. "Are you ready, gentlemen?"

"Always ready," said the Assistant Under Secretary of War, "although that resembles the motto of a rival service."

"Semper fidelis!" exclaimed General Fessel, and everyone laughed heartily.

Captain Newman led them to the big iron door. Inside, Wardmaster Kopp saluted and reached for his key. Consternation oozed across his features. There was no key on the clip attached to his belt.

"Key!" Captain Newman whispered.

Consternation changed to horror as Sergeant Kopp, with masterly surreption, indicated the fatal absence.

Francie closed her eyes.

Captain Newman cleared his throat. "Wardmaster," he said loudly, "you may now go and fetch the key." I must say that I admired Captain Newman at that moment, for he acted as if no key near the entrance was a feature of Ward 7's security precautions. "While we wait, gentlemen," he announced, "some— er—facts may serve to increase the interest of your visit. Ward Seven was opened, with only four patients, on . . ."

Sergeant Kopp was hustling down the aisle, moaning, *"Key!* Come on, fellas. *Who's got the key?"*

"Today, our patients come from every theater of war. . . ." Captain Newman dilated loudly.

"Key . . . *key* . . ." I could hear Arkie plead.

"Removal from combat is itself a form of therapy. . . ."

I could swear that the Assistant Under Secretary of War was watching Sergeant Kopp, rather than listening to Captain Newman, with the utmost fascination.

". . . in some fifteen per cent of our cases Sodium Pentothal . . ."

General Armstrong was turning choleric. Colonel Pyser was studying Newman like an evil cat about to swallow a goldfish.

Francie groaned demurely. Newman orated on, in a glaze.

"No ice cream!" I heard Arkie mutter hoarsely. "No pie, no butterscotch, no malts—"

In Bed 19 Corporal Rusty Scofield, who had not uttered a word for three weeks, got out of bed with dignity (he loved butterscotch), reached under his pillow, and marched to the barred portal. He unlocked the door, marched back to his bed, and did not speak for three weeks more.

"One of your assistants?" asked the Assistant Under Secretary of War politely.

"No, sir," said Captain Newman. "One of my patients."

"Pilot?"

"No, sir. Gunner."

"Combat?"

"Thirty missions."

"Fine chap."

"Very fine, sir."

The official party entered.

The inspection of Ward 7 passed without further incident, and certainly achieved its high purpose: our visitors felt nobler for having done their duty, and our patients felt better when they departed.

Only at the end, as the battalions outside were heard tramping to the parade ground in massive unison, did anything noteworthy happen. The Assistant Under Secretary of War for Air was shaking Captain Newman's hand, precedent to formal commendation and departure, when a plaintive "Baaa" bleated through the air. This "Baaa" was followed by another "Baaa," then another, as an unseen Hammerhead herded the sheep back into the yard, returned from their orgy of freedom.

Colonel Pyser's eyes darted to Brigadier General Armstrong, who glanced uneasily at the Assistant Under Secretary, who cast his compassionate orbs on Captain Newman. "Good-by, Captain," he sighed. "Thank you for a most instructive visit, and for the earlier—uh—dramatization of Psalm Twenty-three."

The Twenty-third Psalm, as anyone knows, begins: "The Lord is my shepherd."

XV
MR. FUTURE

It was raining, *mirabile dictu,* raining. For three days the Colfax *Courier* had no headline problems. Ten miles from our installation a rancher and his wife were drowned—drowned on the desert, when a flash flood roared down a bone-dry *arroyo* to sweep their car into the terrible inundation.

The rain began with a cloudburst, so sudden and so violent that no one thought it could last. But it lasted. It lasted and it fattened and it turned into tropical torrents. Rain sluiced down our tin roofs, raced across the sandy stretches of the post, hammered on a thousand coffee-colored puddles between the gates and the flying field, deserted and silent now. Across our grounds, only apparitions in ponchos scurried. In our barracks, the GIs played nonstop poker, shot craps, communed with sleep. In the B.O.Q., the officers fretted and wrote letters and read the same magazines three times a day. In our ready rooms, the pilots grumbled over the skull sessions that replaced aerial maneuvers. In the Officers' Club, the drinking began much sooner and ended much later. And mostly, and above all, from every barrack, morning and afternoon, the snores of *ennui* ascended.

But I loved that rain, that blessed armistice with the blinding sun. The earth dared breathe again and gave us sweetness in re-

ward: the fragrance of wet sagebrush, ironwood, palo verde. The
mesquite danced with droplet bells and the Spring Deer Horn
Cactus wore filigreed liquid jewels. The entire baked, seared
land was magically transformed: grays enveloped the world now,
and against their unaccustomed monochrome all the strident
colors of the desert went muted. It was as if a Van Gogh had
been repainted by Corot, or Matisse softened by a Chinese hand.

It was oddly fitting, I think, that out of that sovereign rain
the man with the red beard first appeared.

It was quite early, I remember. I had hung up my poncho and
shaken the water off the plastic cover of my cap. I was standing
at the window, my back to the door, gazing with contentment
into the falling sea.

I did not hear the door open behind me. I heard nothing, indeed, until a musical voice murmured, "You may terminate your
reverie, Lieutenant."

I jumped.

Leaning against the door, which he had closed noiselessly behind him, was a figure who might have stepped out of Dostoev-
sky: a tall man with a red beard, a shock of red hair, baby-blue
eyes, a thin blade of a nose. On the left breast of his maroon
bathrobe a colonel's eagle was pinned. He looked about fifty-five.
"Sharp now, lad. Sharp!" He waved a swagger stick and seated
himself with a flourish that swirled the bathrobe around himself
tightly, poking the stick into one of the folds to carry it across
the arm of the chair. "You may be seated." Those blue eyes—
very bright, mocking, vaguely maniacal—gleamed with pierc-
ing clarity. "Proceed to interview me, in the customary fashion,
antecedent to my admission into your woebegone ward. Close
your *mouth*, Lieutenant! I am quite aware that you can breathe.
You resemble an idiot."

I opened a drawer nervously and rummaged around for an
admission form, stalling for time, saying, "Quite a rain we're having, Colonel."

His eyebrows formed inverted "Vs." "Colonel? Colonel? I see no colonel in this dreary chamber. What evidence warrants your absurd attribution of rank?"

"The eagle, sir," I said in astonishment. "On your robe."

"Correction!" he barked. "There is *an* eagle on *a* bathrobe."

"Oh. Isn't it your eagle?"

"No."

"Nor your bathrobe?"

"No!"

I cleared my throat. "Sir, would you mind telling me—"

"*De*lighted!" He threw his head back and exploded in laughter. "One encounters similar contretemps with the cluttering, clamorous clods in the unmedical corps upstairs. Oh, that the Army of the United States should come to this! Selective service, inductees! I wrote an exposé of the farce for the Chief of Staff, an old friend. It upset him deeply. But of course it was too late. *Millions* of incompetents had already contaminated our ranks. Well, I did my duty, that I did. No man can aver that Mr. Future did not his duty do."

"Is that your—name, Colonel?"

He jerked his head from side to side owlishly. "You are clearly hallucinating." He pointed that blade of a nose at the ceiling and shook with glee. "Brav*o*, Mr. Future, brav*o!*"

I found myself hoping that someone would enter the room. I started to excuse myself, to step across the hall, but remembered that Captain Newman and Stacy Mathieson were at Lubbock Field for a two-day conference. Captain Jarvis would be starting on morning rounds. My hand wandered to the phone. The man with the red beard leaned forward. "I detest stupidity," he murmured. "There is no need to seek reinforcement. Fear not; I am unhomicidal."

I remembered something Captain Newman had said a long time ago: "Never show you are afraid of a patient. Even a violent one. Your fear is more dangerous than his hostility. He wants the reassurance that you are not frightened by that in himself which frightens himself and threatens to overwhelm him." I arranged the admission form in front of me. "May I ask how you got here?" I tried to sound brisk.

"You may ask; I may not answer. Remove the ambiguity, sir."

"Who—sent you here?"

"A malignant M.D. upstairs, one Captain Robling. He is perbophoric."

"I beg your pardon."

He winked slyly. "You do not understand the word?"

"No, sir."

"Neither did that idiot Robling. He would not know how to track a hippopotamus through the snow!"

"Did he give you permission—"

"He? Give? Me?" The desk shook under the blow of his fist. "It is *I*, sir, who gives permission. I informed Dr. Rhubarb of my destination. Get on with your *questions,* man."

I poised my pen. "Name, please."

"Mr. Future."

I cleared my throat. "First name?"

"Objection! Immaterial and irrelevant. Put down any name you wish. Yes. Any-name Future. Next."

"Date of birth?"

He leaned forward. "The day he left."

"Who's he?"

"A friend," he whispered, "a very close and special friend. Mr. Past. Would you like to know about him, where he went, why he will never return?"

I leaned back in my chair. "All right."

"Ah . . . You restore yourself in my good graces. Mr. Past is gone, sir, far from these primitive, puerile purlieus. You have observed, I trust, my skill in alliteration. Where is Mr. Past? I gave him my word, as an officer and a gentleman, never to reveal his whereabouts. Lips sealed. Ozymandias." He winked again.

"Ergo. Your hospital has me, Mr. Future, about whom they know nothing; but in their files rests a dossier on Mr. Past, who is nowhere to be found. One patient with no case history; one case history, but no patient. What a paradox! What a triumph! . . . At this point you should inquire about my age."

"How old are you?"

"How gullible you are. . . . Why must I be surrounded by dolts—dupes, drones, depressive dumbbells? I am excellent on 'd's today. Decidedly. There's another." He put both hands out in supplication. "Do not be deceived by my façade. I have been diagnosed as psychotic: paranoid-schizophrenic. I do not mind. I do not *agree,* mind you, but mind I do not, though I detest psychiatric jargon. *I* put it to you simply: I am sick, sir. Sick of the Army to which I gave my life and my brilliance; sick of this panatropical pesthole; sick of being questioned, probed, doused, spied on; sick of the disgusting charlatans who masquerade as physicians—at least two of them upstairs are latent homosexuals; be on guard, lad, on guard. I am also sick of you!" He reached across the desk, picked up the admission form, tore the page down the center, turned the parts, tore them across and, rising, holding his arm out high above his head, let the fragments flutter down from his hand in a paper snowfall. "Now, sir, you have my permission to escort me to Ward Seven."

"But I can't—Captain Jarvis will have to authorize it."

"He will," whispered Mr. Future, "he will. Swiftly, swiftly, for I feel the fearful furies closing in." He drew himself up to his full height and lifted the swagger stick, signaling me to follow him. As he strode out, even in that drab and shapeless robe, he looked majestic.

Captain Jarvis, after a sardonic lecture from Mr. Future on dementia praecox ("which, sir, I warn thee, may at any moment turn into three-dimensional postcox"), assigned Mr. Future to Room E.

An hour later, Jackson Laibowitz slouched into my office to growl: "It's some democratic-type army that puts the privates in public and the officers in private."

The case history I got from the files of Main identified Mr. Future as Colonel Norval Algate Bliss. A professional soldier for almost thirty years, he had seen service under Pershing in Mexico and France, and had completed tours of duty in the Philippines, the Canal Zone, Guam. After Pearl Harbor, he had been an executive officer in the Fourth Interceptor Command, San Francisco. He flew to Australia on a liaison mission in the spring of 1943.

In Port Moresby, New Guinea, his aide found him in his quarters one morning, entirely nude, cursing and ripping the sheets to shreds. In the base hospital, said the psychiatrist's report, he developed a peculiar facial tic and "onomatomania," dwelling on certain words compulsively, as if they contained hidden meanings or were endowed with magical powers. He often invented words, words entirely without meaning. During a hurricane he had become homicidal, almost choking an attendant to death. He was put in a strait jacket. "E.C.T." was initialed under "Treatment." After six sessions of electroshock in a general hospital, he was shipped back to the States. . . .

The ward was proud to have a full colonel in Room E—at least Arkie Kopp was proud of it: it added luster to his responsibilities. Laibowitz's favor was not won so lightly; he regarded "the Moses with the red beard" as a telling example of the well-known dictum (well known only to him, it turned out) that the regular Army turns out more psychos than what he called "the civilian lifeblood." Gavoni was overawed by Mr. Future and offered him no salami. Hammerhead Lawrence hated him.

When Captain Newman returned from Lubbock he made me repeat every word I could remember from that extraordinary first interview with Mr. Future. He did not seem impressed by the *bizarreries* which had made so vivid an impression on me.

He asked me whether Mr. Future had referred to himself in the first person or the third person, if he had perspired much, if he showed spasmodic tremors. Then he brooded and paced back and forth. "Did he identify the two doctors upstairs—the ones he called queer?"

"No. He didn't, by the way, say they *were* queer; he called them 'latent homosexuals.' "

"I know. Overt homosexuals are rare among M.D.s."

"Why is that?" I asked.

He grinned. "Someday I'll try to find out if that's really so."

Captain Newman went into the ward, where he got Mr. Future's chart from Francie. "How's he doing?"

"Don't ask me, Joe. He avoids me like the plague."

"Does he sleep much?"

"Not a wink during the day—and from what Lieutenant Blodgett tells me, he stays up most of the night, too: talking, arguing, making speeches—to no one."

"No one?" Newman echoed. "Maybe no one you can see . . ."

"I'm just as glad," said Francie. She gave him a curious glance, but he didn't seem to notice it.

"Let's talk to Arkie," he said absently.

Sergeant Kopp said, "Doc, we'll have to watch out for him. He *hates* Hammerhead."

"What do you mean?"

"Hammerhead was doing the old man's room this morning, real nice, like he likes to. The Colonel watched him, then grabbed a pillow and began beating him on the head. Laibowitz and me had to jump him."

"What had Lawrence done?" asked Newman.

"*Nothing.* I asked him what did Hammerhead do? He gave me a hundred-proof octane glare and yelled, 'It's in his eyes! Can't you see what's in that little swine's eyes?' "

Captain Newman frowned. He entered Room E. Mr. Future was propped up in bed, the sheet drawn up under his beard, a book in his hands. "I granted no appointment for this hour!" he snapped. "Dismissed!"

"'Dismissed'? Before I've even come in?" Newman sighed elaborately. "That's not very friendly, is it? I'm Captain Newman."

The book lowered in Mr. Future's hands. "*Ahhh* . . . the perceptive one of whom I hear the baboons babble brightly. At last. Come in, sir, *do* come in." He waved regally. "Forgive the antiseptic aroma and the dreariness of the décor. Neither, of course, did I choose. . . ." His crystal eyes were dancing. "Making observations on the patient, eh, Captain? You should learn to control your expressions. I await your first question with the keenest anticipation."

"How do you feel?" asked Newman.

Mr. Future winced. "Tsk, tsk! Standard opening. You disappoint me. Have you no imagination?"

"I'm holding it in reserve. You've got enough for both of us."

"Clever, clever . . . Consider: First, you bestow a compliment on the patient, to establish rapport; then you attempt a tacit alliance—with that oh-so-innocuous 'both of us.' A lesser man than I would walk into your trap." He indicated the wicker chair. "Do sit down, Captain Boo-man, *do* sit down."

"Thank you, Colonel," said Newman wryly.

"Colonel? Colonel?" The red head bobbed from side to side. "Where?"

"What do you prefer I call you?"

"It is a matter of fact, not preference!" he glared. "The name is Future, not Colonel."

"And mine is not Boo-man."

"Excellent, Captain, *ex*cellent! I underestimated you. But you are beset and beleaguered by blockheads—brainless, benighted blockheads. I am in a mood that bursts with 'b's this morning."

"Brilliant!" Captain Newman got his cigarettes and held the package out.

Mr. Future's eyes gleamed as he murmured, "Are you mad, sir?"

"Not at the moment."

"Offering a cigarette—in a psychiatric ward? Matches, sir! Damnably dangerous in the hands of demented men."

Newman nodded. "I was going to light it for you."

"You were not going to let me hold the matches?"

"Certainly not."

"Bravo! I commend your candor. I believe I shall like you."

"That shouldn't be hard; I'm a likable type."

Mr. Future grinned. "I believe we shall understand one another."

"You'll understand me, all right," said Newman. "I'm not so sure that you want me to understand you."

"Then we understand each other already!" The head went back; a laugh boomed out; the red beard shook. "Capital, sir! You are shrewd in appraising my resistance, and canny in trying to effect a transference. My insight takes you by surprise, eh? You *must* learn to control your expressions. I happen to be a student of psychiatry, sir. By necessity, not inclination. It is child's play for me to use your silly mumbo-jumbo. Oh, what a pity Mr. Past is not here! He would be amused by you and enchanted with me. Enchanted, sir, beguiled. No, I am tired of 'b's; they contain 'boring' and 'banal.' I shall favor 'e's for the remainder of our talk. Elementary, my un-dear Watson! I feel euphoric."

Captain Newman looked at his watch ostentatiously. "We have thirty minutes before my next patient. You can use it up trying to show me how skillfully you play with words, how cleverly you produce verbal smoke screens—and waste my time and yours; or you can lower your guard a couple of notches and tell me a few things which might—just possibly—help me alleviate some of your misery."

"Misery, sir? Mr. Future? Bah! You are considerably more miserable than I!"

Newman shook his head. "I'm only impatient. You—" He stopped.

"Yes? Go on, go *on*." Mr. Future leaned forward eagerly.

"Nothing."

"You must be fair, sir! You are deliberately inciting me. It is *I* who am impatient, not you. What were you going to say? I have certain rights; I insist upon them. Complete your thought!"

"You," said Captain Newman, "are afraid."

Hate flared up in the blue eyes; then they widened in a parody of dismay. "Afraid? Bless my soul, O penetrating pharmacist of the psyche: of what?"

"Of what you may reveal."

"Careful!" Mr. Future whispered. "Do not overplay your hand."

Captain Newman groaned. "Can't you stop being clever? This isn't a fencing match. We're not trying to score points, or win—"

"But you are!" cried Mr. Future. "You *are* trying to win."

"What?"

"My confidence!" The head shot back; the whole body shook with glee.

"Hooray. Hooray for Mr. Future," said Newman. "How cunning he is. If it's flattery you want, here's a bushelful. You are an extremely intelligent man. You are erudite. You have an excellent brain and a remarkable sense of words. Now—can we go on from there?"

Mr. Future was beaming, nodding, chuckling into his beard, stroking his mustache in vast self-satisfaction.

Captain Newman sighed. "But what a pity that such intelligence, such energy and skill should be wasted on such trivial gestures. For what? To impress an Air Force psychiatrist you hardly know, in an obscure Army hospital—"

"You flatter yourself!" laughed Mr. Future. "I am not trying to impress *you!*"

"No? Then you must be trying to impress him."

Mr. Future smiled slyly.

Newman shrugged. "How strange."

"Eh? Why?"

"Why should one have to try so hard to impress one's dearest friend, the one who really understands you—"

Mr. Future's features went dark. "Do not meddle, sir! You will never understand certain things!"

"I think I understand; but I don't agree."

"That which exists between Mr. Past and Mr. Future is sacred! You want to destroy it!"

"Change it," said Newman.

Mr. Future licked his lips. "How?"

"I want to put Mr. Past where he belongs, in the past. And all your ingenuity and pyrotechnics—do they really change anything? Do they really help you? You're so miserable, Mr. Future, so very miserable. Running, twisting, turning, fleeing—from what? You, and Mr. Past, you're both men, aren't you? You've constructed it that way. So you can live, in secret, with another man—"

"Goddam your eyes!" Mr. Future shouted. "God shrivel your heart and consume your monstrous brain. You are vile, vile, vicious and contemptible. I scorn your solicitude!"

Captain Newman nodded. "Most people talk in order to express themselves. But you—" He stopped.

"Continue," said Mr. Future. "Go on. Finish your thought! How do *I* talk?"

"You," said Captain Newman, "talk to conceal yourself."

Mr. Future's eyes burned. He spat on the floor. "Nor will you penetrate the place where Mr. Past hides. Never!"

"Maybe you're right." Newman tapped a cigarette on the back of his hand and struck a match, observing how greedily the man in bed followed the flame as it came up to light the cigarette.

"One day," Mr. Future whispered, "I will show you what I can do with fire. Ectomorphic ectonesia. The triumph of spirit over matter . . . But we digress, sir. You were asking me to describe Mr. Past."

"I was not," said Newman.

"How direct you are."

"You *want* me to ask you."

"Excellent, Captain! You are not one to be ambushed." Mr. Future grinned. "Ask me."

Newman shrugged. "Would you care to describe Mr. Past?"

"I care very much. But to care is not to comply."

"Can you describe him?"

"I can, but shall not. . . . Do not be discouraged."

"How old is he?"

"That's better. He is as old as Mr. Future."

"How tall?"

"As tall, too."

"What does he do?"

"Be more specific."

"Does he have a profession?"

"He does not practice what he professes," Mr. Future chortled.

"It's your time you're wasting."

"It is not wasted. I wish to frustrate you."

"Congratulations. I am now frustrated."

"You delight me."

Captain Newman pointed to his watch. "Twenty-two minutes left. Use them or fritter them away."

"You are at my disposal," smiled Mr. Future.

"But not at your mercy."

"Oh, fudge. Return to Mr. Past."

"Does he wear a beard, too?"

"No! Are you not perceptive, sir? Beards bespeak bravado, and bravado is beneath—but you have bedeviled me back to the 'b's, blast you, and soon I shall be angry with you."

"You already are." Captain Newman stubbed the cigarette out on his heel and got up. "Well . . ."

"Wait! I am enjoying your visit."

"I don't doubt it. But I didn't come here for the purpose of providing a patronizing patient with a plethora of private pleasure."

Mr. Future laughed uproariously. "How shrewd of you. Seven 'p's! Yes, you are swift and see through many disguises; but I am swifter. I make the case insoluble, sir; confess it! For Mr. Future has no past and Mr. Past has no future!" He threw his head back and roared, "Ho, ho, ho, sir, ho, ho, ho! Ha, ha, ha, sir, ha, ha, ha! I shall answer but one more question."

"I have nothing more to ask you today." Captain Newman started for the door.

"But you *must!*" cried Mr. Future. "Wait! That is not fair! I still have twenty minutes!"

"I'll see you tomorrow."

Mr. Future leaped out of bed. "Goddam you!" He hurled himself between Newman and the door. "You will stay!" He raised his fists over Newman's head. "Go back! Sit down before I—"

"Behave yourself!" said Newman sharply. "You won't do that, Mr. Future. You don't want to be put in restraint, do you? And I don't want to commit you, not yet. *I'm* a friend of Mr. Past's, too. . . . Now, put your arms down. Go back to bed. Tomorrow, we'll talk. . . ."

Mr. Future lowered his arms slowly, blinking, chastened and bewildered. "Oh, dear. Oh, dear . . ." Then he glanced at Captain Newman covertly, winking. "That orderly, Lawrence. Do transfer him, sir, lest I be compelled to strangle him with my bare hands."

When Captain Newman finished his rounds the next day, he studied Mr. Future's chart for a long time. Mr. Future had refused to swallow any pills. He had refused medication. He had refused sedation. He had sat up in bed, in the dark, all night long, carrying on an animated conversation with Mr. Past.

Newman entered Room E. Mr. Future was sprawled out on the bed, wearing his khaki shirt and tie and the pants of his pajamas. *"Bon jour, Capitaine,"* he called brightly. "Also *Guten Tag, Bon giorno,* and *God morgen,* which is Swedish. I speak four languages fluently. Well, no matter; the correlation between languages and intelligence is negative. Any idiot can learn Chinese —if he is a Chinaman. Won't you be seated?"

"Merci."

Mr. Future laughed. "You delight me. Oh, I do hope you survive."

"Survive what?"

"Me."

Captain Newman smiled. "I suppose you know that you are somewhat paranoid?"

"Oh, yes."

"Do you know what that means?"

"Bah! Your patron saint, Sigismundus Freud, has taught you, no doubt, that in all paranoia there is a homosexual base."

"Do you agree?"

Mr. Future regarded him slyly. "The dismal doctor was projecting, was he not? All seems jaundiced to the jaundiced eye."

"I see that you won't take any of the pills I prescribed for you."

"I do not need to sleep! I have surmounted the call to oblivion."

Again, as on the preceding day, Captain Newman offered him a cigarette and this time, his eyes gleaming, Mr. Future took it. Captain Newman struck a match. Mr. Future lighted his cigarette, then gently removed the match from Newman's hand. He did not blow out the match. He did not even look at it. The flame began to burn his fingers, but Mr. Future made not the slightest response or grimace or movement.

The two men eyed each other in silence.

The smell of burning flesh made Mr. Future cock his head to one side with an expression of amusement.

Captain Newman pointed to the match.

Mr. Future grinned.

Newman leaned over, blew the match out and removed it from between Mr. Future's fingers. "What am I supposed to do now? Hail you as prophet? Start a new religion?"

"Bah! You do not grasp the point of my demonstration."

"You showed me the triumph of mind over matter."

"And you think me mad. Do you not?"

"Well, you certainly *act* mad," Newman replied.

"And am I not?"

"What do you think?"

Mr. Future punched his pillow in exasperation. "A cheap device! You evade the point. I asked what *you* think, sir. Am I not entitled to direct response? I repeat: Is Mr. Future mad or is he not mad?"

"Mr. Future," said Newman, "is an invention."

Mr. Future smiled. "Is he incurable?"

"I'm trying to decide."

The red beard waggled. "At least you are honest. Not like the others. They persecuted me."

"Who are 'they'?"

"The doctors."

"Oh, come now. Doctors don't go around persecuting patients."

Mr. Future grinned. "Your equanimity does not deceive me, sir. You are simply maintaining professional detachment. Oh, you do it quite well, that I grant you. Yet someone *is* persecuting me!"

"I agree."

The eyes filled with astonishment. "Yes? Then you see it? Who?" Mr. Future whispered. "Who is persecuting me?"

"You."

"No!"

"Part of you is persecuting the rest."

"No. Oh, no." Suddenly tears welled into the pale blue eyes. "Oh, if Mr. Past were only here. If you could but know him."

"But he *is* here," said Captain Newman.

"Where? Look—search—examine every nook and cranny of these ghastly quarters! Where can anyone conceivably find Mr. Past?"

Newman pointed at Mr. Future without a word.

"You lie, sir!" Mr. Future shouted. "Mr. Past is gone—far from here. I sent him away."

"Not entirely. You can use the past, learn from it, build on it. You can reshape it, even surmount it. But you can't abolish it, not even you; and even with the most powerful will in the world, you can't will it away."

"Mr. Future can," whispered the man with the red beard. "Mr. Future did."

"And is this where you wanted to end? In a mental ward?"

"It was not I who consigned Mr. Future here!"

"This is where men end who split themselves in two."

Mr. Future was silent for a moment, lost, for the first time since he had come to Ward 7, in sadness. "Shall I tell you a story, Captain? It was years ago. I was on extended leave, in mufti, which permitted me to indulge my fancy and grow this hirsute badge. I was walking through a long tunnel in Central Park, one cold winter day, and as I emerged, the sun struck my hair, my beard. A little lad, perhaps five, perhaps six, saw me, astonished, open-mouthed, his eyes like china saucers. 'Santa Claus!' he cried. 'Are you Santa Claus? Are you?' I hesitated not one moment, sir, and bowed: 'That, son, is who I am.' The lad caught his breath: 'But you are so *tall;* you are so big and *tall*. How will you ever come down my tiny chimney?' The question gave me but slight pause. 'Watch,' I said, and lighted a cigarette and blew out a cloud of smoke. 'This smoke, son, is like the smoke in your chimney. Watch.' I puffed and puffed and blew out smoke. 'See? The smoke gets larger and larger, but the cigarette gets smaller and smaller. And that's what I do, too, on Christmas Eve. Part of me turns into smoke, so I can come

down your chimney.' . . . Then I heard someone cry out—and
she came along. Slut. Nurse. Slut. Like all the rest. She clutched
that little golden lad, and tore him away, jabbering, 'Naughty!
Bad, bad boy. Talking to that filthy, crazy man!'" Mr. Future's
head dropped to one side, and though he made no sound, no
sound at all, the tears gushed down his cheeks.

"*'Reach'* him? How the hell can I? How does anyone 'reach' a
psychotic?" Captain Newman looked tired that staff meeting; his
voice had that irascible edge I had come to recognize, the edge
of discontent—with a colleague, a patient, above all, with himself.

"What about trying Pentothal?" asked Captain Jarvis.

"Pentothal breaks down the defenses. And that's the one thing
Mr. Future doesn't need. He needs all the defenses he's got—
and more. He's afraid to lower his defenses, even for a moment.
Why else his inability to tolerate silence? Why his fantastic bar-
rage of words, his obsession with letters, alliteration, puns? He
has to obliterate an internal threat, drown it in symbols, suffocate it with words. He has to escape from the terrible tempta-
tion to perversity by compulsive preoccupations—with verbal
games, puzzles, rituals. He's afraid to listen. He's afraid to relax.
He's afraid to reverie, to sleep, even to be quiet. To be quiet is
to be passive, too. To be passive spells danger; in his mind, it
invites attack. Remember his rage about Private Lawrence. . . .
He even has anxieties about taking sedation. He'd have more violent fears of a hypodermic needle. That can represent an invasion
of the body. . . . No, Bill, to accept flak-juice means to surrender control. And every move he makes shows us that he is
overorganized around that one threat. He must keep control. By
the way, has he had any surgery?"

"He had a lot of dental work upstairs," said Francie. "His
teeth were in pretty bad shape when he got here."

Captain Newman grunted. "Bill, suppose you find out what
happened."

At our next staff meeting, Captain Jarvis reported, rather sheepishly, that when Mr. Future had seen the hypodermic needle in the dentist's hand he had gone wild. It had taken three men to pin him into the chair. Then he sat through hours of drilling for a week in a row, without any anesthesia, not even Novocain, his arms folded defiantly.

One day Captain Newman asked me to come to Room E with him. Mr. Future was standing before the window, staring out. His back to us, he exclaimed, without turning: "Halt! It is useless to try to catch me unawares. I have exceptionally acute hearing. There are two of you: Captain Know-it-all and Lieutenant Bewildered. I have made a lifelong study of footsteps." He threw his head back, turned to face us, and laughed. "Gentlemen, your questifications. Bequest them, I beseech you. I always burst with 'b's before breakfast."

Captain Newman did an odd thing. He sank into the wicker chair and gazed at Mr. Future steadily, saying not a word. Mr. Future cocked his head to one side. Newman did not move. Mr. Future frowned. The moments passed. Mr. Future shot me a glare of suspicion, then glanced back to Newman. He had not stirred. I think he wanted to see what Mr. Future would do if offered no comment, no cue, no foil, no words to turn against their user, no distractions to seize upon as respite from an insupportable self. As the silence spun itself out, I saw a bead of sweat form on Mr. Future's brow; he put on a smile, but it was a ghastly grimace and I could see it was an effort; his eyes were anxious. Suddenly a sly, sidelong expression formed on his features; recognition tried to allay anxiety as the self mobilized itself against betrayal. "Careful, Captain," he murmured.

Newman waited.

"Who is playing games now?" cried Mr. Future.

Newman did not stir.

Mr. Future shouted, "You, goddam you! You think you're smart because you make the rules, don't you? It's you who's mad.

You!" He towered over Newman's chair and his hand slashed through the air, back and forth, as if wielding an ax, a few inches from Newman's head. He began to sob, like a child in a temper tantrum, enraged and thwarted, then sank to the bed and buried his face in his hands. "You bastard," he cried hoarsely. "You dirty, scheming, clever bastard."

At last Captain Newman said, "How do you feel now?"

"You know how I feel. You won't meet Mr. Past this way. Never." He glanced up. "You know, I presume, that Mr. Past once floated for thirty-seven hours in a sea of burning muck before they rescued him."

"When was that?"

"After a certain troopship was torpedoed. I will also tell you this: He can do anything Jesus did."

"Can you?"

"You mean, 'Can *he*'?" rasped Mr. Future.

"No, Mr. Future, I mean 'you.' "

Mr. Future grinned. "I, sir? Why, at this very moment am not I, like our blessed Saviour, being crucified—between two thieves?"

This is a copy of the report Captain Newman submitted that afternoon:

> TO: *Lt. Colonel Michael Larrabee,*
> *Commanding Officer, Colfax A.A.A.F.B. Hospital*
>
> FROM: *Josiah J. Newman, Capt., M.C.*
> *Ser. #0-1-785-902*

In re: Norval Algate Bliss, Colonel, U.S.A. (0-169-621)

(1) The undersigned requests the summoning of a Retirement Board meeting to authorize a medical discharge for the patient named above.

(2) The patient is a 52-year-old male in an acute psychotic phase of schizophrenia, paranoid type. He exhibits pronounced homicidal drives.

(3) The patient has received maximum hospital benefits and requires custodial care.

(4) The patient should be committed to a veterans' hospital.

(5) Insulin-coma therapy, under competent supervision, may be indicated—in more doses than attempted in previous E.C.T. (see attached).

Diagnosis: Schizophrenia, paranoid type; acute, severe.

L.O.D.:   No.   E.P.T.S.

Prognosis: Requires prolonged hospitalization.

(signed) JOSIAH J. NEWMAN

Mr. Future's appearance before the Retirement Board was brief but memorable. He strode into the room like an emperor, head high, carriage superb, left hand on hip. He had brushed his beard carefully. A braided *fourragère* encircled the upper left sleeve of his dress jacket. On his breast were pinned four theater-of-war ribbons, three battle decorations, an oak leaf with palms, a rosette on a bar (from a foreign government). He had demanded the return of his swagger stick, which, he insisted, he had a right to carry, but Captain Newman had talked him out of it.

Mr. Future nodded to me, and with a slightly superior air bowed to the officers behind the green table.

Colonel Pyser, presiding, tapped his gavel on its wooden base. "This board is now in session. . . . Colonel Bliss, will you please state your name, rank and serial number?"

Mr. Future gazed at Colonel Pyser stonily.

"Colonel . . . would you please identify yourself?"

Captain Newman rose and said gently, "Mr. Future . . ."

"*D*elighted! Alonzo Archimedes Future, United States Army, World Victory II. Expert on tactics, tautology, logistics, semantics."

Colonel Pyser's brow furrowed. Mayor Wyzanski coughed. Major Durant examined his pencil.

"The patient's name is Bliss, Norval Algate. Colonel. Serial number—" Newman read it off.

"Proceed with the medical report," said Colonel Pyser.

Captain Newman rose. He gave a résumé of Colonel Bliss' medical history since the episode at Port Moresby. He read passages from a case folder. To all of this, Mr. Future listened with the keenest interest, his head moving in birdlike movements to indicate approval. Captain Newman said, "I should now like to question the patient before you, gentlemen."

"Proceed."

Captain Newman turned to face Mr. Future, who donned an expression of mock gravity. "Mr. Future, I think you understand the nature of this hearing, and its purpose?"

"I understand your purpose." The bearded figure smiled. "You do not understand mine."

"I want to ask you some questions."

"Permission granted. Caveat: the right not to answer is reserved."

"Of course."

"*Pro*ceed."

"Mr. Future, how do you feel these days?"

"*Feel*, sir?" Mr. Future beamed. "My mood may be described, in technical jargon, as hypomanic." He winked at Colonel Pyser. "You, sir, realize I am here through a gigantic hoax. It is Mr. Past you seek, of course. He spurns your invitation and invites your inquisition. These proceedings are patently illegal—"

"One moment," Colonel Pyser interrupted. "What do you mean, you're here through a hoax?"

"The hoax is mine," smiled Mr. Future, "on you."

Colonel Pyser cleared his throat. "We will dispense with sarcasm. You mention a Mr. 'Past'? To whom were you referring?"

"To Mr. Past, you silly ass."

"Mr. Future—" Newman cut in quickly (only Colonel Bliss' rank spared him Pyser's reprimand)—"would you tell these officers a little about Mr. Past?"

"I will not."

"It is important that they know."

"It is important that they be befuddled!"

"Was Mr. Past's legal name—formerly, that is—Norval Algate Bliss?"

Mr. Future braced his shoulders and stared straight ahead.

"Was Mr. Past a patient in this hospital?" asked Newman.

Mr. Future snickered.

"Are you not taking Mr. Past's place because he—'left' here?"

No answer.

Colonel Pyser wrote a note and passed it to Major Wyzanski.

"Mr. Future," said Captain Newman, "I have a medical history on Colonel Bliss in my hands. You have often told me that that history refers not to you, but to Mr. Past. Isn't that so?"

Mr. Future nodded solemnly.

"And you have often told me that we have no data on Mr. Future. . . ."

"Precisely," Mr. Future smiled.

Captain Newman placed the folder on the table. "Do you think you are mentally ill, Mr. Future?"

Mr. Future cocked his head to one side. " 'Do you think you are mentally ill, Mr. Future?' Do you think *you* are mentally ill, Dr. Boo-man?" It was extraordinary how he mimicked Newman's voice and inflection. He turned to address his peers. "You are losing the war, gentlemen. Mark these words. You are pawns in a putrescent conspiracy, persecuting professional soldiers, driving them from the ranks, breaking will and reason on the rack!" He raised his hands in a travesty of supplication. "More need not be said. Duty has been done."

"You think these officers are persecuting you?" asked Captain Newman.

"Of course."

"Why?"

"Because I am intelligent and they are ignorant. Because I know what they fear and do not fear what they know."

"Is anyone else persecuting you, Mr. Future?"

"All the psycho-pseudo-psychiatrists—excluding you. You merely wish to trap me."

"How do you think I wish to trap you?"

Mr. Future pointed that thin blade of a nose toward the ceiling and laughed. "Trap, trap, clap-trap."

"Do you have any physical complaints?" asked Newman.

"None."

"Is your appetite good?"

"Too good for the culinary crimes committed in these kitchens!"

"Do you suffer from any diseases you know of?"

"I suffer fools and frauds you know not of."

"Do you feel any pains?"

"Only in the ears—from the prattle of idiots."

"How do you sleep?"

"Miserably."

At this point, Colonel Pyser, who had been listening with amazement and discomfort, suddenly leaped forward, glad, I suppose, to intervene. "You say that you sleep miserably? Why?"

"How would *you* sleep, Colonel Numbskull, in a room full of howling maniacs?"

Colonel Pyser's cheeks went livid. "You will refrain from—"

"I will quote you Samuel Johnson!"

Pyser's gavel came down sharply. "You will respect the dignity of this board—"

"I will quote the learned doctor!" shouted Mr. Future. " 'Boy, let us be grave; here comes a fool!' " He wheeled on Captain Newman. "Why was I exposed to this tristomic farce? That man is a fraud, sir, a *fool!*"

Colonel Pyser was rapping his gavel on the table insistently. "The hearing is concluded!"

"No!" roared Mr. Future. "Coward! Craven!"

Captain Newman stepped to Mr. Future's side. "Norval . . ." he said quietly.

"They shall not rob the worthy, nor act Ahab to the whale!" He winked at Captain Newman. "Paranoia, eh? Let them contend with that!"

Colonel Pyser signaled the MPs and strode out of the room. Mr. Future shouted scornfully after him. But all he said to the MPs who led him out was: "Lads, do not quote scripture to the heathen, for he will eat you alive."

No relatives were listed in Colonel Bliss's file—no wife, no children, no parents. The only name cited under "In case of emergency, notify . . ." was a Mrs. Leslie Orkum Cluett. The address was a small town near La Jolla, California.

It took several hours before Captain Newman's call went through. A soft, pleasantly husky woman's voice answered, "Mrs. Cluett's residence."

"May I speak to Mrs. Cluett, please?"

"And who may I say is calling, please?"

"My name is Captain Newman. I'm calling from the hospital at Colfax Army Air Force Base."

"Oh? . . . One moment, please. I'll see whether Mrs. Cluett is in." A moment later the same unmistakable voice said, "Hel-lo. This is Mrs. Cluett."

"Mrs. Cluett, I'm sorry to bother you, but I don't know whom else to call. It's about Colonel Bliss."

"Who, please?"

"Colonel Norval Bliss. Your name is given in case of emergency, and—"

"Norry? Norry Bliss—gave *my* name? Are you sure?" The mellow voice quickened, almost girlishly.

"Oh, yes. I've got his file in front of me."

"How strange. Did you say you were calling from an Army hospital?"

"Yes. Colonel Bliss is my patient."

"Are you a doctor?"

"Yes. Mrs. Cluett, are you related to Colonel Bliss in any way?" There was a moment's silence, so dead that the connection seemed to have been broken. "Hello . . . Mrs. Cluett . . . are you there?"

"Yes. I'm here."

"I was asking if you—"

"I heard you, Captain. No, Norry and I are in no way related. We were married, many years ago. It was annulled."

"Oh. I called because I hoped someone, perhaps you, might come here, to the hospital, I mean, to see him. It's not too far, and I thought that if someone he knew, a friend, someone he cared about, showed an interest in him—"

"What is wrong with him?"

Captain Newman said carefully, "He's in a psychiatric ward, Mrs. Cluett. He's going to be committed—"

"A mental ward? Norry?" The charming, husky voice rippled. "Oh, that *is* rich, really. That's too good to be true. That's certainly where he belongs."

"What did you say?"

"You heard me, Captain. I said he belongs in a lunatic asylum, and I hope he stays there! I hope you never let him out! I hope he goes through the same torture he put me through—"

"Mrs. Cluett—"

"Don't 'Mrs. Cluett' me, Captain whoever you are. You telephoned *me*, didn't you? Why that filthy swine had the gall to put *my* name down there I'll never know. If my husband were alive I'd send him to your camp—with a pistol, so he could blow that smutty brain out of Norry's head. Who are you to judge? What's your first name? St. Francis? Is that it?"

"Good-by—"

"Don't hang up. I want to know your name!"

"Josiah," he said impatiently.

"What?"

"Joe."

"Joe? Joe Newman? And you want me to rush out to a hospital and hold poor Norry's filthy hand—"

"Not any more, Mrs. Cluett—"

"I'll tell you what you can do. Just go out and dig a grave and throw Norry in, and save the taxpayers all the money you Jews and Democrats are wasting in Roosevelt's lousy war—"

Captain Newman put the phone down. His hand was shaking.

The day before they were to put Mr. Future on a train for the veterans' hospital in Canandaigua, New York, Captain Newman went to Room E. Mr. Future was seated in the wicker chair, facing the window, his arms folded rigidly, staring out at the cottonwood trees and the parade ground. It was a dank, oppressive day, the sky gray and leaden, and all the flags hung limp and spiritless. Mr. Future made no sound as Newman entered, no movement when Newman came beside him, not the slightest response when Newman greeted him. The blue eyes were fixed, hard and cold, with no light in them.

"This may be the last time I'll see you," said Captain Newman.

Mr. Future might have been a statue.

"You understand, don't you, that they're going to take you to a veterans' hospital now?"

Silence.

"I chose the one nearest to where you were born and went to school. I thought—you can be sent to another, if you want. You've got that privilege. If you'll tell me, I'll arrange it."

No response.

Captain Newman sat down on the bed. "I'm sorry, Mr. Future, I'm sorry as hell I couldn't help you. . . . More hospitalization might help you. I've recommended it. There have been some surprising recoveries in cases like yours. . . . Maybe I wasn't the right doctor for you. Maybe I didn't really understand. I couldn't get through to you, could I? But maybe another man . . . I just hope that you won't give up. You're an officer. You've had a brilliant career. You've got a lot to be proud of."

Not a muscle stirred.

Captain Newman lighted a cigarette and held it before Mr.

Future's lips. "We could have one last smoke together. . . ."

Nothing.

"Are you angry with me?"

Silence.

"Well, I want you to know that I respect you—for the fight you're putting up. . . . Yes, you are. If you weren't, if you had just surrendered to what has put you into this terrible conflict—" He paused, waiting.

No sound, no movement.

Captain Newman rose. "This is good-by, then." He felt awkward—inept and defeated. "Good luck, Colonel Norval Algate Bliss."

The arms stayed folded, the head high, the eyes frozen.

Captain Newman was halfway out of the room when he heard a whispered, "Captain . . ." Quickly, he stepped back to the chair. "Yes?"

Mr. Future did not shift that frigid pose by so much as a hair as, in a monotone, he whispered, "Tell her—I tried."

"Who?"

"The one—whose name is written."

Captain Newman forced a cheerful note into his voice: "Sure. I'll telephone her. Maybe she'll come—"

"I am now entering a state of catatonia. These are the last words that shall ever pass my lips."

"Wait! What about Mr. Past?"

There was no answer.

"Don't do this to him!" exclaimed Newman. "He's part of you. Where can he go if you leave? Where? To whom?"

A shield, glazed and impenetrable, covered those blue, blue eyes.

"Think, Norval! Mr. Past—he has *no place to go,* no place on earth, except to you. He understands you. He needs you. You need him. Together, you can be whole—"

Not even a tremor touched the lips or eyes or beard.

Mr. Future had entered the future, and would not return.

I was asleep, restlessly, tossing, vaguely aware of the heavy, stifling air, of wheels of thunder rolling across the heavens, when my ears were split by a thunderbolt. I leaped out of bed. My room, for a startling moment, seemed on fire, then blacked out, then lighted up again in a flash of lightning. I heard something crash overhead and voices cursing in the next room.

I yanked my trousers over my pajamas. There would be trouble in the ward; there always was during a storm, especially with lightning, worst of all with thunder.

I could hear windows slamming all around me. Thunder cracked out close to the barracks, and, as lightning serrated the sky, the post became a surrealistic set on some strange, forbidding stage, lighted up and blacked out in a flash.

I ran down the porch steps, cut across the corner of the parade grounds. Clouds—muddy, restless, angry—churned across the moonless firmament.

Phantoms were hurrying to the hospital, a looming presence in which patches of light were popping. I heard the agitation inside, the wails of fear, the whimpers of pain reawakened.

As I went through the swinging doors, even before I hit the ramp, I heard the screaming in Ward 7.

No one was at the iron door. Through the bars, I saw the ward in turmoil. Nurses and orderlies were hurrying from bed to bed, trying to calm the men. Some had pulled sheets over their heads, several had covered their heads with pillows. Carbo Wilkes was sprawled on the floor, face down, hands clapped over his ears. Nick Ives was running around, babbling and laughing. Nasty Nevers was standing on his bed, shaking his fist, howling about the avenging angel and cesspools of corruption.

Hammerhead let me in. His face was the color of milk.

I saw Captain Newman head for Room E, where Laibowitz

was pounding on the door. When I got to them, Laibowitz was saying, "He's got the goddam bed jammed against the door or something!"

Captain Newman motioned him aside and tried the door. It did not budge. "Mr. Future!" He knocked on the door. "It's Captain Newman! Open the door!"

Room E was silent.

Francie Corum came down the aisle. "I found him at my locker this afternoon, trying to jimmy it open."

Captain Newman rattled the door. "I know you can hear me. Listen! I have news! Important! I just heard from Mr. Past!"

A rustle inside the room.

"Mr. Past—is on his way! To join you. He says he'll never leave you again! Do you hear me? *He'll never leave you alone again.*"

We heard the bed being shoved away. The door swung back on its hinges. Francie shuddered.

Against the dim light, Colonel Norval Algate Bliss stood silhouetted. He had shaved off his beard and mustache. He was clad in a feathery kimono, stolen from one of the nurses' lockers. There was rouge on his cheeks.

"Come in, dearie," he smiled.

XVI

THE

LAST CHRISTMAS

Fourteen sun-blackened, woebegone Italian prisoners of war, guarded by five MPs in helmets, shuffled down the ramp to Ward 7. Their boots were caked with alkali, their uniforms shapeless from innumerable rubbings on desert rock. Some had sun-bleached knapsacks slung across their shoulders; some clutched bundles, ponchos, greasy canvas tied with rope. At the head of the column was an officer in the once-dashing garb of Mussolini's legions.

The MP in command, one Lieutenant Farkus, bellowed, "Prisonerrrs HALT, hut-*two!*" in so loud a voice that it rolled down the aisle of Ward 7, where it created pandemonium. Some of the patients, thinking the war had come to an end, began to dance up and down and slap each other on the back; others, mistaking the MPs for prisoners and the prisoners for conquerors, began to weep or wail or dive under their beds. Punchy Holt assumed the posture of a pugilist and cried, "One at a time, you yellow-belly wops!" Luther Cousy jeered, "Lousy Fassists! Spaghetti guzzlers!"

Lieutenant Farkus stepped to Captain Newman's door and knocked. . . .

You may ask what fourteen Italian prisoners of war were doing five thousand miles from a European theater of war, and why, in particular, they awaited admittance to an N.P. ward? The answer is simple, though you may have trouble believing it.

In November, 1942, our expeditionary forces, under a General named Dwight D. Eisenhower, landed on the northwest coast of Africa and overran Oran, Algiers, Casablanca. Between the valiant British and ferocious Aussies to the east and the clamoring Americans to the west, between the planes that hammered them from the sky and the tanks that chewed them up on the sand, the enemy took a terrible clobbering. At Kasserine Gap, so did we. By May, the "master races" lost almost one million men, eight thousand aircraft, uncounted thousands of tanks and cannon. General Rommel's *Afrika Korps* alone surrendered a quarter of a million prisoners.

As for the Italians—ah, the Italians! They simply were not cut out to be the empire-builders their strutting Duce yearned for. Italian troops began surrendering whenever they could get close enough to the Americans to hold their hands up. They were anxious to surrender only to Americans because they felt inferior to the British, were terrified of the Aussies, and had so many relatives in America that they had confidence in our ingenuous and benevolent nature. They also believed our radio, our leaflets and our mobile loudspeakers, which promised all who laid down their arms instant forgiveness, excellent provender and boundless understanding. What our propaganda did not achieve, our P-38s did: the Italians went green with panic at the sight of one of our "twin-forked devils," which made a hair-curling whine when they dived and a blood-chilling scream when they strafed. The Italians surrendered in droves.

All this is simple. What borders on fantasy is how 270 of the vanquished Latins got all the way from North Africa to Camp

Colfax. It was because of the way some idiot in high station in-
terpreted the Geneva Convention of July 27, 1929, which is entitled "Convention Relative to the Treatment of Prisoners of
War." Section II, Article 9, paragraph 2 of that historic covenant,
in case you want to look it up yourself, reads as follows:

> Prisoners captured in districts which are unhealthy, or whose climate
> is deleterious to persons coming from temperate climates, shall be re-
> moved as soon as possible to a more favorable climate.

Anyone who thinks about it must be impressed by the
wisdom, to say nothing of the humanity, which inspired that provision. It would, after all, be barbarous to send Hottentots to a
prison camp in Alaska, or Eskimos, say, to a stockade in Yucatán.
Among civilized nations, prisoners of war are surely entitled to a
climate as much like their native habitat as their captors can
provide.

Since the Italians had been captured on a desert, the idiot mentioned above thought it necessary to incarcerate them in a similar
climate. So boys raised in the verdant Dolomites or the fertile
valley of the Po, lads from the vineyards of Tuscany or the
heavenly lake of Maggiore, soon found themselves on the Atlantic
—bound for shuttered trains which were bound for the broiling
sands of the Southwest. Our quota, at Colfax, was 270.

They were put to work, with meticulous respect for the rules
of war, as labor crews on the miniature base (where everyone
slept in a tent) some twenty miles from our post, which General
Armstrong had set up for special training in desert maneuvers.
Our GIs called it "Death Valley," which was, in fact, a good two
hundred miles away. The Italians referred to it with phrases from
Dante.

It has often been alleged that Italians, a self-dramatizing people, are matchless hypochondriacs, and that even the hardiest
among them express heart-rending anguish over the most minor

aches, pains and twinges. I do not know whether this applies to all of the sons of Romulus and Remus, but I can vouch for the fact that *our* Italians were practitioners of suffering without peer.

Some PWs, of course, suffered real injury in the line of their bondage—hernias, fractures, blows on the head. But a whacking proportion of the rest swiftly acquired ailments that were distinguished by two salient traits: they were pitiful to observe and impossible to disprove. Our first-aid unit in Death Valley was soon deluged by epidemics of aching backs and athlete's foot; putative nauseas, heat rash and ringing ears; disturbances of skin, liver, heart or stomach that were as subtle as they were exotic. The complaints of our prisoners were of a range and a complexity before which medicine could only stand dumfounded. Even Corporal Laibowitz, no tyro in convenient *krankheit,* was astounded by the Latins' symptomatic genius.

Some of the doctors in Main insisted that the Italians were strong as horses and had simply discovered that they could lighten their servitude by rolling their eyes and moaning *"Mamma mia."* This did not alter our solemn obligations: No civilized power denies medical care to the ailing. And under military regulations, even a sick PW must be confined in a well-guarded area. The only guarded area in our hospital was Ward 7. That is why fourteen hot, dirty, more-or-less sick sons of Rome were dispatched to us. . . .

MP Lieutenant Farkus, having knocked so resolutely on Captain Newman's door that he brought him to it with a scowl, now presented him with a formal receipt, which Captain Newman was to sign, acknowledging the transfer of fourteen bona-fide PWs from the jurisdiction of the police to that of the healers.

Captain Newman was flabbergasted. Our facilities were overtaxed enough without taking on fourteen ambulatory aliens whose symptoms, save for one bandaged and one lame, he regarded more with admiration than alarm. Before Captain Newman would sign any document, he telephoned a protest to Lieutenant Colonel Larrabee.

In five minutes, Colonel Pyser called Captain Newman and told him to get the hell on with his duties. "There's no other place in the hospital I can put those Dagos," was the way Colonel Pyser phrased it. "Examine them, dose them with castor oil for all I care, and get them the hell back to Death Valley! And Newman . . ."

"Yes, sir?"

"The United States is at *war* with Italy, goddamit!"

"Thank you, Colonel."

"Don't give me any of your sarcasm, Newman. You know damn well what I mean: I don't want you to mollycoddle these jokers just because they fake a toothache and sing *Pagliacci*."

"I will not permit vocalizing in the ward, sir."

"That's not what I'm driving at! Just don't start psy-cho-ther-a-py on those baboons, for God's sake. They are enemy, not house guests. Treat them as if you were in a battle zone, not a goddam health resort, and get them back to their picks and shovels!"

Captain Newman signed the receipt.

The fourteen PWs were assimilated in Ward 7 with no difficulty. They were not all malingerers. One ran a fever of 103; another had a vicious infection, from some rusty barbed wire, that threatened to require a leg amputation. The youngest, a sixteen-year-old whom the others called "Bambino," cried for his mother, hour after hour. The other PWs made a great fuss over him, sharing their mail and their Red Cross packages and trying to entertain him with foolish clownings. They even improvised a Punch-and-Judy show out of old socks stuffed with paper. But Bambino's anguish did not abate until one of the Italians got a rubber glove from Francie Corum, filled it with milk, punctured one of the fingers, and put it in the boy's mouth. Bambino sucked on it greedily and fell asleep. The comments some of the Americans made on this infantile regression were brutal; but Bambino's terrible weeping stopped, and for that everyone in the ward was grateful.

In due course, twelve of the PWs returned to Death Valley. Their places were promptly taken by others. How could it be otherwise? Ward 7's mirific attractions—sheets, soft beds, revolving fans, good food, devoted orderlies, pleasing nurses, a radio, ping-pong—were glowingly extolled by the twelve who returned from the hospital to the 258 who still labored out in the desert. Ailments promptly broke out among those 258 with a speed not seen since the Black Plague. The first-aid unit in Death Valley threw up its hands and called for the delivery truck. In two days we had nineteen more Italians in Ward 7. And when *they* were discharged—well, it soon got so that a regular shuttle ran between Death Valley and our hospital. Every armed truck that conveyed PWs out of Colfax transported PWs back. On any given day, we had anywhere from ten to twenty-five Italians in the ward—wheezing with "asthma" or groaning of constipation, fluttering their eyelids over "heart murmurs" or thrashing about in the throes of "bladder trouble." "This place is like Bellevue on New Year's Day," said Francie.

Yet the Italians turned out to be a blessed addition to our lives. Lovable by nature, they were so glad to be in the cool, clean ward that they knocked themselves out trying to please us. They laughed readily, leaped to offer everyone help, and seized on any excuse to burst into song. They made beds, washed dishes, scrubbed floors. Several even began to sew curtains. They would do anything to avoid being discharged.

They also left no doubt in anyone's mind as to what side they were on. They prayed aloud for the death of Hitler, whom they loathed, and the disgrace of Mussolini, whom they despised. For good measure, they threw in disgust with the Japanese, about whom they knew nothing. They realized that the sooner their country was defeated, the sooner would they be reunited with tneir loved ones. Nothing was more precious, more dreamed of, more beseeched of the Almighty.

Few of the Italians spoke English, but that presented no problem in communication: there was always one or another patient in the ward who spoke Italian. (Pepi Gavoni did not, to Laibowitz's astonishment.) Besides, the gestures of our PWs were so eloquent, their pantomime so descriptive, their speech so melodious, that few of us had difficulty in understanding what they were trying to express.

It was two weeks before Christmas, 1944 (the last Christmas most of us would ever spend at Colfax, though we did not know it), when an Italian Major named Marcello Fortuno and sixteen of his talented countrymen were vacationing in our ward, that Corporal Laibowitz asked Captain Newman for an audience "with me and a committee of the boys," at his captain's earliest convenience.

"I'm up to my ears today," said Captain Newman.

Laibowitz looked at the ears unsympathetically.

Captain Newman consulted his calendar. "Oh, hell, come in at four-fifteen."

At exactly 4:14, Laibowitz entered Captain Newman's office with Gavoni and Lawrence. The three lined up before the desk. They even saluted.

"At ease," said Captain Newman, surprised that they had not already taken seats. "Now, what's this all about?"

"It's about Christmas," said Laibowitz. "There's a beaut of a tree in the Rec Hall, from General Armstrong in person, but regulations don't allow our patients out of the ward."

"We feel our boys ought to have their *own* tree," blinked Gavoni. "Agreed, Doc?"

Captain Newman said, "I see no reason why we shouldn't have our own tree. What else?"

"Santa Claus," announced Hammerhead. "Why can't our boys have a Santa Claus of their own, too?"

"I see no objection to having our own Santa Claus, too."

"That brings us to a serious problem." Laibowitz pursed his lips profoundly. "Right?"

"I don't understand," said Captain Newman.

"That's why I raise the point. Doc, what about the PWs?"

"I don't see what problem they can present."

"That's because you're not a PW. The Italians feel they should be allowed in the Rec Hall on Christmas Eve for the big show, with the whole hospital. They want to be treated like friends, not neurotics."

"That's interesting."

"I'm glad you agree."

"I didn't say I agreed! I said the Italian position is interesting." Captain Newman massaged the small of his back. "Who raised the question about the PWs?"

"Major Fortuno. I told him he had my backing all the way."

"That was decent of you," said Newman sourly.

"I was only giving my opinion."

"I didn't think it was an order of the day. . . . The C.O.'s office will have to grant formal permission for the Italians to be taken to the Rec Hall."

"The Italians can put plenty of life in the celebration, Doc! They sing like maniacs. And they can sing an American song in the C.O.'s honor. Tell him that and we're in!"

"Jackson, I've got to hand it to you. Your recommendation has merit."

"That's because it makes sense," beamed Gavoni.

"That," said Captain Newman, stealing a page from Laibowitz's book, "is why it has merit."

Laibowitz looked startled; he was accustomed to laying, not exploding, dialectical booby traps.

"Is that all?" smiled Captain Newman.

"Yeah—"

"Dismissed."

"—except for the collection."

"What collection?"

"The collection for buying the *tree,* for the ward," said Hammerhead.

"A buck a head from the nurses and orderlies, and two from each doctor," said Gavoni.

Captain Newman reached into his pocket.

"Three bucks from you, Doc," said Laibowitz. "On account of your being chief of the ward."

"Get a nice big tree," sighed Captain Newman.

The tree he saw in the sun lounge several days later was not very big and even less impressive. It was, indeed, a rather puzzling tree—at least it puzzled Captain Newman. It puzzled him more and more the more he studied it, and he found himself studying it more and more as the day wore on.

The tree was, for one thing, only five feet high; for another, it looked undernourished. The more Captain Newman thought about that tree, the more he tried not to think about it; and the more he tried not to think about it, the more he did. When he found himself thinking of the tree instead of the patient in Bed 5, who was suffering from hyperacusis, he decided to go to the sun lounge.

The tree was in the far corner. The Italians, Francie Corum and the Three Wise Men were bustling around it, festooning it with tinsel and trinkets under the direction of Major Fortuno, who was supervising their efforts with narrowed eyes and the hand signals of an orchestra conductor. "No-no-no-*no! A sinistra! Bene! Un altro poco. Si! Bravo! Perfettamente!*"

He was a splendid figure of a man, that Major Fortuno. He had black hair with natural waves in it, a silky mustache and goatee, and eyes that invested even his "gooda mora-ning"s with passion.

"Excuse me," said Captain Newman.

"*Per favore!*" bowed Major Fortuno, clicking his heels.

Captain Newman called, "Laibowitz . . ."

Something in Captain Newman's tone warned Laibowitz that no good was being boded. "He is busy with the tree," observed Laibowitz.

"He is also wanted by Captain Newman," said Newman.

"He is coming," said Laibowitz.

Captain Newman stepped into the orderlies' bull pen, which Laibowitz entered with an aggrieved expression.

"Jackson," said Captain Newman carefully, "couldn't you find a—uh—bigger tree than that?"

"If a man could get a giant would he settle for a midget?"

"Don't play volley ball with my questions! Where did you buy that tree?"

Laibowitz studied the ceiling. "Who said I bought it?"

Captain Newman felt a prickle of apprehension. "You went into town three days in a row—I okayed the passes myself—for the express purpose of buying a tree—"

"A man can start for paradise and end up in Flushing," cried Laibowitz. "The trees in town are a disgrace—crummy and all picked over; only anemics left."

"Then where did you get—"

"Doc, some things a man is better off not knowing."

"I'll be the judge of that," said Captain Newman sternly.

"To be judge and jury at the same time is a mistake."

"*Where did you get that tree?*"

"From another tree," said Laibowitz dourly.

"From 'another'—! What tree? Where?" An awful possibility loomed in Captain Newman's mind. "Jackson, is there any connection between the tree in the Rec Hall and the tree on our porch?"

"Not now . . . Doc, you are turning pale. I'll get you an aspirin."

"I don't need an aspirin. I need a gun!"

"Can I put on a blindfold?"

"Answer my question!" snapped Newman.

"You should of been a district attorney."

"Did you get the tree which is on the sun porch—"

"Doc—"

"Yes or no?"

"Yes."

Captain Newman sank into a chair. He was wrestling with all sorts of emotions. "How did you do it?"

"With a saw."

"A *saw?* What kind of saw?"

"How many types of saw *are* there?" cried Laibowitz. "A saw. For sawing."

"Where did you get it?"

"From surgery."

"From *surgery?*" Newman exploded.

"You sound like an echo."

"You *stole* a surgical saw—"

"Such an accusation is not fair! The saw was borrowed."

"You *borrowed* a delicate, expensive instrument—"

Laibowitz raised a hand. "Doc, do me a favor. Bust me, to civilian. I prefer it to this chewing out."

"You'll get both! I want the details."

"The details will make you madder."

"That's not possible. You 'borrowed' a surgical saw—"

"It's already returned!"

"Dull as a board, no doubt—"

"No!" protested Laibowitz. "Just bent."

" 'Bent.' That's nice. Nothing could be better for a surgeon, of course, than a bent saw. For crooked patients. It will cut around corners."

"Doc, I can see you are getting upset."

"Upset? I?" Newman laughed hollowly. "Simply because my orderly broke into surgery—"

"I didn't. Don't be hard on Pepi, Doc! He was doing it for the

ward. I tell him to get a saw, thinking he'll go to the tool shed, but the poor four-eyed slob sneaks upstairs—"

Captain Newman rose. "Let's quit all this stalling. Tell me the whole story."

"It isn't so interesting."

"I find it fascinating."

"You better sit down."

"I stay mad better when I'm standing." Captain Newman put his hands behind his back.

"You look like Captain Bligh."

"That will be enough, Laibowitz!"

"That tree in the Rec Hall was a good twenty-five feet high!" cried Laibowitz. "The top didn't even clear the overhang from the balcony. They had to ease it down, under and up, to get it in. And then the top couldn't even be seen, unless a guy laid flat on his back! Doc, is that a way to enjoy a Christmas tree?"

Captain Newman wrapped himself in ice.

"The rest," muttered Laibowitz, "is obvious."

"*Be* obvious."

"So I took the saw and climbed the ladder and cut the goddam top off!" cried Laibowitz. "Doc, I made that tree look ten times better! It was a cockamamy tree. Ask anyone. The top *leaned*." Laibowitz illustrated the deplorable deformity of the tree quite vividly.

"And are you so damn stupid," Captain Newman fumed, "as to think that General Armstrong won't see that his tree has had its top chopped off?"

"How will he see?"

"With his eyes!"

"Doc, do I look like a meathead? Would I leave a tree with a flat top? A Christmas tree comes to a point, right? Well, it still comes to a point, because that's the way I trimmed it, after I cut the top off. Doc, so help me, the only difference in the General's tree now is I improved it!"

"It's merely five feet shorter," glared Newman.

"Looks are more important than height," observed Laibowitz.

"Be sure to remind General Armstrong of that when he throws you into the guardhouse. How did you get it out of the Rec Hall?"

"Out a window, through the sheep pen, up the back stairs. No one even got a peep what was going on!"

"Not one of the five thousand blind men on this installation saw you carrying a five-foot tree—"

"We didn't carry it."

Captain Newman closed his eyes. "What did you do?"

"We used an ambulance."

"An *am*bulance? Where the hell did you get an ambulance?"

"Near Emergency."

"Where was the driver?"

"Shooting craps, with Pepi."

"Did *you* tell Pepi to—"

"Certainly. How else could I get the ambulance? . . . This driver is a nut for galloping dominoes."

"Then who drove?"

"Cooshy."

"Cooshy? Cooshy *Finn?*"

"He is a very careful driver, Doc."

"Cooshy Finn is a patient!" exclaimed Newman.

"That's why I chose him!" said Laibowitz. "We can always claim he stole the ambulance when he was off his rocker. Hammerhead told me—"

"Hammerhead?"

"He was in charge of the stretcher."

"The *what?*"

"The stretcher we put the tree on. You would never know it was a tree!"

"Why not?" asked Captain Newman bitterly. "Did you dress it in a uniform?"

"No, I covered it with a blanket. Doc, you would be the first to swear it looked like a corpse!"

Captain Newman put his head between his hands. His groans were many and heartfelt, but they did not make him feel better. They did not seem to affect Laibowitz either. After some piteous sounds, Newman muttered, "You may go—no, wait." He raised his head. "Excuse my asking so hostile a question, Corporal Finaglowitz, but just for the hell of it, and because you didn't spend one red cent for that wonderful, perfectly pointed tree you wrapped in a blanket and conveyed in an ambulance: What did you do with the money you collected?"

Laibowitz drew himself up with dignity. "What we *saved* in not buying a crummy tree went for presents—for my patients."

The days sped by in the pleasant turmoil of the season: the Italians decorated Ward 7 with green branches and imitation holly; patients received parcels from loved ones throughout the land; plum puddings piled up in a corner. Advance scouts from Special Services (I. and E.) came in with tape measures to survey the ward, preparing for the Christmas show they would bring us—a short version of the gala program ballyhooed on posters all over the post:

COLFAX CHRISTMAS CAPERS

with

THE SINGING SECRETARIES

M/SGT. PETE POLANSKY'S ONE-MAN BAND

THE GREAT HOODUNIT AND HIS MYSTIFYING MAGIC

*   *   *

SONGS! CAROLS! COMMUNITY SING!

*   *   *

EXTRA STAR ATTRACTION!!

(courtesy the "Blue Cave" Night Club, Colfax)

AMY BEAUREGARD

"The Pride of the South"

As I walked around the installation those days, I could hear the new spinet in the Rec Hall banging away in relentless re-hearsals: choral run-throughs, close-harmony WACs—and carols, carols, carols. From every radio on the post came glutinous rendi-tions of "Silent Night." Day and night, "I'm Dreaming of a White Christmas" drifted, most incongruously, across the desert air.

In our ward, song after song ascended from the Italians, who exercised their happy voices on the sun lounge. There was a cer-tain mystery about some of the songs they were rehearsing, for they always stopped when an officer was around. Gavoni or Lawrence patrolled the entrance to the ward and signaled back to the sun porch when enemies were approaching. When Francie asked Laibowitz, who seemed to spend every moment he could whispering to Major Fortuno, what all the secrecy was about, the lugubrious Corporal studied a nonexistent spot on her uniform and replied, "The PWs are preparing a surprise."

"I'll bet it will be a good one," she smiled.

He favored her with one of his most enigmatic moues—inscruta-ble, yet patronizing: "You said a mouthful, Lieutenant."

How can I describe, to those who have not themselves experi-enced it, what Christmas is like away from home? At no other time does memory serve men so cruelly.

On the battlefields around the world, Christmas partook of paradox to confuse the heart. On military posts in the States, depopulated by fortunates with home leave, it was bittersweet, at best. And in the Army hospitals, where men may lay locked in pain, torn by wounds, contending with the accursed heralds of death . . . Many of us offered silent thanks that Christmas "comes but once a year."

The morning of Christmas Eve—perhaps in the spirit of the season, perhaps because Colonel Pyser could not hope forever to prevent it—Josiah J. Newman, after three solid years as a captain, was informed that effective January 1, 1945, he would enjoy all the privileges, perquisites, honors and increased base pay of a major in the Army of the United States of America. I must, in truth, report that the promotion both pleased Newman, who was not exactly modest, and depressed him, for the same reason. "Three *years*," he grumbled, as he invited us to join him and Francie at the Officers' Club that night, to salute the Army's wisdom with revelry.

The Eve was officially inaugurated in Ward 7 after an early dinner, when Clarence ("Armpit") Garopy, dressed in a preposterous Santa Claus suit, crawled in through a window, unlocked by Lieutenant Grace Blodgett on this special occasion, bellowing "Ho, ho, ho!" through a false beard and hauling three duffel bags, bulging with presents, over his shoulders. Garopy, a scullery helot, was the biggest, fattest soldier Arkie Kopp could recruit for the role. He had a little trouble getting through the window, partly because the duffel bags kept banging against each other like unanchored buoys in a storm-tossed sea, and partly because while Pepi and Hammerhead kept trying to yank him in, two hypomanic patients kept trying to push him out. But Armpit kept bellowing those "Ho-ho-ho"s and charged down the center aisle, snapping a paper whip and shouting, "Hi, Dumbbell! Hey, Blitzen!"

Armpit emptied the bags under the tree and the Italian PWs scrambled around, yelling *"Ecco! Ecco!"* arranging the packages, each of which had a patient's name on it.

At this point the Special Service crew dollied in some spotlights and rolled in the spinet. The ward lights flicked on and off. The piano banged out some chords. The patients sat up in their beds. Nurses and doctors took to the folding chairs at one side. A Master of Ceremonies stepped to the mike. . . .

It was, all things considered, not a bad program. "The Singing Secretaries," four WACs from Fiscal, were generously applauded, not least because one of them developed trouble with her brassière and kept fumbling around under her blouse until a loud male offer of help, from the rear, brought the house down. "The Great Hoodunit" turned out to be Corporal Tepaska, from Crash Crews, dressed in a top hat and improvised tails. He made cards disappear, lighted cigarettes by snapping his fingers, pulled American flags out of the air. I could not help admiring his poise in the face of the kind of adversity a magician would encounter only in Ward 7: The patient in Bed 16 kept announcing that he could make *Tepaska* disappear any time he put his mind to it; and Snitchy Bruner, whose hallucinations had lately taken the form of seeing Japs emerge from an invasion tunnel near the PX, kept looking under all the beds for anything Tepaska prestidigitated.

The *pièce de résistance* was, of course, Amy Beauregard, the night-club *diseuse* who was the only professional on the program. Her entrance was spectacular: a blackout, a rattle of drums, a blue spotlight—and there stood Miss Beauregard, in the closest-fitting of low-cut gowns, all sequins and spangles. The ward rang with mating calls.

Amy laughed deep in her throat and sang "Blue Skies." She had a husky soprano and a magnolia accent. She was admirable. She was admirable on every count and through three numbers. For her encore, she touched the sentimental strings in every male's heart with the song which extols Mother, cataloguing her virtues in acrostic form (" 'M' is for the many things she gave me, 'O' means only . . ."). As she trilled the Oedipal phrases, Miss Beauregard moved between the beds, kissing each patient on the cheek.

It was a superb notion, of course, a sure-fire show-stopper, and it was acclaimed as fervently by our men as it ever was in a night club. But on the line about what "E" stands for, a painful thing happened. As Miss Beauregard turned to Bed 5, she missed a note: the man due to be bussed next was Coffee Dewhurst, and Coffee was a Negro. He was lying flat on his back. His eyes were bandaged. Silence fell on the ward. "The Pride of the South," whose eyes were dazed by shock, could pass Coffee by; he did not know that she had kissed the others. She swallowed hard, recaptured her rhythm, closed her eyes and touched Coffee's forehead with her lips. No one even heard what "R" stood for. . . .

The program for Ward 7 ended. Iona Finch and Hammerhead began to bed the ward down for the night. Outside the iron door, a squad of MPs waited. We watched the Italians file out proudly. The MPs bracketed them. "Pris-onerrrs, for-ward *march*!" roared Lieutenant Farkus.

Off they marched, Major Fortuno in the van, up the ramp to Main.

The Rec Hall was so decorated and pretty that I hardly recognized it. A huge "MERRY CHRISTMAS—HAPPY NEW YEAR" was strung across the entire width of the auditorium, beneath a canopy of interlaced red and green streamers. Silver stars and balls and twinkling lights gleamed everywhere. Every door and window was framed with greenery, in which poinsettias nestled.

The auditorium was jammed. Men in wheel chairs lined both sides of the hall, right up to the stage. Only the first row of folding chairs, reserved for the C.O. and his party, was empty. We found seats in row two, which early comers had unanimously avoided. Officers and nurses filled the next six rows; behind, the GIs and patients were packed in.

Down the corridor a clarion "Ten*shun*!" echoed. We stood up as one. Came the rustle of commotion antecedent to order, the pregnant bustle that precedes, and the awesome silence that succeeds, the entrance of Command, mighty and incarnate. Entered General Armstrong, smiling, laden with decorations, his wife on his arm. None but a C.O. could nod with such practiced grace. Immediately behind: Colonel Pyser, two lieutenant colonels with wives, four majors without. What a fine sight our H.Q. staff made as they filed into the front row!

As the ladies seated themselves, with girlish sounds and gestures, I saw General Armstrong nudge his wife. "Honey," he said proudly, "did you ever see such a magnificent tree?"

"Oh-oh," whispered Francie, beside me.

The General's tree, which I had entirely overlooked, looked magnificent indeed. It was a fine, thick evergreen, heavily adorned and topped by a big star.

"Mason," replied Mrs. Armstrong, "that *is* a beautiful tree."

"Great tree, General!" said Lieutenant Colonel Liston.

"Perfectly *love*ly," chirped Mrs. Glock.

"Best tree we ever had, sir," grinned Major Frisby.

Fondly, General Armstrong's eyes took in every branch, every string of snow and silver until—he frowned, turning to Major Hornaday. "Say, does that tree look right to you?"

I heard Newman moan.

" 'Right,' sir?" asked Hornaday.

"I could swear—"

"Gentlemen, our national anthem!" proclaimed Captain Frolich (Special Services), from the stage.

A ruffle of drums: we snapped to attention, Newman with particular alacrity, and the hospital orchestra played "My Country, 'Tis of Thee," which is not our national anthem.

General Armstrong was staring at the Christmas tree intently. "Hornaday," he whispered, "I could swear that tree was bigger!"

"Bigger, sir?" Hornaday echoed.

"Taller."

"Perhaps it was the angle from which you originally viewed it, sir."

"Don't be a jackass, Hornaday."

"Sorry, sir."

All during the singing of the carols, General Armstrong kept eyeing that tree, interspersing his singing with side-of-the-mouth comments. His rendition of "Adeste Fideles" went like a descant:

Oh, come all ye faith-ful
   (They said that tree measured twenty-five feet.)
Joyful and tri-umphant
   (That tree's no twenty-five feet!)
Oh, come ye, oh, co-ome ye
   (Think it could've shrunk indoors?)
To Be-eth-le-hem;
Come and adore Him,
   (How high d'you figure that tree to be?)
Born the king of a-angels
   (I make it nineteen—twenty, tops!)
O come let us adore Him
   (Next year, Hornaday—)
O come let us adore Him
   (—send one of our trucks—)
O come let us adore Him,
   (—pick up the tree instead of accepting delivery from—)
Chri-ist, our Lord.
   (—those goddam scoundrels in town.)

"On with the show!" the M.C. cried, and the auditorium rocked with applause.

The Singing Secretaries got a riotous hand, Hoodunit was extravagantly acclaimed, and Amy Beauregard created near-pandemonium, of course, when she sashayed down the aisle in her sequin *décolletage,* blue-lighted by a baby spot, pressing kisses on foreheads as she extolled Mother in subsyllabic detail. Amy held a good ten-second beat at the end of "Put them all to-gether they spell Mo-o-other . . ." looking around the hall as if she did not quite know on whom to bestow her final osculation. In a faultless stroke of showmanship she not only selected General Armstrong, but kissed him right on the lips. It would have created a sensation even if the smack had not been amplified through her portable mike.

"And now, a surprise!" announced the M.C. "Our Italian PWs!"

The orchestra struck up "Funiculi, Funicula." Down the aisle, up the stairs, onto stage, flanked by MPs, marched Major Fortuno and sixteen compatriots. Never had the Major looked so elegant: his hair shone, his goatee gleamed, his teeth sparkled.

"Prison-errs, HALT!" Thus Lieutenant Farkus.

"Molte grazie," bowed Major Fortuno.

The Italians arranged themselves in a semicircle. Major Fortuno stepped forward, clicked heels, and, reinforced by a slip of paper, orated: "Generale Arma-strong, officers, *medici*, beautiful *signore:* Ina my country is saying: '*Molte grazie!*' It mean: 'Thanka you varry moch.' Alla my man say *molte grazie* you! We prisoner—buta no slafe! We lose—buta no punish! We Italian—buta horray America!" The applause was so deafening that Major Fortuno had to bow three times. "America! What it mean? It's come from Amerigo Vespucci! America! Who discovred? Cristoforo Colombo! New York! Who boss? Fiorello La Guardia!" After naming other great Italians linked to our glory, from Arturo Toscanini to "ball-playing Tony Lazzeri," Major Fortuno concluded: "So ina you honor, Generale Arma-strong, we singa special song!" He raised his hands; sixteen pairs of lips were wetted; sixteen pairs of lungs inhaled; sixteen pairs of eyes burned at their *maréchal*. And when his hands pumped downward, out of sixteen grateful throats poured: *"Oh, di, puoi vedere alla prima luce dell'alba . . ."* They were singing "The Star-Spangled Banner" in Italian.

How can I hope to convey the effect this had on us? We were on our feet at once. We had never heard our great hymn sung in another tongue; nor have I, for one, ever heard it sung with such feeling. After the final, stirring strophe, *"sulla ter-ra dei liberi-i-i, E sulla casa dei coraggiosi!"* our prisoners could do no wrong.

And perhaps that was just as well. . . . Major Fortuno announced their next selection as "olda American Indian song." Again he raised both hands; again they dropped; and this time from the sixteen fervent throats ascended a melody that puzzled me, in accents certainly not Comanche. Nor were they English, Italian, French. They contained a good many gutturals. . . .

Newman's eyes got wider and wider, his cheeks paling, and when Francie turned to him for enlightenment, from one side, as did I from the other, I heard Newman curse under his breath. "Laibowitz!"

Then I knew. Major Fortuno's proud choir was singing a song Laibowitz had taught them in those secret sessions—a Jewish song, a Chanukah song, every sound and syllable of it!

If the Italians thought they were singing an Indian lyric, the Americans had no reason to doubt that, like "The Star-Spangled Banner," the words had been translated into Italian, too. (I leave out some lads from Brooklyn, whose expression suggested that the world was coming to an end.)

Captain Newman turned, surveying the rows of GIs behind us with an expression such as I never expected to see on a psychoanalyst. Corporal Laibowitz was nowhere to be seen among the seated. That was because he was not seated. He was standing—leaning against the wall under the overhang, one hand fondling a branch of the Christmas tree he had made foal another, the other keeping time to the song his innocent agents were singing. His face was a study in rapture.

General Armstrong whispered, over his shoulder: "Newman!" Francie winced.

My chief leaned forward. "Yes, sir."

"Got to hand it to those Italians, Newman."

"Yes, sir."

"Damn beautiful language!"

"It—certainly is."

"You understand it?"

"I—don't speak Italian."

"No lingo like it, Newman."

"There certainly isn't."

At this point Mrs. Armstrong murmured, "It's so beautiful it makes me want to cry."

It did not make me want to cry, because I was lost in admiration for Newman, who had not uttered a single untruth during a colloquy bristling with dangers.

I could not help thinking that there was a moral in what I was witnessing. If the Italians thought they were singing Indian, and the Americans thought they were singing Italian— Reality, I concluded, is not what is, but what men think it to be.

The Italians finished in a polyphonic climax that got a rising ovation.

The program was over.

General Armstrong called *"Molte grazie!"* to the Italians on stage.

"Viva il Generale!" they cheered in ecstasy.

We followed *il Generale* up the aisle as he dropped "Merry Christmases" right and left. I stayed close to Newman and Francie. His eyes were searching the crowd and he was muttering, "See you at the club, Francie. Start the party."

"Joe!" she protested. "It's Christmas Eve!"

"I want to deliver a present," he said grimly.

"You look more like you're going to commit a murder."

"That's the way I ought to look, sweetheart. See you later, Barney."

"Not on your life," I said.

"I'll change into something black," said Francie.

Corporal Laibowitz was not in the corridors.

He was not at the punch bowls.

He was not near the coffee vats.

He was not at the milk bar.

He was not at the cookie counter.

He was not at the Coke corner, the Pepsi booth, or the Seven-Up redoubt.

Newman cursed and sped to Ward 7. I was right with him.

Laibowitz was not in the reception area.

He was not in the open ward.

He was not in the orderlies' bull pen.

He was not in the kitchen or the shower rooms or the commissary.

Where he was, I do not to this day know. The only sign of him was the note we found pinned on Newman's door:

> Dear "Major":
>
> I couldn't pass up the chance.
>
> Jake
>
> *P.S.* Get some rest, Doc. You look terrible.

EPILOGUE

Not long ago, I was looking through the part of my library where I keep the books about the war which I have collected over the years. I was browsing through the pages of an anthology on combat, and I began to think back over what the war had meant to those of us who never saw combat, and to those who, like me, saw only portions of its consequence.

I thought of Oatmeal McKee and his roaring and reprobate ways. I thought of Little Jim, with his pinched face and corroding guilt, and the heroism of his end. I thought of Laibowitz and his fellow pirates plundering the commissaries for the sake of patients to whom they felt such a passion of loyalty. I thought of Coby Clay, who prevailed against the entire majestic array of military power that tried so desperately to persuade him to—make his bed. I thought of Gino McGraw, who took his life over a remorse that was no less tragic for being senseless. I thought of the maddened sheep and the insolent ducks, of Captain Vinson and his wife, of Hammerhead's profane compulsion and Pepi Gavoni's benevolent salami. I thought of Mr. Future, lost in the silent storm of an identity he both sought and feared, possessed at last by that other self which, like a vengeful woman, could not be denied. I thought of the singular Hrdlicka, who tried to steal a jeep via the U.S. mails. I thought of Francie Corum, so cool, so lovely, and of that wicked, blessed nurse called Katy who gave love to men who needed nothing more. Mostly, of course, I thought of Newman.

I remember many things I have not written in these pages: Newman's defense, in a court-martial, of a boy who had gone AWOL and was on trial as a deserter—because he had taken a toothbrush along on a three-day bender, which proved, the Adjutant General's prosecutor maintained, that he had planned never to return.

I remember coming into the ward one night, shortly after a fighter instructor named Brexel had been found behind one of the hangars. He had taken a plank, painted on it:

CHARLES W. BREXEL
Capt. U.S.A.
Ser. No. 0-1-668-349
B. June 3, 1920
D. June 3, 1944,

hammered the plank upright in the ground, dug a grave before it, crawled in, slashed his wrists, covered himself with sand, and waited for death, which soon claimed him. No one knew why Brexel had done it, nor why on his twenty-fourth birthday. He had been so popular an officer, handsome, healthy, happy-go-lucky, on whom fortune had showered so much: wealth, distinguished parents, a beautiful girl to whom he was engaged. . . . They had put Brexel's body under a sheet on a cot in Emergency.

"That damn fool had everything to live for!" Captain Jarvis exclaimed.

Newman looked up wearily. " 'Everything' for you, Bill; nothing for him—or something he could not endure." He shook his head. "Oh, hell; we all see life through our own special lenses—rose-colored, black, the green of envy, the yellow of fear —because of what the past has done to us. Somewhere each of us is ridden by some damaged moment, some skewed sense of proportion, somewhere, about something. The whole human race—who said: 'We go through life seeing things as we are and not as they are'?"

And Captain Jarvis smiled to himself. Poor Bill Jarvis: cynical, naïve, romantic, hopelessly adolescent. He was sent to India early in 1945, to the Tenth Air Force, after long insisting on his right to earn his wings as a flying officer; and some of us scoffed that the real reason he wanted to get away was that he had exhausted the supply of WACs on the post, and the dreary, foolish girls in town, or that he had a new and all-too-familiar crush on Joan Daniels, a luscious nurse who had passed through Colfax on her way to the C.B.I. Jarvis got his wings, all right; and on his next flight, the plane in which he was hitchhiking to a forward base (a fast, hard-to-handle model the men called "the flying prostitute" because it had no visible means of support) crashed against a Himalayan pinnacle beyond the Ledo Road, and not a single body survived the holocaust.

They are all gone out of my life, the soldiers and officers who were so much a part of it for so many days and nights and hours. Occasionally, I get a note, a wedding announcement, a Christmas card from one or another of them.

I ran into Pepi Gavoni five or six years ago, at the La Salle Street station in Chicago: he was twenty pounds heavier and no less nearsighted; and though we found each other with pleasure and excitement, our meeting soon turned awkward. There seemed little for us to say to each other beyond our first fitful resurrections of the past, and the awesome lieutenancy I still occupied in his mind made him rush off with relief, I suspect, when the loudspeakers announced the next train to Terre Haute.

I got a letter from Laibowitz once, after the war: he had made a stab at higher education, under the GI Bill of Rights, but soon quit. I was not surprised. Jake was one of those whose genius lies in the unique and critical assertion of an untutored vision; he could not, I think, bear that alteration of preferences which education demands. I do not know where he is now, nor what he is doing, but I hope that he found a wife worthy of his melancholy affections, and friends worthy of his antiseptic creed.

Newman and Francie were married after V-J Day. They settled in San Francisco, where he quickly became a most successful psychoanalyst. But Ward 7 had made it impossible for him long to accept such lucrative rewards, or so parochial a practice, and in 1953, making the most sardonic comments about his stupidity and his damnable conscience, he went back into the Air Force he had so long fought and fumed against. He is a lieutenant colonel now, in charge of the N.P. division at the huge Air Force hospital in ———.

They are all gone out of my life, I say, but I think of them often (how could it be otherwise?) and often marvel at how much I learned from them and from my time at Colfax.

I learned that you can understand people better if you look at them—no matter how old or important or impressive they may be—as if they are children. For most men never mature; they simply grow taller.

I learned that in some way, however small and secret, each of us is a little mad. If we want to stay sane we must moderate our demands—on ourselves and on others; for those who do not understand mercy cannot escape that Ward 7 which waits within each of us.

I learned that everyone is lonely, at bottom, and cries to be understood; but we can never entirely understand someone else, no matter how much we try, or want to; and each of us remains part stranger even to those who love us.

I learned that the dimensions of suffering, of anguish, of pettiness, resentment, rancor, recrimination, envy, lust, despair exceed the wildest imaginings of those who have not themselves witnessed men in conflict. I learned, too, that man's capacity for sacrifice, for devotion and compassion and that most miraculous of all virtues—simple decency—can forever hearten and surprise us.

I learned that it is the weak who are cruel, and that gentleness is to be expected only from the strong.

I came to believe it not true that "the coward dies a thousand deaths, the brave man only one." I think it is the other way around: it is the brave who die a thousand deaths. For it is imagination, and not just conscience, which doth make cowards of us all. Those who do not know fear are not really brave. Courage, I think, is the capacity to confront what can be imagined.

I learned that life—so precious, so variable, so honeycombed with richness and delight—is held cheap and trivial in the scheme of impersonal events. When a human life is snuffed out in an instant, without reason, without justice, as so many were in Colfax, how can one deny that all our lives hang by threads of nothing more than luck? A vagrant microbe or an oil slick on the road, an open door, the leak in a gas line, a madman encountered by chance—against these what matters all our painful accumulations of virtue, knowledge, nobility, sacrifice? There is no answer to death, nor to many of the problems which perplex us; there are only rueful accommodations to reality. And what is reality but a fortuitous play of circumstance, indifferent to our hopes or our unutterable aspirations? And what is wisdom but the capacity to confront intolerable ideas with equanimity?

I came to see that every man is subject to fantasies so obscene, yearnings so mendacious, drives so destructive that even to mention them shakes the gates which we have erected against the barbarian within. Nothing in nature, not the wonders of the firmament nor the enigmas of the atom, is half so strange as man's unconscious—that hidden, heaving sea of primordial impulse in which the most confounding contradictions live side by side: the insatiable hunger for love, the boundless rage to kill; the clamorous Now, preserved from the most distant Then, in scornful obliteration of time; the yearning to be known, the conspiracy to remain unrevealed; the male, the female, their tragic amalgams. . . . Not Xanthus nor Xanadu, for all its measureless caverns, provides so stupefying a landscape. I sometimes think there is a dimension beyond the four of experience and Einstein: insight, that fifth dimension which promises to liberate us from bondage to the long, imperfect past.

In Ward 7, I learned that no despotism is more terrible than the tyranny of neurosis. No punishment is more pitiless, more harsh and cunning and malevolent, than that which we inflict on ourselves. And in later years, I came to see that no oppression is more vicious than that of the more neurotic among us over the less. "For some not to be martyrs is martyrdom indeed." There is an imperialism in virtue, which compels us to acquiesce to those who exploit it. For each of us is a slave to guilt, and acts out lifelong expiation—however disguised, however symbolic.

I learned, with some reluctance, that men like Colonel Pyser, whom we loathed, or Colonel Crowther, whom we despised, or Captain Howard, that silly mint-sucker, were nevertheless among those who did their share to save our civilization; and that it was men like Newman, Laibowitz, Arkie Kopp, Pepi and—yes—Hammerhead who make that civilization worth saving.

It is many years now since the war ended. Colfax is a deserted place on a desert few would even want to visit. But what happened there lifted ordinary men into a kind of grandeur, because they were dedicated to a purpose larger than themselves. Most men debase "the pursuit of happiness" by transforming it into a narcotic pursuit of "fun." But there are those sublimely cursed by discontent, and to them happiness comes only when they push their brains and hearts to the farthest reaches of which they are capable. Nothing is more rewarding than the effort a man makes to *matter*—to count, to stand for something, to have it make some difference that he lived at all.

I often remember a Sunday picnic, one rare spring day on the dunes many miles from Colfax. Newman and I were stretched out, our shirts and shoes off, soaking up the sun, watching a continent of clouds drift toward the crimsoning horizon. Francie was sitting beside us, in the partial shade of a saguaro, her honey hair flecked with light, picking up handfuls of sand with that amused composure which rarely failed her, watching the golden grains trickle through her fingers. We had taken a solemn oath, as we drove away from the post, that we would not for so much as a moment think about the war or the ward. From Francie's portable radio, we heard the joyous arpeggios of a Mozart concerto.

We reveled in the beauty of that day. The war, we knew, could not go on much longer. Hodges' troops had punched through to take the Roer dams. Further north, Montgomery's British and Canadians were slashing their way up to the Rhine. Patton's magnificent wildmen had their armor cocked at Trier. Our entire front was alive, rolling for the great river. The Russians were chewing up German armies in the Polish marshlands.

The strains of Mozart cut off abruptly. "We interrupt this program to bring you a special news bulletin. . . ."

On an island called Iwo Jima, only eight hundred miles from Tokyo, soon within range of our P-51 Mustangs, after seventy-two successive days of unparalleled "softening up" by aerial bombardment, our Marines, pinned down in treacherous volcanic ash, were being massacred. The Japanese had concealed their cannon in a thousand ridges and terraces and underground pill-boxes, connected by subterranean tunnels, covered with eight, ten, twelve solid feet of cement. Another disaster, more slaughter, men bleeding, cursing, weeping, dying, in mud, sea slime, filth.

"Oh, God," cried Francie. "Will it never end?"

Newman reached over and snapped off the radio. "Sure; everything ends," he said and put his hand out, pulling her down beside him. She buried her face in his shoulder. For a moment the unearthly stillness of the desert enveloped us.

Then Newman said, "My father once told me a story I always think of, when the going gets rough and things look hopeless. It's about Destiny. . . . Destiny came down to an island, centuries ago, and summoned three of the inhabitants before him. 'What would you do,' asked Destiny, 'if I told you that tomorrow this island will be completely inundated by an immense tidal wave?' The first man, who was a cynic, said, 'Why, I would eat, drink, carouse and make love all night long!' The second man, who was a mystic, said, 'I would go to the sacred grove with my loved ones and make sacrifices to the gods and pray without ceasing.' And the third man, who loved reason, thought for a while, confused and troubled, and said, 'Why, I would assemble our wisest men and begin at once to study how to live under water.' "

I, too, never forgot that story. When our cause seems doomed and the future lost, when despair becomes unbearable and the heart is on the edge of breaking, let men summon hope and honor and high resolve in yet one more stubborn affirmation: Come, let us assemble our wisest men and begin at once to think, to study, to try to learn—even to learn, if we must, how to live under water.

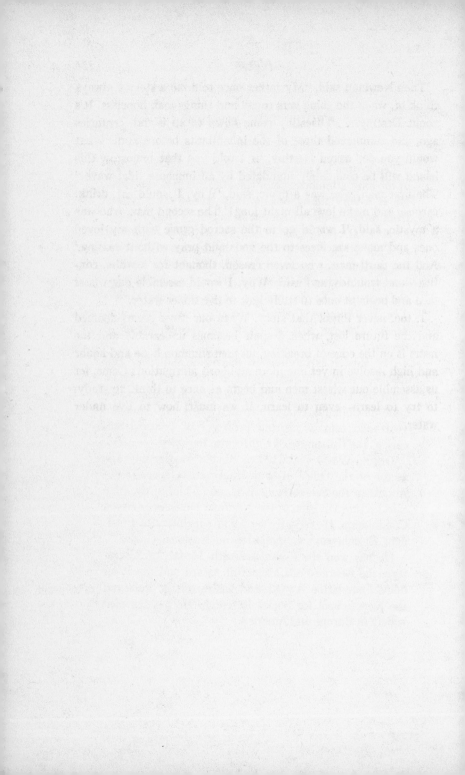

ABOUT THE AUTHOR

Leo Rosten is known to many different publics as one of the most stimulating and versatile minds of our time. He is a very funny serious man whose work ranges from those classics of American humor, *The Education of H*Y*M*A*N K*A*P*L*A*N* and *The Return of H*Y*M*A*N K*A*P*L*A*N*, to short stories, movies, melodrama, essays, travel books. He is Special Editorial Adviser to *Look* magazine. As a leading social scientist, he has written these standard works: *The Washington Correspondents; Hollywood: The Movie Colony;* and *A Guide to the Religions of America.*

Mr. Rosten is familiar to television audiences and has been a favorite participant in *Open End*. A Ph.D. from the University of Chicago, he is a faculty associate at Columbia University and spent the academic year 1960–1961 as visiting Professor of Political Science at the University of California, Berkeley.

During World War II, Leo Rosten was Deputy Director of the Office of War Information, special consultant to the Secretary of War, and Chief of the Motion Picture Division of the National Defense Advisory Commission. He recently served as consultant to President Eisenhower's Commission on National Goals.

He has won the Commonwealth Medal for Literature, the George Polk Memorial Award and the Freedoms Foundation Award, and has taught at Yale and the New School for Social Research. He has traveled widely in Europe and America.